What Readers Are Saying About

By the Light of the Silvery Moon

"*By the Light of the Silvery Moon* has everything I adore about Tricia Goyer's writing—emotion that pulls me in, a plot that keeps me turning pages, and characters that won't let go of my heart. Even now."

—Tamera Alexander, bestselling author of *A Lasting Impression* and *Within My Heart*

"Tricia Goyer has a wonderful way of crafting a novel that the reader has a hard time putting down. She took the beautiful woman with secrets in her past and a future in America, a heart-broken father, a dutiful—but resentful—son, and a son who has wasted his inheritance and thrusts them onto the maiden voyage of the *Titanic,* the unsinkable ship. The lives are skillfully interwoven with major conflicts that kept me guessing. No one will want to miss this amazing tale."

—Lena Nelson Dooley, author of *Love Finds You in Golden* and *Maggie's Journey,* book one of the McKenna's Daughters series

"*By the Light of the Silvery Moon* is officially my favorite Tricia Goyer novel. The story is filled with characters who will steal your heart. Take this voyage on the *Titanic*. You'll be glad you did!"

—Robin Lee Hatcher, bestselling author
of *Belonging* and *Heart of Gold*

"Be still my heart! A shipboard romance, a prodigal son, Tricia Goyer's rich historical research, and all the *Titanic*'s lushness and impending doom—*By the Light of the Silvery Moon* is everything a historical romance novel should be."

—Sarah Sundin, award-winning author
of the Wings of Glory series.

By The Light of the Silvery Moon

TRICIA GOYER

Dedication

To my mom, Linda, and my grandma Dolores. When I was at my darkest moment you pointed me to Jesus and reminded me of His love. It was that love that rescued me and gave me a hope and a future.

Acknowledgments

$\mathcal{I}$ am thankful for my friend Kristen Gaffney who read this book as I wrote it and was the first one to care about the characters along with me. Also, thank you to those at the Titanic Experience in Branson who treated my family to your amazing museum. Months and months after being there we're still talking about it. We have recommended you often.

I also appreciate my editors, Rebecca Germany and Traci DePree, and the rest of the Barbour team!

I'm also thankful for my agent, Janet Grant. You not only brought this idea to my attention, but your influence and encouragement keep my afloat. And my assistant, Amy Lathrop, who takes care of everything business-like so I can write!

And I'm thankful for my family: John, Leslie, Nathan, Alyssa, Cory, Katie, and Clayton Goyer. Also my grandma Dolores who does all my laundry and covers me in prayer daily. My family means everything to me, and I love when I can reunite families within the pages of a book.

Finally, to my best friend, Jesus Christ. None of this would be possible without You. Thank You for rescuing me from the depths and giving me a new life in You....

Greater love hath no man than this, that a
man lay down his life for his friends.
JOHN 15:13

But without faith it is impossible to please him: for he
that cometh to God must believe that he is, and that he
is a rewarder of them that diligently seek him.
HEBREWS 11:6

Table of Contents

Prologue · xiii

Chapter 1 · 1
Chapter 2 · 16
Chapter 3 · 26
Chapter 4 · 37
Chapter 5 · 54
Chapter 6 · 63
Chapter 7 · 79
Chapter 8 · 93
Chapter 9 · 114
Chapter 10 · 121
Chapter 11 · 132
Chapter 12 · 154
Chapter 13 · 167
Chapter 14 · 175
Chapter 15 · 183
Chapter 16 · 193
Chapter 17 · 200
Chapter 18 · 210
Chapter 19 · 216
Chapter 20 · 220
Chapter 21 · 225

Chapter 22 · 232
Chapter 23 · 242
Chapter 24 · 248
Chapter 25 · 253
Chapter 26 · 263
Chapter 27 · 274
Chapter 28 · 293

By the Light of the Silvery Moon · · · · · · · · · · · · · · · · · 307

Prologue

"Quentin, honey, don't get too close to the dock."

Quentin's footsteps stopped short as he looked back at his mother. His bright smile faded. Her gaze had already returned to the party on the top of the hill. He had run as far as he could, but even here at the edge of the estate pond, the high-pitched laughter and constant chatter followed. Even here those voices, those people, held his mother's attention.

Quentin had cheered when his mother agreed to take him away from the party for a while. Now he panted, out of breath. He bent over and placed his small hands on his knees, sucking in an especially large gulp of air at the sight of the house, their house, on top of the hill. Though it was not yet dark, Quentin's eyes widened at the patio lights sparkling in the distance. They danced in the wind like forest fairies in the books his mother read to him.

Chords of laughter rang in the distance, stirring Quentin back to reality. It was most likely his brother, humoring the crowd, charming their parents' friends. Quentin stuck out his tongue at the party, almost wishing his mother saw him do it. She hadn't. He wiped one hand down a red, sweaty cheek and ran to her side.

"Mama, 'Ring around the Rosie'? 'Ring around the Rosie'?" His fingers glided over her silky dress and the long curls that trailed down her back.

"Not right now, son. Maybe later." She offered a half smile. Her fingers mindlessly played with the strand of pearls clasped around her neck.

He grabbed her hand. "Please … please … please?"

Her blue eyes met his gaze. "Quentin, honey, just run around for a bit, yes? We need to get back up there soon. I already feel bad for leaving the party. I'll give you two minutes. Go." She patted his bottom.

Quentin didn't answer, and he didn't run. Instead he walked to the edge of the pond where the water lapped against the grassy shore. He folded his arms across his chest, stuck out his bottom lip, and plopped down. Dampness seeped through his good pants.

Why did they have to move to this big house? At their old place, his mother used to play with him. She used to hold him— hold him tight—snuggled close to her heart.

With no more than a glance in his mother's direction, Quentin jumped to his feet and scurried down the dock. Down to the very end. He eased himself onto the last wooden plank and dangled his feet over the dark green water. Tall lake grass quivered just beneath the surface, waving ever so slightly at him. Quentin moved his legs back and forth, allowing the tips of his black dress shoes to skim the water. The thrill of it took his breath away.

"One more minute," his mother called without looking back.

Quentin frowned and considered kicking off his shoes. He imagined them hitting the surface and then descending through the lake grass until they plopped onto the slimy bottom. Maybe if he kicked them off, he wouldn't have to go back to the party. Maybe he'd have to go to his room instead and Mama would have to talk to him, spend time with him. Even a scolding would be worth it.

A small green turtle surfaced and snapped at his shoes. He jumped with surprise. Quiet laughter escaped Quentin's lips as he wiggled his shoes, luring the turtle closer. Instead it swam the other direction.

He reached toward the small form. "No, wait!" he called, and suddenly the air had more hold on him than the dock. With a splash, he fell into the water. Cold wetness enveloped him, pulling him into its depths.

Quentin's hands opened, fingers splayed. He reached toward the surface, toward the dock, but the lake grasses held him tight. His eyes widened. Legs kicked, body twisted. Lungs burned. The light so far, far away.

Someone called his name.

Help me! He opened his mouth to scream. Water poured into his lungs, burning, choking him. A fuzzy blur filled his vision. The force of a body jumping in next to him stirred the waters.

Mama. He reached for his mother and grabbed a piece of her, but his grip gave way. *Mama.*

Hands unwrapped the tangled weeds around his legs and propelled him toward the dock. His numb fingers grabbed the rough wood. His face surfaced. Coughing, he struggled to suck in air.

He pulled with all his might, but lifting himself onto the dock was impossible. Quentin dragged his body along the wooden edge toward the shallow water. Only when his shoes hit the slimy, muddy bottom did he look back. Where was she? Quentin struggled onto the grass.

"Mama!"

No response.

"Mama!" he screamed again, louder.

He searched the dark water. There! Bubbles surfaced no more than ten feet from the dock. His heart pounded as he retraced his steps down the weathered wooden planks. Wet and shaking, he leaned down and reached one hand toward the water. His mother struggled just beneath the surface.

Crying, he called to her—but she would not come to him. She would not come.

It wasn't until the bubbles ceased that Quentin turned and ran to the house as quickly as his legs would carry him. Held tightly in his fist was the strand of pearls from around his mother's neck. When had he grabbed it? He couldn't remember. The clasp broken but the pearls intact, it streamed behind him like a trail of tears.

Chapter 1

April 10, 1912
Wednesday

Almost on board. Amelia Gladstone took a step forward, her hand wrapped around Aunt Neda's elbow, leading the way. Her aunt leaned heavily on her cane, and Amelia moved with slow steps. She had never given much thought to leaving Southampton, and those few moments she'd considered it, this picture wouldn't have crossed her mind. This excitement.

Full. The pier was full. The boarding ramp. The decks. Her heart and soul.

Porters hauling luggage. Men and women strolling. Children, faces bright with excitement. Some in fine dress from tailor's shops, most in handmade frocks. Reporters snapping photos. Everyone talking at once. The shrill whistle of the train that had just arrived from London to the docks. Laughter. She looked down at her arms. Prickles. Goose bumps raced up them as if her skin attempted to absorb the energy of people around her and the regality of the ship before.

Amelia lifted her head and craned her neck. The RMS *Titanic* was larger than her sister ship *Olympic*. She blocked out most of the sun and sky with four smokestacks jutting into the air. Even from the dock the *Titanic*'s promenade deck could be seen below the boat deck. Butterflies tumbled in her stomach. Not long from now she'd be walking those decks.

There'd never been a ship like it in the history of the world, which seemed fitting for the occasion. *Titanic* filled the horizon with more than just evidence of men's great feat. It symbolized *promise,* the promise of seeing her cousin Elizabeth again. Elizabeth was her closest friend—the daughter of her aging aunt, whom Amelia again tried to encourage to move just a bit faster toward the loading ramp.

"Come, Auntie. Watch your step. We don't want you tripping over anything or anyone. It's mighty busy here today."

Amelia stepped closer to her aunt as a mother with two small children passed. The younger boy clung to a ragged blanket, tucking it under his chin. His fist gripped the hem of his mother's traveling jacket as his wide eyes focused on the ship. The boy's mouth curled into a circle at the sight of the *Titanic,* and Amelia nodded in understanding. *I feel the same.*

"I cannot wait to tell Elizabeth about this." Aunt Neda pointed a thin finger to the smokestacks high above. "I wish she were here to see it herself."

Laughter tumbled from Amelia's lips. "Oh, she'll see it, Auntie, on the other side. This grand ship won't lose its luster in one crossing."

They stepped forward just as a lady dressed in a tailored red wool coat hustled past, moving to the front of the line. Her dark hair flowed in soft waves to her shoulders. She carried a purse on one arm and a hat box on the other.

The woman paused before the steward at the end of the gangplank. "Excuse me. Is this the way to first class?"

The steward's jaw dropped. He swallowed hard, composing himself. "No, ma'am." His finger pointed to a gangplank farther down. "That is the one, there."

The woman glanced over her shoulder, scanning the crowd. Amelia offered a smile, but the woman's gaze passed over Amelia as if her kind offering was of no consequence.

"Yes, of course. I should have known." And with that she moved toward the far gangplank, her feet gliding over the rough wooden dock as if she walked on a puff of air.

Amelia touched the collar of her yellow dress. She'd been so pleased with her garment this morning, but now she fretted. How did others see her? As simple? Plain? Dull?

How would Mr. Chapman see her?

The promise of meeting Mr. Chapman—the friend and neighbor of Elizabeth and her husband, Len—caused Amelia's stomach to flip even more than the excitement of the ship. Mr. Chapman who'd written her no less than a dozen letters and ended each one expressing an eagerness to meet her in person. Mr. Chapman who'd purchased the second-class tickets, for her, Aunt Neda, and…

Amelia lowered her head, the excitement of the day interrupted by the heat of anger flushing her cheeks. He'd even bought a ticket for her cousin Henry who'd been foolish enough to land himself in jail just last night.

Mr. Chapman wasn't her intended—not yet. She had hopes, though, of a future together. And from the letters he wrote—so did he. She wouldn't let Henry's getting arrested sink that happy thought.

Truth be told, Amelia was thankful for her cousin's absence. Even her aunt seemed somewhat relieved that they wouldn't have to put up with Henry's foolishness aboard the ship. If trouble brewed, Henry found it. Amelia blew out the anger and sucked in a breath of fresh ocean air. Without Henry she'd be able to enjoy herself. To find a bit of peace before a change in her life situation.

She took one step closer to the gangplank.

"Almost there, ladies," the steward called. "Jest wait till you see what this beauty offers inside." The steward talked to her without really looking at her—a stark contrast to the attention he'd paid to the lady in the wool coat.

Suddenly Amelia felt self-conscious. *Will Mr. Chapman be disappointed?*

Amelia pushed that thought from her mind. There was no turning back. Mr. Chapman would be waiting at the docks in New York. Would he be even a smidgen as impressed with her as he would be by the great ship? At least, she comforted herself, he had already been impressed enough in her correspondence to ask her to come in the first place.

"Thank you, sir. I'm looking forward to walking the decks." She smiled at the steward. "I've heard so much from the papers. I'm eager to see such grandeur with my own eyes."

Aunt Neda gripped her arm, leaning close to Amelia's ear. "It is a large vessel, but do you believe they'll all fit?" Aunt Neda scanned the quay teeming with people.

"Not all of them are coming on, I suppose. Some are watchers. Others goers."

"Yes, I can see the difference now. Shiny faces. Bright smiles. All things new. Well, except for that man. Pour soul."

Amelia followed her aunt's gaze up the gangplank. Two stewards in white uniforms dragged a man between them, escorting him off the ship. He was thin. Matted hair clung to his head. His face was lowered, ashamed as the crowds looked on. Amelia's heart went out to him. She clutched her gloved hands together and pulled them to her chest. Then she stepped slightly to the side as the stewards approached.

"Excuse me, ma'am," one steward said, his gaze falling and holding hers. "Thank ye for letting us past."

"Yes, of course." She eyed the stowaway. Blood dripped from a gash in his cheek. They passed, and she took a step to follow them. Follow *him*.

Aunt Neda's hand tightened on Amelia's arm. "Where are you going?"

She glanced back over her shoulder. "I'll be right back. The man ... he was injured."

Her aunt's eyes widened. "Now? Here?" She looked to the large ship and then back to Amelia. "Can't one day pass without you running off to tend to the unfortunate? America surely has plenty of poor souls for your mercies—"

"I'll just be a moment."

"But the ship. We're set to board."

Amelia took another step. "We have hours before it leaves the dock. I won't miss it. I promise."

Aunt Neda sighed then pulled a few small coins from her pocket. Coins they'd scrimped and saved for the trip. Coins to finance their new life.

"Thank you, Aunt. I'll be right back." Amelia grasped them in her hand and hurried off. A smile filled her face as she scanned the crowd for the stewards.

There. Over by the train station. The stewards threw the man to the ground and kicked his side for good measure. She raced their direction, lifting the hem of her traveling gown as she jogged toward the man. Ignoring how quickly she became winded. Ignoring the stares of the people watching.

"I don't blame ye, miss," one viewer called as she passed. "I'd run away, too, if I were you. I have a bad feeling about this ship."

Amelia wasn't about to pause to set the record straight. Only as she neared the man, crumpled into a heap on the damp dock, did she slow. Then, just as she was about to speak to him, he

5

rose—his back to her. He was taller than she thought. And as he strode away, confusion filled her. He walked not with the slumped stagger of a beggar but the straight, confident gait of a king.

She rubbed her eyes, unsure of what she was seeing. She almost second-guessed her plan, but something inside told her to be brave. To balm the man's wounds with her smile—and her gift. She slid the coins into her pocket and instead pulled out the ticket. "Sir?"

The man continued on, as if not hearing her.

She hurried after him, placing a hand on his arm. He paused and turned, eyes widening.

"You talking to me?" he mumbled. Dark brown eyes met hers and a light of interest filled them. They were beautiful eyes that reminded her of lamplight glowing on cobblestone streets after the rain. His gaze remained steady on Amelia, and her throat muscles rose and fell as she swallowed. There was something familiar about this man.

Do I know him? No, that was impossible. Her lips fell open as she tried to remember what she was going to say.

She looked to his cheek and pulled her handkerchief from her pocket, reaching up and dabbing it. At the feel of her touch, he jerked his head back. She held out the handkerchief, stained with blood. "You're bleeding."

He took the cloth, pressing it to the wound. He lowered his head, looking to the ticket in her opposite hand.

"Sir, I have this ticket we are not using and—"

"I'm sorry. I have no money," he interrupted, speaking so softly it was a murmur. "If I had, I would have bought—"

"No, sir. No purchase. A gift."

He ran a dirty hand through his hair. "I—I don't understand."

"A second chance." The words escaped with a breath, and she willed her heart to slow its wild beating. "All of us need a second chance."

"All of us need a second chance."

Her words replayed in Quentin's mind as she walked away. Her smile—well, it warmed him even more than the sun overhead.

Only when she disappeared among the crowd did he again look at the ticket in his hand. A gift? Who was he to her? What had he done to deserve such an offering?

He struggled for a breath and moved to the brick wall of a nearby building. Stepping into the shadows, he fingered the small piece of paper. Such a simple thing that offered so much.

Quentin rubbed the spot on his ribs where the steward had offered a firm kick. He deserved it—littering the ship with his filth. Everyone saw him as he was: a beggar, a vagabond. But her—he felt valued when he looked into her gaze. It was a feeling he'd long forgotten.

Who was that woman? She no doubt had seen the stewards dragging him off. Quentin lowered his head. His stomach ached as he thought about her seeing that. Or maybe the ache was because he hadn't eaten for a while. How many days had passed? One? Two? He wasn't sure.

He fingered the inspection card—which also served as a ticket—wondering if he could pull it off. Would the stewards really let him on?

Something inside told him to forget the idea. *It's no use to try.*

Then again, the woman had approached him. He had a passage in his hand. If he walked away now, he'd always wonder.

He rose and looked at his dirty slacks and coat. No, they'd never let him on looking like this.

Quentin scanned the docks filled with people, and then his eyes moved to crates and trunks being boarded. A large stack was piled high, with stewards hauling them one by one up to the hold. Each piece of luggage was marked to be stored or taken to the passenger's room.

He checked his pants pocket, making sure he still had his most valuable possession, and then he slid off his dirty jacket, tossing it into the crook of his arm. Noting a barrel of rainwater next to the wall, he quickly washed his face and hair, using the woman's handkerchief to dab the gash on his cheek once more. Then he moved to the suitcases and eyed the stack. He had one shot to pick the right one.

A black scuffed trunk sat on the far edge. It wasn't the trunk of a wealthy man, and that was what he was looking for. On top of the trunk was a bag containing a sweater with a wooden hanger sticking out the top. The tag on it read McHenry Rm. B124. It looked as if Mr. McHenry would have his sweater hand delivered to his room this morning.

Quentin hurried over and grabbed the sweater from the hanger. Before the steward noticed his presence, he had the garment in his hand and had hurried around the side of the building. He glanced down at the simple white sweater. It wasn't his style, but he slipped it on. The sleeves were a bit short, so he pushed them up, nearly to his elbows. Then seeing a muddy area at the building's corner, Quentin sank to his knees in the mud.

Satisfied, he rose, lifted his chin, and approached the line waiting to board. His eyes scanned the gangplank, but the woman wasn't there. Good thing. One slip of her lips—one wrong look—and she could give him away.

Finally, his turn. He approached the steward and handed him the ticket with a heavy sigh.

"Sir?" the steward asked, eyeing him.

"Dratted motorcars." Quentin spoke with a lilt. "My friend offered a ride and the beast broke down." He shook his head, looking at his pants. "And guess who was the one on the ground, checking the motor? Yessir, you guessed it." Quentin smiled. "At least I can be guaranteed this ride. No break downs, right, lad?"

"Uh, no sir." A smile lifted the steward's rosy cheeks. "I do say you're in for a fine ride from here on out." The steward studied the ticket and then handed it back. "Glad to have you, Mr. Gladstone. Your room is on B deck. At the top of the gang-plank, continue down the hall, and then take the grand staircase up one level. Enjoy the voyage. I can't imagine anything but smooth sailing today."

Amelia stepped into the second-class room. Two mahogany beds were bunked, one on top of the other. A sitting bench and cupboard filled the opposite wall. In the center, built against the wall between the two, was a wash basin with running water, drawers, a mirror, and a lamp.

Imagine that, running water!

It was far nicer than she'd imagined. For so long she'd never thought she'd board any ship, and now she was a passenger on the finest ever built. What would her mother think of this?

Her hands quivered as she set down her aunt's small suitcase on the floor. Most of their things—all they owned—had been crated up and stored below, deep in the ship's belly. A few more of their suitcases would soon be delivered to their room.

Amelia bit her lip. She told herself again that she was making the right choice by leaving what she knew to venture into a future in America, and possibly a future with Mr. Chapman. It wasn't as if her mother had ever come looking for her in Southampton. Twelve years she had stayed with her aunt—her mother's sister-in-law. Aunt Neda had married her mother's brother, but they'd only been married ten years when sickness took Uncle Rupert.

While Uncle Rupert had stayed on land and had married Neda and had two children, Amelia's mother had taken to the sea. She'd worked as a stewardess from the time she was sixteen, until Amelia was born when she was twenty-two. She knew that good mothers settled down, and she'd tried that for a time. They moved near Aunt Neda and had provided comforting arms during Uncle Rupert's passing. But as Amelia grew, her mother often took her down to the docks to watch the ships departing.

Then one day, with little more than a brief explanation that "the sea is calling," Mother's things were packed up and Amelia—only six years old—was taken to live with Aunt Neda. As Amelia grew, she wondered if it was more than the sea that called. She never knew her father, but her mother had told her once she met him on a ship. Was it love—his love—that had drawn her mother away? A love even deeper than that for her own daughter?

In the last twelve years, not a day passed when Amelia didn't wonder if it would be the day she'd hear a soft knock on the door and she'd open it to see her mother's smile.

But that had not been the case, and all Amelia had left from her mother were memories of her first six years and stories of her mother's many trips across the sea as a stewardess.

Mother had told Amelia about sleeping on a thin bunk with rats as her bed mates, and Amelia thought that on a ship like this, even the rats would be forced into coats and hats.

"This is a fine room." Aunt Neda settled onto the sitting bench and removed her hat pin, placing her simple bonnet on the bed. "There is even a small desk where you could write letters to your Mr. Chapman."

"Yes, Mr. Chapman." Even as she said that name, Amelia couldn't help but think of the man she'd given the ticket to on the dock. Had he boarded? Was he situating himself in the room next door even now?

Amelia lowered herself onto the sitting bench. "I do suppose I could take time to write a letter, although since Mr. Chapman is the one meeting us in New York, a letter couldn't possibly beat us to him."

Her aunt's eyes locked with hers, and Amelia could see questions there. Questions whether they'd made the right choice leaving everything. Questions if he was the right man for Amelia. They were the same questions that stirred in Amelia's heart.

"Yes, that is true. I just supposed that if you had any romantic notions, quickened by the ocean breeze, you very well could write them down."

"Of course, Aunt, if I have any romantic notions." Amelia breathed out a soft sigh, wishing it could be so.

The problem was she didn't know the man's first name. She had yet to see a photograph. She'd been so sure of her decision to leave Southampton, but her and her aunt's future now depended on the man who'd sent their passage. Surely her cousin Elizabeth had decent taste and a sharp eye. Amelia's whole future depended on that.

Tears filled Quentin's eyes as he sank into the bathtub in the common bathroom. His first real bath in weeks. Or was it months? He didn't know. And that bath had only been in a public fountain.

Time had become a flowing river. He slept under whatever bridge wasn't already occupied. Worked menial jobs with hopes of a decent meal for supper. And along the dark, raging river of time, he left behind so-called friends, vengeful enemies, regrets, curses, tears.

He lifted his hand from the warm water and looked at it. His knuckles were cracked and bloody from more than one bar fight. He lifted his arm farther. Thin, covered with sores. His fingers probed his chest. Only a layer of skin, not an ounce of fat, covered his ribs. Amazement filled him that one could fall so low and still live. Still hope.

The ship. The *Titanic*. News of its arrival had spread through London. Many had traveled to Southampton to view the sight. From the first moment Quentin saw it, he desired to be aboard its maiden voyage. London had robbed everything from him. Maybe returning to America would reverse his fate.

A memory of other voyages he'd taken filled his mind. He cupped his hands and filled them with the warm, fragrant water, pouring it over his head as if the water could wash away the past. Wash away recollections of how things used to be—before.

A knock sounded at the door and Quentin tensed. Had he been discovered? As soon as he boarded he hadn't taken one moment to explore the ship like everyone else. Instead he dropped off the borrowed sweater in front of Mr. McHenry's door, found his room, dropped his coat on the bed, and then hurried to the modest second-class bathroom and locked himself in, lest anyone question what such riffraff was doing aboard. Only when he and his clothes were cleaned up would he dare show his face.

Would anyone bother him if he stayed in his room? He'd hole up there if he had to, leaving only in the darkest part of the night to steal food. If he'd excelled at anything over the past two years on the streets, that was it.

Another knock sounded. "Sir, a delivery," a man's voice called.

A desire to protect himself battled with curiosity. He rose from the bath and slid on the white cotton robe he'd snagged from an opened, unoccupied room on his way to the bath—telling himself he'd return that later, too. He hurried to the door, his wet feet sliding on the white tiled floor. He opened the door a crack.

A steward stood there. One of the two who'd carried him off. But instead of anger flashing in the man's eyes, the steward's lips lifted in a slight smile.

He doesn't recognize me.

The steward held up a small, cardboard suitcase. "So sorry to interrupt, sir, but there is a delivery from a lady. She asked that this be brought to you right away. When I told her you weren't in your room, another steward mentioned he saw you enter here. Your friend was certain you'd want your things."

Quentin reached for the handle of the suitcase. "Yes, of course. Thank you. I was—uh—in need of this." He rubbed his forehead. "And I forgot where my—uh—friend told me she was staying. The excitement of the journey has emptied my mind of every other detail, I'm afraid." He took the suitcase from the man's hand.

The steward cocked his eyebrow. "In the room right next to yours, sir—toward the stern. Although the young lady is not present in the room at this moment. She's stepped to the upper deck for the cast off."

"Yes, of course. Thank you again."

The man didn't leave. The steward perhaps expected a coin, and he had none.

Quentin took the suitcase and put it inside the door, noticing the steward eyeing his cut cheek. Then his hair. The steward looked closer and his brow furrowed.

Without another word, Quentin shut the bathroom door. He touched his hand to his face then looked at his fingers. Blood. He hoped the gash hadn't stirred the man's memory. To have his identity questioned. Then again, why should he worry? He had a ticket. He had the woman to back up his story that he was indeed Henry Gladstone.

Not that the steward could do anything about it even if the truth was discovered. They'd be out at sea soon. The worst that could happen was he'd be locked up or watched over. Either way, he'd make it to America. He considered opening the suitcase and going through its contents, but his instinct kicked in, telling him to leave, to run back to the safety of his room, to hide.

Quentin finished bathing, dressed in his dirty pants and shirt, and then hurried back to his room that had two beds and a mahogany bureau. His heartbeat quickened at the thought of sleeping in a bed again. Of sleeping with a pillow, between fresh, clean sheets that had never been slept in.

He placed the suitcase on the white bed covering. With a slight quiver of his hand, he opened the latches. Clothes. He pulled out a pair of new pants, a white shirt, and a jacket. A modest pair of shoes were tucked beside them, and under those yet another outfit.

He lifted the jacket. A note fluttered to the ground. He picked it up. It smelled like the woman—soft and sweet like her perfume. Then he read:

Dear Sir,

My cousin has no need for his boat passage, nor for these garments my aunt sewed for him for the trip. Please accept these as our welcome aboard this beautiful vessel—have you ever seen such opulence in your life?

The pants might be a bit short in length, the jacket a smidgen large. But I do hope you make use of them. Who knows, maybe we'll see you at the dining hall later tonight. I'll save a chair next to us just in case.

With hopes of friendship,
Amelia Gladstone

"Amelia," he whispered, refolding the note and placing it on the bed. So that was the name of his angel of mercy.

He looked at the jacket, and eagerness filled him. He would dress in these clothes and perhaps meet her and her aunt for supper. His only worry, though, was that his lack of excitement over this fine vessel would give him away. Amelia was wrong—he *had* seen such finery. Lived in places grander than this. But for a ship, he guessed, it was the nicest he'd seen.

With a damp hand, he fingered the white cuff of the shirt.

I'll pretend to be awed by it all. For her.

Chapter 2

Freshly bathed and in his new clothes, Quentin made his way to the second-class deck, amazed at the number of visitors and reporters who still strolled the decks so close to casting off. An older gentleman strode by in a white pinstriped suit. Even if the man was in second class, he dressed the part of someone from first class. Quentin was no stranger to playing the part of someone he wasn't. He'd done it for years, living on the streets of London. He did it now. The ticket in his pocket read HENRY GLADSTONE. He wondered what had caused Henry to skip the ship. *Poor Henry, missing out.*

Many people browsed the library, which still smelled of fresh paint. Quentin glanced into the room filled with books and polished wood, looking for the woman who'd given him the ticket. In addition to those who strode around the library, two men sat at a small table, relaxed and talking as if they spent every afternoon in such a manner.

Quentin stepped back out onto the deck. A woman nearly walked into him. Her face was white, and she gripped a blue shawl around her shoulders. She had dark hair and a touch of gray at her temples. She longingly looked at the gangplank that would take her safely back to land.

"I have a bad feeling about this. A bad feeling," she muttered under her breath.

"There is no need to worry, ma'am." A red-haired deckhand cocked his chin and spoke as if he'd built the ship with his own two hands. "*Titanic* has been inspected bow to stern and declared man's finest creation. God himself cannot sink this ship."

Quentin smirked as he heard the man's words. He'd thrown more than enough boasting words into God's face—and look where it had brought him. Yet while he shook his head, the woman stopped her pacing, relieved.

Quentin scanned the sea of men in suits, women in fine hats, and children who wove in and out of the flow of bodies with their parents' calls nipping at their heels.

When he didn't see the woman, he strolled along the second-class promenade deck, walking in step with the orchestra playing festive ragtime tunes that welcomed those who continued to board.

He'd seen the advertisements—Titanic, Ship of Dreams. To him it wasn't the ship that was so impressive but the fact he was on it. Being gifted the ticket was his first piece of good luck in years, and that was why he'd decided to risk walking the decks. The more he thought about hiding away, the more he felt drawn to walk boldly in his borrowed clothes. No one here would know him. From the moment he stepped out of his room, clean and shaven, he had presented himself as if the last two years on the streets hadn't happened.

He straightened his shoulders and lifted his chin slightly higher. Many people looked his way, and with each glance he battled the urge to look away. He wasn't used to people looking at him, smiling. Over the last two years, most had ignored him or had looked the other way. Some had even paused their steps, turned, and walked the other direction if he was in their path. It was amazing what a bath, haircut, and a shave could do. He ran a hand down the smooth skin of his cheek, thankful that a shaving kit and scissors had been packed in the suitcase.

Quentin didn't see the woman anywhere, so instead he turned his attention to an arriving boat in the harbor. As he watched, a long line of people departed the luxury boat ferry and boarded the *Titanic.* Color drained from his face as he recognized many in the group—Isidor Straus, owner of Macy's department store and former congressman of New York, and his wife, Ida. Major Archibald Butt, military aid to President Taft, and Colonel Archibald Gracie. Each of them Quentin had dined with, knew personally, not just as figureheads. Of course, that had been then—in his old life.

As more of the world's wealthiest men and women boarded the *Titanic,* Quentin stepped into the shadows. Even though he knew none of them could recognize him at this distance, he didn't want to take the chance. Of course, even if they thought he looked familiar, they would never expect him in these hand-made clothes or on the second-class deck. They'd expect him to be in first class, mingling and strolling the decks with a beautiful woman on his arm. Here, now, the only beautiful woman he cared about was his angel of mercy, and she'd seen him at his worst.

He lowered his head as he imagined what she thought of him—his ragged attire, his unkempt hair, his stench. She was thoughtful enough to provide him with passage, and perhaps she would sit with him at a meal—as she'd written in the note—but he knew nothing would come of it beyond that. Why would someone so wonderful and kind be attracted to a man who couldn't even provide a roof over his own head or bread for his table? A man who'd tried to sneak onto the ship and had been dragged off in shame. She wouldn't be interested, and that was that.

A fellow second-class passenger, who looked to be in his mid-twenties, approached, gripping Quentin's arm as if coming upon an old friend. "Sir, you wouldn't believe my luck. I was ticketed for the *Olympic,* but because of the coal workers' strike, my ship was canceled and I was transferred here. My ma breathed a sigh of relief. She'd been worried about the dangers of crossing the ocean but was pleased when I told her I'd be on the *Titanic.* This ship, they say, is unsinkable."

Unsinkable. That's what he'd thought about his life up until two years ago.

Quentin blew out a slow breath. It was easy to make claims, to have a vision, but few things were as perfect as they seemed. "I'm not sure any ship is unsinkable."

The man cocked an eyebrow. "Yes, well, let's not test that. I'm excited to get to America again."

"Again?" Quentin asked.

"My sister and I visited America six years ago. She stayed, so I visited her three years later. She's living in Minnesota now. It's there I have a job as a horse trainer."

Quentin nodded. How long had it been since he'd had a simple conversation with an average citizen? "It's easier to work with wild horses than people—that would be my guess."

"Precisely." A chuckle split the man's lips. He extended his hand. "Charles Bainbrigge from Guernsey."

Quentin nodded, gripping the man's hand in a tight handshake. "Nice to meet you. I'm Que—" He cleared his throat. "I'm Henry Gladstone."

"How about you, Henry?" the man asked. "Is this your first trip to America?"

Quentin tucked his hands into his pant pockets and leaned back against the deck's rail. "I was born there, actually."

"Sure enough, gov'nor, I can hear your American accent now. Have you been in England long?"

"Five years. Five long, long years. I left my father's home and moved to London to start my own business when I was only twenty-one. But we don't need to talk about that. Tell me, can you tell a horse is wild just by looking at him? Or is there something you see in his eyes?"

The man cocked an eyebrow. "All horses are wild to some extent. The key to taming them is being mindful of the present moment. It does no good to approach the beast with an agenda. He'll see you coming from a mile down the road. Instead, accept him for who he is. Then gently lead him in a way that shows how he can be different."

"Seems like good advice, and not only for our animal friends."

"That be right, gov'nor. There's truth in that. I feel like a wild stallion at times, and the more I have friends who push for their way…the more I want my own."

The man continued on, talking about the unruly temperament of the last horse he'd trained. And as he talked about the importance of not getting angry or frustrated with a horse since it just made matters worse, Quentin's mind wandered.

It seemed one hundred years ago that he'd traveled from his father's estate in Maryland to Europe. If his father could find such success in America, Quentin had been sure he could replicate it in London, England, The Square Mile. For a time it had worked. His steel supply business flourished. Everything he'd set his hand to had succeeded. Then—not weeks after his twenty-fourth birthday—everything changed. An English competitor came in, and most of Quentin's customers turned to that man for their supplies. Lavish living took all that remained of Quentin's wealth. Within months he went from having everything to having nothing at all.

He lowered his head, not wanting to think about how far he'd fallen after that—lower than he ever thought possible. Did things. Unimaginable things.

Charles finished his story and then hurried on to talk to the next passenger who dared to make eye contact. As Charles moved on, Quentin turned to the rail, noticing the ships' guests were now departing the gangplank. Wistful looks radiated from their faces, and he still could not believe he wouldn't be one of the thousands watching the *Titanic* sail away. Instead he'd be waving to them from the rails. A simple slip of paper Quentin carried in his waistcoat pocket told him he could remain. He took it out and looked at it, reading the name again: Henry Gladstone. If going by another identity offered a chance to start a new life in his homeland, then Henry Gladstone he would be.

Amelia stepped into the narrow hallway just outside their stateroom, smoothing the soft fabric of the yellow dress her aunt had sewn for the voyage. She looked to the door of the room next to her, wondering if the man from the dock was there. She had yet to get his name. She also hadn't told her aunt of the gift. She wouldn't understand that Amelia had given her cousin's passage to a beggar and drifter. In fact, there was much Amelia did that she didn't reveal to her aunt. Sometimes safety, Aunt Neda believed, was more important than helping people.

Should she knock on the man's door, just to check on him? She raised her hand to knock, but an excited gasp from behind her caused her to pause. She turned to see a dark-haired woman who looked to be her age. The woman's cheeks glowed pink, and she hugged her arms as if trying to hold in her excitement.

Amelia turned, and the woman paused before her.

"Can you believe this? Such an amazing ship!"

The woman's excitement was contagious, and laughter slipped from Amelia's lips. "I just unpacked. I'm off to explore the second-class promenade."

"Second class? Haven't you heard? The first-class decks are open to us until we launch." The woman wore a simple dress and clutched a book to her chest. "My husband, poor dear, has a headache and told me to go ahead without him. I was heading up to the deck to read, and then I heard about the chance to explore. Care to walk up with me to first class and look around?"

"Yes, wonderful." She extended her hand. "My name is Amelia."

"And I'm Ethel Beane. My husband is Edward. We were married just a few days ago."

"So is this your first time on a ship?" Amelia asked.

"It is for me, but Mr. Beane has made the journey several times." She tucked a stray strand of hair behind her ear. "Are you traveling alone, Amelia?"

"Oh no, my aunt is with me. We were awoken early with news that my cousin wouldn't be joining us.... It overwhelmed her. Aunt Neda told me she needed to rest—to calm herself."

Following the crowd, they walked down various passageways to a grand staircase that led to the first-class promenade. On the top of the grand staircase, a glass dome cast muted light down the stairs. A cherub lamp guarded the way, and a carved clock displayed the time. Eleven twenty-six, it read, just over thirty minutes until the launch.

They walked side by side as they took in the dining area with white walls and oak furniture. They gazed at the books in the library, and Ethel placed down Edward's tattered book and picked up one from the bookshelf. She held it in her hands, exclaiming over the leather cover and pristine paper. Yet even the beautiful books couldn't keep them from further exploring. They walked from room to room, exclaiming over each one.

Amelia's favorite room was the Verandah Café, decorated in modern "Art Nouveau" style. Their eyes grew wide as they viewed the swimming pool, gymnasium, and squash court. It seemed to Amelia one could live a year on this ship and not be lacking for luxury.

Two men in fine suits approached and eyed them boldly. Heat rose to Amelia's cheeks, and if she had been carrying a fan, she would have covered her face with it. The men smiled at her reaction, and though they continued walking, their gazes lingered as they passed.

"I am married, but maybe we should stop and make introductions," Ethel said a little too loudly for Amelia's comfort.

The men turned and smiled, but instead of pausing, Amelia hurried her pace.

"Please, I am not looking for romance upon this ship." Amelia smoothed the soft fabric of her yellow dress. Her shoes clicked on the polished floors, and she forced herself not to look back.

"Do you have a suitor?" Ethel tucked her shoulder closer to Amelia's as they walked, as if they'd been dear friends their entire lives.

"I do...of sorts. Nothing we have written in our correspondence has made it official, but I have a dear friend named Mr. Chapman who lives in America. We enjoy each other's company through letters, and he suggested that my moving there would make it possible for us to strengthen our friendship face-to-face. And also to see if our friendship could lead to...more." The last word dropped from her lips like a loosened rose petal. "He even paid for the passage for my aunt and me." Amelia failed to mention that he'd paid for her cousin's passage, too, and that another man—a beggar no less—now occupied that room.

"Is he handsome, your Mr. Chapman?" Ethel asked.

Amelia conjured up an image in her mind. As she'd read the letters, she pictured a tall, dark-haired man with broad shoulders, but unfortunately, Elizabeth had commented little about his appearance. Mr. Chapman had spoken nothing of his looks within the letters, and Amelia had been too shy to ask.

"Handsome? I have yet to see a photograph, but I am certain he is. He is a businessman and also highly respected in his community." *Looks aren't everything,* she'd decided. What mattered more than a man's chiseled jaw or handsome eyes was a giving and caring heart, which Mr. Chapman seemed to possess.

"If he's highly respected, that means he's a man of means—which seems certain since he paid for you both to come." Ethel sighed. "My Edward is a bricklayer, but I'd rather have love than money. And truth be told, I've never known a more devoted man. He returned to England to marry me, and being his wife has brought my happiest days."

Amelia studied the soft glow about the woman's cheeks and neck. A twinge of jealously tightened her gut. "Yes, well, I hope I will find that type of love someday."

Ethel turned to Amelia, taking Amelia's hands in hers. "You will." Ethel smiled. "God has a special man for you. And from that sparkle in your eyes, I have a feeling it will be your Mr. Chapman."

Amelia blew out a huge breath, and the tension left her shoulders.

Ethel glanced into the gymnasium where the two handsome passengers had retreated. "Then again they call this ship *The Millionaire's Special.*" She laughed. "With a husband like that, you can travel in this style the rest of your life."

Amelia wrinkled her nose. Out of all the things she hoped for in a future husband, wealth wasn't one of them. Compassion and a gentle spirit were traits on the top of her list. And eyes that drew her into their depths. Eyes that expressed love and acceptance. That's what she wanted most of all—for someone to love her for who she was. Who didn't care where she came from—who didn't expect her to change.

For some queer reason, it was the homeless man's face that filled Amelia's mind as she considered someone she wanted to get to know better. He wore rags, but she could tell there was much—much more—hidden within him. She had seen a gentleness in his gaze, and he'd truly appreciated the gift of the ticket. He seemed honored that she cared—that she'd thought of him.

She glanced around. Had the man gotten dressed in her cousin's clothes? Did he now walk the decks? She didn't see him. Would she, on this voyage? She hoped so. She wanted to hear his story. Why would he have the walk of a king but wear the rags of a beggar? On the streets of London, she'd learned not to be surprised by the type of people who were down on their luck, but this man surprised her.

With a gasp, Ethel turned. "Amelia, look! Another group of passengers boarding. I believe I recognize some of those faces from the society section of the *London Times*. Do you wish to take a look?"

"Yes." Amelia nodded, but it was not those from the society section she wanted to see. Was the man from the docks around here somewhere?

Chapter 3

*T*he first-class passengers' boat ferry arrived from London's Waterloo Station at the dockside. Damien Walpole glanced up at the majestic ship, preparing to board and more impressed than he thought he would be. The *Titanic* rose into the horizon, gleaming under the light of the sun. Men and women, wearing their finest, strolled on the first-class decks high above them— wanting to be seen and to rub elbows with some of the wealthiest men and women in the world. Damien took a deep breath and prepared for that. There was no relaxing when there were important people to engage in conversation and an image to uphold. The approval of his fellow high-society passengers had taken his father far, and because of his brother's unwise choices, Damien had to prove their trust of his father and his business was not in vain.

Travel had never been relaxing, with his father to give companionship to and his father's friends to entertain. Yet there were times he allowed himself to relax—a beautiful woman on his arm helped with that. But for once he wished he could get lost in the crowd. He longed to be known more for himself than his name or the size of his father's bank account.

Behind him sat Colonel Archibald Gracie, a former colonel in the Seventh Regiment of the United States Army. Colonel Gracie filled the boat with his commanding presence. While

Father and Gracie chatted about their recent London adventures, Damien's mind was drawn away. Gracies presence took Damien back to the worst day of his life—the day they buried his mother. His stomach tightened.

It had been a bright, sunny spring day. He'd been only ten years old. The sun seemed to taunt him with its warmth. Everything had changed that day in so many ways.

Damien had always shared a room with his younger brother, but before their maid had brought his suit for the funeral that morning, he'd packed up his things and moved them down the hall. He'd always gotten along well with his younger brother, but after what happened, he didn't even want to look at him. His brother had taken away their mother. Damien didn't know if he could ever forgive him for that.

Damien looked around. Most of the first-class passengers on this ship had been friends with his father even back then. They vacationed in the same locations and stayed in the same hotels. The problem was whenever they were around, Damien couldn't escape the memories—not that the loss of his mother was ever far from his thoughts.

Whenever Damien remembered his mother's funeral, he couldn't forget Colonel's Gracies face leaning low. Gracie's mustache had twitched as he'd attempted to keep his composure. "Son, your mother is gone. Your father needs you now. He needs your strength."

Other men—wise and wealthy men—had mimicked those words. "You need to be there for your father. He only has you to count on." And as the days and weeks and months followed, those same men had watched him. They'd nodded their approval to see Damien attending dinners with his father, traveling with him, standing by his father's side at public functions, transformed from a boy to a man before their eyes.

And they watched him still.

It was a heavy load to carry. The load hadn't lightened over the years. Yet he also knew his father wouldn't have been able to continue without Damien by his side. Father especially wouldn't have been able to deal with Quentin's foolish ways on his own. For every step of responsibility Damien had taken, his brother had taken a step backward, until he'd sunken to lows that even Damien never expected.

Colonel Gracie's voice interrupted his thoughts, and Damien turned to see the older gentleman speaking to four women.

"Mesdames, I see you are traveling alone." Gracie tipped his hat to the women. "It would be my honor to offer my services to you."

Damien watched. *Why didn't I think of that?* It was the gentlemanly thing to do to offer services to unprotected ladies. He glanced at his father, wondering if he'd see a hint of disappointment that Damien hadn't offered first, but Father seemed more intent on hearing the story of the women—three of them sisters—who were returning to America after attending a family funeral in England.

"I am Mrs. E. D. Appleton, and these are my sisters, Mrs. R. C. Cornell and Mrs. John Murray Brown," one woman announced. "And, of course, our friend Miss Edith Evans."

At the pronouncement of "Miss," his father glanced over at him, but Damien cringed. His father didn't hide his desire for Damien to find a good woman to marry, but this woman was not what he had in mind.

The woman was an old maid with a dour expression and condescending manner—not anything like the type of woman he wanted to spend his life with. Besides, he'd accepted his fate long ago. As long as his father needed him, he'd have to put off his own pursuit of a wife and family. Maybe next year—when his father had some time to realize his brother was lost to them forever—he'd be able to follow his heart. Even then, only the most stunning, most caring young woman would do.

"Father." Damien cleared his throat. "Why don't we head to the back of the boat ferry? We needn't rush to board the great ship. Ladies first, isn't that what you always told me?"

His father nodded, approval reflected in his eyes. *That's my son,* his gaze seemed to say.

As the boat ferry approached the *Titanic,* ten stewards stood at the gangplank, a small army of troops ready for service, but Damien's eyes were not on the stewards. Instead he was drawn to a spot of yellow. A beautiful woman in a buttercup yellow dress stood like a rose among a meadow of thistles. Unlike most of the high society ladies who hid their hair under extravagant hats, her blond hair was pinned up on her head, and a few soft curls slipped from their hold and blew in the wind. As he watched, her head tossed back, and although he couldn't hear her laughter, he saw the way it brightened and transformed her face. He wished he knew the joke her friend at her side shared. Wished he could see that laughter again. He envied her joy and her easy manner. An ache stirred deep inside wanting that for himself.

"Is it everything you expected?" his father asked, speaking of the great ship.

It wasn't a difficult question, but Damien felt himself at a loss for words. "Yes…no. I expected this…but it's also so much more."

His answer, of course, not only spoke of the ship, but of the woman. He'd lived among the same circles for so long he usually wasn't impressed by those he met on voyages. Yet this woman. He knew he hadn't seen her before. A face like that—her fine features and smile—those he would not forget. His heartbeat quickened, and he wasn't sure if the sun had brightened or if it was simply her presence that caused him to warm.

Damien looked at the long line of people ahead of him and willed those walking up the gangplank to hurry. He knew he couldn't make his introduction yet, but...

Please look this way.

He wanted to get close enough to look into her eyes. To see if there was any spark of interest as she looked at him. One thing Damien had learned was that the best business deal was one with mutual interest and investment. He wasn't one to chase a customer, and he had the same opinion about finding a woman to share his heart with. Yet even as he neared, the woman's eyes weren't on him. Instead she looked to his father's maids with an interest that Damien could not understand.

Look this way. Look this way, he willed. But as he neared, the woman lowered her wistful gaze and then turned to her friend who was standing by her side.

His only consolation was they had the whole voyage to get to know each other. And Damien made it his goal to do just that.

Amelia watched as the group of men and women climbed aboard. Men in their proper gray coats and matching caps. Women in dresses that looked fine enough for tea at Windsor Palace. Her knees buckled slightly, but she resisted the urge to curtsy as they passed. And then there were the maids. She saw the eagerness in their eyes. Yes, they boarded as servants, but they, too, experienced the same luxury. Had her mother felt a similar hint of excitement as she traveled to distant places? Mother had served those who traveled upon the seas, but she'd been carried along just the same over the rippling waves.

She glanced to Ethel. The woman's mouth dropped open at the sight of the maids who followed, clutching fresh flowers to their chests. "Even they dress finer than the rest of us," Ethel muttered under her breath.

One of the maids carried a dog who yapped at the gathering crowd, as if warning them to keep back. It was as if the small creature realized those who watched weren't worthy to wait in the shadows of those who walked aboard.

"Serving girls, aren't they lucky?" Amelia murmured. She lowered her head and turned away.

A strange emotion stirred her—a longing for her mother. Being here, on this ship, made her feel closer to her mother than she had in years. Perhaps because she now experienced all the things her mother spoke of. How many nights had Amelia fallen asleep to the gossip from her mother's past, juicy revelations the serving girls had shared with the stewardess from journeys long ago? More than she could count. Those stories had been to her like tales of knights and dragons, godmothers and queens, but being here on the *Titanic* made it all real. She sucked in a breath of salty air and clutched her hands before her. Her lips straightened into a thin line. Her chin quivered and the tendons in her neck tightened as she held back the tears.

Ethel touched her arm. "Are you feeling ill?"

Amelia forced a smile. "Just thinking of my mother."

"Come..." Ethel swept her arm as if offering the deck—all of the *Titanic*—to Amelia. "Let's go listen to the orchestra. That will surely lift your spirits!"

Amelia walked beside Ethel. She tightened her stomach muscles and held a pent-up breath, willing the engines to roar to life and the ship to slide out into the channel. Maybe, if the shore disappeared behind them, the memories would fade into the horizon, too. That would make all things easier.

It seemed only right that she should launch a new life without the old one dragging her back as an anchor.

Damien stepped onto the polished wooden deck, and a chief steward hurried forward. "Welcome, sir, welcome. We are glad to have you upon the *Ship of Dreams.*"

He craned his neck and brushed the man aside. The woman was gone. He let out a disappointed breath and balled his fists at his sides. If only they'd had a chance to make eye contact. Then again, they were on the same ship, with almost a week to run into each other. *Unless.*

He shook his head. *Unless* the woman wasn't a first-class passenger.

"Of course she is," he mumbled to himself. She had to be. If she wasn't—that would be the end of that.

As much as Damien wanted to know the beautiful woman, he also had a standard to uphold. People watched him. They had expectations. He not only represented himself, but his father, too. His brother had done enough damage to the family name. It was his job to rectify all that his brother had tarnished.

Damien remained one step behind his father. Their head butler, Arnold, strode by his father's side, as if creating a buffer between his boss and any commoners who happened to cross his path. Damien followed as another steward led the way to their first-class stateroom, located on the promenade deck. It was almost directly below the bridge near the first smokestack—one of the finest rooms on the ship, he'd been told. Ocean air followed him, filling the corridor with a delightful breeze.

Inside the stateroom, the room's mirrors were trimmed with gold. Real gold. He'd been around it enough to know the difference. Instead of the usual bunks, his and his father's rooms had full bedsteads, a telephone for shipboard communication, and a washstand with hot and cold running water. Hand-carved oak, teak, and maple wood paneling decorated the room in modern style. He eyed the rich velvet drapes and luxurious bedding. There was a sofa and a desk with a lamp. The dressing table looked to be hand-carved as well. If he hadn't known better, he would have guessed they were in a luxury hotel, not on a ship. It was the finest passenger room he'd ever seen.

"Your room has electric lights and heat, sir," the steward said, pushing the switch on and off. "Please let me know if you have any needs."

As his father conversed with the steward and Arnold, Damien walked to the desk. A note sat on the marble top. His name was written in perfect script on the envelope. Who could it be from? One of his father's friends sending an invitation for supper?

He picked up the envelope. The scent of a woman's perfume wafted up to his nose. He knew that scent, and with the whiff of it came a dozen memories of the dark-haired beauty in his arms as they twirled around the dance floors of East Coast estates. In his arms as they kissed in the gardens of English castles. His heartbeat quickened, but he told himself not to get excited. The woman who wrote this note was everything his flesh desired, and for that very reason she did not meet his father's approval.

Swallowing down desire, Damien slipped the piece of monogrammed paper from the envelope.

Damien, imagine my excitement to discover we are on this grand adventure together. I'll meet you at supper. I'll be the one in red.
                                                                Love, Dorothea.

He didn't know whether to smile or to wince as he read the note. Dorothea was one of the most eligible women on this ship—of "old money," his friends reminded him, which meant that her prestige was accompanied by social graces. His friends often forgot he was "new money," which meant their means came from their own hard work rather than investments and inheritances. Though Damien had worked hard to ensure that they forget. So diligently he'd strived to make his manner fit with those who'd been trained to live elegantly, nobly since birth.

Yet for the first time, it didn't bother him that his friends and his father disagreed. It didn't bother him that he'd most likely have to fend off Dorothea's advances. As much as the woman's beauty and allure interested him, there had to be someone else out there who could be his companion in life.

Dorothea was beautiful, yes, but she was painfully spoiled. She expected the best and received it. She was kind...most of the time, but her favor could turn at any moment. Did a woman exist who had a pure heart and good intentions? Someone like his mother.

His father told him often that the right woman was out there, but as the years passed, he'd questioned if such a thing was true. That was why he'd found Dorothea in his arms more often than not. When one felt lonely, the companionship of another was like balm to an aching soul. His only concern was that she took their relationship more seriously than he. The note she'd left on his desk proved that fact.

Damien moved to his trunk that had been delivered to the room and pulled out the jacket he'd picked up from the tailor in London. The fit and style favored him, the tailor had exclaimed.

As he hung the jacket in the wardrobe, he again thought of the blond woman on the deck. Perhaps she was someone worth getting to know. After traveling the same circles for so long, a new face was always a welcome sight.

He removed his hat and placed it on an ornate hook on the wall, glancing at the crystal chandelier. His emotions over returning to the States were mixed. He was eager to return to their fine estate, but he'd be lying if he didn't admit he carried the burden of his father's pain. They'd traveled to London for business, but more than once Damien had overheard his father's command to the servants. "Please, while you go about your tasks, be on the lookout for my son."

Damien sighed and finger-combed his hair as he looked into the gilded mirror. His father hadn't been the same since Quentin's departure. Yet Damien was glad they were returning to America without him. Quin had been a fool. He'd demanded what he had no right to receive—and walked away from all he knew—trampling their father's heart with each step. His father's fortune, though they lived well, had never quite recovered from being cut in half. Quentin's greed insured those left behind would have to watch their own accounting more closely.

Damien left their room and strode toward the first-class deck.

He found his way to the gentleman's first-class smoking lounge, taking in the mahogany paneled walls and mother of pearl inlaid work. Painted glass windows displayed pastoral landscapes, ancient ships, and mythological figures. Potted plants offered the room color, life.

A bartender wiped down an immaculately clean bar, and two young men dressed in new suits chatted about jobs waiting for them in New York as they smoked cigars. Damien sat in the tall-backed chair, and thankfulness flooded him. They were on the *Titanic*. They would be leaving London, and hopefully when they returned to Maryland, thoughts of his brother would stay far away.

His knee bounced. He was eager for the ship to place an ocean between them. He tired of his father's craning neck and wide-eyed pursuance of every tall, young, dark-haired man. What his father didn't know was that Quentin wouldn't be found in the restaurants and museums they visited. While his father had hired investigators to find his son over the years, Damien paid double to make sure their findings never met his father's ears. The newspaper clippings after Quentin first moved to London had been bad enough. It pained his father to see how Quentin had wasted his fortune on wild living. It would kill him to know his son slept in the gutters and ate out of trash cans. What he hid was for his father's protection. His peace.

Damien scanned the crowd, and a bit of color caught his eye from the doorway to his right. The woman in the yellow dress—as soft and delicate as a rose in the queen's garden—peeked into the room. Another woman walked by her side. Would it be too forward for him to make an introduction? He took a step and then paused.

As they passed, he heard the woman speak to her friend. "Could you imagine crossing the ocean in first class? Maybe someday, Ethel, we'll experience such a thing."

Her words caused his head to jerk back as if she'd slapped him across the face with her gloves. She wasn't first class, thus she wasn't suitable. The two ideas, in his mind—and in the minds of those of his peers—went hand in hand. Damien considered introducing himself to the woman despite her social standing. The more he thought about it, the more he liked it. All those in first class knew who he was, knew who his father was. But what about someone in second class? He doubted it.

Damien stroked a hand down his chin. What would it be like to spend time with someone who would look at him as just another man instead of an heir to a fortune? At thirty-one years of age, he'd never known such a thing.

From the moment he'd boarded the ship, all eyes had been on him—on his father. He knew over the days to come their every need would be met. He'd be introduced to beautiful, eligible women and engage in talk of politics, science, and literature. It wouldn't be necessary to introduce himself. All would know who he was as clearly as if he'd had his name pinned to his chest.

Yet she hadn't even glanced over to try to get his attention as she passed. If he introduced himself, she wouldn't know who he was, and even if she did, it wouldn't matter in the slightest.

And for the first time ever, he liked that.

Chapter 4

The excitement of their launch soon lifted Amelia's mood. Tonight, as she snuggled in her bunk, she'd think or Mother and wonder, *Why couldn't things have turned out differently?* But today—today she was going to let the joy of the occasion push those thoughts to the side. Today she would celebrate being part of a new era of history—being a passenger on a new league of ship.

She'd decided something else, too. On this trip aboard the *Titanic,* Amelia would strive to live in the present. She wouldn't let the anchor of her mother's memory sink her spirits. She wouldn't let the waves of worry over what waited on the other shore crash against her heart.

Dear God, she prayed within her mind, her soul. *Help me live in this moment and be open to what you have for me. New friendships or new insights ... new relationships and a stronger faith.* Amelia smiled. That prayer was a first step. It wasn't that she didn't believe in God. She did. She loved Him greatly. But with the many needs that always presented themselves, Amelia often worked in the strength she could muster. While many knew her to be a caring and capable woman, she hadn't been as bold in sharing her faith in God as she wished.

"Give me a chance to do that." She whispered the words, only to have them swallowed up by the noises blaring all around on the deck.

The docks and gangways buzzed as the final passengers and crew members hurried on board.

The ship's whistle caused Amelia to jump, and laughter spilled from her lips.

The man next to her pulled a pocket watch from his waistcoat. "Precisely noon." He nodded. "Time for the RMS *Titanic* to launch." A smile filled his face, and he walked among the other passengers as their cheers grew.

"RMS *Titanic*," she whispered. How many times had she heard that name? Tens, hundreds of times.

A locomotive could pass through each funnel that jutted into the sky, she'd read. A double-deck tramcar could pass through each of its twenty-nine boilers that were tucked away far under her feet.

Those who had been visiting the ship hurried back to the docks with waves and final good wishes to travelers. The gangplanks were drawn, and Amelia looked around for the first time, noticing how little room the *Titanic* had to maneuver out of the bay.

"Why are there so many ships at the dock?" she asked Ethel.

"A coal strike. I heard many passengers who were supposed to be on other ships are now on the *Titanic*. I feel bad for those other ships, but I'm sure those who were transferred here don't mind one bit."

Amelia waved to those on the quay.

"Do you have any friends or family wishing you off?" Ethel asked.

"No, I said all my good-byes over the last few weeks."

She didn't tell Ethel that most of her friends were children or those who cared for children. Either that or hardworking widowed mothers who did all they could to put food on the table. She'd gained their friendship as she'd ventured into the slums to offer a helping hand. To spend half the day at the docks, wishing her farewell, would be time those poor mothers could not afford to be away.

Over the last few weeks, she'd spent extra time with the children at the orphanage and other friends around town. She promised them all that she'd write letters about the voyage. Many of her friends were more interested in hearing about Mr. Chapman who waited on the opposite shore than they were excited about the *Titanic*. She'd read them his letters, and most had approved. All except one, her dear Marguerite.

"He seems kindly enough," Marguerite had said with a wrinkle of her nose, "but the man works in a bank. He has his supper precisely at six o'clock and attends the orchestra each Saturday. You are a woman who knows not what her day holds until she wakes and scours the city for the most pressing needs. I'm afraid you'll find him a bore."

"A bore? How could you say that? He's the type of person I've been looking for," Amelia had declared. Marguerite, more than anyone, should appreciate not having to worry for one's next meal or being an old maid without the hope of a family or children of her own.

"Jealous, that's what she is," Amelia muttered.

"Excuse me?" Ethel said over the noise of the crowd.

Amelia turned her attention back to the matter at hand, reminding herself that thoughts of whether Mr. Chapman was suitable could wait until she reached the distant shore. "Uh, I was simply commenting that I feel bad for all those on the docks. I am sure they are jealous they aren't on the ship."

"Next voyage." Ethel pushed back the strands of dark hair that had slipped out of her pinned-up bun. "They can book a ticket on *Titanic's* next voyage."

There were no flags flying or bands playing, but the excitement was contagious. Laughter and talking filled the air, and a sharp whistle caused the volume to grow. Within moments a rumble below deck told her the enormous luxury ship would be venturing out into the channel of the River Test. Six tugboats escorted the ship, blasting their horns. Then, as if in slow motion, *Titanic* floated away from the quay slowly, gently.

Amelia and Ethel leaned against the railing. Stretching out from either side of them, straw hats and handkerchiefs waved in the air. Children stood up on the rails, waving at the crowds on the dock.

Shouts rose from those who waved them off. "Godspeed! Godspeed!"

"I can't believe I am so lucky. To be one of the first." Ethel sighed.

The *Titanic* moved majestically down the dock, and the crowd followed it. On its way out, it passed beside the steamer *New York,* moored to the dock.

As Amelia watched, the displaced water pushed nearer the *New York* and lifted it upward. The ship passed, and within seconds three sharp sounds filled the air.

Amelia jumped. "Sounds like gunshots!"

"Look!" Ethel pointed.

Like whips splitting the air, the *New York*'s mooring ropes flung themselves into the waiting crowd on the dock. Screams erupted, and Amelia saw sailors running to the aid of some of the bystanders who must have been struck by the recoiling ropes. Exclamations of worry rumbled through those on *Titanic*'s deck, and they watched with worry as the *New York*'s gangway crashed into the water. Then, as if being pulled by an invisible force, *New York*'s stern swung out toward the *Titanic.*

"What's happening?" Amelia asked no one in particular.

She didn't need an answer. It was clear the suction and waves caused by the *Titanic*'s huge propellers had caused the other ship's thick ropes to strain and break. And now there was nothing keeping that same suction from pulling the *New York* into *Titanic's* hull. The *New York* grew closer, closer.

Amelia pressed a hand to her chest. "We're going to be hit!"

A small tug boat got a line onto the *New York*. It strained with all its might, attempting to hold the ship. The tug rocked side to side as it pulled, and Amelia held her breath, wondering if the tug's efforts would do any good.

At the stern, officers with sharp black suits with gold buttons and sailors in white uniforms shouted out commands. The men rushed past to various stations, ringing bells and telephoning the bridge. White and red flags were hauled up and down a line, and within a minute the *Titanic* came to a stop. Now that the large ship had stilled, the suction ceased and the tug was able to pull the vessel farther down the quay. Then, as if tugged by a magnet, the *New York* slipped back into its place at the docks.

Amelia released the breath she'd been holding. That had been a close one. Only a few yards had separated the hulls of the *New York* and the *Titanic*. She hated to think of what damage the *Titanic* would have done to the smaller ship.

The tug continued on, carrying them toward the open waters. Only when they were clear of danger did the *Titanic's* engines once again come to life. She and Ethel watched as they slowly passed a second ship, the *Teutonic*. That ship also strained at its ropes so much that it heeled over several degrees, attempting to follow the *Titanic*. Amelia placed a hand over her mouth, expecting its mooring lines to break also. Just then she felt the slightest touch on her wrist. She glanced over to notice a handsome man standing next to her with concern in his gaze.

"Don't worry," he commented. "The lines will hold, and all our troubles will soon be behind us."

There was something familiar about the man's handsome face—his eyes. She peered into their dark depths and then sucked in a breath. It was the man from the dock.

"You've shaved." She stammered. His eyes remained steady on Amelia as she swallowed. It was clear he'd done more than shave. His hair was shorter. He wore Henry's clothes, but if it weren't for his beautiful dark eyes, she never would have believed it was the same man.

Her heart beat faster. Her hand self-consciously patted her hair, making sure her hair pins were still in place. She forgot about the ships they passed. And it wasn't until she heard the sound of a clearing throat that Amelia remembered Ethel standing by her side.

"Ethel," she piped up, remembering her manners. "I'd like to introduce you to a friend..." Her voice trailed off. "I'm sorry, sir, but I believe I've forgotten your name."

"Henry Gladstone." The man winked at Amelia and then extended his hand to Ethel. "Nice to meet you, Ethel. I have to say I do love your brooch."

Ethel placed a hand to her neck and fingered the small cameo brooch. "Thank you. It was a wedding gift from—oh, Edward." She placed a hand on her cheek. "I've been so caught up in the launch. I must go. I must check on my husband. I'd love to meet up again soon, Amelia... with both of you. Maybe in the dining room? Sometime for supper?" She offered Amelia a quick hug and then waved back toward the man—whatever his real name was—as she hurried off.

Amelia turned back to him, gazing up into his face, wondering why being in his presence unnerved her so. As strange as it was, she'd felt far more comfortable near him when he'd been in rags than when he was dressed neatly in Henry's clothes.

"I'm glad to see you found the items in Henry's suitcase useful," she said. "No one would doubt you really were Henry Gladstone now."

"Are you saying I'm not?" He gasped, and his brown-eyed gaze held a startled expression.

As she wondered how to respond, a smile spread over his face, and she released the breath she'd been holding.

"I'm sorry. I don't want to appear ungrateful," he said. "The items in the suitcase were very handy indeed." He glanced out at the water, and his hair ruffled against his forehead from the noonday breeze. "I wouldn't be here without you, Amelia."

Her lips fell open when he said her name. Goose bumps rose on her arms, and she pretended it was from the cool breeze that picked up as the ship's speed increased.

"Thank you for everything," he whispered softly.

She tilted her head, attempting to keep her heart from leaping from her chest at his nearness. She tried to remind herself who this man was. Tried to picture him as he was on the dock—in rags and slumped between the stewards—but that image faded with his smile. It was only the gash in his cheek that confirmed his true identity, evidence to her that he would have been sleeping under one of Southampton's bridges tonight had she not approached and offered the ticket.

"You are welcome, of course, and I will say we're even if you give me a gift in return."

His eyebrows furrowed, and his eyes cast downward. From his worried expression, she knew he hadn't a coin to give, but a coin—or what it could buy—wasn't what she wanted.

"And what would this gift be?" he asked.

Somewhere down the deck, a child's laughter filled the air, and Amelia smiled—partly from the laughter and partly because this man's complete attention was fixed on her.

"Tell me your real name," she finally said.

He released the breath he'd been holding and ran a hand through his dark hair. "Quentin."

"Is that all of your name or only part?" she asked, waiting for him to offer his last name, too.

He didn't answer right away. Looking up at him again, she pouted. It was the playful kind of pout she'd seen young women offer their beaus. Of course he wasn't her beau. Still, she couldn't help but notice that her playfulness added color to his cheeks.

She absently played with the ruffle of her dress collar and wondered why she was acting in such a way. Why did her mind scurry to find something else to ask him? Something to keep him from turning and walking away along the deck that was filled with lingering passengers.

"It is only part of my name." He tugged at the too-short sleeves of his jacket. "It is enough." He leaned closer, his mouth next to her ear. "And whatever you do, you *cannot* mention my name to anyone on this ship. You cannot reveal my presence."

She nodded, accepting that, yet what was he hiding? What secret could his name reveal? Unless he was worried about getting in trouble for taking the identity of another. Maybe she could, too, for offering the ticket. Perhaps his resolve was a means of protecting her.

They stood facing each other, and he leaned by degrees until his hip connected with the deck's rail. She could see that he was relaxing in her presence, but she felt anything but relaxed. She'd worked with many homeless people before, but this man no longer appeared homeless. She wanted to ask him his story. She wanted to know why he'd been down on his luck, what had brought him so low, who he'd been before. It was clear there was more to him than she'd first imagined. If she were to guess, he was educated, cultured. But how could that be? More questions than answers filled her mind. She opened her mouth to ask but then closed it again.

"I received your note, but I don't think I should join you for supper," he said matter-of-factly. "I do appreciate your kindness, though, with the offer."

She squared her shoulders as she looked at him. "Don't you think people will question if one of our party is missing from supper? I'm sure the dining staff will be expecting Henry Gladstone to join us. If you're going to play the part, you should play it well," she teased.

He eyed her. His jaw tensed. It was not his choice to play a part, and she could tell that if she pushed him on any matter he'd shrink off for certain.

"But more than that," she hurriedly continued, "I'd like to get to know a little more about you, Quentin."

His head jerked back as she said his name, as if he hadn't heard it spoken in a while.

Beneath his direct gaze, she felt her face flame. He was so utterly handsome. A brief smile filled her face as she quickly turned her attention to where the stewards set out deck chairs. Not willing to part just yet, she placed a soft hand on his arm. Was her eagerness to spend time with him evident in her gaze?

"Would you like to take in some sun?" she asked. "It looks like a lovely afternoon to get to know each other."

That afternoon Quentin felt as if he were part of a dream. Yesterday he'd first seen the *Titanic*'s tall funnels from the train station in Southampton, and today he sat on its deck, enjoying a time of leisure with a beautiful woman.

Children's laughter filled the air. Two small boys chased each other while their father looked on amused. Wholesome families enjoyed time together. A mother carried a baby on her hip and pointed to the lifeboats on the deck. "Boat, boat," she said, attempting to teach him a new word. Even on the second-class deck where they sat, there was plenty of space for passengers to take a stroll or relax.

People laughed and chatted as they enjoyed the sun. A man in a wrinkled suit walked alone, appearing out of place but also excited. Quentin understood. Just being on the ship made one feel important, part of a new community. From this day forward, the story of the *Titanic*'s first day at sea would always be one to tell.

The *Titanic* moved its course down the English Channel, and Quentin guessed they'd be docked in Cherbourg by night.

"Look how that ship is rolling! I never thought the sea was so rough." The comment came from a lady at the rail. Quentin sat up straighter, and from his view between the lifeboats, he noticed a large three-masted sailing vessel. It rolled and pitched in the waves as if a string were attached to its bottom and a great force from underneath attempted to pull it under.

Yet far above the waterline, those on the deck of the *Titanic* felt no movement. The ship was like a steady rock in the tempestuous sea. It was only the brisk breeze that brushed Quentin's cheeks and pulled Amelia's hair from its pins, blowing it now and again across her face, that hinted of their movement at all.

As if feeling his gaze upon her, Amelia turned from watching the crowd and studied him. Her gaze lifted and lingered on his face.

Come on, Quentin, think of something witty ... something wise. Nothing came.

"So Amelia, is this your first time across the ocean?" It was all he could come up with.

"Yes, I've watched the ships come and go many times, more than I could count. It's great to be on one."

"Have you lived in Southampton all your life?"

"All of it. I've only been out of the city a few times, too. It's all I've known ... so this is quite the experience." She eyed him. "How about you?"

"I've been on a few ships. Traveled all over. Like to Italy."

She nodded and waited for him to continue.

"And to Germany, but of course I didn't get there by ship." He forced a chuckle and wondered why he struggled with his words.

Why does she unnerve me so? The weight of her gaze penetrated into deep, hidden places. He looked away and stared up at the expansive blue sky dotted with clouds. His stomach ached with the old familiar tension of uncertainty. His desire to get to know her wrapped around his heart like sailing ropes and cinched down.

"Did you live … well, did you live on the streets then, too?"

"No. That was before."

She waited for him to continue, but what type of excuse could he give?

"You're probably wondering how I ended up as I did. You have a right to know," Quentin said. "After all, you are the reason I'm here."

"I'm just curious. Don't feel as if you owe me an explanation. You just don't seem like a street person, that's all."

"I'm not—" The words blurted out. "Well, I was, but I shouldn't have been. I made some poor choices. Stupid mistakes."

Part of him wanted to share his heart with her. Another part wanted to run. He'd lived too long in the shadows, and the truth was Quentin didn't like being watched, questioned.

Being on the streets it was better not to be seen. He shifted in his chair and refused to look her direction to see if her gaze was still on him. He didn't understand why she was being so kind. She knew the type of man he was.

Ever since he was a child, he'd had eyes on him, especially after his father became wealthy. His mother made sure he dressed properly from head to toe. His brother had always been an entertainer, and each time after Damien's song and dance, all eyes had turned to Quentin. What could the younger brother do? How could he entertain?

For a time—when he was on his own—he didn't have to worry about living in his brother's shadow. He had his own money. His own friends. Yet when his money disappeared, his friends did, too.

If he enjoyed anything about being on the streets, it was that no one paid him any mind. People didn't look long on someone so unlovely. It had been easy to find a dark corner under a bridge or in a wooded park.

But now—he couldn't explain why he appreciated Amelia's presence. He hated that she'd seen him at his worst, but deep down he was thankful. He didn't have to put on airs and try to be something he wasn't.

She had a contagious inner joy, and when she rested her caring eyes on him, he forgot who he'd been just hours ago. He still felt uneasy, but as the minutes passed, Quentin welcomed the bright thoughts that filtered through the clouds of gray that often stormed through his mind. He allowed himself to consider what he could be. And perhaps what they could be together.

No, it's too soon to think of that. He pushed that last hope from his mind.

It had been so long since a woman had taken interest in him, he had to remind himself that just because she offered her friendship didn't mean she thought more of him than that. Why would she? Why would anyone?

Squinting into the lowering sun, they watched the children play. The rail cast shadows that lengthened, nearing the chairs where he and Amelia sat as the minutes ticked by. The long shadows of the boats, rigging, ropes, and rails became artistic creations splayed on the deck.

When was the last time he'd paused to look at such things? For too long he'd only been worried about his next meal or where to lay his head.

"So, I have to ask," Amelia was saying. "I can tell by your accent you're American. I won't ask how you got to England." Amelia looked over him and narrowed her gaze. "Not yet anyway." She smiled. "Have you traveled around the States much? I have spoken to a few people who have visited, and it seems like a beautiful and expansive place."

"Beautiful, yes, at least most places. I've been all over the States. My father's...uh...work saw to that. I grew up in Maryland. I've been to Florida, California by train, and all the States the train took me through to get there."

"Have you been to New York?" Amelia's voice rose an octave.

"Yes." He chuckled at the joy on her face. "Why?"

"Have you seen the Ziegfeld Follies?"

Quentin thought back. The last time he'd been in the city he'd only been a teen. He'd been more interested in the tall buildings and their construction than the musicals.

"No, why?"

"Oh, no reason really. Except that I love the music." Enthusiasm bubbled out with her words. "Tin Pan Alley songs is what they call them."

Quentin furrowed his brow. "I'm sorry, Amelia. I haven't really kept up with the latest music ...."

"The name comes from music publishers set up in Manhattan. One of my aunt's neighbors had a phonograph. He didn't have money for meat from the butcher, but he always had the latest records. I would often go to sleep at night to the music drifting through the walls. He told me about the Ziegfeld Follies in New York, too. Famous stars sing there, and they have beautiful chorus girls called Ziegfeld girls. Once I fell asleep to the music and dreamt I was singing in the chorus."

She smiled and hummed a tune. Her face lit up as she did, and he imagined taking her to a place like that. In his old life he could have seen to that. Now it was only an impossible dream.

As she continued humming—slightly out of key—Quentin vaguely recognized the tune. A few times over the last two years, he'd slipped into small pubs and had a chance to listen to a few songs before they'd kicked him out. The song she hummed must have been one of the popular ones. If he wasn't mistaken, the lyrics said something about a moon.

"Manhattan. That's pretty close to where the docks are in New York. Do you think you'll get a chance to visit the follies while you're there?"

"Oh no." The words blurted from her lips. "I won't stay in New York. I'm heading to New Haven, Connecticut. I have...uh...my cousin is there."

"Your cousin. I see." From the guilty look on her face, Quentin could tell there was more to her story, but he decided not to press.

"Besides," she quickly added. "To go to such a show like that would cost a lot of money. Money that could be used to help people."

Tingles ran up his neck, and memories of this morning crashed down upon him. For a little while he'd forgotten who he was and how he'd lived for the past two years. Her words reminded him again how she saw him, how she rescued him.

"I see." He whistled under his breath. "So I'm not the only one who calls you my angel of mercy."

Pink rose up her cheeks, and he could see that she liked his pet name.

"Well, I help where I can."

He folded his arms over his chest. "It seems to me that it's not necessary to always give and care. Everyone needs a chance to relax, to listen to music they like and enjoy a good conversation."

Amelia nodded. "It makes sense, but I'm finding it hard even now to sit here." She smiled. "Even though I enjoy it, I know there are beds that need to be made somewhere. Maybe there's a tired mother who would appreciate an extra pair of arms to help her with her children...."

"I understand." And deep down, he truly did. From the time he left his father's home, he'd worked. When he wasn't working, he spent time with friends, enjoying the good life. That had kept him busy in a different way.

Even after he lost it all, he didn't sit. He ran. He lived on the streets and knew each passageway. He walked them. Heading where, he didn't know. To sit meant he had time to remember, and remembering was the hardest of all.

Amelia nodded and settled back into the lounge chair, letting her eyes close briefly. Quentin felt himself settling in, too. Here, with her, he found a glimpse of peace he hadn't known for as long as he could remember.

Then, just as Quentin felt himself relaxing into the lounge chair, he glanced up to notice an older woman approaching. The woman's eyes studied Amelia, and then the woman looked to him. Her eyebrows furrowed as she glanced from his shirt and jacket to his pants and even his shoes. Thoroughly displeased, she turned her attention to his face, and Quentin knew that she saw right through him. To her he wasn't simply another passenger on the ship. He was someone who wasn't worthy to be here. She looked at him as a thousand Londoners had looked at him over the previous two years—with disapproval.

Amelia was saying something—asking a question about supper—but he didn't make out all her words. He only saw the disgust in the older woman's eyes—the silent accusations. More than anything, Quentin wanted to run again—to find a hidden corner in the bowels of the ship. For Amelia's sake he remained, but it took everything within him to stay rooted in place.

"So, Quentin," Amelia asked, "what do you suppose they'll serve for supper? On a ship this nice, I'd guess it will be something delightful."

The words were no more out of her mouth than her aunt approached. The thin, older woman leaned heavily on her cane as she walked down the deck. Amelia sucked in a breath and stood to hurry toward her. Guilt over not attending to her aunt weighed on her with every step. More than that, lounging with a handsome man was shameful. After all, what would Mr. Chapman say? Amelia didn't want to think of that.

"Aunt Neda, please tell me you didn't take the stairs alone. I'm sorry I didn't come for you sooner. I suppose I got carried away with the launch." She felt Quentin's presence as he rose and stood behind her, but she didn't know what to say. She felt like a child who'd just snuck a biscuit from her mother's plate. Her aunt tilted up her head and eyed the tall man. Recognition filled her face, and something else—disbelief. Maybe she should have confessed to her aunt that she'd given the man the ticket and Henry's clothes instead of letting her discover it for herself.

Instead of commenting to him, she turned to Amelia. "I see your cousin's property has not gone to waste. I assume the room is also being put to good use."

Quentin stepped forward. "If it is a problem—"

Her aunt's lifted hand halted Quentin's words. "It is not a problem. I know my niece, and I'm not surprised."

He lowered his head like a child who'd just been scolded, even though Aunt Neda's disapproval was directed to her niece and not him.

"I do appreciate it," he said. Then he turned to Amelia. "I will leave you to enjoy the day. Thank you again." He hurried away before Amelia had a chance to respond.

Her lower lip puckered.

"Do you think I should go after him—to invite him to supper? I'd hate to have him feel as if he doesn't have a friend on the ship."

"Amelia. Just because you helped him once does not mean you need to have any further responsibilities. What do you know of the man? He could be a scoundrel or a crook. He was trying to sneak on this ship after all."

"As any poor man would," she said in his defense. "Just because one does not have sufficient means does not mean he has an evil heart. I have a good feeling about him, Aunt. I believe there is more to Quentin than what's on the surface."

Her aunt nodded but did not respond, and with careful steps Amelia led her to one of the lounge chairs and helped her to sit. Quentin reminded Amelia of the young children who'd come to the orphanage after living in poor conditions. He was wounded—that she knew—and he was scared. Mostly, he was looking for a friend, one person he could trust. She could see that deep in his gaze.

If only I could do more for him.

Amelia hoped to be that friend. Maybe in their weeklong journey she'd get the opportunity. It was a ship of dreams—of hope—after all.

Chapter 5

Clarence Walpole walked onto the first-class deck of the *Titanic*, gripping the handrail with each step as if he held on to his last ounce of faith. Leaving England's shores meant he left his youngest son. Deep regrets churned in his heart, just as the large *Titanic* propellers churned up silt from the bay floor.

He stared into the water. His heart ached. His eyes blinked back tears. How could he still have tears? He'd cried enough to fill this channel—to fill the Atlantic.

His throat felt on fire as he attempted to hold in his own muted cries. It was as if stokers shoveled in smoldering coals and he was forced to keep them down with one swallow. But he did not cry. He had to be strong. He had to prove that God's strength carried him; otherwise, what hope could he offer?

Clarence stared into the water. The light played on the ripple of waves flowing away from the ship, stirring a memory. He gripped the rail tighter as he was taken back to that place again— the place that never left his thoughts.

Jillian's still form under the water. The shock of jumping in and pulling her body to the shore. Her blond hair splayed— tangled and limp on the grass. Her beautiful dress clinging to her frame, and her arms limp at her side.

Yet it was her face Clarence could not forget. Pale yet serene. Perfect, as if someone had cast a porcelain doll to model his wife. He'd never seen her so still. Even in her sleep, Jillian had been restless, as if sleep was an interruption to her full and fulfilled life. She'd always been excited for what the next day held, whether it was ordering uniforms for their sons' new school or gathering flowers in the garden to fill the crystal vase on their dining room table. He'd never been one interested in attaining wealth for himself. Clarence had worked for all he had for her—for their sons. Yet what joy was work without Jillian to celebrate in the rewards?

Even after almost twenty years, he couldn't help but think of how excited she would have been to be on such a fine ship as the *Titanic*. They'd traveled across the Atlantic Ocean a number of times in their twelve years of marriage, but those steamers could not hold a candle to the opulence he found here. It was like comparing a simple wedding band to queen Victoria's jewels. And because of her—because of the memory he carried in his heart—he'd booked one of the finest rooms he could afford for the joy of imagining Jillian experiencing the richness and comfort with him.

Besides, Damien would enjoy it. His eldest son reminded Clarence of the boy's mother. He appreciated fine things, and Clarence worked hard to see he enjoyed them often. Unlike most of the other wealthy passengers who prided themselves in stacking up their riches, filling the banks and growing their worth in figures, Clarence knew that money was fleeting. He'd seen much lost with little effort. Since then he'd decided to enjoy what he had while he could—and share each treasure-filled day with Damien while he had the chance.

Cold air nipped at his cheeks, and Clarence turned so his face met the breeze full force. It was no use looking back to England. The sight of the land slipping into the horizon would remind him he was returning yet again to America without Quentin. With each step through the London streets, Clarence felt his youngest son's presence, yet just when he believed he was close to finding Quentin, his son again disappeared like a reflection of the moon on a still pond at daybreak.

"Clarence Walpole, is that you?"

Clarence turned to find Thomas Andrews, designer of the *Titanic*. A smile filled the man's face, and Clarence wondered if Thomas's buttons would burst from his chest puffed out with pride.

"Thomas, I expected to see you here. I have to say, son, you've built one amazing ship."

Thomas lowered his head bashfully then lifted it, meeting Clarence's gaze with a twinkle in his eyes. "I didn't build the ship. That was a task for a large crew, but I do believe my design turned out well."

"Well? I'd say that is an understatement. Is it true there are watertight steel compartments supposed to render her unsinkable?"

Thomas laughed. "Clarence, that is just the beginning. Have you ever heard of a ship with submarine signals with microphones? Their job is to tell the bridge by means of wires when another ship or any other object is at hand. Not to mention the collision bulkhead to safeguard the ship against an invasion of water should the bow be torn away. The *Titanic* has both!"

Clarence offered a low whistle. "Who would have ever thought it possible? I'm planning on doing more exploring— I'm eager to see the Turkish baths and photography darkroom— although I'd better wait for Damien to lead the way. You've heard rumors, no doubt, of how dreadful I am with directions."

"Who needs to find his own way with a staff such as you have?" Thomas glanced at his watch. "Speaking of business, I told Mr. Ismay I'd give him a private tour, so I must be going. Please do tell your sons I hope they enjoy the trip." And with a quick wave, Thomas Andrews hurried away.

Sons. Clarence guessed it was simply a slip of the man's lips. Most people he knew didn't mention *sons.* Most spoke as if Damien was his only child. The same thing had happened after Jillian's death. No one—not even her closest friends—spoke her name. It was as if she'd never existed. That bothered Clarence, but it was understandable. To mention someone meant mourning their death in the same breath. The difference was he had not buried Quentin. Five years had passed since his son had walked out the door, his pockets full of his inheritance—five long years.

But his youngest son still lived—he was sure of it. Something deep in his heart told him to hope. He had faith in God that somehow, somewhere that fact would be confirmed.

Clarence dared to turn. He glanced back at the narrow strip of land. His last glimpse of England. Somewhere back in that all too familiar place his son walked the streets. If only he could know Quentin was well. That would have been enough. If only he could have seen a glimpse of him. It would have appeased his father-heart.

But until then he could only trust. God saw his son. God loved Quentin, and at this moment that had to be enough.

The sea air chilled to the bone, or at least that was what Aunt Neda said as they strode out of the breeze, heading inside to the glass-enclosed second-class promenade deck.

"Yes, this is much better." Aunt Neda tucked stray strands of gray hair into her bonnet.

"It's to keep you dry. You can take in the sea air without being splashed by the spray." Amelia spoke to her aunt, but her eyes scanned the passengers, looking for Quentin. Men, women, families walked along the enclosed deck. An older boy ran by in suspenders and cap, but Quentin was nowhere to be seen.

"I feel as comfortable here as I would walking down Market Street." Aunt Neda smiled. "I can barely feel the vibration from the engines."

Amelia nodded an acknowledgment, but her mind wasn't on her aunt's words. Aunt Neda had meant no harm, but Quentin hadn't heard her aunt's words that way. She saw the shame on his face as her aunt had pointed out his borrowed things—and that memory caused Amelia's heart to ache. Amelia had seen the same look hundreds of times, if not more, on the faces of those she'd tried to help. Her greatest joy was to offer help to someone in need, yet many people accepted her gifts feeling worse about themselves. Charity was hard to accept sometimes, no matter if the hand that offered it did so with a noble heart.

Aunt Neda patted Amelia's hand. "As delightful as this is, I'd like to return to our room to write a few letters to our friends back in Southampton before supper."

"Yes, of course." Amelia tried not to smile too broadly. With Aunt Neda writing letters, she'd be able to find Quentin and apologize. To clear the air and maybe get to know him better.

They used the lift to take them back to D deck. She marveled at the contraption and smiled at the kind young man who seemed as excited about operating the lift as they were about riding in it.

"It seems you enjoy your job," she said, taking in his wide-eyed gaze.

"I enjoy meeting all our guests the most. And what is your name, ma'am?"

"Amelia Gladstone, and this is my aunt Neda."

"Gladstone?" he chuckled. "Are you related to our former prime minister?"

Amelia laughed as if she hadn't heard that question every day of her life. "If I were, I'd be riding in first class. I have no doubt about that."

"What do you think of the magnificent *Titanic,* Miss Gladstone?"

"It's like nothing I've ever seen. If I weren't looking out the windows, I'd never know it was moving, so smooth the ride."

They chatted until they reached their deck. As soon as the lift doors opened, she stepped out and scanned the hallway. Her heart fell. There was no sign of Quentin. A steward in a sharp white suit was the only one who walked down the long passageway.

Once her aunt was settled back in the room, Amelia shut the door of their stateroom behind her and moved to the next door. Amelia took a deep breath and knocked—quietly enough so her aunt wouldn't realize what she was doing, but hopefully loud enough for Quentin to hear. She thought she heard rustling inside but wasn't sure.

Was Quentin hiding from her? She wouldn't blame him if he did.

Amelia turned as footsteps approached. An older stewardess neared with a pile of fresh linens in her arms.

The stewardess paused before Amelia, tilting her head to the side. "Emma?" She tossed her gray curls as soon as the words were out. "Nah, that's not possible."

"I'm not Emma, but surely you couldn't mean…Did you believe I was Emma Gladstone?" Amelia took a tentative step forward. A thousand butterflies fluttered in her stomach. Her hand covered the spot where her racing heart was sure to jump from her chest. "That's my mother's name. She was a stewardess on many ships. Did you know her?"

The woman nodded, and the look in her eyes told Amelia she was thinking back to a distant past. "Oh, I did." The stewardess was short but erect, with a pert nose and full cheeks. An Irish lilt softened her words.

"Have you seen her lately? By lately, I mean the last twelve years?" Amelia's words were eager, intrigued and worried at the same time.

"Darlin', it's been eighteen years at least. Emma looked as young and beautiful as you the last time we worked side by side. Ye look exactly like her, you know. But when I remembered how many years had passed since I'd seen my friend, I knew you could not be. In fact, I remember when she was with child—she tried to hide her age to keep her job, but she could only do it for so long." A memory sparked in the woman's eyes.

Amelia touched a hand to her cheek. She had a hundred questions about her mother—what had she been like? Had she been happy on the ship? It would make Amelia feel better to know that if her mother chose her work over her daughter she would have been happy doing so, yet one question rose to the top.

"Since you knew my mother before she had me, do you know who my father is? Did she ever mention him?"

The older woman shook her head. "I'm sorry, child. If she told me, I do not know. It's been many a year—too long. I've sailed many voyages. I've worked with so many friends. The stories run together, you see. And maybe..." She let her voice trail off. "Maybe it's best to enjoy the present rather than worry about the past."

There was something in the woman's gaze that told Amelia she knew more than she offered up, yet Amelia didn't press. She remembered the prayer she'd just prayed—to let go of the past and let it sink to the bottom of the sea. It was enough to have met this woman, wasn't it? To know she looked like her mother. To experience a taste of what her mother had experienced as she sailed away from the quay at Southampton.

"This is a great privilege meeting you on this ship, of all the ones," the stewardess continued. "Your ma would have thought something great of this. That's why I remember her when so many other stewardesses are lost in my memory. Emma got excited over the smallest things. Old sugar lumps from the kitchen and tea in chipped china cups. She loved the sunsets over the ocean. She'd sit by me in the evenings as we put our tired feet up and say, 'Geraldine, you'll never imagine what I saw today.' I feasted more on her stories than even the food put before me."

"Yes, I remember that about her." Amelia twirled a blond curl around her finger and slowly released it. "As a child I never knew how much I lacked, because dinner was always a party." She chuckled softly. "Partly from the stories...and partly because my mother's obtaining enough food for the day was something to appreciate." Amelia's voice caught in her throat. Her mother had worked so hard for the simplest of things.

Geraldine offered a sad smile and lowered her voice. "Since you're asking, my child, I suspect you haven't seen her recently?"

Amelia's eyes grew moist. "No. She left for work...years ago...saying she'd only be gone for one month. I haven't heard a word since. At least I am grateful that she stayed around, caring for me until I was six."

Emma patted Amelia's hand. "I am certain she's out there somewhere, getting caught up in the thrill of the voyage. Never much of a land lover was she. I'm surprised she stuck around as long as she had—says something about her love for you, I suppose."

Emotion tightened Amelia's throat. If her mother had really cared she would have stuck around longer. She wouldn't have left at all. "Well, thank you." Amelia took a step back, and another smile filled Geraldine's face.

"What is it?" Amelia asked. "Did you remember something more?"

"No." The woman clucked her tongue. "I was just thinking Emma wouldn't know what to do with herself if she saw the glory hole of this place."

"Glory hole?"

"Oh, just the name of the stewards' quarters—the name given because there's nothing glorious about them. A foul place, most are, but not here." She offered a low whistle. "The most comfortable room I've ever slept in on the seas ... and speaking of sleeping, there are a few more beds I need to make up. Ones I didn't get done before the launch. You should have seen us hustling to get everything ready for the guests. We're still not done. In fact ... be careful what walls you touch—some places still have wet paint!" The stewardess's smile lifted her round cheeks. "I'll be seeing you, dear. And if my old memory surprises me and offers up another occurrence, you'll be the first to know!"

"Thank you," Amelia said as the woman shuffled off. The words were insufficient for her depth of gratitude. To have met someone who'd known her mother .... Tears filled her eyes. Her lower lip trembled, and she wiped the tears away.

Amelia let out a soft sigh and leaned against the paneled wall next to Quentin's door. Did he have people in his past whom he missed and wondered about? To know and be known. To love and be loved. Was there anything in life greater than that?

Chapter 6

Quentin sat with his back pressed against the door. Even though solid wood separated him from Amelia, he could hear every word as she talked to the stewardess. He listened as they talked about Amelia's mother. He listened as she'd questioned about her father. That was what had really choked him up. Maybe because he knew who his father was, and he had failed him in every way. Quentin pressed his hands to his forehead as the pain of that ache stabbed him yet again, wishing that wasn't the case.

When she'd first offered him the ticket, he assumed much about her that he now knew wasn't true. She was so beautiful, so kind. He'd assumed that she had no problems. Even as he'd talked to her on the deck, he guessed this grand voyage to be a vacation for her. What he now understood was that being on this vessel caused Amelia to do some searching of her own. Much as he did.

He looked around. The room seemed to press in. He needed to get out of there, but where could he go? Not to the first-class decks. Those were off-limits to second-class passengers. Besides, there were too many of his father's friends and acquaintances who'd recognize him there. It wouldn't take long for them to get word back to his father in Maryland about spotting Quentin.

And he couldn't stroll the second class. He wasn't ready to face Amelia. As much as he knew she'd make a good friend, it would be better for her if he stayed away. First, because her aunt disapproved. Second, because his heart was softening to her. And third, because her aunt was right. He was trouble. He'd run from those who truly loved him, and when he did stay around, he always ended up breaking their hearts. While it was too early to consider if he and Amelia could ever be more than friends, he had noticed there was a sparkle in her eyes when she looked at him.

Whether simply as a friend—or by a slim chance something more developed—Quentin knew he wasn't good for her. Somehow he'd hurt her, too, and that was the last thing he wanted. She'd already faced too much heartbreak.

Quentin rose, opened the door slightly, and then strode down the hall, determined to find a way to third class. He could make new friends there without having to worry about disappointing anyone. He fit better there. Among them, he didn't have to worry about his status.

He could talk about the future without reliving the past.

Amelia's mind was still on her mother as the *Titanic* finished the channel crossing and arrived at Cherbourg, France, at 6:30 p.m. Amelia found her way back to the second-class deck to get fresh air, and also to keep an eye out for Quentin.

She'd thrown a shawl over her shoulders to fend against the chilled air. She looked forward to having space to think. Her mind felt as full as the heavy trunks she'd packed. First there was Quentin who didn't cease to surprise her, then meeting the stewardess Geraldine. As much as she appreciated the grand ship, its opulence didn't touch her nearly as much as those two events.

The early evening sun filled the sky as the *Titanic* anchored in the breakwater. It was Amelia's first time away from England,

and just this crossing seemed like a big enough adventure. How many friends could say they'd been to France? None that she could think of, except Mrs. Merryweather, one of her neighbors, who'd traveled there on her honeymoon twenty-five years prior. Most of the people she knew hadn't left Southampton. Their world consisted of a mile in each direction.

The sun was moving lower in the sky as she braved the cooling evening temperatures to watch as more passengers boarded the ship by way of water ferry. She'd heard France didn't have a harbor large enough for the *Titanic* to dock; she supposed not many places would.

Most of those who boarded looked as if they were as wealthy as the queen herself. They walked the gangway in fine clothes, with maids and butlers carrying trunks piled high. One young fellow even had a dog. Amelia didn't recognize any of their faces, except for one: John Jacob Astor. The man stood ramrod straight and tucked a hand behind his back as he walked the gangplank. She'd seen his image in the newspaper. One of the wealthiest men in the world, he'd divorced his wife and married an eighteen-year-old, the same age as Amelia. They'd left the States to vacation and leave the rumors and finger-pointing behind. Yet if she'd read about it in the paper, the scandal had already followed them across the Atlantic.

But it wasn't Mr. Astor who was most prominent in her thoughts. It was Quentin.

Where was he? Yes, it was a large ship, but there were only so many places to hide.

When the bugle sounded announcing supper, Amelia found her aunt on the promenade deck, and they entered the second-class dining room on the D deck. The elegant room stretched before her. The mahogany chairs were cushioned in rich crimson cloth. As she approached, she noticed they were swivel chairs, bolted to the floor.

Aunt Neda stroked the fine varnished wood and sat regally, as if she'd just been offered a throne. "I suppose they bolted them down in case of bad weather at sea."

"But do you really think anything could cause them to move an inch?" Amelia asked. "Outside the channel was horribly choppy today, and we…I…didn't feel it in the slightest." Her thoughts darkened some when she remembered the words her aunt spoke in Quentin's presence, but she tried to push away ill feelings toward her aunt. Amelia knew deep down it was her fault. If she'd mentioned what she'd done—had confessed to offering Quentin the ticket—her aunt wouldn't have been caught off guard, and Quentin's feelings wouldn't have been crushed.

She glanced at the paper menu, and though the items sounded delightful, she wasn't very hungry. The chair beside her sat empty, and she worried about Quentin not eating. He looked painfully thin as it was.

The sounds of footsteps filled the room as others walked along the tiled floor to their seats. Hushed voices exclaimed over the chandeliers, white linens and china, and the handsome stewards there to attend them. As soon as Amelia and her aunt were settled, one of the stewards took their orders and cared for their every need. A hint of a smile touched her lips. She couldn't imagine living in such a manner all the time. What would it be like to have someone to cook for you? Serve you on a daily basis?

Amelia enjoyed lamb's head broth, roast pork, and apple sauce with a jam tart, while Aunt Neda had the Ragout of Veal.

Sitting near them, Amelia enjoyed conversation with Mrs. Alice Christy, a widow from London, and her daughter, Julie-Rachel. They were accompanied by Sidney and Amy Jacobsohn, and all were on their way to Canada. Their new friends spoke of London, and with each mention of their neighborhoods and friends, Amelia wished Quentin was here to join in the conversation. Then again, Quentin's London had no doubt been very different from what these fine folks had experienced over the years.

Amelia was just about to excuse herself and her aunt—having only taken a few bites of her dessert tart—when Ethel Beane rushed to her side.

"Amelia, there you are. I need your help." Ethel's eyebrows formed a V, and worry filled her eyes. "I had Edward's book this afternoon when we visited first class. I believe I mindlessly set it down in the library. Would you walk up there with me? Inside, Edward had tucked our receipt from the purser. We won't be able to get the money we deposited in the purser's safe without that receipt."

Amelia bit her lip. Upon boarding the ship, everyone had been asked to deposit all their money with the purser. She and her aunt had done so, even though it hadn't amounted to much. Amelia did remember seeing Ethel with a book, but only at their meeting in the passageway. It could be anywhere.

"But we're not allowed in first class. There are signs posted telling us to keep out. There are stewards watching the passageways."

"We can talk to them." Ethel grasped Amelia's hands. "You don't understand... without that receipt we'll lose all we have." Tears rimmed Ethel's eyes.

She squeezed Ethel's hand. Even if they were reprimanded for going where they shouldn't, she had to try.

"Yes, of course I'll join you, but first I must see my aunt to her room."

"Don't worry about that, dear child," Mr. Jacobsohn piped up. "Please be off and help your friend. We'll see that your aunt is taken to her quarters... but of course we'll insist she join us in listening to the orchestra in the lounge first."

A smile filled Aunt Neda's face at those words, and Amelia rose. "Thank you then. It was a pleasure to make your acquaintance."

She joined Ethel in walking toward the entrance nearest to the grand staircase. That would be the easiest path to again find their way to first class.

When they arrived at the staircase, a steward was guarding it.

"Lift your head and pretend you belong," Amelia whispered to. her friend. From the corner of her eye, Amelia noticed Ethel straightening her shoulders. Ethel's lips lifted into a smile, and Amelia's did the same.

The steward watched as they approached, and Amelia hurried to him. "Sir, could you please tell us the way to the first-class library? I'm afraid we got turned. This ship is so huge," Amelia started in.

"No, ma'am, unless you are first class, and I don't think—"

"Have you ever gotten lost on this ship?" Amelia interrupted. Then she placed a hand to her neck. "Of course not. I am sure you figured out all the passageways and decks—everything—within hours. But we'll be in New York before I find my way to our room." She laughed.

The steward lowered his hand and offered a sly smile. "Actually, I've gotten lost a few times myself." He sighed. "To find your way to the first-class reading and writing room, follow the staircase up to promenade deck A."

"Thank you." Amelia took Ethel's hand and led the way. "We appreciate your help!"

They hurried up the flight of stairs and made their way to the library. Amelia's hands quivered as they strode into the room. Men and women were dressed in their finest. She felt like a peasant who'd snuck into a royal wedding. She gripped her shawl tighter around her shoulders and walked a few steps behind her friend.

Ethel walked with purpose, scanning the shelves. From the corner of her eye, Amelia studied the women with their large hats. Their full, ruffled skirts and blouses with high collars were finer than any clothes she'd ever seen. The men, circled up in groups, were dressed in fine suits and top hats. Some of the men wore white gloves that flashed as they moved their hands. No one seemed to give Ethel or her any notice, so intent were they on mingling—walking around in small groups, like proud peacocks with splayed feathers. Amelia's heart ached to realize a small portion of the fortune of the dozen people in this room would be enough to feed all the poor in Southampton—and maybe London, too.

"Here it is!" Ethel's voice rose, and she pulled the book from the shelf. She opened it hastily and flipped through the pages, looking for the claim ticket. Ethel released a heavy breath when she came upon the ticket. A smile filled her face, and she pulled it out. "It's here. Let's hurry before the steward in charge of this room accuses me of attempting to steal one of his books."

Ethel moved toward the door. Amelia turned to follow, but someone caught her eye. He stood aloof from the other passengers who stood sharing in some type of story. The man's eyes were focused on hers, and a smile lifted his lips—as if he'd been hoping to see her. Amelia covered her mouth with her hand, and a gasp escaped her throat. She knew that face.

Forgetting where she was, she lifted her hand. "Quentin!"

The man's eyes widened, not with excitement but with surprise. She crossed the room, but as she neared, her footsteps slowed.

The man looked like Quentin but not exactly. He looked older with a touch of gray on his temples. His chin had a dimple, too—something she didn't remember Quentin having.

Amelia paused. "I'm so sorry to bother you."

Eyes from the other first-class passengers turned toward her, brows peaked in interest and curiosity. *Who does this woman think she is?* their gazes seemed to say.

She looked to the floor, silently begging it to open and swallow her up, take her back to the second-class berth where she belonged. "I'm so sorry," she repeated.

Amelia turned to move toward Ethel, but the man's hand caught her arm. Amelia waved her friend away, lest she get in trouble, too.

"Wait," he said. "I wish to speak to you. I—"

"I know we're not supposed to be in first class," she interrupted, "but we were simply trying to find my friend's book." Her words rumbled on. "She left it here on the tour...before the launch. Second class, you see, was allowed to look around and—"

The man raised a gloved finger to Amelia's mouth, halting her words. So bold was his touch, Amelia didn't know what to do. How to respond. She looked at him closer. His resemblance to Quentin was startling.

"Miss, please...you don't have to explain."

The scraping of the feet of a chair on the shined wooden floor caught her attention. Not three yards away an elderly man rose from a high-backed leather chair and neared. His shoulders slumped as he walked, as if he'd been carrying around a heavy burden for many years. He clenched his fists to his chest. "Do you know him? Do you know my son?"

She looked from the younger man back to the older man. The younger man held out the crook of his elbow for support.

"I'm sorry, sir. I must have been mistaken. I—"

Tears filled the old man's eyes. "You said *Quentin*," he interrupted. "You called his name. Do you know him?"

She quickly looked away, remembering the promise she'd made not a few hours prior. The promise not to tell another soul that Quentin was on board, or even to mention his name.

What is Quentin hiding from?

She looked back to the two men, now understanding the resemblance. This younger man was his brother, and this older man...

A hundred questions fought for priority in her mind, but two rose to the top. Why would the son of a wealthy man be living in such rags? Why hadn't he gone to his father for help?

Both men ... and it seemed everyone else in the room ... waited for her answer.

Heat crept up her cheeks. "Yes, I have met him."

"Can you tell me when? How is he doing? Did he look well to you?" The older man leaned heavy on his son's arm.

"It was recently, and he did look well. He's been through some hard times, but things are looking up."

"Were you in a relationship?" the young man dared to ask.

"No, not at all." Her words escaped as a gasp. She studied the man who looked so much like Quentin. Yet there was no joy in this man's eyes at knowing his brother's fate—knowing he was doing well.

"He is well." The older man offered a relieved smile. "Did you hear that?"

"Yes, exciting, Father." Deep color rose from the younger man's open, white collar. She stared at the hollow of his throat as his Adam's apple bounced. He had a small book of poetry in his hands, and he opened and closed the cover with quick, nervous movements. Though the old man hung on her every word, the young one looked as if he wished she'd vanish into the waves rippling out from the side of the ship. Was *he* the reason Quentin requested his presence to remain unknown?

She turned her attention back to the older man. "If I may be so bold ... I assume you *both* are related to Quentin?"

"I'm sorry, dear, I did not introduce myself. I'm certain my manners are still in our stateroom waiting to be unpacked. My name is Clarence Walpole. I ask my closest friends to call me C.J. That—my dear—would be you, too." He took her hand and softly lifted it to his lips, kissing it. His fingers trembled. Instead of releasing her hand, he clung to it, as if her grasp was the one lifeline to his son.

"I am Amelia, Amelia Gladstone," she said simply. Then she turned to the younger man beside him, waiting for an introduction.

"This is my son Damien," Clarence continued. "Quentin— whom you have met—is Damien's younger brother. We haven't seen Quentin for five years. During our trip to London, I'd hoped to find him. I wish nothing more than for us to be reunited. Your news is a gift, my dear. Knowing he's doing well does this old heart good."

They fell into an uncomfortable silence, and Amelia glanced around. The women—noses upturned—eyed her simple dress and shawl. The men leaned in, as if waiting for her words. They were curious, and she guessed they most likely knew why Quentin was estranged from his family. Perhaps there was some type of falling out?

Her stomach rumbled and lurched as if everything she'd eaten tonight wished to come up. She placed a soft hand on it, willing it to calm. Why did she have to open her mouth like that? What a fool. She should have walked in, helped Ethel find the book, and walked out.

Even though Clarence's nervous eyes told her he still carried a great burden for his son, his smile was gentle and his manner kind.

Clarence finally released her hand, and she reached out her palm to Damien for a handshake. He twitched as if he'd just been woken up from a dream. He took her hand. It was warm and soft. His fingernails were perfectly manicured. He was just as handsome as Quentin, but his face wasn't touched by the hardship the younger brother had faced.

Her eyes lingered on his, trying to see the emotions that flashed there—anger, frustration, fear? Yes, a hint of fear remained there. He was afraid of knowing more about his brother. Afraid for his father to know.

She bit her lip and looked over her shoulder as if looking for someone. "I'm so sorry, but I should go find my friend...She, uh, might need me. It was so nice to meet you." Amelia pulled her hand out of Damien's grasp.

The old man's eyes widened as if not wanting her to leave. She felt bad for not telling him more. Felt she owed him some explanation. Yet Quentin had asked her to keep his presence a secret for a reason. And his brother, Damien, obviously didn't want Quentin's whereabouts revealed either.

"Nice to meet you, too, dear. I'm so sorry we do not have more time to talk now. Maybe one of these evenings at supper. We'd love to have you at our table."

"Of course," she answered before she remembered she was still in the first-class section. She didn't belong here. She wouldn't be eating with them, not tomorrow. Not ever.

"I suppose I'll see you again." She turned and hurried off, heat creeping up her neck. She walked in the direction of the grand staircase, a sigh of relief escaping with heavy breaths. She would not be seeing them again. She would not be dining at their tables. She didn't belong in first class. She was blessed to have a passage in second. For all she knew, that brief meeting was a gift to Clarence Walpole—a hopeful word of his son that would carry him for years to come. *Unless...*

She considered discussing the situation with Quentin. Surely if he knew his father and brother were passengers on this very ship—first-class passengers—he'd come out of his hiding and reveal his true self to them. Maybe her random act of kindness wasn't so random at all. A shiver ran down her arms, and suddenly she felt as if destiny brushed up against the ship, like the waves lapping against the hull. How did a simple girl from Southampton stumble into this?

The third-class decks were crowded with hundreds of English, Dutch, Italian, and French passengers—from even more countries, too, he'd guess. Everyone seemed to be talking at once in their own languages. He felt more at home here than on the upper decks.

None of the other passengers questioned Quentin when he sat down for supper among the third-class passengers. And when he was asked for his supper ticket, he'd fibbed and said he'd forgotten it in his room. With a few empty chairs around him, no one bothered to tell him to go find it. There was extra room during this supper shift and plenty of food. He closed his eyes and took in a deep breath. Even with the scents of boiled potatoes and beef, the room still smelled of fresh-sawn wood and paint.

When his supper arrived, Quentin stared at the food before him as if he was trying to decide if it was a dream or real. He ran his tongue over his teeth, and he noticed the gaze of a woman sitting next to him fixed on his.

"Shall we pray?" The woman offered one hand to Quentin and another to the man on the other side of her whom he assumed was her husband. Quentin wrapped his hand around hers. He'd forgotten what it was to feel a woman's innocent touch. As soon as the prayer was offered, he dug into his food. He didn't know the last time he'd eaten a meal like this.

Along with the beef and boiled potatoes, there was fresh bread, sweet corn, fruit, and plum pudding. The meat and potatoes were good, but he closed his eyes as he took a bite of the plum pudding and swallowed down emotion with the food. It tasted so much like the pudding Mother used to make.

His body couldn't seem to get enough of the meal, and he ate it faster than he should.

From the corner of his eyes, he saw that the woman watched him eat.

"So, Mr . . . ."

"Qu—uh, Henry, ma'am. You can just call me Henry."

"Yes Henry. Well, you have long fingers that move with grace. If I'm not mistaken, I'd guess you play the piano."

He paused with the fork halfway to his mouth. "Yes, ma'am."

"If I get to call you Henry, then you have to call me Grace, and this is my husband, Sven."

"Nice to meet you," he said between swallows, but even as they tried to make small talk, Quentin cared more for the food, and he was pleasantly surprised when the steward brought him a second plate.

He ate until he felt as if he'd swallowed a piano, and when he set down his fork, he realized nearly the whole table had been watching him. Heat rose up his neck as he saw the pity in their gazes. Understanding, too. If they hadn't been where he now was, they'd seen it just over the horizon.

After a simple meal, he followed the others to the common room. His eyes immediately moved to the piano. Approaching it, he sat down and started to play "Bon, Bon Buddy." Those in the room cheered and swayed to his tune, and when he finished and rose, another passenger stood with his bagpipes and began to play. The music really picked up, and then the dancing started. The music was punctuated by the clinking of glasses.

He moved among the small group of people laughing and talking. In the designated smoking room, the air was thick with what looked like a low gray fog. He thought about walking to the poop deck, but as he headed out the door, he felt eyes upon him. A tall woman with reddish hair stood just outside the door with a cigarette in hand. She took a long draw and flicked ashes onto the polished wood boards. Her dark eyes pierced his, and a slight smile lifted the corners of her lips. So intense was her stare that Quentin paused.

The woman tucked her curls behind her ear. "You do not remember, do you?"

"No, I'm sorry."

A harsh chuckle split her lips, and as she brushed her hair back from her neck, her dress slipped down, revealing a creamy white shoulder.

She lifted her chin and smiled. "I lived in your house in London. In Westminster."

Quentin cleared his throat. "Yes, of course." Then he chuckled. "Many people did. I remember now." He smiled an acknowledgment, but still the woman wasn't familiar. That time had been a blur. He'd had a drink in his hand more often than not. His pockets were full of his father's riches, and the business he'd begun was going well. Many people had filled his home. Many women had filled his bed, and from the sly smile and sultry gaze she offered, this woman had no doubt been one of them.

"It's a beautiful evening on a beautiful ship. It's the type of night one shouldn't have to spend alone," she purred, taking a step closer.

Quentin smelled alcohol on her breath and imagined the taste of her lips. He instinctively stretched out his hand and brushed her hair back from her other shoulder. With his touch, she closed her eyes, and her mouth parted slightly.

It would be easy. He had an empty room. He didn't think this woman—whatever her name was—would resist him sneaking her up to second class. Yet when Quentin imagined meeting Amelia in the hall with this woman's hand in his, his heart sank. He pictured hurt in Amelia's eyes, and for some reason that pained him.

Quentin pulled his hand back and then dropped his head. With a sigh, he turned his back to her.

"We can walk the deck if you would like." Her voice sounded desperate, as if she were afraid he was going to walk away.

He crossed his arms over his chest. "I have nothing to offer you. I lost my house in Westminster years ago."

The woman approached from behind him, gripping his arms with her hands and laying a cheek against his back.

"Do you think I don't know that?" she chuckled. "You're riding in third class. More than that, people talk. I've heard the stories. I assumed you'd be dead by now. I was surprised to see you here."

"Me, too. Yesterday I would have never thought…" He stopped there. He couldn't mention Amelia or the gift, even though her presence felt close. Closer than this woman behind him.

How could that have happened? He'd known Amelia for less than a day, yet just the thought of her caused him to question all he'd known. How he'd lived.

Quentin stepped away. "It was nice to see you again. Maybe I'll see you around."

"Wait!"

He turned back.

The woman awkwardly crossed her arms over her chest. "It was nice to see you, too. I hope America treats you well." Disappointment colored her words.

Quentin walked away, only stopping when he was beyond her view. He sat down on a long bench and lowered his forehead into his hands. The air around him was icy cold, but he hardly noticed. Amelia, only Amelia, filled his thoughts. If he could run from her he would. If she had already pervaded his life this much, what would getting to know her do? Where would spending more time together lead them?

Suddenly he didn't care. At this moment, Quentin could think of nothing more than doing just that. Of returning to second class and finding Amelia. Of risking everything—his heart, hers.

Chapter 7

From the glass windows of the promenade deck, Amelia looked down at the couple below. She'd been hurrying to her room when she saw them, and the way the woman curled up against the man's back—as if they were the only two people on the ship—caused her to pause.

It was only as the man turned that a gasp escaped her lips. She'd been mistaken before, but not this time. It was Quentin who stood there with the woman.

No wonder he'd wanted on the ship. It wasn't just the passage he'd wanted. It was her!

A hot smack of anger came out of nowhere and sent Amelia whirling in a half circle. An older couple strode by, bundled up in warm coats, and offered her a smile. Amelia attempted to smile back, but as soon as they passed, she covered her mouth with her hand.

She felt like such a fool. No wonder Quentin had been so awkward in her presence. Maybe that had been his plan all along—to prey on some merciful person on the docks. Maybe that was why he'd been so fidgety today as they sat on the deck chairs. He was just talking with her out of duty. He didn't want to be with her—but rather another. He only spent time with her out of obligation.

"How foolish I've been," she mumbled to herself. Aunt Neda was right. Just because she'd helped the man didn't mean she needed to get involved in his matters. He most likely knew his father and brother were on board. How could he not? Maybe he had a plan to swindle them again, too. No wonder he warned her not to say anything.

Refusing to watch Quentin with the woman, she turned her head sharply aside and stared out the window at the expanse of ocean beyond. This was the very reason she wanted to start a relationship with someone like Mr. Chapman. He might be simple—boring even—but at least he would be dependable. He'd always been frank with her in his letters. He'd be a steady rock for her to lean on. Committing to someone like that would save her from a thousand tears and much heartbreak.

She made her way to her stateroom. Swinging the door open, she saw it was empty. Aunt Neda most likely still listened to the orchestra with her new friends. Amelia softly shut the door and eased herself onto the sitting bench, leaning her head back against the cushions and closing her eyes. She needed this time alone to think. Needed to remember her purpose for the voyage. How foolish she'd been for trying to forget what she was leaving behind. She'd do wise to learn from her mother's mistakes, lest she repeat them. How equally foolish not to consider what lay ahead. That was the whole reason she was here. Mr. Chapman was the whole reason.

Amelia picked up the stack of letters she had brought with her. They were addressed to her in perfect penmanship. Mr. Chapman's penmanship. She'd read them ten, maybe twenty times, over the previous months. Mr. Chapman had seemed so kindhearted. He appeared to be someone worth getting to know. Yet as she held the envelopes in her hands—letters that had crossed the ocean in the opposite direction—she suddenly couldn't remember what they said. She also only remembered some of the words of Elizabeth's letter. Her cousin had told her that Mr. Chapman had fair features, and that he was a highly respected man in the community and in their church. He was her neighbor, and he was a wonderful conversationalist. Upon first boarding this fine ship, Amelia had wondered if all those things were enough. Now she knew. Of course they could be enough. Relationships that succeeded were ones based on commitment. On stability.

She sat down on the cushioned sitting bench and picked up the letters, deciding to read a few again to remind herself why she'd set out on this journey.

Dear Miss Gladstone,

You asked about some of my favorite things in New Haven. By far I would have to say a fine spot I enjoy visiting is the New Haven Green. It comprises the central square of the nine-square settlement plan made by the original Puritan colonists in New Haven. It is a lovely park where many go to recreate. I often visit to feed the pigeons and sit down with a good book. Remind me when we visit sometime to tell you about when the greens were used as a burial ground for the citizens of New Haven. The headstones were moved to the Grove Street Cemetery, however, the remains of the dead were not moved. My father has a few stories about this, and I'm sure you would be interested in hearing his tales, which brings me to the main point of my letter, dear Miss Gladstone.

This may be much to ask, but it seems that we will never get a chance to truly know each other unless we meet face-to-face. I spoke to Len and Elizabeth about this. They mentioned that your aunt is getting on in years, and they would like to be able to provide for her—if only she were able to make it to America. I have proposed an idea to them, and I wanted to propose it to you as well. I am not an overly wealthy man, but I have saved most of what I've earned. If you and your aunt would consider coming to America for a visit, I would gladly pay your passage on a ship. Elizabeth suggested your aunt consider moving—and you, too, with her—but that will be your decision. Either for a short time or a longer stay, I'll leave the decision to you, but I have faith that once we have the chance to meet in person, the small affections we have found in our letters will grow.

There could be a future for us, Miss Gladstone, a wonderful future.

With true sincerity,
Mr. Chapman

Amelia smiled as she read the man's words. He did seem kind, and oh so thoughtful. She appreciated that he had a close relationship with his family, and it was sweet of him to think of Aunt Neda's wellbeing. And surely Elizabeth and Len's opinion greatly matters.

She set her chin and pulled out another letter. She needed this—needed the reminder of all the reasons she was willing to leave all she knew for this man.

Dear Miss Gladstone,

Before your letter came, there was a knock on the door from Elizabeth. She received your note saying that your aunt has agreed to come if passage for you and your cousin—Elizabeth's brother, Henry—can come, too. Elizabeth and Len offered to pay your cousin's passage, but I insisted I cover that expense. It is such a little thing when it means you'll be coming here soon. A note has already been sent to my bank. The money will be sent soon. I will leave it to your discretion when you wish to come. I read in yesterday's paper that the greatest ship ever built, the Titanic, *is due to set sail in March or April. I will include enough funds for passage upon that grand ship if you so desire. It seems only fitting, such a great woman as yourself should ride upon the very best.*

With care,

Mr. Chapman

Amelia bit her lip. What would Mr. Chapman think to know that Henry didn't make it? That his own foolishness landed him in jail? She refolded the letter and put it back in the envelope.

From what she knew about Mr. Chapman, he'd be gracious—maybe a little put out, but gracious all the same. Len and Elizabeth wouldn't be surprised. Losing his father when he was just a wee boy had hurt Henry the most, and from a young age he spent time with the wrong people at the docks. Still it was she whom Mr. Chapman wished to see disembarking from the ship. As long as she was there—and was eager to fulfill her promise for them to get to know each other in new and deeper ways—she figured Mr. Chapman would not feel so flustered about the rest.

Dear Amelia,

First, I will say with sincerity, thank you for insisting that I call you Amelia. It is a fine name, one you should be proud of.

Many thanks for your Christmas note also; it just arrived. When I told your cousin, Elizabeth, and her husband, Len, that I would be writing you a letter momentarily, they asked that I pass on their good wishes.

I found it of interest in your last note that you do not like to cook. When I discussed this matter with Elizabeth, she confirmed that was the case. She said if you do cook, it is simple meals that you share with neighbors and those in need. I, too, cook simply, but considering the upcoming arrival of you, your cousin, and your aunt, I realized that hiring a cook would be a wise procurement. I stopped by the newspaper during my lunchtime today and put in an advertisement. I will be interviewing cooks Monday next, although I wonder how best to do that. Should I ask each to bring a favorite dish? I believe my stomach likes the idea of such an interview.

In the last letter, you asked me to share a bit more of my life. I have shared about my education, my job, and my friends. I've described my house, and I've told you about my growing-up years, but I realize that maybe I need to go into more detail about our community.

I have lived in New Haven, Connecticut, all my life. If you are not aware, it is part of the Long Island Sound, and my home has a nice view of Long Island, New York, to the south. My father worked from the time he was a young boy at the Winchester Repeating Arms Company. He retired there two years prior and lives one street over from me. Most of my relatives, in fact, live within two miles of my home. They are all eager to meet you.

Also, Amelia, you wouldn't be aware of it unless I confessed, but this letter has sat on my desk a day and a night as I tried to figure out how to write what I am thinking about most. I suppose the only way to say things is to state them clearly. Amelia, you are a beautiful woman, and I am worried you would be disinterested in such a simple man as myself who lives such a simple existence.

Yesterday, just as I had started writing my letter, Elizabeth stopped by with a photograph of you that she had found in her trunk. She described you very well, but your beauty came through in your photo. She said I can keep it, so I have placed it on my piano. As I look at your photograph, more worries now fill my mind. I knew from the beginning I would find you a woman of interest. I've known Elizabeth and Len for many years, and I trust them explicitly. I am more eager now than I have ever been to meet you face-to-face and to settle down on the front porch for long talks.

Were you able to procure a suitable ship passage for your aunt and your cousin? I do hope the money that I sent was enough. I wish to tell you again there is no need to thank me. If we are to get on as well as Elizabeth thinks we are, then your friendship is quite enough. After that . . . we will let matters settle once we are able to discuss things face-to-face.

I will post this letter now and eagerly await your response.

Sincerely,

Your Mr. Chapman

She picked up one more letter and had just pulled it from the envelope when a knock interrupted Amelia's reading. She frowned at the door. Who could it be? She rose, thinking it might be Ethel. After all, her friend had scurried away, leaving Amelia to face those in first class alone.

The knock sounded again.

"Amelia? Are you in there?" Though muffled through the door, she could tell it was a male voice. "Amelia," the voice said louder.

"I know you're in there," she heard Quentin say. "I saw your aunt in the lounge. You weren't with her. I talked to the steward, and he said you entered your stateroom not thirty minutes ago."

She sat there quietly, her fingers playing with the letters on her lap. Amelia bit her lip. If she opened the door, she'd have something to say—too much to say. She'd question Quentin about his father and brother. She'd ask him about the woman in third class, even though it was none of her business. And because she didn't want to get hurt any more than she'd already been, she sat.

She heard Quentin pacing outside the door. Under the lower edge of the door his shadow briefly blocked the light as he passed. The longer he paced, the more she wanted to open the door and talk to him, and that was exactly what he wanted her to do. She would not give in. Not this time.

Another thought stirred, causing her to sit up straighter. Maybe Aunt Neda was right. Maybe he was a con man and a crook.

"This is a game," she whispered. "But what is he after?" She hardly had two coins.

Amelia considered what she *did* have. She did have compassion. She did have concern. And those were things men like him took advantage of most. She'd heard about things like that happening before—women trusting the wrong men, only to end up alone and forgotten.

She also had her heart...which Quentin could be intent on trying to steal. And where would that leave her if he succeeded? She had others to think of—Mr. Chapman, her aunt, even Elizabeth and Len.

Amelia swallowed hard and rubbed the goose bumps rising on her arms. Her mother had warned her of men like him. Even before she was able to understand, her mother had told her about men who played with a woman's affections in order to meet their desires for a time. Well, Amelia Gladstone wasn't that type of woman.

Amelia sighed, closed her eyes, and rested her head against the back of the cushioned bench and willed the *Titanic* to move faster. Willed it to take her to a man who could be trusted—her Mr. Chapman who waited on the distant shore.

Damien guided his father down the grand staircase beneath the opulent, white-enameled, wrought-iron skylight on A deck and descended through the four decks to the first-class dining room entrance on D deck. The expanse of the dining room ran the full width of the hull. He took in the spotless white linen tablecloths, crystal and silver stretching in each direction. Fresh flowers and fruit baskets decorated the tables. A dining steward led them to one of the recessed bays, which allowed small parties to dine in privacy. It was only as they neared that Damien saw the beautiful, dark-haired woman sitting at their table.

"I asked your father if I could join you tonight. I hope you don't mind." Dorothea's red lips curled upward in a smile. She wore a red dress with a black lace shawl that swooped up to one shoulder and was pinned with a jeweled rose. Rubies and emeralds and diamonds sparkled from the pin—and so did the interest in her eyes.

"No, of course I don't mind." Damien forced a smile. He turned to his father but noticed the older man was lost in his thoughts. Father no doubt was thinking about the blond woman they'd met in the library. The woman who'd mentioned Quentin. The lady's beautiful face was still fresh in his own mind. She had perfect features and wide blue eyes. She'd worn the same flowing yellow dress she'd worn earlier, and the shawl about her shoulders gave her a special naïveté. He wanted to be angry with the woman for bringing up his brother's name, for stirring up hope in his father's eyes, but instead he was more intrigued. It was obvious Amelia hadn't known his brother very well or for very long. Her surprised innocence proved that fact.

The dining room steward pulled out a chair decorated in French fleurs-de-lis.

"Your mother would like these chairs," his father proclaimed, speaking of her as if only a few weeks had passed since her death and not nearly twenty years.

Dorothea sat, smoothing the skirt of her dress and touching her wide-brimmed hat that was decorated with bows and flowers, ensuring the arrangement was still in place. "I do think the chairs are exquisite. I was telling my mother just today it would be lovely if we could find something similar for our dining room back home."

"Which dining room?" Damien lifted an eyebrow. Dorothea's family owned three homes in New York and Maryland alone.

"Oh, Damien, you're such a kidder. That's why I love you so. The home nearest to yours, of course. You've known all along that's the home that matters most to me."

Dorothea took a breath and continued on, without even giving him a chance to respond. "I've been eager to see you again. The weeks in Paris couldn't pass fast enough. My mother was intent on acquiring new art for our homes, and she dragged me through gallery after gallery. The only highlights were the shops we visited…have you heard of Paul Pioret?"

Damien cocked an eyebrow. "I can't say I have."

"Really? That's unbelievable. Mother says his contributions to fashion are equal to Monet's contributions to art. In fact, while we were there, a famous photographer came and took photos of gowns designed by Poiret. My mother says I would have done a better job than the models did, but that is of no consequence. They will be published this month in the magazine *Art et Décoration*."

Damien nodded as she spoke. It was no secret that Dorothea's mother considered him husband material for her daughter, but as he sat there, he tried to imagine spending the next five, ten, twenty years having to talk about designers and magazine spreads. Just thinking of it, he already felt the tension tightening in his chest. No wonder all the men he knew retired to smoking rooms after supper. Every man needed peace from such chatter.

"The whole time I was away, I thought of you and our last time together." She leaned close and whispered so his father wouldn't hear. "I'd never been kissed like that night in the center of Times Square. A thousand people could have been walking by us, and I would not have known."

Damien smiled at that memory. He did enjoy Dorothea's kisses. They always had that.

The seven-course evening meal was of higher quality than he expected. Virginia and Cumberland ham, baked jacket potatoes, even corned ox tongue—something he'd only seen in the finest restaurants.

As the meal continued—courses being brought out one by one—he and Dorothea chatted about their vacations and the grandeur of the ship, and by the way she stirred her soup until it was cold, he could tell she was disappointed that the romantic fire that was usually between them wasn't even a flicker.

The scene that played out was no different from a hundred other similar events he participated in through the year. Women wore their finest new gowns, men wore evening suits, and some couples even found their way to the dance floor.

Dorothea leaned forward and grasped his hand. "Do you care to dance?"

Damien lifted her hand to his lips and kissed her fingertips. "To be honest, my dear, I'm not in the mood tonight. There was a strange woman, you see, who found us in the first-class reading and writing room. She called out to me, but not by my name. She called out the name, 'Quentin.'"

Dorothea gasped, and from the corner of his eye, Damien noticed his father lower his head.

She dabbed her linen napkin to the corners of her lips and leaned even closer. "How does this woman know Quentin? Did she say?"

His father lifted his head and met Dorothea's gaze, answering for his son. "She did not. I believe she was as much surprised by the meeting as we were. She thought Damien was Quentin—you know how much my sons look alike."

"Yes, I remember well." Dorothea smirked. "Of course I was always one who thought Damien to be the most handsome of the two." She squeezed his hand tighter.

His father turned his attention to the orchestra that was launching into another number. Seeing she once again had Damien's full attention, she leaned forward to whisper in his ear.

"Damien, if you'd like, we can go back to my stateroom. Mother and Father are most likely in bed. We have a private promenade deck. I thought we could enjoy more privacy—enjoy catching up."

"As much as I'd like to, darling, can I pass on your invitation tonight? You've noticed my father is out of sorts. After a brief stop at the smoking room, I'm going to make sure he gets to bed. He'll get lost in these passageways if he tries to find the way himself."

"I understand. He always seems shaken up with matters that concern your brother." She leaned closer so her voice could be heard by him alone. "I feel badly. Did the woman have any more details about Quentin?"

He noticed something in her eyes—a piqued interest. She wanted him to tell her a tidbit of information no one else knew. Not because she cared, though. She wanted to tickle the ears of the other women who gathered in the lounge with her inside knowledge.

"I'm sorry, dear," he stated simply. "If I am to find out anything else, you'll be the first to know."

When Dorothea excused herself, Damien retired with his father to the first-class smoking room, located on the promenade deck. Leaded glass panels had been inset into carved mahogany-paneled walls. Massive leather armchairs sat beside marble-top tables, but as Damien looked around the room, being there held little appeal. He'd sat with these same men—or others like them—and discussed the same topics: travel, music, art, politics. He'd served his father faithfully, yet he couldn't imagine bearing one more night. More than that, he couldn't get his mind off that woman in the yellow dress.

He strode through the groups of men dressed in silk waistcoats, oxford shoes, gold watch chains. At their command, railroads were laid, news was printed, new factories were built—old ones torn down. As he sat he knew he'd not be able to handle one more story of conquest, so he told his father he was going to listen to the orchestra. Once in the lounge, he pulled up a chair and watched the musicians, but his thoughts weren't on the lively tunes.

Damien couldn't get Amelia off his mind. Her beauty interested him from the first moment he saw her. And her lack of awe over those in first class intrigued him even more. She was nervous in the library, but she didn't look at the men and women there with wide-eyed wonder. He liked that. He liked her. And more than that—he had to know what type of involvement the woman had with his brother.

Clarence Walpole didn't wait for Damien to return from the lounge. Instead it was Arnold who had found him and walked him back to his room.

The opulent stateroom was quiet as he entered. His butler had turned down his bed, laid out his sleeping garments, and retired to his own room. Clarence was glad for that. He could barely make it to his private bedroom before he dropped down to his knees.

He folded his hands in front of him and placed them on the silky bedspread. The tears came, and a groan escaped his lips. His groan was a prayer.

Clarence had told God he'd wanted just a word about Quentin, to know that he was well. He'd prayed the same thing for months, and what had the young woman said?

I've seen him recently. He's doing well. He's gone through hard times, but he's doing better now.

He leaned forward so his forehead rested on his fists, and he uttered thanksgiving to God. After that he prayed he'd have a chance to talk to the young woman again. And that God would put it on her heart to tell him Quentin's whereabouts. Yes, they were on their way back to America, but he could get off the ship in Ireland. They'd be docking in Queenstown tomorrow. He could disembark, return to London, and find his son.

Clarence rose with new energy in his movements. He moved to the bureau and began to pack the things his butler had already hung out. He could use his help, but he could also go alone. If Damien argued, Damien could stay on the ship, too.

Clarence decided then that he'd find the young woman first thing in the morning and do whatever it took to enlist Amelia's help. All he knew was he didn't want to return to America if there was even a slim chance of finding Quentin.

Chapter 8

April 11, 1912
Thursday

Quentin struggled for breath as his mind clawed for wakefulness. Perhaps it was the ever-present vibration of the engines that had caused him to dream about the trains again. The trains that carried away all he'd loved on golden tracks.

He remembered the first time he'd climbed aboard the large black engine. He'd been allowed to sit up front on the conductor's knee. His mother's laughter remained even more prominent in his mind than the sound of the engine. He guessed it had been loud—trains always were—but it was her joy that had made him so happy. She'd been depressed all their months in London. His father had sent them there to stay with her family while his business flourished in America and a home was being built for them in Maryland. His father had wished for his wife to see their home complete—to not have to worry about its construction. Finally, the time had come when he'd sent for them.

Quentin didn't remember the passage across the ocean as much as he remembered his first ride on the train. His father had invested in a raw materials business that provided steel and wood to feed the hungry railroad tycoons like James J. Hill, whose Great Northern Railroad controlled the northwest part of the country. His investment had paid off. The fine home with the pond in the back was proof of that.

Another woman filled his mind, too, one who had some of the same qualities as his mother. Or at least the qualities he remembered most. But what had happened after they parted? Why hadn't she answered the door? He'd heard her inside. He'd heard the rustling of papers. Was she angry with him for not coming to supper? Had Amelia finally realized the type of man he was?

He imagined her aunt talking to her, bringing her around to the truth that he was a scoundrel. Her aunt hadn't been happy to see him. She'd seen through the facade to who he really was.

He walked to the mahogany bureau and opened the top drawer. His filthy rags lay bunched in the corner of the room. They were not worth saving, but the one thing he'd carried in his pocket the last five years—and all the years before that—was worth … everything. Quentin pulled the pearl necklace from the drawer and turned it over in his fingers. No matter how hungry he'd been. No matter how desperate for the drink and some company found seated upon the barstool of a London pub, he'd never been desperate enough to consider selling it.

A shiver moved down his spine when he remembered finding it in his clutched fingers as his mother lay dead on the grass. His father hadn't questioned what had happened to the necklace. And Quentin had never revealed that he had it hidden away. Since that time, he'd carried it around to remember—remember that it was his foolishness that caused her death. He'd looked at it again, remembering that his life had been an unworthy one to risk hers for—his last five years had confirmed that fact.

Fingering the pearls, he told himself he needed to stay away from Amelia. Remaining in her life would lead to her destruction, too, but he couldn't keep his mind off her. He'd walked away from most good things in the last five years. His heart begged him to hold on to her friendship. Last night she'd refused to talk to him, but maybe today would be different.

Instead of shrinking back—as he'd done nearly every day for the last two years—something inside told him to go to her, to lay his feelings before her. Last night her silence had told him she wanted no part of him, but today ... if she still felt the same, she would have to speak the words to his face.

In all her life, Amelia had never eaten breakfast anywhere but at her mother's small table—and later her aunt's—but she could tell from the wonderful scents of food filling the dining room that the staff of the *Titanic* had planned more than her typical biscuits with jam. Scents of ham and bacon and eggs and fresh coffee caused her stomach to growl. As she and Aunt Neda walked along the tables, fellow passengers chatted about the wonderful night's sleep and their nearness to Ireland. Amelia guessed that, like her, this trip was farther than most of them had ever traveled—and their journey was just beginning.

The four people who'd joined Amelia and her aunt for supper had returned to sit in the same spot they had last night, and a new couple joined them, too. But the chair for "Henry Gladstone" still sat empty.

Amelia told herself it didn't matter. It wasn't as if Quentin would come. And she was rather relieved that he didn't—it wasn't as if she wanted to sit by him, to have to pretend to be pleasant.

The couple who'd joined them for breakfast were old in years but young in character. They teased each other about scaling the last funnel on the *Titanic*—the one that was just for show.

The woman waved to a young man serving coffee. "We've traveled the *Olympic* a few times—it's good to see many of the same stewards and stewardesses here. They are like old friends."

Amelia took a sip of her coffee. The woman's mention of the ship's staff intrigued her. Was it possible others aboard knew her mother, had met her?

"Have you been traveling by ship many years? Twelve or more?" Amelia dared to ask.

"Let me see." The man nodded his head. "Yes, maybe a bit longer. My younger brother bought out half of our engineering business, giving me the time to travel and the funds to do so!" He laughed. "I could never be more grateful."

"I'm sure you have many stories of your voyages." Amelia folded her hands on her lap. "Do you remember a stewardess named Emma?"

"Emma is a common name." The woman focused on Amelia. "What did she look like, dear?"

"I'm told she looks like me. Or rather I look like her." Amelia cleared her throat. "You see, she is my mother. She would look older now, of course. Maybe she is still working on the ships; I do not know. I haven't seen her in many, many years."

Amelia glanced over at her aunt, noticing Aunt Neda's surprised expression. She imagined what her aunt was thinking. In the many years that Amelia had lived in her home, they'd only discussed her mother a few times.

The woman placed her fork across her plate and leaned slightly closer, as if she was more interested in Amelia's request than in the fine food on the menu.

"You do not know where your mother is? I'm sorry to hear that, darlin'."

The man scratched his head. "And I'm sorry to say I don't remember a stewardess that matches your description."

"No, surely we would remember." The woman reached for Amelia's hand. "I wish my husband and I could help you. We would remember a stewardess as lovely as you, but know that we will keep you in our prayers. May God fill your heart with a new love—not to replace the love of a mother, but to hold you up when the missing gets too terrible."

Amelia squeezed the woman's hand and smiled. How kind of her to say such words. The older woman released her grasp and looked to her husband. It was clear the woman knew the type of love she spoke of. Amelia spread her cloth napkin over her lap, wondering if she'd find such a love with Mr. Chapman.

The gaiety at their table settled into a subdued appreciation of the ship and their journey. Like children in a candy shop, those gathered around the table pointed out to each other the delightful items on the breakfast menu.

Amelia looked at her own printed menu, trying to decide between the grilled ham and fried eggs or the buckwheat cakes, when she spotted someone out of the corner of her eye.

A tall, dark-haired man stood at the entrance to the dining hall and scanned the room. *Quentin.* She twisted one of the curls that lay on her shoulder, and the slight smile he offered sent her heartbeat thumping. She willed her heart to stop its pounding, but instead of calming, goose bumps rose on her arms.

Amelia lifted the cup of tea to her lips, pretending she didn't care if he was there or not. It did no good. Although the room was filled with people, noises, smells, and conversation around her, she was only aware of him—of his presence. The room around her seemed to quiet. The faces of those seated at their section of the long table blurred as her eyes fixed on his.

Quentin approached with quickened steps and sat down in the chair beside her—the chair that should have been Henry's.

After a quick greeting to everyone at the table, he leaned close to Amelia. So close she felt his breath on her ear. "I came to see you last night after supper."

"Really?" She gingerly unfolded her cloth napkin and placed it on her lap. "Where did you eat? I remember sitting in this very spot, but that chair was empty."

He glanced down at his fingers as they fiddled with the silver spoon. "I ate in third class. I thought I'd be more comfortable there."

Comfortable? Is that what he calls it? She thought of seeing him on the third-class deck—but something even more pressing pushed to the forefront of her thoughts. His lie. Did he think he'd make it all the way to America without the truth of who he really was being discovered?

"Third class? Is that so?" She lowered her voice and leaned close to his ear. Quentin leaned in. "Because, if I wasn't mistaken, I would have guessed you to have a much higher status, like first class. Like your father and your brother. So tell me, Quentin, why didn't you join them at their table last night? The first-class dining room is something to behold."

Quentin jolted to his feet. If the chair weren't bolted to the floor, he would have knocked it over. His eyes widened, and his forehead knotted, as if his mind worked to make sense of her words.

"They're here?" His voice was ragged, shaky.

Amelia pushed down her panic, wondering if she'd just made a horrible mistake. Had she misjudged him? Maybe he really didn't know. Maybe he honestly had just been a person in need and had no other motives than that.

Unless Quentin was as talented as the picture show actors, the news of his father and brother being on board took him by complete surprise. His eyes blinked slowly as he looked to her, as if he was trying to make sense of her words.

She almost stood, too, to offer him an apology, but something else kept Amelia planted firmly in her seat. She may have assumed wrong about him knowing his father and brother were on board, but she had not been mistaken when it came to seeing him with that woman. Amelia's neck tightened in a dozen knots as the image resurrected of the woman from third class curling herself against his back, her arms embracing him.

"Amelia." Quentin's voice quavered. "Can I speak with you for a few moments? In private?"

Her companions turned to her, waiting for her response. The steward approached, but seeing the awkwardness of the moment, he told them he had an errand in the kitchen and would be back soon to take their orders.

"Yes, of course." She placed her linen napkin on the table and turned to her aunt and the others. "Won't you excuse me? I'll be back in just a moment."

The displeasure was clear in her aunt's gaze. If only Amelia could tell her not to worry. She may have fallen in step with this man's schemes yesterday, but today she would not let herself be drawn back in.

They walked out of the second-class dining salon, and she followed him to the boat deck. A few feet out of the doorway, the cool ocean air took her breath away. He paused and turned to her.

"Amelia, are you saying what I think you are? Did you say— are my father and brother on this ship?"

She tugged at the lace on her sleeves, feeling foolish for blurting out the news as she had. "You didn't know? I'm sorry. It's just that... Well, yes they are, but I shouldn't have ..." She pressed her lips together. "I assumed you knew."

Running a hand down his face, Quentin mumbled something under his breath. "How would I know that? Think about it, Amelia. Do you think I checked with the White Star offices about the passenger list before I tried to sneak on?"

"But I thought..." Amelia placed trembling fingers to her lips. She didn't know what she thought. She didn't know why she'd assumed what she had. What had happened between

Quentin and his family? How could Quentin run so far ... fall so low without them reaching out to help?

"When did you find this out?" he asked.

"Last night."

"So when I knocked at your door last night..."

"Yes, I already knew."

He walked nearer to her and sat on a lounge chair, peering up into her face. "You don't know me. You don't have any reason to trust me, but would it have been too hard to tell me?"

"I—I..." She lowered her head. "I was angry. I saw you on the deck with that woman and—"

"On the third-class deck? You were watching me?"

She shrugged, not knowing what to say. The desperation in his face caused her heart to soften. She placed a hand on his shoulder. "You don't have to say anything about her. You don't owe me an explanation. I was glad to help you."

He looked down at the polished deck and blew out a deep breath.

Is he trying to figure out how to explain?

"I'm still trying to figure out my past," he finally said. "There are many things I thought I'd left behind. Things that seem to be following me."

He rose and nervously looked in the direction of the first-class deck.

"Are you going to find your father and brother? Are you going to let them know you're here? Talk to them? Your father, he—"

His eyes darted to hers. "No." The word shot from his lips. "I can't."

A cold rush of ocean breeze ruffled Amelia's hair. The large ship skimmed through the water, and the cloudless sky stretched until it touched the edge of the horizon. When she'd boarded yesterday, she'd been excited to ride amid such luxury. What she didn't realize was what would impact her most wouldn't be the *Titanic,* or its grandeur, but who she'd meet on its decks.

"But you don't understand." Amelia took a step toward him. "I'm not sure what happened in your past, but they were asking about you. They wanted to know how you were."

Quentin's eyes widened. "You talked to them? How did that happen? You didn't tell them I was on this ship, did you?"

"No, I did not tell them. I told your father you were well. I—" She bit her lip. "I saw your brother and thought he was you. I called out to him. I called your name. That was when they approached. They asked about you. You should at least consider—"

"Don't try to convince me. There is too much to understand, Amelia." Quentin tucked his hand into his pocket and seemed to grasp something. "I am not going to tell them I'm on this ship, and I beg you not to utter a word."

Two men in officer's uniforms strode by. Quentin pressed his lips together and took a step forward, closer to her. He took both of her hands in his, and when he looked into her face, she noticed tears in his eyes.

"They can't . . . they can't see me like this, Amelia. Although I wish things were different, this is the way they have to be." And with that, Quentin released her hands and strode away.

After ten steps, his pace quickened until he was nearly jogging. Her heart sank, and she crossed her arms over her chest. She thought about following him, but that was the last thing Quentin needed. If she tried to talk to him, if she pressed, it would just push him further away.

She lifted her face to the sky. She thought about saying a prayer to God, but she didn't know what to pray for. Finally, she decided to pray for Quentin.

Amelia sat down on the lounge chair and folded her hands on her lap. A strange sensation came over her, almost as if someone stood behind her. She quickly turned around, but no one was there. Her stomach flipped. What seemed like a thousand needles pierced her arms. It was almost as if God was sitting there with her on the deck. A warmth filled her, warmer than the sun beaming down. A peace fluttered in her heart, brushing away the tension.

As her heartbeat settled, a deep knowing filled her chest. It was no coincidence Quentin was on this ship. No coincidence his father and brother were, too. There had been times over the years when Amelia had felt used by God, such as when she called upon a friend with a basket of food only to discover that friend had just served her children the last that they had. But now ... this ...

She'd been on the pier for a reason. It was not by chance that she had an extra passenger's ticket in her pocket as she saw Quentin being dragged off the gangplank. She might never evidence the family coming together while they were on the open sea, but suddenly it didn't matter.

Just as the ocean depths stretched under the ship deeper than she imagined, God had a purpose for Quentin. Perhaps she'd play a larger part in the days to come—or perhaps her job was only to offer him the ticket—but as Amelia arose and moved back toward the second-class dining room, faith that God had a plan encircled her, as gentle as the ocean breeze.

She didn't need to run after Quentin. She didn't need to try to fix anything. Even though she did not know where he had run to and she couldn't fathom the depths of the aching in his heart. He was in God's hands. God saw him even when she could not. And she prayed God would soften Quentin's heart and remind him of his father's love.

Thursday
11:30 a.m.

The noonday sun was nearly straight overhead, and the coast of Ireland shone beautifully as they approached Queenstown harbor. Amelia had never seen hills so green. White houses speckled across them. Rugged cliffs ringed the coast. If Amelia wasn't on her way to meet a man who could possibly be her future husband, she would have wished to stay and explore Ireland for a while.

She walked to the deck and noticed the screws of the *Titanic* churning up water brown with sand. Because the *Titanic* was too large to enter the harbor, tenders carried passengers and supplies out to the ship. When the gangplank went down, some passengers departed. Others joined the voyage. Amelia had come to watch, almost expecting Quentin to be one of those leaving. Her chest warmed when she didn't see him. God had a plan for him on this ship. Something deep down told her it was so.

She turned and scanned the expanse of decks and funnels that rose around her. Where could he be? After breakfast, she hadn't bothered to knock on the door of his cabin. And she knew not to expect him at lunch. She hoped to see him again, maybe this evening or tomorrow, but she wouldn't push. What Quentin needed most from her was patience, time, and prayers.

Amelia smiled seeing the new passengers' wide-eyed and gap-mouthed expressions as stewards welcomed them. She no doubt had looked the same only the day before.

Titanic was surrounded by a flotilla of small boats. Vendors hauled all sorts of goods onto the ship and disappeared into the passageways leading to first class. Fashionably dressed ladies waited with their purses on their laps, eager to see the goods Ireland had to offer—small trinkets or jewelry that they could wear back home to show off their world travels.

Laughter carried up from a lower deck, and Amelia smiled. Few others on the ship had funds for frivolous purchases. Most in second and third class were starting a new life in America. Every penny they could scrape together would be used for that, but when it came down to it, Amelia guessed the excitement of those down below excelled those in the highest, fanciest decks. She reminded herself that true treasure wasn't about accumulating more, but about living each day with hope of what God had just ahead.

Bags of mail were also carried up the gang planks. All her letters to Mr. Chapman had taken this type of voyage. And now she herself would be the special delivery. Would Mr. Chapman be disappointed? Would she?

Growing up she'd never thought much of marriage. She cared more to know that she could roll up her sleeves and offer a helpful hand to the orphans around town. Some young men had fancied her, but none of them understood her heart's passion— to care for those who did not have a mother or a father, who were hardly treated better than the dogs on the street. Would Mr. Chapman understand? From his letters it seemed he would, or had she read more into the lines than what had been there? Her aunt always did tell her she read too much goodness into people's motives.

As mail was being carried on, waste pipes poured into the harbor entrance. Within a matter of minutes, hundreds of seagulls fought over remnants of breakfast floating on the water.

Amelia clung to the rail of the ocean liner, staring into the deep, blue ocean. In all her life, she never thought she'd leave Southampton. How many ships had she seen arrive and leave again? More than she could count. For a while she had watched them—waited at the docks and watched the crews disembark. After awhile she knew it was no use. Her mother would never return.

"Awk!" the squall of gulls filled the air. Some swooped around the deck, but most circled the liner's waste pipes. They swooped and turned with hardly a flutter of their wings, so effortless was their rise and fall. As she watched, flutters of her mother's stories filled Amelia's mind.

"In France if you are found strolling along the boulevards without plans for supper, the locals will fight over you, each family welcoming you into their home," her mother had told her once.

"On the *Atlantic,* the captain was so punctual, he visited the lavatory every three hours on the dot."

"In the Overland Route in North Africa, we were forced to travel ninety miles across the desert on two-wheeled omnibuses that held six persons and were drawn by four horses. We traveled through the moonlight, and the only sound was the grinding of the horse's hooves on the sand and the voice of the driver directing them."

These were only a few of a thousand stories Amelia's mother had whispered in her ear. From as long as she could remember, Mother had put her to bed and laid beside her telling her of the places she'd visited, some of the tales more fiction than true.

"In New York a lady greets you in the harbor. She's so tall her crown touches the clouds. In Ireland the hills are covered with emeralds." Amelia had fallen asleep to such stories.

"Is my father in New York?" she'd asked as a young child. "Is my father in Ireland?" Her mother answered "maybe" to all her questions about her father. And then one day—the pull of the water, the ships, and maybe lost love—drew her mother away.

Laughter rose even louder than the gulls' cries, and Amelia strained to listen. She walked to the railing and looked down. Far astern, on the poop deck, the third-class passengers waved at the shore and called out. A man brought out an accordion and struck up a tune. Children gathered around, laughing and danc-ing, chasing each other.

For the first six years of Amelia's life, her mother had worked around Southampton instead of traveling and working out at sea, but all that changed after Amelia's sixth birthday.

They'd shown up at Aunt Neda's doorstep with two card-board suitcases and a tattered rag doll she'd named Ibette. Even though her mother and aunt had argued for a time, Amelia could tell from her aunt's kind eyes she would not be turned away.

As she'd grown, she understood the sacrifice her aunt had made. Not only did her aunt have to feed four mouths—Elizabeth's, Henry's, Amelia's, and hers—as a widowed seam-stress, but the whispers around the neighborhood must have been yet another burden to carry. They were whispers Amelia didn't know about until a neighborhood friend asked Amelia if she, too, was going to be the mistress of a great sea captain like her mother. Amelia didn't know if the rumors had any weight to them, or if they were simply invisible knives, fashioned to cut deep. What she did know was that from that moment she determined to be nothing like her mother. She had stayed away from the docks and the ships—until now. This trip—and the man who waited—changed everything.

Soon the transfers were complete, the tenders cast off, and with screws churning up the sea bottom again, the *Titanic* turned, pointing her nose down the Irish coast. The ship moved grace-fully through the water, moving up and down, over the swells in the harbor. Amelia returned to her room to find her aunt resting.

As Aunt Neda napped, Amelia decided to write a letter to her Southampton friends.

Dear friends at the Seaman's Orphanage at Tremona Court,
    I expect you will be glad to hear about my journey upon the greatest ship ever built. I am not sure how to put all I've

experienced into words. It feels as if I've been on this great vessel for a week, rather than just a day.

When we left, the docks were filled with well-wishers who were envious that they could not join us. Maybe they will get their chance someday. Maybe you will, too. If you do get to ride the Titanic to America, make sure you visit me in New Haven.

The ship itself is lovely. The rooms are paneled in fine wood; the carpets are lush to walk on; the decks polished like a mirror. There is decorative paper on the wall and fine china dishes! And our needs are cared for by an attentive and friendly staff.

Our room is just as large as the one Aunt Neda and I shared back in our apartment, but the linens are of the best quality, and the wood used in the room is polished to a shine. There is even running water for our wash basin. I was allowed to visit first class, and I'm sure even royalty would be impressed with the details. There are leather chairs, leather-bound books in the library, and crystal chandeliers. I wish I had a photograph to send to you!

Last night the food was wonderful and plentiful. The hardest thing was not being able to wrap up what I couldn't finish and save it for another date. The other hardest thing was knowing that each minute on this ship carried me farther from all of you. My consolation, however, is that because we can write letters, we don't ever have to feel as if we're far part.

Looking at the clock, I see it's almost time for tea. I believe I'll take Aunt Neda to the lounge. I'll write more later as I am able.

A friend who cherishes you,
Amelia Gladstone

The sea was calm. Her penmanship untouched by the ship's movements. Aunt Neda's snores filled the room, and Amelia wished it was warmer so she could sit out on the deck.

She also considered going to the library or one of the lounges to write in her journal, but she'd get distracted watching everyone else. Instead she stayed in the room and pulled out the small journal with the brown leather cover and wrote some of the things she'd written in the letter. Then she wrote about the lift, and the grand staircase, and the chairs in the dining room that were bolted to the floor. Her words filled four pages, and only when her hand started to cramp did she set the book and fountain pen to the side.

She smiled as she closed the journal, imagining her children and grandchildren in future years pausing to listen to her read about her journey on the most elegant ship on its maiden voyage. There was only one problem....

Like the letter, the journal spoke little of what mattered most—about the experience that impacted her deeply. How could she write all those pages and not mention meeting Quentin, or running into his brother, or meeting Geraldine—the stewardess who knew her mother?

Yet Amelia hadn't shared most of those things with her aunt either. Perhaps because she was still pondering all those things as she held them in her heart.

After writing in her journal, she wrote a letter to Mr. Chapman. She figured that she'd arrive on his doorstep before the letter, but how quaint it would be to have him read the words she wrote while on the ship with her sitting right next to him.

Dear Mr. Chapman,

It may seem strange that I will most likely hand you this letter in person, but I thought you would like to know a little about my trip. It will also help jog my memory so we can share about my journey from Southampton to New Haven. There is so much to look at and to experience and to see on the Titanic *that I am afraid I will forget something. Forget one hundred things.*

The ship is just leaving Ireland now. This ship has three promenade decks. A lounge runs along each. The ship is delightful, but the crew is special. Each of them seems as excited as we are to be on this voyage. I've never received so many smiles and greetings. As I walk the decks, the sound of the orchestra punctuates each step.

She stopped the letter there, partly because she didn't know what else to say without mentioning Quentin, and partly because these were details she wouldn't forget—no matter how many days passed. It made her nervous to think of Mr. Chapman reading a letter with her sitting right there. What if he had no smile on his face as he read? What if he didn't laugh at the right moments? She'd always assumed he'd be easy to converse with, since he seemed to write well, but what if he was more like her uncle Rupert, God rest his soul, who spoke little and was more concerned with a good book?

The thought of such a thing seized her pen. So she rose and checked her hair briefly in the mirror before leaving the room, taking her finished letter in her grasp.

After finding her way through the correct passageways, Amelia posted the letter to the orphans by the second-class library door.

"This ship is made in Ireland," she heard one man say to another as the ship again slid back into the sea, "solid as a rock." She smiled and told herself she could write about that in the next letter.

With her letter posted, she returned to her room. When she opened the door and stepped in, she saw her aunt was awake. Her aunt's head jerked up and her face flamed. On Aunt Neda's lap were letters from Mr. Chapman.

"Amelia, you're home so soon." Color rose up Aunt Neda's neck.

"Find good reading material, Aunt?" Amelia teased.

Aunt Neda smiled and fanned her face with the letters. "I hope you don't mind, dear. I woke up from my nap and was afraid to venture out to find you. There are so many passageways and levels. I feared I'd get lost."

Amelia laughed, remembering when the roles were reversed and her aunt was the one who used to catch her up to no good.

"Aunt, you know I don't mind. I've read those letters to you a few times each, and I don't blame you. There isn't much to do in the room alone. I apologize for not waiting for you to wake before I walked to the library."

"No problem, dear. As long as we do not miss tea." Her aunt placed the letters on the top of the bureau and spread them with her hands. "And I do hate to mention it, but I've noted something I didn't realize before. Maybe it's because this time I read all of the letters back to back." Her brow knitted and her aunt's thin, age-spotted hands continued to play with the letters.

"What is it, Aunt?" Amelia stepped forward and placed a hand on her aunt's arm. "Do you have a concern about Mr. Chapman? You don't feel we've acted hastily by moving all this way, do you?"

"My dear Amelia, I've never had a concern about Mr. Chapman. Elizabeth's recommendation is good enough for me." Aunt Neda lifted her gaze and looked at Amelia with watery blue eyes. She sighed and then continued, "But don't you feel it strange, dear, that he seems so taken with his cook? That Miss Betsie MacLellan will be someone you might want to keep an eye on."

Amelia gasped. "Aunt, how could you say such a thing? He hired her for us—for me—to make things easier."

"Yes, dear." Aunt Neda smiled. "And although it was a very fine gesture, maybe you should read these three letters and tell me what you think of the way Mr. Chapman favors her so."

Amelia nodded and took the letters her aunt had pulled from the stack, but as she read, she didn't think anything appeared unusual to her.... Well, at least not too much. Instead her heart endeared even more to what a dear, dear man Mr. Chapman was.

Dear Amelia,

It was very exciting news for me to hear that you were able to book your passage to America. You will arrive just in time for spring in New Haven. There is no more beautiful time with the flowers blooming and the trees resonating with the songs of birds.

As I told you in the last correspondence, after talking to Elizabeth, I hired a cook, Miss Betsie MacLellan. She has been practicing, cooking for me breakfast, lunch, and dinner. Elizabeth shared recipes for some of your favorite meals. A few of the recipes were written by your aunt's own hand, and reading them has made me feel closer to you both.

Also, dear Amelia, it must be trying to pack for such a voyage. I believe I've told you before that Elizabeth has a small carriage room behind her home that we are remodeling for the use of you and your aunt. One of our neighbors down the street recently lost his grandmother, and he provided us with extra furnishings. If you bring yourselves, your most precious keepsakes, and your clothing items, that will be enough. And once you settle in, perhaps you can help me choose new furnishings for my expansive home. I've filled the rooms with pieces that others have given me. They are functional for a bachelor but not nearly nice enough for a lady's proper home.

I'm looking forward to hearing more from you.

With sincerity,
Your Mr. Chapman

Dear Amelia,

The weeks seem to creep by as I wait for the calendar month to flip to April. Only two newsworthy events have taken place that merit the ink to write about. First, the ground has thawed, and I was able to plant a garden behind my home. Len and Elizabeth helped me, and we expanded the plot over what I've had the previous years. We all felt we would need a larger plot because of more smiling faces (and hungry stomachs!) around the dinner table. I'm most excited about the onions and radishes. Last year they were plentiful, and I hope this year will be no different.

The second notable event is the fact I had to go to the tailor and have many of the waistbands of my pants taken out. It seems the efforts of my new cook, Miss Betsie MacLellan, have been beneficial to my girth. Len always complained I was stick rail thin. He's been complaining less and less. Although we have continued to try out English recipes, there is nothing finer than a piece of Betsie's apple pie. I'll ask her to make a pie for you for your first dinner in America.

Yours, Mr. Chapman

Dear Amelia,

My hope is that this letter reaches you before you board the great ship Titanic. I saw an advertisement for it in the New York paper. It seems that even more passengers have purchased their passage for the return trip from New York to London than those who have bought tickets to travel from Europe to New York.

I found many of the facts interesting. Did you know it took three thousand men two years to build the Titanic, and only three of the four funnels are working smokestacks? The fourth is hollow and simply for looks.

*My cook, Miss Betsie MacLellan, and I have been wonder-
ing what types of meals they will be serving on the great ship.
We expect that they will be very grand indeed. It seems no
expense has been spared by the White Star Line when it comes
to the Titanic.*

*I am more than eager to see the ship with my own eyes when
it docks in New York. I'm sure half the city will come out for
that. When Betsie and I were talking about it the other day,
she expressed her interest in seeing the ship, too. If Len and
Elizabeth can take their own vehicle to New York to meet you
and your aunt, I might invite Betsie along. She's eager to meet
you, my dear, and to see the ship with her own eyes would be
an event she wouldn't soon forget.*

Sincerely,

Mr. Chapman

Then again . . .

Even after Amelia tucked the letters away, Mr. Chapman's
words played over in her mind. *Betsie and I were talking. Betsie
and I were wondering. Betsie might come with us to New York. Betsie,
Betsie, Betsie . . .*

Was her aunt right? Had Mr. Chapman found a new love in
his cook? Was Amelia coming all this way for nothing?

Amelia sat at the bureau and unpinned her hair, deciding to
put it up in a new style. Not because she was displeased with the
way it looked but rather to occupy her mind so she could stop
thinking of Betsie MacLellan spending so much time with *her*
Mr. Chapman.

Chapter 9

Quentin stared into the water. Even after all these years, he could see his mother's form in the ripple of the waves. The pain of that day at his father's party wrapped around his soul like the anchor of the *Titanic*. Yet his feet were rooted to the deck. Part of him hated the water. He hated the fact that something so beautiful could suck away the life of a person so easily.

Another part of him was drawn to its power. For a time—before he lost all his riches—he lived at a cottage near the ocean shore and would fall asleep to the pounding of the waves. It was one of the few things that had helped him sleep over the years. The sound of the waves had helped to dull out the other noises. It had helped him drift away. But it was the sight of the water that caused him to remember. It took his mind back to that place as quickly as if he'd walked through a passage back into time. The pain ripped at his heart, the memories of his mother's embrace. The embrace gone. How could loving someone hurt so much? He'd told himself long ago that he'd never allow himself to go to that place again. By keeping people at arm's length, he was protecting himself.

His eyes moved to the tall cliffs along the coast of Ireland. Hills rose above them, the fading light casting gray shadows. He watched until the last of the Irish coast slipped out of view and they were once again on the open water.

He questioned whether he should partake of his meals in the dining area or ask the steward if one could be brought to his room. He decided on the latter. It was best not to bother Amelia again. The poor girl. She had a habit of trying to help people fix unfortunate situations. But there was no fixing him—no rectifying what he'd done.

He touched his hand to his cheek, fingering the cut and remembering the way the stewards had dragged him off. He deserved that. He had no right being here—not with these good people.

Quentin entered his stateroom and sat heavily on his bed. He'd pushed the thoughts of his father out of his mind, but doing so sapped more strength than he could muster. Unwilling to fight the memories any longer, he allowed his mind to go there. To think back to the day of his mother's death.

The house seemed miles from the pond as his weak legs had struggled to run up the hill. The orchestra was still playing when he ran into the house. Men and women mingled—wearing their finest clothes. He'd tried to find his father in a sea of dark-colored suits. He'd finally found him near the fireplace. Damien had been at Father's side entertaining the partygoers by reciting memorized poetry. His father's face had been bright with joy as he'd listened to Damien, but then his mouth dropped as he'd turned to Quentin.

"Son, what happened? Why are you wet?" Concern transformed into horror as he hurried to the nearest window that overlooked the pond. "Quentin, where is your mother?" he'd asked only loud enough for Quentin to hear.

Father turned back, dropping to his knees and grasping Quentin's hands with vicelike grips. "Son, where is she? Where is she?" he whispered, his face pressed close.

Quentin barely squeaked out one word. "Under…"

Without waiting for more of an explanation, his father darted to the pond with Quentin trailing. The laughter and music had continued as though nothing had happened. His brother most likely recited another poem. Only the maids and the butler—whose job was to be alert to his father's needs—realized something was wrong and followed.

Then, from the soft, muddy grass at the edge of his pond, he'd watched his father struggle to pull his mother from the water. He'd heard his cries and saw his moans, and then when Quentin knew she was dead, he approached. He stood there wet, quivering. His father only had to take one look into his eyes to guess what had happened. Quentin would never forget the expression on his face when his father's gaze met his—one of pure pain.

And that was when Quentin had found it easier to look away—to run away, because it was easier to forget when he didn't have to look into his father's eyes.

Clarence Walpole gazed at his clothes that were once again arranged in the bureau. His butler, upon seeing Clarence had packed to return to the shore, had set matters right. As he'd packed his things in his trunk the night before, all he'd thought about was the fact that young woman had seen his son. He had to see if what the woman said was true. He longed to see for himself that Quentin was all right, safe.

To Clarence's surprise when he'd awoken in the morning, he knew he was no longer supposed to disembark in Ireland. One thought filled his mind: *"Give your sons to Me."*

The words came as a whisper to his heart.

He'd lain there for a while thinking of that. Wondering if the message was from God. The peace that came with the words told him it was. It pushed away the anxiety that had filled him the previous night when the realization that he was leaving Quentin behind became as clear as the steady vibration from the engines below that stirred his bed.

The new peace didn't soothe all the anxiety he'd been storing up over the past five years, though. It was as if the Spirit of God had opened up the storehouse of concerns and let warm shafts of light in, dusting off the closest burdens. It hadn't yet touched the locked boxes of worries and fears he'd been piling up . . . but casting light on them was a first step, wasn't it?

"Give your sons to Me," he whispered into the room. Silent sobs shook his body. Why was saying those words harder than anything he'd worked at or set out to accomplish in his sixty-one years?

From the beginning, Clarence believed he'd given everything to God. His business. His marriage. He prayed about his decisions and didn't proceed until he was certain of his path. But his sons? Could he trust God with them completely?

He'd done what he could for them, especially after Jillian's death. He'd made certain they attended the best schools. He saw that their every need was met, and when Quentin had asked for his inheritance, nearly as soon as he was old enough to leave home, Clarence hadn't argued. His friends tried to tell him he was a fool. Clarence had as many English friends as American ones, and his English friends had been most appalled.

"The things Americans allow their prodigy to get away with!" they'd exclaimed. Never would an English youth ask for such a thing. Never would an English parent indulge a child like that in such a way—even if the child was now a grown adult. No sense of respect or dignity or patience whatsoever.

Damien, too, had cursed his brother—reprimanding him for not being thankful for all he had, saying that he was kicking dirt on their father's grave while he still lived. But Clarence believed in his boy. He trusted he'd done what he could to ensure Quentin had the skills he needed to succeed in his new venture.

It was only later, when his youngest son stumbled, and all he'd been given had started to slip away, that Clarence questioned if he'd given Quentin too much too soon. And after his son lost everything and had slipped into the London nights, Clarence held on tighter. If not with his hands, with his heart.

And now with the young woman having seen Quentin recently, his instinct screamed to find her, to get as much information as he could from her. But he knew he wasn't supposed to do that either.

In Your time, Lord, in Your time.

Waiting, it seemed, was harder. Not pursuing Quentin made Clarence feel like he wasn't really loving with all that he had.

What did it mean to give his sons to God?

Clarence opened his hands and placed them on his lap. Did it mean he stopped worrying about them? Did it mean he would no longer provide?

Or maybe...

Maybe the answer was simpler than he expected, and it came as another whisper to his heart. Maybe he simply had to trust God, and to pray that his sons would seek Him and do the same. Maybe it was taking the worry off of his shoulders and placing it on God's lap for Him to sort out.

Somehow after the years of trying to give his sons everything, Clarence had a feeling God knew what they needed most of all.

"Lord, I am willing." His lips trembled with the words. "Make me more willing, still," he prayed.

Damien Walpole received most things he wanted in his life, but nothing confused him more than his interest in the woman in the yellow dress. She was beautiful, yes, but he knew many beautiful women. She wasn't from first class, but somehow the more he thought of her, that didn't seem to be a problem. She knew Quentin—or at least had known him—and that made her much more intriguing. Of all the women he knew, Amelia was different. Other women would have used their knowledge of Quentin's whereabouts to get the upper hand over him or his father. But she seemed almost regretful to have mentioned it at all. And knowing that made Damien want to spend time with her. Not only for what she knew but also for who she was. Different, unique—unpretentious.

He dressed in simple black pants and a dark blue shirt he'd left unbuttoned at the neck and rolled up the sleeves. He felt like a college boy again, and maybe that was what gave him the extra hop in his step as he made his way to the stairway that would take him down to the second-class accommodations.

Damien approached a redheaded steward who watered some of the potted plants that lined the hall. "Excuse me, but I was wondering if it was possible to take a stroll on the second-class deck."

The man looked confused. "But, sir, once passengers board, each class is supposed to stay in their designated areas."

"I understand why you wouldn't want those in second or third class coming to first class." Damien rubbed the back of his neck. "Heaven knows the passengers pay enough not to be bothered, but the other way around . . . ?"

The young, freckle-faced man shrugged. "I can ask my supervisor. It is not something I've been asked before."

"Or . . . at least if you could get a message to someone for me. I can return with a note. There is a woman, you see. . . . I met her just briefly, and she's traveling in second class with her aunt. I thought about inviting her to stroll the deck with me. The first-class or second-class deck, it really doesn't matter."

The steward eyed Damien, and just when he was sure the steward would deny his request, the young man's eyes brightened. "Is she beautiful?"

Damien nodded. "Yes, very much so."

The steward whistled softly. His green eyes sparkled. "A beautiful woman you say—why that's a different matter. Please, sir, let me lead the way."

Chapter 10

It was just a simple tea with her aunt. The tea was served in white china cups with a blue floral design and the White Star logo. Kindly stewards passed out fresh scones.

The gasp of the young woman seated at the next table over alerted Amelia that something was amiss. She glanced over, and the womans eyes widened—her smile did, too. But it was the pink that flushed the woman's cheeks that told Amelia a handsome man had just walked into the room.

"That is a man from first class. I saw him board yesterday, I am certain," the woman said a little too loudly for Amelia's comfort. "He's very, very rich. Don't let his plain dress fool you."

Amelia turned in her seat, curious. The man's broad-shouldered form filled the doorway, and her heart did a double beat as she spotted him. It was Damien, and he looked finer in his simple clothes than he had the previous night dressed in expensive attire. As their eyes met, a smile filled his face. He patted the shoulder of the steward who stood by his side and strode over with quickened steps.

Pausing before their table, Damien offered a hand to her aunt first. "Dear madame, please excuse me for interrupting your tea, but may I have a moment with Amelia?"

Her aunt eyed her, and confusion flashed through Aunt Neda's face.

"Do I know you, sir? You look familiar. Similar to—"

"Aunt, I met Mr. Damien Walpole last night," Amelia interrupted. She could not allow her aunt to mention Quentin. She could not let Damien know his brother was on the ship.

"I am certain you have not met him before, although there are many handsome men on this ship," Amelia continued. "I can see how easy it would be to get confused." She widened her smile.

Her aunt cocked an eyebrow. "I see. Very confusing indeed." Aunt Neda glanced at Amelia's teacup that was nearly full, and then she looked back up a Damien. "It seems my niece is almost finished here. I don't mind if you steal her away, if you don't."

Amelia's throat tightened at her aunt's boldness, and she tried to swallow down her surprise. Aunt Neda had been the one who had urged her to travel to America to meet Mr. Chapman. "He sounds like the perfect man for you. You cannot miss this opportunity," she'd said more than once. And now her aunt was going to forget about Mr. Chapman and push her into the arms of the first handsome man from first class who showed interest in her? Surely this was not happening!

So much for her tea. So much for trusting her aunt's judgment.

"Mind?" Damien smiled. "You are gracious, and I am thankful for the opportunity." He offered his arm. "Amelia, we just met, but would you give me the honor of taking a turn with you around the ship? It has warmed up outside, and it's a beautiful spring day."

All eyes were on her. The woman sitting across from Amelia nodded as if answering for her. The only excuse she could think of for not going with him was that she wanted to finish her tea. But that would only prolong this tension. And a proper English tea was no excuse for delaying an invitation from a man as handsome and well-mannered as this.

Amelia pushed her teacup back and stood. Peering up into Damien's face, she felt a wash of heat rush from the top of her head to the tip of her toes. His smile was intoxicating, and he smelled like the sweetest dream shed ever known.

He captured Amelia's eyes for a moment, looking deep, and then turned back to her aunt. "Thank you much, dear lady, and what name can I utter my appreciation to?"

Aunt Neda offered her gloved hand, and Damien touched it to his lips. If Amelia wasn't mistaken, she noticed a slight blush on her aunt's cheeks. "My name is Neda...short for Neandra Gladstone, and I do hope you enjoy the afternoon with my niece. The second-class promenade deck this time of day is something to behold."

"I will take your suggestion, ma'am. Thank you again." And with that, he placed a hand on the small of Amelia's back and led her through the lounge. Amelia had never walked in a parade, but if she had, she was sure that their exit was no different. All eyes were on them—following them. Whispers erupted in small bursts. Who was this man from first class? What did he want to do with a woman from their station?

Since this section of the ship was new to Damien, Amelia led the way to the second-class promenade. They strode side by side, passing fellow passengers, including many families with young children. As they walked from the glass-walled promenade to the open boat deck, Damien again offered his arm. This time she slipped her hand into its crook, feeling his warm skin through the thin linen shirt. He held her hand there, tucking it close to his side. When they approached the rail they paused, but he didn't release her. Instead of her senses being overwhelmed with his closeness, Amelia felt herself relax.

There was an ease about Damien she hadn't felt with any man she'd ever known before. From her first impression, Damien knew who he was and he was comfortable with that. Maybe it was because of his money. Or maybe not. Maybe it was because he knew what he had to offer a woman beyond his money.

Her heart pounded faster as he stood motionless. She grasped the railing and looked up at him. The light from the sea cast a warm glow around him. A spray of water rose up, misting the air. Damien laughed and wiped a hand down his cheek, brushed it against the front of his shirt, and continued staring.

"Have you ever seen anything so beautiful?" he asked, staring out at the sea that reminded her of the color of a bluish-gray sky right before a thunderstorm. "The sea is lovely, but not nearly as lovely as the woman on my arm."

"That's kind of you to say, Mr. Walpole." The wind took her breath away—or maybe it was his words. "But I don't think you sought me out just to flatter me."

"Please call me Damien." He chuckled and glanced down at her. "And flattery comes naturally, my dear. It's simply the byproduct of being by your side. My motive is just to spend time with you. To get to know you better." He brushed a strand of hair that was blowing across her face back from her forehead. "And to tell you the truth, I was intrigued when I met you in the reading and writing room, but you intrigued me before that. I spotted you taking in the sights and sounds when I was boarding. It was then I knew this ride on the *Titanic* would be spectacular indeed."

Oh dear, Amelia thought as his lips curled up in a smile. *I believe he's flirting with me.*

She squeezed his arm in response to his words. *And I believe I like it.*

Immediately she thought of Quentin and then Mr. Chapman. Mostly the latter. He'd cared for her over so many months by his kind words. He'd sacrificed to pay for their passage. He even hired a cook to make their lives easier once they arrived in New Haven. Then again, if he spent his time having long conversations with that cook Betsie MacLellan, then it wouldn't hurt for her to build a friendship of her own on this ship—would it? They were just friends.

Still, even if she enjoyed the flirting, how could what he said be possible? How could she have caught the attention of one of the wealthiest men on the ship just by standing on the deck? And how could she like it so?

Amelia lowered her chin. She told herself to treat him as she would any new friend. She told herself not to dwell on the fact that she was drawn to his brother. She wouldn't worry that Damien was from first class. She'd do her best just to get to know Damien for who he was as a person.

"So, Damien." She smiled as she said his first name. "Were you in England long?"

"Three months. It was a nice trip. We spent most of our time in the country, overseeing a construction project. I made it into London as often as I could, though, for sightseeing. It is one of my favorite cities.

Amelia nodded. Had the brothers known they had been so close? Then again, even in the same city they may as well have been in different worlds. It wasn't like Quentin would have frequented the same establishments as his brother.

"A building project, do tell." She raised an eyebrow. "Let me guess, are you building a summer home in the English countryside?"

"No." Damien shook his head. "It was an orphanage, actually."

"An orphanage?" She was stunned. She'd totally misjudged him, thought him vain and selfish given his wealth.

"You look surprised," he said, his smile relaxed, easy.

Amelia's face flamed. "I must confess, I am a bit. I volunteered in one back in Southampton. How kind of you to give so generously—especially being American and all."

125

"My grandmother—my mother's mother—was from England. Father wanted to do something he thought she'd appreciate. When a friend told him about the need in one community, well, we did what we could."

Amelia tilted her head. There was a softness in Damien's voice as he talked about helping others. From the moment she first saw him, she considered him handsome, but it warmed her to discover the goodness he had inside.

An officer strolled the deck. He wore a sharp, dark black uniform with two rows of gold buttons on his lapel. Under his jacket was a white dress shirt and tie. A black cap with a gold insignia topped the uniform.

Damien offered him a wave. "Thanks for all you do." He called out to the man.

The officer smiled in surprise. "Thanks, lad, but 'tis not hard on this ship. The *Titanic* runs herself, but I appreciate you saying as much."

"Do you know him?" Amelia asked as the officer strode off.

"Now I do. Now we both do." Damien winked.

"Yes." She nodded. "I suppose so."

"My mother is to blame for that. Growing up, I'd hear her thanking our drivers, our cooks. She smiled and chatted with the sailors on the ships and the conductors on the trains. To strangers she seemed an awful flirt, but that was simply her nature."

"Trains, ships…So, do you travel like this often?" She glanced at the handsome deck chairs with lush fabric cushions. "This is quite a sight for me to behold, but maybe you're used to it."

"My father does love to travel, but I've always told him it's the company we travel with that makes the trip worthwhile. So tell me, Amelia, what are you doing here? And where are you headed?"

He paused, leaning one hip against the deck's rail.

"I'm heading to live in America. My aunt and I will be living near my cousin. It will be great to reunite—and there is a man there my cousin wants me to meet."

Damien cocked an eyebrow.

"Are you interested in opening your heart to this stranger?" Damien asked.

"I don't know many strangers, only friends I haven't gotten to know well yet. Similar to you." She chuckled. "Or at least that's what my aunt Neda has told me many times." She shrugged. "I'm not committed, yet I'm open. I'm open to see what's out there—who's out there."

Damien smiled. "Yes, I see. I'm finding myself in the same place." And with that he let out a long, low sigh.

Quiet fell between them. Their eyes met, looked away, met again. There was an attraction there she couldn't deny. What would it be like to spend her life with someone like this? Someone who traveled the world yet didn't seem caught up in the trappings of luxury as others she observed and read about. Damien was easy to talk to, was outgoing and kind to strangers, yet he also did his duty to help mankind. She never thought a man like him existed—not until now.

The way his dark eyes embraced her made her trust him as she hadn't trusted any other man. It also made her want to reveal what she knew about Quentin.

Damien would help his brother... if Quentin would only give him a chance.

"I appreciate your invitation. Also, if you were wondering about your brother—"

"I wasn't." His words interrupted.

"But I assumed that was what you wanted to talk to me about."

"You assumed wrong." His eyes fixed on hers. "When you say that you knew him briefly, that there was no relationship, I believe you. It's good he's out of your life."

"But how could you be certain? I could have lied."

He shook his head. "My brother, Quentin, ruins all he touches. He has not touched you, my dear, for there is nothing tarnished about you."

"I'm not sure whether to take that as a compliment for myself or as a jab at your brother. He seemed like a very nice fellow the times we talked."

"He lies. He cheats. He ruins.... You have no idea how he's ruined my father. My father's name—his pocketbook—would be greater than John Jacob Astor if not for my brother, Quentin." He spat his brother's name as if it were poison on his lips. "If not for my brother, we'd be able to afford the largest stateroom on this ship. The one with a private deck."

She felt the hairs on the back of her neck bristle. *Maybe I judged him too favorably.*

"Are you complaining about your accommodations? That you don't have the biggest or best? I'm sorry, sir, if first class does not suit you. I'm sure if you have a moment you can travel down a few more decks and explain to the men and women in steerage that you would have the largest and most luxurious suite had it not been for your brother's betrayal. You seem rather spoiled to me." Her eyes narrowed, but instead of indignation in his gaze, Damien's laughter filled the air.

The sound came from his gut, and his face reddened. He paused, attempting to catch his breath.

Anger bubbled up inside Amelia, and she placed her fists on her hips. "I'm so glad you find me so amusing." She turned, but his soft grip caught her arm.

"No, wait." He sucked in a breath and gently turned her around. "I'm laughing at myself. How foolish—how spoiled

I did sound. I'm laughing because in all my days I've never had a woman speak to me that way, and amazingly I found it refreshing."

Amelia felt heat rising to her cheeks. She sat down in the nearest lounge chair and took a sudden interest in running her hand over the curve of the armrest. "Yes, well...I suppose you did need to be put in your place."

He laughed again and then sat down in the chair next to her. The toe of his shined leather shoe tapped along to music that drifted out from one of the nearby rooms.

"This is a short voyage," he said, "and I'm not allowed on your deck—or you on mine—but I'm going to talk to someone to see if we can rectify that problem. And if we can find a way, I'd like to spend more time getting to know you. As much time as possible."

"It's a wonderful thought, but I hardly know you, sir. I am sure you are very nice, but..."

But what? How could she argue that she couldn't spend time with him because she didn't know him well enough? Wasn't that the point?

"Also, I do have my aunt," she hurriedly continued. Her anger of a moment before dissipated with the smile that lit up his eyes. She tried to ignore his gaze. Mostly she tried to ignore how that gaze made her feel seen, truly seen, and wanted. "I must spend time with my aunt," she repeated. "And you have your father."

"I've spent nearly every day with my father for the last five years. I think he'll be fine if I spend a little time wooing a beautiful woman."

"Is that what you're doing? Wooing?"

"Only if you don't mind."

"I'm not sure what to say."

"How about you say yes to supper tonight...in first class?"

"Really?" She thought of the peek she'd gotten into the first-class dining room. The fine linens and silver and crystal and fresh flowers. *Oh my!* Just looking into that room was the closest she'd ever been to feeling like royalty.

"Yes, really." He laughed.

Goose bumps rose on her arms as she considered accepting his offer. But she also chided herself for getting so excited about it.

"I'm not sure." She cocked her chin, rising and moving back to the rail. Damien followed. "One minute I'm calling you spoiled, and then—"

"And then you accept my invitation to be spoiled alongside me?" He folded his hands as if in prayer and pulled them up close to his lips. She couldn't help but laugh.

Amelia blew out a sigh and fingered the pearl buttons on the wrist of her sleeve. "Yes, I suppose so. How can I resist that? Then I accept your invitation."

He beamed radiantly. "Tonight, then?" He placed his hand on hers and turned her so their backs were to the deck rail. As he did, she again caught the intoxicating whiff of his cologne. Most likely something from one of those pricey shops in London. Or Paris. It probably cost more than her aunt made in six months...and from the way it caused her stomach to flip, it might just be worth it.

They walked back to the enclosed deck. Why had he approached her? Why was he being so flattering? What did he really know about her other than the fact that she'd seen his brother?

His brother. The lightness that danced around her heart sank a bit. He pretended he didn't care about Quentin, but was that the truth?

Maybe he was causing her to lower her defenses so she'd freely give up any information she had. Did she dare let Damien know Quentin was a passenger on this very ship? Even though she'd promised Quentin she wouldn't tell them, it was a valid question. Even though they were still stuck on the same boat, Quentin was still running from his family. A family who worried about his wellbeing.

If she tried to talk to Quentin about the need for reconciliation, it would do little good, but if his older brother approached—maybe he'd listen then. She'd need time to think about that—to figure out what to do, what to say. For now she decided to enjoy this time with Damien.

"Yes, tonight I'll join you for supper," she finally relented. "It'll be quite a challenge, though, to keep you off your high horse."

"You're right, and I'm glad you're up to the challenge. I have a feeling, Amelia, you'll keep me on my toes."

Chapter 11

Aunt Neda didn't wait for Amelia to find her. Instead, as Amelia sat on one of the lounge chairs on the promenade deck, she lifted her face to see her aunt hurrying toward her. A smile tugged at Amelia's lips, as she was sure she hadn't seen her aunt move so quickly in years.

"Amelia, dear, you do have to let your dear aunt know more of your comings and goings on this trip. Our friends at tea wanted to know all the details of your acquaintance with Mr. Walpole, and I had nothing to share with them. One dear woman seated next to me pointed out that Mr. Damien Walpole looked very similar to the man who'd approached you at breakfast, but I assured her there was no connection."

Amelia nodded. "I'm sure you're right, Aunt," she said simply.

Aunt Neda sat down on the cushioned chair next to her. "So tell me, dear, where ever did you meet Mr. Walpole?"

"Yesterday when I went to first class, I met Damien and his father there."

"And you spoke to them? Amelia, dear, I thought you were only going to find your friend's book. You shouldn't have bothered those dear people in first class. Then again, I shouldn't be surprised."

Tension stirred in Amelia's chest. How could she explain what had happened? It wasn't as if she tried to be a bother. She'd made an honest mistake and believed Damien to be Quentin. She sat a little straighter, flustered by the displeased look in her aunt's eyes.

"And what do you mean by that, Aunt? What aren't you surprised about?"

Aunt Neda sighed. "If there is a side of town where you hear it is too dangerous, you will find yourself there. If you know someone has a contagious disease, you are the first taking food. If there is a sign saying, FIRST-CLASS PASSENGERS ONLY, you're going to cross it. Not only that, you're going to strike up conversations. We've only been on the ship one day, and you've already stuck your nose into quite a few places."

"But it's not like that. It's not that I'm trying to bother anyone. I never asked for any of this. I promise I will try to mind myself better in the days ahead."

Her aunt nodded, as if she was finally satisfied that Amelia was put in her place. And as Amelia watched, her aunt's concerned look turned again into one of curiosity. "So, dear, it is clear you shouldn't have talked with the man and his father. But since you did, I'm curious to know what happened. More than that, what did he wish to speak to you about?"

Amelia shrugged and blew out a soft breath. "He didn't want much. Damien Walpole just wanted to know if I'd join him for supper tonight … in first class."

Aunt Neda's eyes widened. "Did you agree to it?"

Amelia smoothed the fabric on her skirt. She pressed her lips together, suddenly feeling like a fool for accepting. "Well, I did. I mean, how often will one get to experience such a thing?"

Even as she spoke, Amelia knew she wasn't convincing, not even to herself. "But I could send a note…. Maybe a steward could get a message to him saying I changed my mind." The stirrings of attraction and interest in her chest told her she was doing the right thing by saying no. She should never let silly, girlish attraction for a man like that grow. He most likely was someone who dated often. Who knew, maybe Damien had a girlfriend on every trip. Maybe asking her to dinner was part of his onboard entertainment.

"No." The word shot from Aunt Neda's lips, interrupting her thoughts. "I wouldn't do that…just yet."

Amelia scratched her head. "You don't want me to cancel?"

"It's only dinner…."

"I know that, but part of me worries. I mean, I wouldn't be here without the help of Mr. Chapman…."

"'Tis true." Her aunt looked away, pretending to be interested in two young women who paused near them on the deck, chatting about their family members who were waiting for them in New York. "But this is a once-in-a-lifetime opportunity. I was talking to the women at lunch. They were from America. They said the Walpoles are well known and have endeared themselves to the community in which they live. This Damien sounds like a nice man, Amelia."

A nice man. Amelia already knew he was much more than nice. She only hoped she wasn't setting herself up for heartbreak.

"Well, I suppose I should keep my word…." She let her words trail off as she noticed approval in her aunt's gaze.

Amelia was wistful as she, too, watched the young women at the railing—the wind whipping through their hair. If only she could just enjoy the journey. When had everything become so complicated? How was it possible she was juggling feelings for three men?

"And, I have to say," her aunt continued, "someone like Damien Walpole would make a very nice catch."

With long strokes, Amelia brushed out her blond curls, still questioning if she was making the right decision by going to dinner with Damien Walpole. No matter what her aunt thought, she wasn't out to catch anyone. She wanted to find someone to spend her life with, sure. Someone to love, who would love her back. Someone who'd share her dreams. But she was no gold digger.

For as long as she could remember, she told herself she wanted to find a good man who could love her and support her. She hadn't really thought much of being swept off her feet. Could she love a simple, uncomplicated, steady man like Mr. Chapman? She always assumed she could. She never dreamed she would be wooed in a way that the songs spoke about, but the romantic gestures by Damien today stirred a longing within her she hadn't known was there. Maybe she did want to be desired, pursued by a man such as him.

Being on this ship took Amelia into different worlds than she'd ever been in before. She couldn't get her thoughts off of Damien. She tried to imagine what life with someone like him would be like. He offered more than stability. He offered adventure, travel, and a life beyond the small area of Southampton where she lived her whole life. And a life far beyond any she'd ever imagined before.

And while what Damien offered was intriguing, she couldn't help but think of Quentin. He was nothing like she wanted. He had no idea what his future held, but there was a hidden jewel deep inside of him. He carried a library of stories within his gaze. Under his hard exterior he had a tender heart.

"Amelia," her aunt's voice interrupted her thoughts, "would you be bothered if I told you I had a surprise for you?"

"A surprise?" Amelia watched her aunt open up her suitcase and move things aside to pull something from underneath. A gasp escaped her lips when her aunt pulled out a white dress and then a soft blue one after that.

"I was going to wait until we got to America. I thought it would be nice to have a new dress for your meeting with Mr. Chapman. But I cannot wait. You have been invited to a nice supper."

Amelia smiled and patted her aunt's hand. "But, Aunt, are you sure? It doesn't bother you that I'm not wearing this for Mr. Chapman?"

"Amelia, as wonderful as Mr. Chapman seems, tonight is a special night. You aren't engaged to Mr. Chapman, and having supper with Mr. Walpole doesn't mean you're throwing your heart that direction. It is not by chance you met Mr. Walpole." Aunt Neda wrinkled her nose. "And whether there is a spark there or simply a new friendship, don't think about anything except enjoying yourself, relishing in this new experience. Give God a chance to guide your heart. Now"—Aunt Neda held up the two dresses—"which one do you choose?"

Amelia glanced in the mirror, disbelieving it was her reflection she saw there. It seemed she was looking at someone else. Someone older and more dignified.

The dress was beautiful. Out of all the ones she'd seen her aunt sew over the years, she wasn't sure she'd ever seen one like it. It was what her aunt called a "tunic dress." The top layer of fabric went to her mid-calves, and the longer, sheer fabric under it went to the floor. The sleeves had the same style, with the silky blue fabric reaching her elbows and the same sheer fabric down to her wrists, fastened with pearl buttons. Her aunt had helped her with her hair, too. She'd pinned it up in the back, and soft curls fell around her face. She appeared like one of those models in the fashion magazines, and Amelia had to pinch herself so she knew she wasn't dreaming.

Damien had told her to meet him at the entrance to the first-class dining room. He must have cleared it with the steward who guarded the passageway between first and second class, because as she approached, the red-haired young man simply stepped aside. "Enjoy your supper, miss," he said with a tip of his hat.

She told herself to breathe as she entered the dining room. Even though she felt as if she didn't belong, no one seemed to pay her any mind as she entered.

White linen draped the tables. White napkins were poised upon each china plate. Empty crystal goblets waited to be filled, and stewards stood by waiting to fill them.

Her eyes scanned the room, and she noticed a man rise from a far corner. It was him. Damien hurried toward her. He extended his arms as he neared and immediately took her hands into his.

"Amelia." Damien leaned forward and kissed her cheek. She pulled back slightly, shocked from his closeness, and as he pulled away, Amelia didn't turn to look into Damien's face. Instead her attention was drawn to a woman who stood just behind him. She was a bit taller than Amelia, with dark hair, and her beauty made Amelia feel like a daisy next to a prize-winning rose.

Amelia recognized her immediately. It was the woman in the red coat from the docks. She'd pushed her way to the front of the line. She'd treated the others in line as if they were of no consequence. Amelia wished for that now. Wished she could fade into the paneled walls.

The woman's gaze bore into Amelia. It was as if bullets shot from her piercing eyes into Amelia's heart. Amelia sucked in a breath and took a step back. Noticing her response, Damien looked over his shoulder. His smile faded.

"Dorothea," he stated flatly. "I should have known."

"Damien, darling!" Her gaze softened, and she rushed forward, falling into his arms. He seemed startled. He offered her a quick hug and then stepped back.

"Dorothea, I would like to introduce you to Amelia Gladstone."

Amelia smiled. "Nice to meet you. I love your dress—"

Dorothea glanced to her quickly and then dismissed her with a nod of her head.

What am I doing here?

"Damien," Dorothea said, turning her attention back to him. "I've been wanting to show you the art pieces my father picked up in Paris. We didn't get a chance to do that last night. What do you think about having supper in our private promenade deck and looking over them? I know how you like art."

"I'm sorry." Damien stretched a hand to Amelia. She placed her hand in his, and he pulled her closer. "I have asked this beautiful woman to join my father and me for supper, and my hope is that our date lasts late into the night."

Dorothea's mouth fell open, and she glanced to Amelia once again. "Oh yes, I heard about you. You're that girl from second class that Clarence was talking about. So nice of you, Damien, to invite her." She leaned forward and patted his cheek with a soft hand. "You were always one to lend a hand to riffraff." With that, she turned and walked back to a table where an older couple sat. Amelia assumed they were Dorothea's parents. Partly because she looked like them, and partly because they peered at her with the same expression of disdain. Their gazes caused her stomach to tie into knots, and any confidence she had entering the room disappeared.

Damien placed a hand on the small of her back and led her to a far table. She focused on her walk, on not tripping on her dress, on appearing as though she belonged.

As they moved, Damien leaned close. "You're tense," he said into her ear. "Ignore them. You are better than them, Amelia. Their worth is based on their wallet, and yours ... on your heart."

She paused and turned to him, studying his face. "Do you really mean that?"

"Of course I do. Why would you ask that?"

She released the breath she'd been holding. "You say kind things, but I'm not sure you're really looking at me ... or if you just know what to say to a woman to cause her knees to quiver."

He studied her face for a moment, and she thought she would melt under his gaze. "I'm looking at you, Amelia. And the more time I spend with you, the more I'm amazed by what I see. I'm looking forward to introducing you to my father. He's going to like you. He's going to see the kindhearted person that I see."

"Really?" she smiled. "I'm looking forward to getting to know him—and you—too."

"Wonderful." Damien smiled. "Wonderful."

They continued on to the dining room table. Clarence Walpole rose and greeted her with a smile. "Amelia, it's so good to see you again."

"You too ... C.J." She offered him a smile and took the chair between the two men.

As soon as she sat, Clarence Walpole leaned forward. His hair, a shock of white, was perfectly combed—not a strand was out of place. A handlebar mustachio curled up at each end, giving him a distinguished look. For a man of means, his face was tan and leathery, as if he spent more time out in the sun than indoors. He dressed in fine clothes, but she could tell by his presence, by his attitude, that he was a man who knew hard work.

"So, Miss Gladstone, I know we should wait until the meal is served, but I have to know. Have you seen my son Quentin recently, within the last month?"

"Yes, I've seen him, and it was rather recently." She looked to Damien, unsure of what else to say.

"My father has tried to keep track of Quin," he said. "While we were in London, we discovered a trail he left behind—bad investments, a long line of riffraff, of friends. We heard many sad stories...."

"None of that matters, though." Mr. Walpole lowered his head. "No matter what he's done, he's still my son. His photo will always be on my mantel. He will always carry my name."

The pain in those words sent a stab to Amelia's heart. Everything within her wanted to tell him—tell Mr. Walpole that his son was not only alive but on this ship. But she'd made a promise. This was not her matter to solve. She could only pray for Quin. Pray he'd stop running. Pray he'd trust in his father's love.

"He has a good heart." She stated it simply. "The world has not ruined that."

Tears filled the older man's eyes. He pressed his lips tight and then swallowed. "Thank you," he finally managed to say.

They dined on cream of barley soup, lamb with mint sauce, green peas, and creamed carrots. The stewards came around to refill their glasses, and even though the food was delicious, Amelia found herself having to force it down.

Tension pervaded the table. Mr. Walpole wanted her to say more—she could see it in his eyes. He wanted the details of where she'd seen Quentin, how she knew him, but he was a gentleman and didn't press.

She spoke instead of her aunt and her skill as a seamstress. She spoke of the shop Elizabeth would set up with her aunt once they got to America. Yet from their bored expressions, it was clear no one was interested in the conversation, not even her.

Amelia struggled to form the correct words. Struggled to not appear a fool. She moved the food around on her plate with a fork. She was certain it was the finest meal she'd ever eaten, but she couldn't concentrate on the taste of it for the likes of her. She looked to Damien. What would a schooled, proper woman say? Would she talk of art and music? Of her travels or great literature? Amelia was sure one would, but she had no knowledge of any of those things.

She placed her hands on the chair's armrest, preparing to rise. To excuse herself. But a man's approaching steps halted her. He had light hair and a mustache. He wore a blue serge suit, tailored perfectly. Amelia recognized his face. She'd seen it in the papers many times.

John Jacob Astor approached, and though his walk was that of a millionaire, his face was a map of worry lines. "C.J.!" He opened his arms to the older man. "It is so good to find you here. I needed to see a friendly face."

Clarence motioned to the empty dining room chair beside him. Without hesitation, John Jacob sat.

"John," Clarence offered him a smile. "It's good to see you. How's business?"

"Business. I believe it is going well. I have been vacationing, my friend. I am not quite sure what is happening in the world. Leisure has been my main responsibility."

"I heard a man jumped from an airplane in Venice Beach, California. He floated to the ground in something called a parachute," Damien commented. "Maybe you should have patented that."

"My question is, what would have happened if the contraption had not worked?" C.J. wrinkled his brow.

"I have known many who have done much more foolish things." John Jacob nodded. "But that is not something I would choose to do ... or want to put my name on."

Damien laughed. "Good choice."

"So how are you enjoying your accommodations?" C.J. looked around the dining room.

"The company looks familiar, but the ship is exquisite. Yesterday when I awoke, I thought I was in my Astoria Hotel. Madeleine practically had to remind me that we were on the ship."

"I could see how you'd make that mistake. I've never ridden on a ship finer than this." C.J. took a sip from his water glass, his eyes still focused on John Jacob. "Speaking of your new wife, Madeleine, I hear congratulations are in order. You have a new baby on the way." C.J.'s face brightened.

John Jacob lowered his head. "It seems you're one of the few that has offered a kind word. It's the reason for our long vacation—you know—trying to stay one step ahead of the commentaries."

A heaviness weighed on Amelia's chest. Even though she hadn't gossiped about this man, she'd judged him with her thoughts as she'd read the paper. She'd judged him, too, when she saw him boarding the dock with his young wife. Yet seeing him here—close up—he was a man like any other.

"Listen to me." Clarence placed a soft hand on John Jacob's arm. "As long as you try to run from the past, it will keep trailing you. What you've done cannot be undone. A child is a gift—remember that."

"Yes." John Jacob focused on Clarence's face as if clinging to a lifeline. "Thank you, I will."

"More importantly, today is a new day," C.J. continued. "You've made mistakes aplenty. All of us have. God will forgive you for any wrong deeds. You know the hurt you've caused others, but the truth is, your misdeeds hurt God's heart even more."

John Jacob nodded, and from the look on his face, he appreciated C.J.'s words. Amelia guessed that most people in his life were more apt to talk behind his back than to speak to him heart to heart.

"Take time tonight to talk to God about all that's bothering you," C.J. continued. "Also remember the next step you take can be a step in the right direction."

With the soft tone of Clarence's words, the lines in John Jacob's face softened.

"Thank you. You've given me something to think about."

While most would bristle to have such a sermon shared in a public setting, John Jacob clung to the hope—the truth—C.J. offered. And with relief on his face, they turned to new topics of conversation—the stock market, their time in Europe, and the weather.

"It seems as if you've met a lot of interesting people," Amelia said to Damien as the two older men continued their conversation.

He took a sip of the water in his crystal glass and nodded. "These are the influential ones. The interesting ones are something very different." He chuckled. "Like the railroad man who taught me how to kill a man in a poker game with a flip of my wrist and make it look like he'd just passed out. How to hop a train without being seen. How to scale the outside of a building..."

"Have you done any of those things?" Amelia's eyes widened.

"No, of course not, but at least I know how." He chuckled. "You may note how my father fits well here, but I guarantee if we were to walk down to the third-class gathering room, he'd enjoy himself just the same. There are days he'll attend great luncheons and then at night join some of the men at the railroad yard for hobo stew. He sees the worth in people when most just focus on their worth—as money."

"Sounds like a great man."

"Yes, well, many think so. But sometimes I think he cares too little for his holdings. He's made foolish decisions and put his trust in the wrong places. The wrong people."

She squirmed in her seat, wondering if it was his brother that Damien spoke of. From the pained expression on his face, she had a feeling it was.

"You're nervous, Amelia."

"Yes, I am."

"That's to be expected, I suppose. I'm sure you've never sat amongst such a gathering."

"No, I haven't ... so near to the likes of these types of folks."

She blinked slowly, trying to decide if she should tell him the truth. She picked up her fork with quivering fingers. It wasn't them—the people in the room—who intimidated her. It was Damien. His presence made her feel impatient and exhilarated in a way she hadn't known before. She wanted to get to know him better, while at the same time she feared knowing more and being disappointed. Or maybe it was the secret. How could she share an honest conversation with Damien when she held back telling him the one piece of information that could change everything?

"You're right." She looked around. "I've never been in a gathering like this, but that's not what is making me uneasy."

"Then what do you have to be nervous about?"

She thought of a dozen things she could say. It was the people, in a small part. The names and faces she'd studied in the newsprint were living, breathing, fleshy people moving around her, laughing and talking. It was this fine dining room and the food on her plate. It was his father, C.J., who looked at her with such intensity it was as if he could read the joys and fears that had been embossed upon her heart. But the one thing that outweighed them all was that Damien's brother was on this very ship. And before that he'd been a thin man in rags without a coin to his name. Did Damien really understand that? Did he understand how his brother had been living?

She bit her lip—remembering the defeat on his face as he was dragged off the ship. Why had things come to that? Why hadn't Quentin allowed his own family to care for him when he needed care? They could have purchased a ticket for him in one of the finest rooms on this ship. Why had it come down to her mercies that had brought him on board?

It was a story she didn't fully understand. Quentin had wanted to keep his presence a secret, but what would keep a poor man from seeking help from a father who seemed to be caring and compassionate in every way?

As she sat there, quiet tension mounted between them.

Damien picked up the menu and placed it to his chest. "Don't worry. If you refuse to tell me what the matter is, I refuse to tell you what we will have for dessert," he said with a playful smile. She supposed he was trying to ease her nerves, but all his teasing did was make her heart flip over in her chest and provide her with another thing to worry about. *Could a man like him honestly be interested in me?*

Surprised laughter bubbled from her lips, and she briefly closed her eyes, sending up a quick prayer for guidance. Damien seemed like a fine man, and his father, too. She could guess why Quentin didn't want them to know his fallen state—it was his pride that kept him at bay—but if she had a family member in such a situation, wouldn't she want to know?

C.J. and John Jacob Astor finished their conversation, and John Jacob excused himself to check on his young wife who was resting in their room.

Just when Amelia considered telling both C.J. and Damien about Quentin, the older man rose.

"If you'll excuse me, this old man has occupied your supper long enough. I can see you have much to discuss. It was a pleasure meeting you, Amelia; honestly it was. As Damien can tell you, when thoughts of Quin arise I can think of little else. It's a surprise I can even run a business."

He rose and patted Damien's shoulder. "In fact, without my eldest son, I couldn't."

Just when Amelia was sure C.J. was going to ask Damien to walk him to his room, he looked at her and paused. It was as if his mind were someplace other than this room—in a different time. Finally, he sat down again, scooting his chair close to her. "I've been battling within myself all evening, my dear. More than anything I want to ask you questions about my son. I can tell by your reluctance that at some time he told you we are estranged ... and maybe he even made you promise not to share his whereabouts. Is that correct?"

As C.J. spoke, her heart ached as much as if he pierced it with his words. She nodded. "Yes ... yes to both of those."

"I won't ask you to tell us more than you feel comfortable saying, but I want you to know I'm also praying that if God releases you ... Well, I can imagine nothing greater than hearing more about Quentin—what he said, how he looked, everything you can tell me. My heart aches ..." He paused and placed a hand on her shoulder. "No, I won't burden you with that, but—"

"Do you need me to see you to your room, Father?" Damien interrupted.

"No, oh no. I'll have one of the stewards show me the way." He shook his head and stood again. "You know I'll get lost if I attempt it on my own."

Amelia opened her mouth, but before she could say a word, C.J. walked away with quickened steps. With each step Amelia felt the tension in her rise. Why had she hesitated?

C.J. exited the room, but instead of relief at seeing him go, the truth grew in her mouth, pressing to be released. If only she could tell him.

If she were in their shoes, she'd want to know. Quentin was a drowning man. How could he succeed in America with nothing, no one? He didn't want her to toss him a lifeline, but she knew his father and brother could be just that to him.

"Damien, I have to tell you something." The words spilled from her lips. "I have to tell you. I cannot hold it in. Quentin is here. He's on the ship. That was when I met him, just yesterday...that's how I am certain he's well.

His breath rushed out in a ragged gust. "Oh no." He propped his elbows on the table and covered his face with his hands.

"I promised him I wouldn't tell your father or you, but you need to know. You need to help him. He's so thin. He was in rags when I first met him."

Damien reached out his hand and took hers. He tenderly ran his thumb over the back of her fingers. "You did the right thing by not telling my father. My father has faced more loss because of my brother than anyone should. Quin most likely wanted to get back to America so he could work himself into my father's life. If you care for anything right and good, you will urge Quin to let my father be. He's already faced enough heartache—"

"But wouldn't it help to see him?" she interrupted.

"You don't understand. You don't know my brother. He will cry and say he's been a fool, but as soon as the social circles press, or as soon as anyone questions where he's been and what he's done, he'll be gone. He'll disappear just as he did before. I'm not sure my father's heart could take that."

She nodded, and sadly she had a feeling Damien was right. She'd seen how Quentin tried to keep everyone at arm's length. Even when he'd sought her out, there had been a barrier there, as if he wanted to get close but was fearful of that very thing.

Damien cleared his throat. "I appreciate your telling me, Amelia." He offered her the beginning of a smile. "That means you trust me. And I will do what I can to not violate your trust."

She gazed at him, taking in the handsome man and his fine suit. She looked around the room at the people in their expensive clothes. "*Give God a chance to guide your heart*," Aunt Neda had said, but here ... how could this be part of God's plan?

A dining steward cleared their empty plates, and Damien rose. He was solemn, but Amelia could tell he wanted to finish off the evening well for her. "Would you like to have dessert at the Café Parisien? I hear the orchestra will be playing in the reception room there."

"Yes, of course, I would love it."

A few minutes later, they entered the Parisien, and Amelia sucked in a breath. It was decorated like a French café with wicker chairs and large picture windows.

"Did you know the Prince of Wales is in Paris as we speak?" Damien asked.

"Yes, actually. He invited me to go with him, but I told him I didn't want to be civilized. I decided to travel to the United States instead."

Damien chuckled. "I beg your pardon. Are you saying Americans are uncivilized?" "Not all Americans. Not you."

Amelia touched her stomach. She felt bad that she'd told Damien about his brother. Wasn't he concerned about Quentin? How could he hear that his brother was on board and act as if nothing had changed?

Her stomach tightened into a knot, and she wanted to excuse herself. But where could she go? If she walked the decks, she could run into Quentin. She didn't want to face him. Didn't want to explain why she'd betrayed his confidence.

She also knew if she returned to their room her aunt would want to hear every detail about their evening. Maybe if she stayed out a bit longer, her aunt would be snoring, and Amelia could slip into bed without too much fuss.

A dining steward approached, and Damien ordered vanilla eclairs for them both. When the steward walked away, he placed his cloth napkin on his lap and looked at her with a soft smile. "I wonder if the éclairs are as good as my favorite café not far from the Louvre. Then again, I hope the baker here treats us more kindly. You should have seen that other man's outburst when my father left part of his pastry on his plate," he said, launching into a story.

She studied Damien's calm appearance and wondered if he was more bothered than he was letting on. Seeing his indifference made her wary of any emotions that he expressed. Did Quentin know this was how his brother would react?

I shouldn't have said anything. What was I thinking?

Amelia's hand trembled as she added cream and sugar to her coffee. The steward returned with their desserts, and nearly as soon as he set them down, she took a bite of her pastry. She needed something to distract her. Something to focus on other than her worries. The pastry was light and sweet, but in her mouth it felt as dry and tasteless as cobblestone. *Why did I tell him? What have I done?*

She glanced up, meeting his eyes, noticing that his face was lit with color. She dabbed her mouth with her napkin, wondering if she had food on her face or if she had done something else to embarrass him.

"It is all right to eat this pastry with a fork, isn't it?"

When he didn't respond her eyes widened. "Or did I say something? Do something?"

"No, it's not that. It's just that you aren't saying anything. I was wondering if I was a bore."

"No, no not at all. I just...well, I shouldn't have told you about your brother. I don't want to cause any trouble."

"Trouble?"

"Telling you about Quentin being on the ship...and with your father finding out."

"My father won't find out."

"Really?"

"I won't tell him. I refuse. My brother chose to walk away. He chose his own path. I told Quentin it was a mistake when he left. I told him I wouldn't chase him."

Unblinking, she stared at him. "And you don't think he'll seek your father out?"

A curt laugh burst from Damien's lips. "And reveal once and for all how he lost everything? How he ended up on the streets with nothing?"

"Then you know?"

"Everyone in our circle knows. There are many eyes on us always, Amelia. The eyes of those of the same status. And then common people, too—those who look to us with awe, wishing they could live our lifestyle."

She set down her fork and leaned closer. Her body felt hot, flushed, and she wasn't sure if it was from anger at how Damien treated his brother or sadness that Quentin had lost so much—by his own hand. Then again, what did she know, being one of those "common people"?

Damien's face flushed even deeper. "I'm not heartless. I don't hate Quin for what he's done. Sometimes he gets into trouble...with the law, with owing money to the wrong people. I've helped him in—" He paused. "Never mind." Damien took a sip from his water. "Just forget I said anything."

She nodded, but she also knew she wouldn't forget. Damien cared for his brother without Quentin's knowing. Had he paid off bad debts? Had he assisted his brother in other ways?

She looked deeper into his eyes and noticed something new. She saw anger and maybe a bit of relief.

"He's not all bad." Damien sighed. "Quentin is just lost."

Damien glanced from her to the paneled ceiling.

She understood then why Damien hadn't been peppering her with questions. He didn't say anything, because he was relieved that he knew where his younger brother was sleeping tonight.

Her heart warmed at that thought. Maybe she was being too hard on him. Maybe she should just enjoy spending an evening with a handsome man.

Amelia picked up her fork again. "You mentioned the Louvre. Did you go there? I would love to go someday. But now, going to America, I doubt I'll get the chance."

Damien fixed his gaze on her again. Relief flooded his face. "Maybe someday. You never know what the future holds, Amelia." He smiled. "And to answer your question, I greatly enjoyed the Louvre, although there was far too much to see in one day. The *Mona Lisa* was the highlight of the trip." He chuckled. "But I guess that's what everyone says."

"I'm so glad she found her way back to the Louvre."

"I know! I couldn't believe it when I heard she'd been stolen. And for her to be gone for so many months. Was it three months?"

"No, nearly six." His face shone with excitement as he talked. "But I said from the beginning that she'd be found. I knew the thief would try to sell her, and when he did the end would be near for him."

As if punctuating Damien's words, beautiful music filled the air. It was a popular American tune that she often heard her neighbor playing in Southampton. Amelia tapped her toe to the beat.

"So true." She glanced around, noticing that the musicians had moved just outside the doors of the café. Crowds followed the music—long lines strolled in from the decks and from the dining room, packing into the smaller space—and she understood why. The musicians' skill was like none she'd ever heard.

Yet the more people entered, the more she noticed something else, too.

As he talked about his knowledge of how the thief had gotten away with the perfect crime, Damien took on a new air. He sat straighter, talked with more conviction. Then again, maybe it wasn't the conversation that had stirred him. Maybe it was the people. Rich people that everyone in the room seemed to know. She was never one to keep up with their adventures that the newspapers loved to commentate on.

From the corner of his eyes, Damien seemed to be watching the first-class crowds as much as they were watching him. Even though she sat across the table from him, she no longer felt as if they were on a date. Damien seemed to be courting the whole room.

Was this how the wealthy lived? Enjoying fine foods and exquisite music and studying each other—wooing each other with their manner in hopes of gaining everyone's approval?

French waiters served coffee and pastries to the other guests. They moved in and out of the kitchen with quickened steps through the revolving doors. Amelia wondered if the attendants were used to this display. She guessed if they spent any time serving first class, they were. Had her mother noticed?

"You know, Amelia," Damien continued, interrupting her thoughts, "if I believe in one thing most of all, it's doing what is right. The thief who stole the *Mona Lisa* will get what he deserved. Even those on this ship ..." He glanced around. "They can act one way, but the truth of who they really are will always come out."

Is he talking about his brother?

Amelia sat straighter in her cushioned chair, and a strange sensation came over her. What if ... what if Quentin didn't want anyone to know his whereabouts because he was in danger or feared being caught yet again hiding away on the ship?

What if Damien went to the bridge and told the captain of his brother being on board? More than that, just how far would Damien go to make sure his father didn't know of his youngest son's presence?

Would he sacrifice his brother to protect his father's heart? His wealth?

Chapter 12

*D*amien was thankful Amelia had agreed to stroll the decks with him. Thankful for the quiet. Thankful to leave curious eyes behind. Dorothea had watched him from across the room. Others had, too. *Who is this woman?* He spotted the question in their eyes.

And from those who knew that Amelia was from second class, he saw judgment, too. *What is she doing on our deck? She doesn't belong.* To them, kindness and gentleness of heart were not traits to be valued. But after spending time with women who cared more about their latest custom hat than whether their cutting words wounded, Damien found Amelia a breath of fresh air. And she was beautiful in her own simple way.

Damien eyed Amelia as she studied the deep, dark water. The light freckles on her nose beguiled him. He imagined her walking off this ship on his arm. He imagined taking her to his father's estate and showing her the property, seeing the joy the beauty of the place would bring to her.

He shook his head, wondering why he dreamed up such ideas. His chest grew heavy, as if *Titanic's* anchor settled there. He didn't know if he could continue on with the rest of the evening without telling her how he felt.

"Amelia?"

"Hmm?" She looked up to him, and he saw interest in her eyes. Perhaps the same emotions that were surging through him tossed around in her heart, too.

"I know this sounds like a line, but being with you this evening is one of the best nights of my life."

She crossed her arms and pulled them to her. "Yes, Damien, I have to agree." Her eyes blinked slowly, and a smile touched her lips. "I enjoyed it very much. Enjoyed getting to know you. You're a very special person."

Her words—her contentment in being there with him—stirred something within he couldn't contain. He lowered his lips to kiss hers. He touched her lips slightly. They were soft, cool from the night air. His heart exploded inside his chest. A rush of heat moved through his limbs.

But instead of returning the kiss, she pulled back. Her face registered surprise, shock.

"I'm sorry. I've been too bold. I'm overstepping my bounds."

"Well, if you want me to disagree, I won't. I haven't spent time with someone like you before." She swept her hand toward the room they'd just exited. "I am not accustomed to your lifestyle. I'm not sure how these women respond, but...I do not give my kisses away so freely. In fact, I don't wish for that to happen again unless it's with the man I plan on marrying."

"I'm sorry." Heat drained from his face. "I never thought...." He let his words trail. *Foolish, foolish.* Most women were eager to accept his kisses, but they also understood and appreciated his standing and his bank account. A kiss to them meant access to both—or at least that was their hope. This woman seemed unconcerned with either. He liked that. He liked her. And at that moment, this was the woman he wanted more than any other. He'd let his shipmates entertain the women who had high standards and low morals. This was a woman to whom he wished to give his heart.

"Tomorrow? Do you think we can meet again soon? Tomorrow for breakfast?"

"I should spend some time with my aunt. I'm afraid she's growing tired of engaging in conversation with strangers rather than her niece. But perhaps tomorrow afternoon... or maybe supper tomorrow night. You could come down to second class." Her eyes studied him as she said that—as if she was testing him—but to Damien it made no sense. Why would he partake of an inferior meal when his first-class passage had already been covered?

"Or we could try the A La Carte Restaurant. I hear that's something," he suggested.

She nodded and bit her lip. "That's in first class, isn't it?"

"It is. The meal there isn't part of the ship's fare; it's an extra charge, but I imagine it's worth it."

"I suppose that will work. Let me talk to my aunt and see if she has any plans," Amelia said with a sigh.

He noticed her breath when she spoke, and he saw her lips shudder.

"We had better go inside," he said softly. "We don't want you to get a chill."

"Yes. Yes we should." She quickly rubbed her arms.

"Unless you would like to stay. I can offer you my jacket." He unbuttoned the top button.

"No." She raised a flat hand toward him. "I'll keep warm enough until we get inside."

Why did I waste so much time talking about Quentin? he wondered.

He wanted to know her. Really know her better. Maybe then she'd take his jacket if he offered.

He walked her from first-class down to second. People were dressed in their best clothes, too, yet their garments hardly compared to what she'd just seen in the first-class dining room. Music played on this deck, too, and laughter was carried along with the melody through the halls.

As they strolled by, Amelia's eyes skittered to the second-class lounge. "If you'd like to stay, we can find some chairs inside. They have a three-piece orchestra that I've enjoyed greatly." But as they entered, he noted a man in the far corner. He knew the back of Quentin's head well enough that he recognized it even though he hadn't seen his brother in five years, give or take. Maybe that sight was so familiar because as long as he could remember Quentin had always been walking away. Running away.

Damien paused in the doorway. "Actually, I need to get back to where I belong. On my own deck."

"Oh, yes," her voice was aloof. "I'm sure you are used to much grander furnishings."

He was about to tell her that wasn't the case. He remembered the days when his family lived with little and struggled for their daily bread—before his father's hard work paid off—but before Damien had a chance to explain, Quentin stirred in his seat as if he was going to stand. Damien took a step backward through the doorway.

"I'll see you tomorrow then." With that, he turned and strode off. He was not ready to face his brother. If luck had its way, they'd make it off this ship without meeting, without confrontation. For if he were ever to come face-to-face with Quentin, his brother would surely not like to hear what he had to say. He also couldn't guarantee the encounter would stop at words alone.

Damien balled his fists at his sides. His brother had ruined everything—more than once—and the years only fueled the fire flickering within.

Amelia was halfway across the second-class lounge when she noticed Quentin seated at a table in a far corner. He sat with a group of older women, and from their bright faces, she could tell they were happily telling stories. Quentin threw back his head in laughter, and she paused. Joy filled her heart to see him like this—enjoying himself without a care in the world. Amelia found an empty chair nearby to watch. The tingle of Damien's kiss was still on her lips, but her heart warmed when she saw Quentin's smile.

A young girl rushed by Quentin's table and tripped on the leg of a chair, tumbling onto the floor. Without a pause, he rose and went to her, scooping her up in his arms. The girl wrapped her arms around Quentin's neck and buried her face into his cheek. He gently carried the girl to her parents. Only after seeing that she was all right did he turned to make his way back to his table.

Amelia smiled seeing that. He didn't care for the girl to put on a show. His tenderness came from a deep place within. She hugged her arms to herself, realizing he'd make a great father someday.

His eyes scanned the room as he walked, and his gaze fell on Amelia. He paused.

She smiled and lifted a hand, offering a wave. He tilted his head as if unsure if he should return to the ladies or approach her. Amelia thought of their conversation that morning. He'd been so upset to know his father and brother were on board. Her shoulders trembled slightly. He'd hate her for certain if he knew that she'd told Damien about his presence—not that Damien was going to do anything about it.

Amelia sucked in a breath and then motioned for him to approach. She wanted to see him, to talk to him. She wanted to be near him, even though she risked the chance of him being angry with her.

He glanced at the older women, offering them a parting wave, and then hurried her direction. His steps faltered slightly when he noticed her dress.

"You look fancy." He offered a tentative smile. "Did you go dancing tonight? Was there a party I didn't know about?"

"Just supper...with some new friends."

"Well, you look very lovely." He motioned to the table farthest from the music. "Do you have a minute or two to talk?" She looked back over her shoulder toward the door she'd just entered. She almost expected Damien to be there watching them. But he wasn't. Only the darkness of the night and the black sea beyond filled her view. Amelia touched her lips, feeling like a traitor. Then again she hadn't asked for the kiss.

She brushed a blond curl back from her face. "Yes, Quentin. I'd like to talk. I'd like that very much."

They made their way to the table, and he scooted the chairs close together so they sat shoulder to shoulder.

Like first class, the room was filled with people who'd come to enjoy the music. An older woman walked by, leaning heavily on the arm of a steward. It made Amelia think of her mother. She focused her eyes on the carpet just beyond the table, attempting to picture her mother's face.

"I don't think I mentioned it to you, but my mother used to be a stewardess," she finally said when she realized Quentin was watching her. "Maybe she still is." Amelia shrugged. "I really don't know."

"So you aren't some well-to-do lady as I first thought after I met you on the dock." He touched the cut on his cheek, and she could see it was healing nicely.

A giggle rose up, and her eyes widened. "You thought that?"

"Yes. A ticket isn't cheap. I had no idea your mother was working class."

"Does it surprise you?"

"Maybe it would have yesterday, but today ... No, not really."
She lifted her eyebrows.

"I heard you talking in the hallway with one of the stewardesses," he confessed. "She said she knew your mother."

Tears filled her eyes, and Amelia didn't know where they came from. It wasn't as if she'd been dwelling on her mother continuously. She tried to quickly wipe them away. "I'm so sorry. I do not know what has come over me."

Quentin wrapped a comforting arm around her shoulder. "It's all right. You have a right to cry. It's a sad thing to have a loss like that. I would think something was wrong if you weren't sad."

She nodded. Emotion filled her throat, and the words refused to come.

Quentin squeezed her shoulder. "Let me guess. Being on this ship, hardly a moment passes when you don't think of her. When you look at the water, you wonder what your mother thought as she looked at the same view. When you see the stewards interacting with the passengers, you imagine your mother doing the same."

She lowered her head, trying to hold in the emotion that pushed its way up from her chest. "How did you know?" she finally whispered.

"I know because I do the same thing. When I walked around my father's estate, I would try to picture things through my mother's eyes more than I was my own. That was one reason I had to leave. I ran from that. I entered a world completely different than hers."

They sat there in silence for a while, each lost in his and her own thoughts. The small band played. They were good, but their music wasn't as showy as the music in first class. The audience seemed to be enjoying themselves. They mingled more with each other. They didn't behave as if they were competing ... or jockeying to be the most important person in the room.

"My mother would be smiling to see me here," she finally said. "What would she think of her daughter dining in first class and..." As soon as the words were out, Amelia caught her mistake.

"First class?" Quentin's eyes narrowed. Glancing at her dress, he understood. "Were these 'new friends' that you had dinner with my brother...my father?"

She sat there for a moment, fiddling with the edge of a cloth napkin. Finally, she nodded. "Yes, and they are very lovely people." The words rushed out of her mouth, as if speaking them quickly would hurt him less. "Your father told me to call him C.J. He's really a wonderful man, Quentin."

He balled his fists at his sides and then scooted a chair closer to her. "They're not going to come looking for me, are they?"

She shook her head. "No." It was the truth. She tried to calm her pounding heart with that fact.

He leaned forward. "Does my brother care about you?" Quentin's eyebrows lifted. "I know my brother well—I have a feeling he's extremely attracted."

"Yes, he does care, but my feelings are not...Well, I don't feel the same as he does." She sighed. It was mostly the truth. Damien. Walpole had stirred emotions within her she'd never felt. How could she not be enchanted by a man such as that? He was smart, handsome. Yet she couldn't imagine spending a life with someone like him—so concerned about his social standing.

The fancy parties and social functions would be hard to stomach, too, especially when there were so many people in need. Living lavishly was such a waste. And she doubted he would understand if she wanted to spend her time assisting the poor.

"I'm glad he cares about you. You should try to return his feelings." Quentin ran a hand down his chin. "My brother's a good man. He's always been there for my father. He's made wise choices, unlike..." Quentin let his voice trail off.

"But what if I'm not interested in someone like Damien Walpole? What if my feelings lean more toward someone like … you?" Amelia covered her mouth with her hand.

Did I just say that? Yes, she had. And it was the truth. It was Quentin she looked forward to seeing the most. He was the one who had found his way into her heart.

"That's not a good idea," he spouted.

She lowered her hand and pushed guilty thoughts of Mr. Chapman out of her mind, focusing instead on Quentin's dark-eyed gaze. "I think it is."

"Don't you understand, Amelia? I hurt everyone I meet. I am a thief. I am a liar." He ran a hand through his hair and narrowed his gaze on her. "In fact … if you want to know the truth, my kindness to you has simply been out of obligation." His tone was sharp.

Her head jerked back. "Obligation?"

"Of course. You rescued me off the docks. You provided my passage. I *had* to be kind to you."

She rubbed her hands up her arms, trying to brush away a sudden chill. "And that is it, obligation? Is that what our time together has been about?" His face was blurry through the thin film of tears in her eyes.

"Yes." The word burst from his mouth.

Her stomach ached, and her heart did, too, yet when she looked into his face, she noticed his eyes were not as unkind as his words. In fact, they were just the opposite. "You answered too quickly. I don't believe you."

"Believe what you'd like. I can play the part of a considerate, caring guy when I'm wearing another's clothes. It would be easier for you to believe me—that I was no good for you—if I were wearing the rags from the dock. I am certain of that."

"It's the opposite. I believe the new clothes have helped what's truly on the inside come out. I saw you just a moment ago." She pointed to the table where the older ladies sat. "You listened and joined in conversation with those women. You didn't need to do that. You helped that little girl, and I'm sure that most guys in first class, your brother included, would have just looked away.

"Quentin, you're a man of honor who fell on hard times," she continued. "For so long people saw the rags. You didn't have the chance to show your real self. Now these clothes have given you a chance to be who you really are."

His eyebrows narrowed. "You aren't listening to me."

"I did listen. I just don't believe you." And with that, Amelia rose. "I'll say good night now…and tomorrow—if you want to tell me you care for me, too—I'll be around." She sighed, remembering that she'd be with Damien again for the evening. At least he cared about what she thought. "Yet this voyage lasts only so long, Quentin, and then I'll be gone. Your father will be gone, too."

Silence met Amelia as she entered their stateroom, but she could tell Aunt Neda was still awake. Her aunt had cared for her since she was a child, and they'd shared the same room for most of her life. Snoring meant Aunt Neda was asleep. Silence meant she was thinking.

"Auntie, are you waiting up for me?" Amelia teased.

"Amelia, dear, you can turn on the light. You know I am still awake. I'm curious how your time went with Mr. Walpole."

Amelia turned on the light, and her aunt partially sat up in bed, making sure she didn't bump her head on the overhead bunk. Aunt Neda was wearing her gown and white sleeping cap. It reminded Amelia of the illustration of Little Red Riding Hood's grandmother from her *Grimm's Fairy Tales* book. Aunt

Neda's eyes were as big as saucers, and Amelia guessed she'd been imagining all types of romantic story lines in her mind as she waited for Amelia to return.

She told her briefly about their dinner, and then Amelia searched her mind for something interesting to tell her. The truth was, she didn't remember much about what Damien had said. Her mind was still focused on Quentin. Her last thirty minutes with him had caused the supper with Damien to grow fuzzy in her mind.

"Oh yes. Damien did talk about Paris and the Louvre," she remembered. "He said he greatly enjoyed *Mona Lisa*. We both agreed that we were thankful for the painting's safe return."

Her aunt's eyes sparkled, and a sinking feeling came over Amelia.

"Aunt Neda. You seem excited about my date tonight, but to be honest, I thought you'd disapprove."

"Disapprove? Why would I disapprove of you getting to know someone so handsome, so kind?"

Amelia placed a hand on her hip. "Maybe because this whole journey has been about meeting Mr. Chapman—about the possibility of me starting a life with him in America."

Her aunt smiled. "Dear child, don't you see? Mr. Chapman is a kind man, and perhaps God is leading you to him, but he is not the reason for all this." She patted the bed beside her, and Amelia sat. "The reason for this journey is that you needed something to believe in, to hope for. I'll be thrilled if you discover Mr. Chapman is for you, but I'll be just as thrilled if you find joy with someone else. Love, my dear, isn't often as scripted as we plan."

"But why did you do it, Aunt? Why were you willing to sell most of what you had, pack up the rest, and come with me?"

"Child, I knew you'd never come alone. You're too dutiful to leave an aging aunt in London with your troublesome cousin as my closest family. I do wonder how Henry's doing." She breathed out a sigh.

Amelia wasn't about to allow her aunt to change the subject. The topic at hand was too important for that. "But was there ever a time you believed Mr. Chapman was the one for me?" Amelia asked.

"I do not know the answer to that, and I can't know until you meet the man." She smiled and patted her sleeping cap. "But what I do know is that you would never find out unless you traveled the distance and risked your heart. What if Mr. Chapman *was* the one, and you remained in the safety of what you'd always known?"

Amelia fiddled with the pearl buttons on her sleeve. "Elizabeth *does* say he's a good man, and he does speak kindly in his letters," trying to convince herself into having the same enthusiasm for meeting Mr. Chapman as when she started this trip.

"That's a start. But is he a good man *for you?* Will you become all God made you to be if you join with him in marriage? And in the joining will you help him be all God made him to be?"

Amelia stared at the pattern on the carpeted floor. For so long her aunt had been the simple, caring woman who spent her days sewing in her back room. The most commentary she'd offered was what sounded good for supper or what to do about the recent trouble Henry had gotten himself into. When had her aunt—her mother's sister-in-law—become so wise?

"I am no stranger to love," Aunt Neda continued, as if reading Amelia's thoughts. "You have little memory of him, but Uncle Rupert was the sparkle of my eyes, the patter of my heart. He died too young of a heart condition, but I would rather have had those fifteen years with him than more time with someone else."

"I'm glad you had that, Aunt." She placed a kiss on her aunt's soft cheek. "Now, will you pray for me? Pray for God to show me who is to be the patter of my heart."

"Of course, dear, I will continue to pray. You should know…as soon as you moved in with me as a child, I've been praying for that very thing. I wanted you to have what your mother never found, what many people never find because they're too afraid to risk their hearts."

Amelia slipped into her nightgown, and then she turned out the light, climbing into her bunk. Weariness came over her as she climbed between the cool linen sheets.

She turned to the wall, knowing on the other side of it sat Quentin. She doubted he was sleeping yet.

Outside the room, Amelia heard the murmur from the stewards and the voices of other passengers in adjoining cabins. She bit her lip, wondering if Quentin had heard her, too, when she talked to Aunt Neda. The finely constructed walls wouldn't allow him to make out her words, but did he hear her voice? And if he did, did it bring joy, frustration, anger, or something in between?

If she could guess, his mind was on their conversation, as was hers. Even though she had told him flatly that she didn't believe that he was a crook and a liar, deep down was there more truth to his words than she wanted to believe?

"Dear Lord," she whispered softly, "my aunt has been praying for many years, and I join her tonight. Show me the man for me. The man you've designed to help me become the best me as I join with him in life." Amelia sighed. "Oh Lord, show me which man creates the patter of my heart."

Chapter 13

Friday
April 12, 1912

Amelia was pleasantly surprised when the first person she saw in the morning as she walked out her stateroom door was the cheery-faced stewardess, Geraldine. Amelia rushed forward and wrapped her arms around Geraldine's shoulders, offering her a quick hug. The truth was, as she'd awoken, Amelia's thoughts had been on her mother again. Maybe it was because of her aunt's words, *"I want you to have the love that your mother never found ...*

It saddened Amelia to realize that. Her mother had been in at least one relationship; she'd given herself completely to another and had his child, but how sad it was that she hadn't found a marriage partner to spend her life with and to enjoy love and family together.

"Oh, dear lass," Geraldine said with a quick release of her breath as if Amelia had just knocked the air from her lungs. "Good morning to ya. What a beautiful day it is on this grand ship, isn't it? A day so full of promise."

"Yes, Geraldine. I hope for a relaxing day and perhaps time to explore new friendships."

"Oh, I hope that's not all you explore. You should take time to traipse around this ship. I've never seen a thing like it."

"Well, I've covered most of first and second class . . . ."

"Yes, but that is just the beginning." Geraldine waved her feather duster in Amelia's direction. "It is a shame for you to be on this ship and not see the third-class accommodations and the boilers underneath. As those on the high decks are lounging, there are men down below who can't pause for a moment's rest."

"Although I'd love to see it all, I couldn't ask such a thing. You have your duties, Geraldine. I wouldn't want to bother you."

"And I can't let you refuse, my dear." Geraldine's gaze grew serious. "No, I surely cannot neglect to give you a tour of this place. As one of us workers, your mother would have wanted you to see it—see how the rest of us go about the ship."

Amelia swallowed down sudden emotion that grew in her throat.

"I can almost hear your dear, sweet mother now. *'Gerri'*—as she used to call me—*'remind my daughter that the wealthy do what they do because they have the rest of us caring for them.'* And it's the perfect timing for you to be here, too. Like Captain Smith, I'm retiring after this voyage." Amelia noticed a quiver in her words. "I've had a good life on the sea, but when my bones start creaking more than the sway of the ship, I know it's time to stop." She patted Amelia's arm. "Besides, this is a grand way to end things. I get a fresh thrill every time I clean the beautiful staterooms."

Amelia nodded, and her chin quivered slightly as she imagined her mother at Geraldine's age, still working, still caring for those who most likely didn't give her a second glance. Was her mama out there somewhere doing that very thing?

"I would like such a tour, and I do have time while my aunt rises and prepares for the day, but don't you have your own duties to attend to?"

"What are they going to do? Fire me?" Geraldine winked. "Come, let us go meet the other stewards and stewardesses. I don't believe any were around who knew your mother, but they'll be glad to know that she was one of our own. That you are one of us, deep in your heart where it matters."

"Yes, of course." Amelia smiled at those words, and she followed the older woman with quickened steps, surprised she was so spritely at her age. Amelia liked that Geraldine saw her as one of them. That was how she wanted to be seen—as a simple woman who took all that was offered to her and freely shared it. That was very different than the type of woman she felt when she was with Damien. In her fine dress and in the polished setting, it became easy to forget that all men and women were created equal. Last night she hadn't paid a bit of mind to the dining stewards who'd served their table. Had there been one server? Two? Were they young? Old? It shamed her that she didn't know.

Amelia followed Geraldine through a doorway that read, STAFF ONLY. Down a hall, she found a washroom. Inside, a group of women were busy folding towels.

They all paused, eyes wide, as Amelia entered, their laughter stopping. They seemed almost worried, as if they'd all been caught robbing a bank window.

"Ladies, I'd like to introduce you to someone. This is Amelia Gladstone. Her mother, Emma, was a good friend of mine. We worked together as stewardesses many moons ago, back when the great liners were no more than tin cans." Geraldine chuckled.

"Your mother, you say, was one of us?" a red-headed woman asked. The pinned cap on the top of her head did little to keep her mass of curls in place. She wiped damp, sweaty hair back from her face. "How special, then, for you to be a passenger! Third-class? Second?" The woman stepped closer.

"Second." Geraldine puffed out her chest with pride. "But last night our dear Amelia was the guest of Mr. Damien Walpole in first class. He's staying in one of the grand suites, but he ventured down to the second-class lounge to invite her to dine with him."

The women's mouths circled into Os, and Amelia glanced over at Geraldine in amazement. "Gerri, how did you know such things? Did you talk to my aunt?"

Laughter filled the room, echoing off the steel walls.

"Oh, Amelia, you have much to learn about your mother's work. We have eyes and ears. We have friends from bow to stern."

Amelia nodded, unsure how to respond. She looked deep into Geraldine's eyes. What else did the woman know? Did she know about Quentin? Did she know that the man who called himself Henry Gladstone was the long-lost son of none other than C.J. Walpole in first class?

Amelia didn't have time to ask. As the women continued their work, Geraldine led her to meet many of the other stewards and stewardesses who worked on the various decks.

For most of her life, Amelia had pictured her mother's job a romantic one, but as she watched the stewardesses work, there was nothing romantic about making beds, cleaning bathrooms and cabins, sweeping, dusting, and bringing trays for breakfast or tea.

As they strolled the first-class area, Amelia kept her eyes peeled for C.J. or Damien, but she saw neither. Instead Geraldine provided commentary on many of the passengers they passed.

"Margaret Brown joined our liner after touring Cairo, Egypt. She vacationed with the Astors and with her daughter, Helen. She's heading home because her grandson has taken ill. One of the stewards overheard her talking with a friend at tea. Apparently, in Cairo she visited a fortune-teller. After studying her palm, he said, 'Water, water, water,' and predicted a sinking ship surrounded by drowning people. They were laughing because, of all ships, they were booked on the *Titanic*. Poor thing, I hope she didn't pay him too much for that prediction." Geraldine shook her head.

Amelia nodded but didn't know how to respond. She didn't think much about fortune-tellers, but she wasn't going to tell Geraldine that.

Geraldine pointed to an older man and woman. "Isidor Straus there is the co-owner of Macy's department stores. He's traveling with his wife, Ida. I hear the Strauses are very charitable and kindly. Many of the first-class stewardesses like waiting on them best."

As they walked past the exercise room, Geraldine pointed to Mr. Astor exercising on one of the mechanical machines.

"Do you see that man?" Geraldine said. "John Jacob Astor. And his bride of a year." His young wife sat next to him, watching him.

Amelia looked closer at the quiet, sullen young woman, wondering if it was just morning sickness that made her look upon the opulence so indifferently.

"The wealth of the world does not bring joy," Amelia's mother had told her once. *"I've not seen more miserable passengers than those in first class."*

The more she walked through life—and through the decks of this ship—the more Amelia understood what her mother meant. Maybe people seemed sad because wealth separated them from others. There was always the question of whether others wanted to spend time with them—or with their things. There were expectations of how to live, what to say, what to wear, and how to act. And the more one owned, it seemed, the more the desire grew to achieve and acquire.

In her own life, Amelia knew she felt no greater joy than to make up some potato soup and take it to a family in need. Even on days when she was feeling tired or depressed by the gray Southampton clouds that blocked out the sun, getting out and thinking of another's needs was the best way to bring a little sun into her life.

She felt awkward, too, to hear Geraldine commenting about the indiscretions of those in first class. Even though Geraldine was their servant, she talked about them as if she were far better than they. Amelia understood the men and women in first class better after last night. They were just people, like the rest of them, trying to find love and acceptance. Sitting among them, watching and listening to their conversations, had given her a different view.

How hard it must be to live one's life with one million people looking on. She remembered the weary look on John Jacob Astor's face when he'd come to C.J. for an encouraging word. Yes, he was the richest man on the ship, but it was clear the treatment of others—their judgment on his indiscretions—had worn him down.

As Geraldine and Amelia continued their tour, two affable and well-groomed men strolled past them toward the smoking room. Both of the men stared at Amelia as they crossed paths, causing Geraldine to chuckle.

"Child, I'm sure they believe that you are a fine lady from this deck and I am your maid."

"Probably so, but I do not like the way they stare." She sidled closer to Geraldine. "It was like this the last time I walked these decks, too. Geraldine, do you know why?"

"I can guess." The woman clicked her tongue. "They're wondering if they know you and to which wealthy family you belong. They wish to know if you are unattached. If so, they might consider you someone to pursue. And finally"—Geraldine squeezed her arm—"because you're beautiful. You've received many of the same stares in second class, dear, but here you're more aware."

Amelia felt herself blushing. "Yes, I do feel more self-conscious here...."

"Then perhaps it's time to take you to third class and then to the decks below that. Some of my favorite friends work down there."

Amelia followed Geraldine through a maze of passageways. "I hope your plans are to take me back to my room, too, because I'm afraid I'll never be able to find my way on my own."

"It is a complex maze, isn't it, dear?" Geraldine pushed open yet another door that led down a long hall. "Most of us staff didn't come on board until three days before the launch. Many, myself included, have gotten lost every day. The worst is trying to give directions to a passenger. I can never tell someone which door to take or which stairway to climb."

Finally, as they walked a long, quiet passageway, she couldn't help but ask, "Geraldine, I have a question for you. Have you remembered anything more about my mother? I'd love to hear news that seems unimportant even from long ago."

"I'm sorry, Amelia. I am afraid I haven't. We were good friends, but that was when my hair still had color and my face wasn't all wrinkled up. I don't even remember exactly when Emma stopped showing up. There are usually more workers than jobs available."

"I bet there were many who wished they could be on the *Titanic*."

"Yes, yes, indeed." Geraldine nodded. "And I was one of the lucky ones."

"So when you didn't see my mother at work, you didn't think much of it?"

"No, I just believed she didn't get an assignment."

"And after that?" "After that, I was certain she found a special man. Got married. Started a life. It was common. Most young stewardesses do."

"What about you, Geraldine? Did you ever find love?"

"I did once." Her voice grew wistful. She glanced up at the ceiling, yet Amelia could see a story in her gaze. "I found it, but it was lost." She let out a sigh.

"Did he not feel the same?"

"He did, dear, but I did not trust the emotions. I didn't think they could come on so strong. I thought it would be prudent that we wait, to get to know each other better. We wrote letters for a while, but many weeks would pass in between. I'd have to wait to mail the letters—or receive them—until we got to shore. Two years passed, and he got tired of waiting for me. Waiting for me to trust my heart."

"I see." Amelia swallowed hard, wishing she could let down her guard with Geraldine and tell her that she had the same feelings. She felt drawn to Quentin, but of all the men who were interested in her, he seemed by be the worst choice. Damien Walpole offered her the world. Mr. Chapman offered a good but simple life. But Quentin? He didn't have anything to offer, nor had he shown much interest. If anything, he pushed her away. But it was him her thoughts trailed to.

She opened her mouth to talk about that, but the words didn't come. Instead she turned her questions to Geraldine.

"So you say this will be your last voyage. Why's that?"

"I've enjoyed my time on the sea, but I've saved enough for a small apartment. I even found one with a garden area in the courtyard. Because of the prolonged coal strike, jobs have been harder and harder to find. I told myself if I somehow made it on this liner, the *Titanic*, that it was God's message to me that I'd done my good duty and now I could settle down. I told myself after that I'd only make one bed each day"—she chuckled—"my own."

Chapter 14

Geraldine led Amelia to the third-class area, and though the staterooms were smaller and there was much less luxury, she was pleasantly surprised by the quality of the accommodations. Amelia also saw far more smiles there than she saw in first class. People sat in small groups, laughing and talking. Children chased each other, played, and sang songs from their homeland. Musicians gathered together, and although it was clear they didn't understand each other's language, they communicated through happy tunes.

They passed the third-class smoking room. Men's laughter rang out from behind the glass door, along with the clinking of glasses. A song began on the piano. It was a happy tune, and a smile lifted Amelia's lips.

After walking through the third-class berth, Geraldine led her through the cargo area to the powerhouse in the deep, dark belly of the ship. The mood down there changed, and Amelia no longer felt like she was on the same liner. With cautious steps, she moved into the boiler room. Huge coal-burning furnaces supplied power to the ship's engines. Stokers stood with shovels in hand, and then a gong sounded. In unison the stokers shoveled in more coal. The men worked as one.

"See those dials?" Geraldine pointed to the gauges on the boilers. "They tell you which boiler needs coal next."

The floor beneath Amelia's feet quaked, not nearly as smooth a ride as it was up top.

Amelia looked at the faces of the men, wondering what they thought of the passengers above. Or did they think of them? Maybe not. Maybe it was easier to do one's work and not think of those who lounged and dined.

They left the doorway, shutting it tight, and reversed their path. "I doubt many passengers know, but there was a fire in boiler room six. It was smoldering when we left the dock in Southampton, and I wouldn't be surprised if it's smoldering still."

Amelia's eyes widened. "Isn't that dangerous?"

Geraldine shrugged. "The firemen keep an eye on it. And the truth is, every time we head out to sea there's a certain level of danger. Fire, storms, ice, human error. What surprises me is when we make it to port without incident."

Amelia grew weary from all the walking. She didn't know how Geraldine could stay on her feet all day every day. The stewardess returned Amelia to her stateroom, and they paused at the door.

"Thank you," Amelia said. "I'm sure I've seen more of the ship than any of the other passengers."

"That is certain." Geraldine offered a quick hug. "I just hope it'll help you, Amelia. Help you know your mother in ways you haven't before."

"That it will. Have a good day, Geraldine," Amelia said, and gathering up her strength again, she stepped through the door into her stateroom.

"Where have you been?" Aunt Neda asked. "Did you have breakfast with Mr. Walpole by chance?"

Amelia was surprised by the smile that played on Aunt Neda's lips. Perhaps Damien's wealth was drawing Aunt Neda more than she wanted to admit. After all, if one married the likes of him, one would never lack for anything....

Except ownership of oneself, she thought. *Gain the whole world and lose your soul, not necessarily to damnation, but to the masses who desire to know all about your life and who live a bit of their dreams through you.*

As Aunt Neda finished pinning up her hair, Amelia sat down to read yet another letter from Mr. Chapman, hoping beyond hope that his words would draw her again to his heart.

Dear Miss Gladstone,

I am grateful to receive your correspondence today. Your thoughtful dialogue and conversational tone made it seem as if you sat beside me at dinner, sharing your favorite stories, which I greatly appreciated. I do confess I have no great tales of today's interactions. I work with figures at the bank most of my day. I suppose I could tell you I caught an error that one of my colleagues had overlooked, but that is not nearly as interesting as your tales of taking fresh bread to a poor widow who'd eaten her last crumb the night prior. I do agree with you that it was our good Lord who put her face within your dream. I also agree that there are plenty of needy people here in New Haven. I cannot go out to visit them during the day, but I weekly provide some coins to the nuns at a nearby church who see to it that they are given to those with the greatest need. Know, dear Amelia, that I understand the caring heart God has given you. Know that I will support your efforts in all the ways that I can.

Your cousin Elizabeth searched through her trunk and indeed found the photo of the two of you taken a few years ago. I was pleasantly surprised by your symmetrical features and bright eyes. If only you had been smiling. Elizabeth claims your smile lights up a room. I believe it would.

I showed your photo to Miss Betsie MacLellan, the cook. She agreed you had fine features and guessed you are the same age as she. I regretfully could not remember your birthday, but

*Bessie's is June 21, 1887. Since that is the first day of summer,
I sometimes call her* flower. *And when she is baking, I call her*
flour, *although since the word is spoken, I don't believe she
notices the change.*

Amelia laughed out loud, and Aunt Neda turned. Then,
almost immediately, she realized again whom he spoke of... that
Betsie MacLellan. Was *flower* or *flour* a term of endearment?

"What is it, Amelia? What do you find so humorous?"

She pushed the smile back onto her lips. "Uh, I forgot how
witty Mr. Chapman is.... If you are going to read any more letters from him, Aunt, you should start with this one."

"Yes, well, I'll have to keep that in mind." Aunt Neda rose,
patted her hair as she looked into the mirror, and moved to the
door. "But for now I'd like my breakfast. And maybe we'll be
greeted by another one of your suitors, Amelia. It seems we
never know who to expect at the table, do we?"

It was Quentin who waited in the second-class dining room as
Amelia and her aunt approached. He rose and greeted them with
a smile. Amelia smiled back at Quentin and noticed again what
a truly nice man he was when he wasn't attempting to push her
away.

Aunt Neda didn't seem overjoyed that Quentin was there,
but she didn't completely ignore him either. Instead she eyed
him, and as they ate their breakfast, Amelia saw he could be just
as fine a gentleman as his brother, Damien, when he wanted to.

"So, Amelia, when did you start being an angel of mercy to
the people in your neighborhood?" She could tell he was trying
to be playful with his question, but she didn't want Quentin to
think he was just another person she took pity on.

"I didn't set out to do that." She spread fresh butter on a roll. "I suppose it started when I was twelve or so. I remember seeing one young girl walking down the street with her mother. Her dirty dress was far too small for her. I followed them to see where they lived, and then I rushed home to ask Aunt Neda if she could help them in some way."

"That she did." Aunt Neda nodded. "She wouldn't let me get a wink of sleep that night until I sewed up a simple frock."

"We took it to them the next morning." Amelia smiled as the memory played in her mind. "You should have heard the girl's squeals of joy as she clutched the garment to her chest. Then her mother made us stay while she tried it on. The girl pranced around the room as if she were Queen Victoria herself. Do you remember, Aunt?"

Aunt Neda smiled at the memory. "I remember, but I believe you forgot something. Your generous spirit started long before that. I remember when you were six years old. You'd only lived with me one or two weeks when I discovered a small stash of food in your room. You'd hidden it inside your cardboard suitcase."

Amelia tried to picture what her aunt was talking about, but as hard as she tried, she couldn't remember. Amelia laughed. "Was I saving it for later?"

"Actually, no. You were saving it for the little girl who used to live in the apartment next door to your mother's place. You said she didn't have much food, and you wanted to take it to her."

Quentin's mouth dropped open as he studied Amelia's face. "You don't remember that?"

She shook her head. "No...I don't." Then Amelia turned back to her aunt. "So did we take her food?"

"Yes, although I made fresh bread instead of the stale biscuits you'd hidden away. But—" Aunt Neda lowered her head.

"But what, Aunt?" Amelia placed her hand over her aunt's.

"Well, we got to the right floor, but instead of going to your friend's house, you ran to your mother's door. You pounded and pounded—" Aunt Neda's voice caught in her throat. She covered her mouth with her hand and shook her head, unable to continue.

Amelia looked from her aunt to Quentin, unsure of how to respond.

Quentin leaned forward, resting his elbows on the table. "Did anyone answer the door?"

Aunt Neda shook her head. "No, and Amelia never asked to go back to that part of town—well, not until the day when she saw that little girl in need of a dress. I had a feeling that bread was simply an excuse. After that she accepted the fact that her mother was gone. Her little heart just needed to confirm it was true."

Amelia's heart ached for the sad girl she used to be. It ached for all the lonely years, but in a strange way her aunt's story caused thankfulness to grow in her chest, expanding and filling every part of her. The truth was that despite her heartache, God had been faithful. He'd watched over her and given her a wonderful aunt and cousins who loved her. He brought her to this ship. Led her to a new hope for her future. It was a turning point, she supposed. She'd learned as a young girl there was no use thinking of what was past—but rather she needed to focus on what she'd been given. She looked to Quentin and smiled. He was one of those gifts.

After the meal, he rose again, this time offering her his arm. "Would you like to stroll?"

Amelia glanced over and noticed her aunt's disapproving look. By her aunt's standards, she was an eligible woman, but he—of all men—was far from acceptable. Still, as Amelia peered into Quentin's dark eyes, he drew her in. "I'd love to."

Ladies in fine attire and gentlemen in suits strolled along the decks. Their clothes weren't near the caliber of those in first class, but the second-class patrons mustered their finest duds for the trip, and to Amelia they looked just fine. The sun rose behind a bank of clouds with pink-tinged edges as if they, too, were putting on their finest display.

As they walked, Amelia glanced up at the crow's nest. "Can you imagine the view from up there?"

"Would you like to see it?" There was a sparkle in Quentin's eyes.

"No, it's not allowed."

"Do you always follow the rules?"

She nodded. "Don't you?" As soon as the words were out of her mouth, she felt heat rising to her cheeks. "Actually, I didn't mean that. I mean, under the circumstances in which we met, I should know—"

"You're probably wondering why I snuck onto the *Titanic*," he interrupted. "Honestly, it was a last-minute decision. I only wanted to steal a loaf of bread, but when I saw all the food being loaded on the ship ... something told me this was my answer."

"Maybe it's your answer because you have a chance to reunite with those you care about." As she said the words, she saw his form stiffen beside her. "I'm sure there are many jobs at your father's business that you can fill."

"I told you before, that's not going to happen."

"I know." She blew out a sigh. "For someone who has nothing, you sure are a proud man."

"What are you talking about?"

"It's your pride that is keeping you in hiding, instead of strolling up to that first-class promenade. You'll have to humble yourself to face him. Humble yourself to ask your father for a job when you know full well that if you had stayed you would have overseen one thousand jobs.

"But you know what I think already, don't you?" She quickly added. "I won't mention it, at least for this circle around the deck." She smirked. "What I will say is that I'm thankful you still feel *obligated* to talk to me. It makes the days pass much more quickly."

"You aren't one to keep your opinions to yourself, are you?" He glared at her. Then his face softened. "If I weren't obliged to talk to you, I'd walk away for certain. And if I weren't obliged to make sure you stayed on this side of the deck, I'd throw you over for sure."

She drew back and compressed her lips to keep from laughing outright. "Well, I'm thankful you're choosing to let me live." She playfully punched his arm. "Although I have to say you might regret it; there are a number of days between now and when the ship docks."

"Enough time for us to spend together?"

Amelia shrugged. "I'll have to check my social calendar, but I might be able to fit you in. Today, for example, I'm open for lunch. I'm also having afternoon tea with my Aunt Neda and her friends. Do you want to join us?"

He offered an overexaggerated shiver. "Do you think I'm British or something? Lunch sounds good. I'll pass on tea today, but I'll see you tonight at supper."

"Well, actually..." Her eyes widened, and he paused. She could tell her hesitation caused an alarm bell to go off inside Quentin.

"Do you have plans? Let me guess, my brother," he mumbled. "I'm suddenly not hungry for lunch."

She lifted her face toward his. Why had she said yes to Damien? "It is your brother, but if you'd like me to change my plans..."

Tell me you'd rather I have supper with you. Ask me to cancel, her heart begged.

"I'm sure you'll have a lovely time.""

Chapter 15

Quentin wilted back against the chair. He still smelled the ocean air on his skin. He still, too, felt the anxiety of Amelia's presence on his soul. Anxiety because he knew that as much as he longed to grow close to her, that would be the worst thing possible for Amelia. What his heart longed for would ruin her, yet how could he stop his feelings? He didn't know anyone like her, and that made the running away even harder.

His eyes closed as the swell of a memory rose. The day he'd walked out of his father's home. It had been easy to run at first, to get caught up in the women, the parties, the drinking. The problem was, he'd poured himself into the very thing that had taken away his mother—wanting attention and doing whatever he could to receive it, including putting himself in danger. He'd done that as a boy at the end of that dock. He'd done that as a young man, wasting money on his friends, on women, on luxuries instead of investing it where it mattered.

Things had been good in their home growing up until his father had made all the right deals at the right times. They'd lived in a small but sufficient house. Their mother had spent time with them daily, but with the wealth came new friends, new outings. A larger house had drawn her attention and her heart. More than once he'd gotten lost in the corridors of their new and expansive home. He'd cried as he searched for his mother. He usually found her before she found him, but her mind was often focused on choosing the right fabric for the drapes or picking out the menu for an upcoming dinner party.

He'd been a freckle-nosed boy of five when she died. Not only did he have to learn how to live without his mother's presence, but he had to live with the fact that it was his fault she was gone.

His father had told him it wasn't his fault, but he knew better. His father hadn't treated Quentin differently after his mother's death, yet he could see a difference in his brother's eyes. Childhood allies, they seemed more like strangers—enemies—as they grew, and being around the house and the pond where she drowned was too much for him. So instead, he ran, but before he did he asked for one thing—his inheritance, the chance to do things his way.

Quentin hadn't desired to approach Damien in all these years, but it took all his willpower to stay within is stateroom now and not to go to the first-class deck and find him. He had a feeling he knew what caused Damien to find Amelia so attractive. It wasn't that he cared for her. Well, maybe he did care in his own way, but Quentin had a feeling it was the *pursuit* that fueled his steps. Damien loved the chase more than the accomplishment, and since Damien saw Amelia as Quentin's friend, his efforts would no doubt be full-force. His brother pleasured in stripping away every bit of Quentin's happiness. How else would Quentin pay for his misdeeds?

Most of the pleasures Quentin had lost himself—by his own foolishness—but by winning Amelia's heart, Damien could take away something good from Quentin's life, just as Quentin had stripped something good from his.

Amelia dressed in a simple lavender gown and felt every bit the lovely lady as she entered the A La Carte Restaurant for supper. The fine restaurant was located aft on the bridge deck. And as Amelia looked around, she could tell it was where the loftier people in first class ate. *So much for trying to spend time with Damien in common settings.* If only he'd joined her in the second-class dining room. Amelia knew she could get to know him by seeing him around his friends, but she could also get to know him better seeing him around strangers, especially strangers of a lower social standing.

Damien was seated at a center table. Amelia walked to him. He rose as she neared, and a smile filled his face. From the looks of it, he'd already ordered their first course—a plate of lush berries and cream.

"Fresh strawberries in April, in the middle of the ocean." Amelia laughed. "Damien, I do believe you're trying to show off." Still, she sat, dipped a strawberry in cream and then took a big bite. Sweet juices flowed into her mouth, and she couldn't help but smile. "This is the best thing I've tasted so far on this ship."

"Glad you approve, my dear." He winked.

She took another bite and glanced around at the room's French style. It was decorated in Louis VI furniture with red carpet and arched windows. The walls were set off by swags and festoons. The same swag design decorated the plaster ceilings and the borders of the china plates and cups. Overhead, crystal chandeliers swayed ever so slightly with the movement of the ship. Potted plants were perfect final touches to the room, as were the decorative lamps that sat in the middle of each table, casting a romantic glow.

"So have you seen my brother today?" Damien asked. He took a bite of a strawberry, but his eyes fixed on hers.

"Yes, I did. I wish I could say he sent you greetings, but he did no such thing."

Damien nodded, and she could tell he wanted to again warn her about his brother's ways, but instead he held his tongue.

When the dining steward came by, Amelia made a point of asking his name.

"William, ma'am." He offered a slight bow.

"William, has it been a good day for you? Did you get out to get some fresh air?"

He raised his eyebrows in surprise then straightened his shoulders, standing a little taller. "Yes, ma'am. I served hot drinks on the decks. It was a wonderful day to breathe in salt air. The sun was lovely."

Damien offered a patient smile. "Yes, yes it was a lovely day. Now I'm hungry and ready to order. Aren't you, Amelia?"

She didn't have a chance to answer before Damien opened his menu wide before him. "I'll have ragout of beef with potatoes and pickles. And for you, Amelia?"

"Me? Oh the quail with cherries sounds lovely."

Damien nodded and then ordered salads and soups to complement their meals.

After supper, they moved to a reception room just outside of the A La Carte Restaurant, where a violin, cello, and piano played. It was the large room where the grand staircase descended and small groups of tables and settees were scattered.

The small band started with Irving Berlin's "Alexander's Ragtime Band" and followed with "Waiting for the Robert E. Lee." When the song "Shine on, Harvest Moon" started up, Damien rose.

"Amelia." Damien extended a hand. "Would you like to dance?"

She felt like a princess as she placed her hand in his. She followed Damien to the dance floor, stepping into his arms, the most eligible man on the *Titanic*. And although she'd attempted to keep any emotions toward him at bay, when he pulled her closer, her heartbeat quickened. He smelled wonderful, and she couldn't keep her eyes off the soft curl of dark hair than lay on his neck just behind his ear. His dance steps were smooth, and he glided her around the room with little effort. She stepped slightly closer, enjoying the warmth of his presence.

Being in his arms like this was far more intimate than last night's kiss.

"You're a fine dancer, Amelia." His breath was warm on her ear. "Do you attend dances often? Did you take lessons?"

"Oh, no." Soft laughter bubbled up. "But there was a dance studio a few blocks away. My cousin Elizabeth and I would sit outside the large glass window and watch. Then we'd go home and practice, dancing along to our neighbor's gramophone that we could hear through our apartment walls. Lucky for you, Elizabeth always wanted to lead."

"Lucky for me, indeed," he said as his fingers splayed across her back.

"Although I have to say you are a far better dancer than Elizabeth." She laughed again, waiting for him to join in.

When he didn't laugh along, she looked up into his face and understood why. His attention was no longer on her. Instead his eyes swept the room as smoothly and precisely as his feet led them around the dance floor.

They danced three dances and then returned to their seats. Amelia took a long drink of iced water. Her face felt hot but not because the room was warm. In fact, the air held a bit of a chill. There were many things she didn't like about Damien, but there was no denying he was a handsome man and being in his arms had an effect on her.

Around them, the party grew livelier, and Amelia chuckled as an elderly couple drew everyone's attention with their precise steps on the dance floor. In their younger years, she guessed, they'd been professional dancers. She enjoyed watching them, and as she sat there, she found herself growing more comfortable. The only thing that still put Amelia on edge was the way Damien scanned the room.

After ten minutes of his eyes moving from table to table, she leaned close to his ear. "You've been on your best behavior all evening," she whispered. "You can stop trying to seek their approval now."

Damien's head jerked back slightly. "What are you talking about?" He cleared his throat.

"The way you watch everyone. You did it last night and now tonight. It's as if you're trying to make sure you're doing everything right. And making sure they notice you doing so."

"That's not the case." He forced a smile, trying to act as though her words didn't bother him. "I just enjoy seeing that everyone's having a good time, that's all."

She nodded. "Yes, of course." She studied his eyes, wondering if he honestly believed that. He looked around again then caught himself and focused on her with a smile. Since Amelia had already overstepped her bounds and his feathers hadn't gotten too ruffled, she dared to ask one more question.

"I'm not trying to pry, and you don't have to answer if you'd rather not, but why are you so against seeking out your brother?"

"I told you. I'm afraid he's going to hurt my father's heart. He's made a habit of running away. It would be worse for my father to see him again—lose him again—than it would be for him not to see Quentin at all."

She nodded. "That makes sense, and if I were in your shoes, I'd be worried about the money situation, too. I mean, what if your father offers him more only to have Quentin lose that? Then there wouldn't be any money if you needed it."

Damien sat straighter. His eyes narrowed into a fierce gaze. "I have not asked anything of my father." His voice trembled as he held his emotion in. "Unlike my brother who robbed what did not belong to him, I haven't even asked for two pennies that are rightly my own."

She attempted to pick up her water glass. Her hand quivered, and she lowered it again. "Who needs money when you have approval?"

"Excuse me?"

"I am sorry if I am overstepping my bounds. We have just met a few days ago, but I know what it's like to be looked down upon. I heard the whispers of those around town, being the daughter of an unmarried woman and all."

"I'm sorry about your experiences, but what does this have to do with me?"

"No one is talking unkindly about you. Your brother has ensured that. They approve of you, and as long as you continue in all you do—"

"How dare you?" Damien interrupted. "Do you know me? You think I do all that I do to seek others' praise?" He glanced around, as if making sure no one noticed his outburst, and then focused back on her. Amelia took a deep breath and then blew it out slowly. "In the short time I've known you, I've noticed how carefully you watch your words. And even from our first dance tonight, your eyes were not on me. You looked more to those gathered around the room. I should be thankful, I suppose, that they smiled and nodded in approval. They accepted me, even though I'm from second class. And because of their approval of me, I received a second dance, and a third."

Damien combed his fingers through his hair and then shook his head. "Amelia, you've missed your calling. You should write fairy tales for as much as your mind lives in the world of make-believe."

"You're right. I'm sorry. You don't need my input. You don't need anything from me. I can see you lack for nothing."

He was silent for a moment, but she read something in his eyes. It was as if he was trying to decide whether to agree with her or to speak of a deeper truth.

"I have no need of anything. I live a very satisfactory life, filled with art and culture." Then he sighed and his voice softened. "What I want is to have someone to share that with. To find a companion like my father found in my mother." He offered a sad smile. "I was hoping that was you."

"If that were true, maybe you would have looked into my eyes," she whispered, leaning close. "I've been looking into your face, Damien, dreaming, hoping. If you would have looked at me...connected with me...Who knows what would have happened?"

Damien leaned forward, taking her hand in his. It was then she noticed his eyes weren't dark brown as she thought. They were rimmed with green, and they sparkled as he looked at her.

"Like this?" His words were barely a whisper.

A tingle started in her chest and grew, radiating out. "Yes," she managed to say. She tried to think of something else clever to add, but under his gaze she could only repeat the word again. "Yes."

"Tell me this, Amelia." He grasped her hand tightly. "Is there even a small piece of your heart that wants to give me a chance?"

She stroked his fingers with her thumb. "There is a part of me that thinks a man like you would be the perfect type of man to choose." She smiled. "Your devotion to your father captures my heart." She stared into the depths of his eyes, wishing she could be lost there. Telling herself to try. It would be so much easier. She'd get her aunt's approval and no doubt Elizabeth's, too, because, really, how could Mr. Chapman compare with a man like Damien Walpole?

"It would have been so easy to fall in love with you," she continued, "and although I do think you dream of finding love, Damien, I don't think you're ready to step down from being the perfect son to being an ordinary man who seeks the heart of an even more ordinary woman." She looked into his eyes again as she said those words, and she saw a wall within his gaze. Quentin may have run away, but his brother had built a brick wall around his heart—too high for her to scale.

Not seeing even a hint of emotion in his eyes, she pulled her hand away and stood.

He followed her, jumping to his feet, wrapping her in a quick embrace. "Amelia, wait, can't we at least try? I will do better. I—" He pulled her tighter, as if not wanting to let go. She looked up into his face and noticed moisture in his eyes.

"I wish I could. I really do. But I don't want to have to fight for a man's heart. My mother did that, Damien. She might have won it. She might have lost it."

She pulled back from his embrace and left the room. Amelia didn't look back. She didn't need to consider what those people thought of her. They could have their opinions but that didn't matter.

She made her way to the second-class staterooms and focused her eyes on one door, the door next to hers, and knocked.

Not ten seconds later, it opened. Quentin stood there with his shirt partly unbuttoned. She tried to ignore his painfully thin chest and instead focused on his face.

"Amelia, did you need something?"

"Tomorrow can we spend time together? Just as friends. I'm tired of trying to pretend. I'm tired of these fancy clothes. I'm tired of first class."

His eyes focused on hers and he smiled. "Yes, I'd like to spend time with you, but I have one question."

She folded her hands together and then tucked them under her chin. "What's that?"

"Do you have one more pretty dress? I'd like to have you on my arm at supper, and maybe, dear Amelia, it'll be my turn to ask you to dance."

Chapter 16

Saturday
April 13, 1912

Outside on the boat deck, the morning fog had thinned and lifted, leaving behind polished handrails wet with moisture. The sun rose higher, bathing the decks in golden light. Quentin strode at Amelia's side.

They'd eaten breakfast with her aunt. They'd played a hand of cards with new friends in second class, and now Amelia was thankful they once again had time alone to walk, to talk.

"Why did you get on the ship, Quentin? Not when you wanted bread, but when I offered you the ticket? You could have said no. You could have walked away."

"I've fallen far, and I'm tired of wandering." The words released with a sigh.

"Were you going home? To your family?" She thought about what Damien had said, what he feared—his brother finding his father only to leave again and break his heart.

"That was my desire ... someday to find them. But I couldn't return as a man in rags. I figured I could find a job and clean up a bit."

"Do you think it matters to your father that you look more presentable?" She bit her lower lip as she asked that question, hoping he wouldn't get angry with her. She'd gotten enough people angry with her over the last few days.

"You don't understand my family. They have high standards. You walked the first-class decks—you saw. Those types are looking for heaven on earth. There is no room for anything but the finest—clothes, accommodations, food, service."

"But your father, is he that way?" She thought about what Damien said, how C.J. enjoyed the common men as much as the rich.

"He didn't used to be. Nor Mother, but once you have such things you become accustomed to them. The man who collects my father's trash dresses finer, lives better, than I have lived these last years. I don't want to be rubbish on his doorstep. If I at least had a stable job . . ."

Stable. The word played in Amelia's mind. It was the same word her aunt had used with her. It was the same word she'd used to describe Mr. Chapman. Her chest tightened as if it were being cranked down with a turn wheel.

Are you no different, Amelia? She chided herself. *You don't need fine things, but are you willing to forgo your chance of someday finding love for a simple home, regular meals, to carry the last name of a proper man? Is stability worth losing the one man who truly draws your heart?*

"Can I ask—why did you leave in the first place?" She eyed Quentin. "You had everything—more than most people could imagine."

He continued on in slow steps almost as if he didn't hear her. Instead he nodded at the stream of people that walked by. Amelia watched them pass—ministers, bricklayers, salesmen, housewives—from many countries and all walks of life. Each of them had a story, she knew, but Amelia wasn't concerned about them. She only wanted to hear one man's tale.

Quentin paused, turning to her. Amelia halted her steps. He pressed his fingers against his eyes as if trying to hold back tears, and then he opened them, looking down at her.

"My mother died because of me," he stated simply. "I was a boy. I'd grown tired of being at my parents' party. I begged and begged for her to take me outside. It was a beautiful spring night. I was playing at the end of the dock."

"Oh no." She covered her lips with her fingertips.

"I was angry with her. Not just angry because she wasn't paying attention to me that night. There were so many things...."

He stood before her, one man on a ship filled with men. When she'd first boarded the *Titanic,* the ship seemed so large, but as she looked to the side and took in the sea that stretched as far as she could see, she suddenly felt so small. Her ability to listen to the rest of this story and give Quentin the support he needed seemed inadequate.

Quentin balled his fists at his side. "I was angry at the big house. At the servants. At my parents' friends. I didn't understand what the money had done to us, but I knew things had changed. I didn't like the changes."

"Did you fall in, Quentin? Did you fall off the end of the dock?"

"Yes, but not on purpose." He looked down on the wooden deck as if seeing something there. "There was a turtle. I reached for it, and before I knew what was happening, I was underwater. I didn't know how to swim." He let out a shuddering sigh. "My mother didn't either. She jumped in to save me. She pushed me to the surface. I tried to hold on to her, but she was stronger. It wasn't until later—as I was running up to the house—that I realized I had her pearl necklace in my hands. It's the only thing..." Quentin covered his face with his hands. He didn't make a sound, but his shoulders shook.

Amelia wanted to speak words of comfort—to tell him he didn't need to continue. Instead something inside told her to wait. To give him time to tell his story. He needed to get the words out just as dirt needed to be cleaned from a wound, so healing could begin.

After a moment, he composed himself and lowered his hands. His face was red, his eyes bloodshot. "After that it was too hard seeing my father without my mother by his side. I couldn't stay and watch, so I asked for my inheritance. I didn't want to wait until my father died before I could leave my own mark. I got tired of walking in his shadow, mostly because of the pain. It was a dark place to be."

"I imagine you enjoyed the freedom. At first at least."

"Yes, and after that … I didn't plan on losing everything—no one does. I didn't plan on living in rags. Didn't plan on going to bed more often hungry than full. I wanted to prove to my father I could do something right. That I could make it on my own." He sighed. "That failed, and I don't know why I even tried. I robbed my father twice—of his wife and his wealth."

"You're not the person you think you are. You didn't mean to cause your mother's death, and just because you're a poor businessman and chose the wrong friends doesn't mean you're not worthy of loving and being loved. You being here—me being here—is proof of that."

"What do you mean?"

She paused, trying to collect her thoughts.

A couple strolled by arm in arm. They appeared as if they didn't have a care in the world. For a moment, Amelia was envious. She wished that were her and Quentin. What would it have been like if they'd boarded this ship as two whole people, without all the invisible burdens? What would it have been like if they could start a relationship without so many walls built around their hearts, so many pin pricks causing tender places?

Then maybe we would have had a chance at love.

Then again, because of the past—the pain—she was learning more about Quentin than she thought possible. How many people could say they got to know another person—truly know his heart—in such a short amount of time? She placed a hand on Quentin's arm, thankful. She knew what she wanted to say— what she *had* to say.

"It is no accident we met. God caused those men to unload you at the same time I was loading up. This ship is large, to be sure, but for a man who likes to run…it seems you have nowhere to go."

He listened but didn't answer. She looked to his hands at his side. His fingers curled as if holding an invisible necklace within them.

"It's time for the truth, Quentin…. You need to go to them."

"You don't understand. The truth is that I ruin all I touch."

"That's your truth, but what is God's truth? How does He see you, Quentin? Not only who you are, but who you *can* be."

"You're the only one I've encountered who sees me like that—as what I should be. You see the promise, not my faults."

"Yes, well, just keep looking into my eyes, then. Until you trust that's how God sees you, too, Quentin, just keep looking into my eyes."

The day was nothing like Amelia planned. She thought it would be a day of walking with Quentin and exploring the ship together. But after their first walk on the deck, they mostly sat. Even during lunch they found their own table instead of sitting with everyone else. Amazingly Aunt Neda didn't seem to mind. Maybe she'd been praying about matters—just as she'd suggested Amelia do. Maybe God was giving them both peace about the situation.

TRICIA GOYER

With Damien she'd enjoyed all the luxuries the ship had to offer. With Quentin they explored each other's hearts, feelings, and emotions. She knew they could explore the whole world, and no matter where they went and what they saw, what they'd appreciate most was each other.

"Why did you go to London?" she asked as they enjoyed the afternoon tea a steward had brought to the deck.

"We lived in a small cottage on our property when my father was having our house built. I remember one day as my mom sat and drank tea, she was staring at a postcard of the London Bridge that a friend had sent. I asked what she was doing, and she told me she was pretending she was there, pretending she was sitting at an outdoor café gazing at the London Bridge."

"And she never went there, did she?"

Quentin shook his head. "And..." A sly smile crept up his face. "There is the fact that they speak English there. I was never one for foreign languages."

They talked about the differences between London and America, and with each comparison excitement bubbled in her chest. America, it seemed, was a place where anything could happen. And as Quentin talked, she saw new hope in his eyes, too.

"Is the music different, too?" she asked.

"Well, there were some songs that came from The World's Fair that I really liked. I attended it in St. Louis with Father before I...left. I learned to play quite a few songs."

"Can you play one? Or two? There's a piano in the second-class reception room."

Quentin nodded. "One or two, I suppose."

They made their way to the reception room, and Quentin sat down to play. He played a song called "On the Pike" by James Scott, and Amelia marveled at the way his fingers moved over the keys. A small crowd gathered, and smiling faces looked on. The group clapped along as he played.

The song ended, and Quentin's hands poised motionless above the keys. Seeing him pause, Amelia wondered if it was because he'd heard the beating of her heart. As she watched him, she ached with a joy she didn't understand. There was no place she would've rather been.

While Damien's face had been so confident, so determined as he'd asked her to dance, Quentin's eyes registered surprise when he looked up at her, as if he couldn't believe she'd stayed to listen—or that the crowd had stayed. It was as if he felt unworthy to have her attention at all.

Her heart fluttered like a captured bird. Her breath came short. Her mouth dried up. Her mind searched for sufficient words.

"That was beautiful," she finally managed. "Can you play a few more?"

Quentin did, and when the music finally stopped, the crowd dispersed with murmurs of praise. Seeing their smiles as they left caused Quentin's face to glow.

Amelia felt her stomach rumble. Supper would be served soon. She didn't want this day to end. In fact, she hoped it would go a new direction.

"Quentin, was there a suit included in that suitcase—Henry's suit?"

He glanced over at her, and his gaze narrowed. "I don't like the sound in your voice, Amelia. You're up to something."

She shrugged. "You're the one who asked me to save a nice dress. I was just hoping for a date—supper and music and a handsome man at my side."

"Yes, but... Well, I'm not sure if that suit will fit me."

Amelia clapped her hands in front of her. "Will you try?"

Quentin let out a deep breath. "Yes, I suppose I can."

She smiled and noticed a smile on his lips, too. "Wonderful. I'll meet you in our dining room in an hour. I do believe you'll look dashing in a suit."

Chapter 17

Quentin scanned the tables of the second-class dining room, looking for Amelia. He didn't see her, but Aunt Neda met his gaze and waved. She seemed happier to see him tonight than she had previously. He hoped that was because she'd noticed the joy on her niece's face.

Neda Gladstone sat with a group of older women dressed in bold colors of red, blue, and green. Each wore a simple gown, and a hint of rouge colored their cheeks.

He waved to Aunt Neda and then continued to scan the room. A sad smile lifted on his lips as he heard the older women's voices rise in laughter. *Mother.* She would be near that age if she were still alive.

Quentin let out a low sigh. Although he'd missed the past twenty-one years with her, he cherished that his last memories of her were when she was young, beautiful. With long blond hair and large brown eyes, his mother had caught the attention of all whenever she entered the room. A farmer's daughter from North Dakota, his father had met her when he went to talk to her father about building a water tower along his creek for the steam engines. Dad said she had worn a simple dress and had been harvesting potatoes in their garden when he first saw her. He claimed it was love at first sight.

His mother had seemed all too happy to leave the farm, and she'd been content with her simple house until her father's business grew and grew. Then, even as she entered more prominent social circles, it had appeared to Quentin that her gaze wasn't on what she had or who she was but on what she could get and who she could be. It scared him even as a child.

Was that what had caused him to keep Amelia at bay? She was just like the woman his father had fallen in love with—sweet, simple—but he'd also witnessed how she reacted to this ship. She appreciated nice things. He didn't have anything to offer her today, but what about the future? If he found a decent job, would she be content with that? Or like the fine women of this ship—like his mother—would she always be looking for more?

Quentin didn't have time to worry anymore, for when he saw the eyes of many in the room turn, he knew deep down that Amelia had just entered. Turning slowly, he saw her ten feet away. Next to him, a group of young women traveling together paused their conversation to watch her step through the doorway.

Amelia wore a cream-colored dress that fell from a black bow at her ribcage in soft drapes to the floor. A black velvet bow tied at her right shoulder as well, with more drapes cascading down. Simple sleeves curved over her shoulders, and she wore no jewels. Instead her blond curls were pinned in a swoop at the base of her neck, and a few curls touched her cheekbones.

Had they only been on the *Titanic* four days? It seemed he'd known this woman his whole life—and he couldn't imagine the days ahead without her.

They finished supper and moved to the second-class reception room. Yet instead of following Quentin and Aunt Neda to a nearby table, Amelia turned to the orchestra, hurrying over to them. For a moment, she talked to the bass violinist. He nodded, and then a smile filled his face. When Amelia scanned the room again, her eyes finally fell on Quentin, taking his breath away.

For someone who'd lived in the shadows for the previous two years, his first inclination was to look away, to step back, to run out through the doors and find his way to a far deck. But the way she looked at him ... Quentin's heart pattered as he stepped forward and offered his hand to her.

"I asked them to play my favorite song," she said with a smile.

"And what song would that be?"

A tune began and Amelia hummed along. Quentin cocked an eyebrow, trying to remember the words. It wasn't as if he'd attended any concerts lately or had a gramophone to listen to. It was a newer song than those he'd heard at the World's Fair six years ago.

He led her to the nearest table, and as they sat she started to hum. Soon her humming turned into words, her singsong voice loud enough for only him to hear.

"By the light, of the silvery moon,
I want to spoon,
To my honey I'll croon love's tune.
Honey moon, keep a shinin' in June.
Your silv'ry beams will bring love's dreams,
We'll be cuddlin' soon,
By the silvery moon..."

Heat rose to her cheeks as she finished the last line. "I—I really hadn't thought much of the words before. I just like the tune."

Quentin nodded. "Well, if there is a sliver of a moon left. By tomorrow it might be gone...."

"Yes, that is a shame. The night never seems to be the same without a moon."

Amelia looked around at the happy passengers shined up like new pennies, and she smiled, disbelieving she was really here. Her mother had told her about the people all fancied up in lace and leather. And the music. And the fine furnishings. Often her mother described the fine things—what she'd seen and washed and mended—with such vivid detail Amelia had thought she'd seen it herself. Now she was dressed in fine things, a part of it all.

Amelia touched the silky fabric that draped from her dress. What would her mother think to see her now, wearing these fine clothes on the fastest, most extravagant ship? What would her mother think about a number of Amelia's fellow passengers being some of the most well-known and richest men and women in the world? A humored smile tugged at her lips. Her mother would be far from impressed about the last part.

"I've cleaned the toilet pots of rich and poor alike," she'd told Amelia once. "Waste is waste and people are people, no matter how you fancy them up. It takes no character to show favor to someone whose pocketbook declares their worth."

"The body grows hungry again and cold," her mother had continued, transferring her thoughts from 'back then' to the reality she faced with her daughter. "Clothes dirty and tear and clean water is drunk down. We must take care of ourselves, dear daughter. We don't have enough to give—enough to go around."

As Amelia listened to the music, as she looked around at those in the room, she thought about things in a different way. When she was little, those words had warmed her just the same as her mother's hug. She knew Mother did what she could to provide for her.

But now, as she thought if it, she wondered what would have happened if her mother would have reached out more. There was always, it seemed, someone who was worse off. If her mother would have sacrificed to meet other's needs, would God have filled in their needs with unexpected bounty?

Great character, she now knew, was realizing that the help you offered to a poor person would only soothe their soul for a few hours, but doing what you could despite the brevity of the gift benefited both the giver and the receiver. Character was realizing the need would still be there tomorrow just as fierce but still doing something to give comfort for an hour.

In her mind's eye, she again tried to picture Quentin at the docks. Where would he be if she hadn't offered him the ticket? He would have missed out on this, but she would have, too. The music in the room punctuated her thoughts. Her heart swelled inside her, and she knew that all of it was worth it. All she was and where she'd come from were for this moment. She looked from the fine wood paneling to the carpets to the lines on the table. All she didn't have back then made her appreciate what she had now. It also gave her hope for what was to come.

Who had God planned for her to walk her life's journey with? She didn't yet know, but she was praying—asking God to make the knowing clear. And for now she'd enjoy this time with Quentin. Enjoy that God had brought them together.

"You're thinking of something, someone. Is it your Mr. Chapman?" Quentin's words interrupted her thoughts.

Amelia gasped. "How...how did you know about him?"

"Your aunt. The other day when I was looking for you, she gave me an earful."

Amelia gasped. "What did she tell you?"

Quentin's finger's tapped on the tabletop as if he were playing along to the music filling the room on an invisible piano.

"She told me he was a dear man that had been writing you often and was looking forward to meeting you in America. She told me he paid for your passage—which means my passage, too. And..." He paused for a moment and cocked his head, looking at her as if trying to decide if he was going to say any more or not. Amelia didn't press him. Instead she just waited.

"She also told me that she had a feeling deep down that you were going to exit this ship with a different idea about your relationship with Mr. Chapman than when you boarded."

Amelia chuckled. "What is that supposed to mean?"

Quentin shrugged. "I don't know. Why don't you tell me?"

She eyed him for a moment. She still wasn't sure what her final thoughts were going to be when she disembarked, but she knew they would be different. They weren't halfway through the voyage yet, and her thoughts were already different from when she'd first boarded.

Amelia touched her fingers to her lips. Her smile was larger than she thought.

"I suppose we're just going to have to find out when the time comes. But to answer your question, I wasn't thinking about Mr. Chapman. I was thinking about my mother. If she were here, there would be laughter and dancing, much dancing. She would have thought it foolish to hear such fine music and not honor the musicians by truly enjoying it."

He rose and extended a hand to her. "Well, if a dance is what you want, you could have just asked."

As he pulled her into his arms, his whispered words caressed her ears. "I'd like to think my mother would have been dancing, too." His voice was reminiscent, wistful.

As he led her across the dance floor, Amelia clung to him tighter. She'd known the truth all along, even after spending time with Damien. She could care for a man like Damien. She could appreciate his care for his father. They could talk and laugh, but it was Quentin who moved her. His eyes seemed to reach into her heart and squeeze. He looked at her as if he had nothing to offer, and that was what she appreciated. He did have nothing to offer, except himself. His heart.

When the music stopped, they walked to the glass-enclosed promenade deck and stared into the sky, hand in hand.

The sliver of moon hung there, and Amelia yawned. It had been the most wonderful day, and she didn't want it to end. Yet tomorrow they'd have another day together on this grand liner. And the day after that...

She turned to study his profile that was lit by the lights from the rooms where music played and people danced.

"Have you thought about what's going to happen when we reach New York?" she dared to ask.

He turned to her and smiled. "How did you know I was thinking about that?"

"The plain truth is, Quentin, I want to spend more time with you. I don't want to get off of the docks in New York and walk away and wonder what became of you. But I also know it is no coincidence that your father—that your brother—is on board. You need to—"

"Stop!" he raised his hand. "I don't need to do anything." His voice was sharp, but she didn't back down.

His words came from the depth of pain he'd been carrying. She hadn't caused the pain, but his sharp words stung just the same. The wonderful mood of the evening crumbled at her feet like a dry and dead rosebud.

She cocked her chin higher and crossed her arms in front of her, not intimidated. "All right, tell me then, what's going to happen when you get to New York? You don't have a penny to your name." "I can find work. Maybe at one of my father's railway yards. I know some of the guys. Maybe if I approach them they won't tell my father."

She nodded. "Of course." She didn't want to say more. What she had to say didn't matter. It was up to the Lord now to change his heart. "I'm sure they'll remember you."

Amelia was suddenly weary. Was it worth giving her heart to a man who carried so much pain, so much baggage from his past?

Not knowing what else to say, she reached up and touched his face, stroking her hand down his jaw.

"Quentin, love covers a multitude of sins. I'm not going to be able to convince you of that...but you have to trust that it's true."

Quentin watched the door to Amelia's stateroom close. He stood there, unmoving. If he walked away—even five feet to the door to his room—he would break the spell she'd cast over him.

His heart felt full—fuller than it had in years. Even with her nagging, she spoke those things because she cared. If Amelia didn't care, she wouldn't take the time to listen to his stories. He smiled. She also wouldn't bother trying to boss him around.

He placed a hand over his heart. He could feel its wild beating under his palm. After all the years and everything that had happened, he never thought he'd ever feel like this. He didn't deserve to feel like this. Yet he also knew that to keep her, he was going to have to make some of the hardest decisions of his life. He was going to have to surrender, have to swallow his pride.

Quentin turned to take a step to his room when he noticed a man approaching. A gasp escaped his lips when he saw it was Damien. His brother's bow tie was undone, and Quentin guessed from his brother's swagger that he'd had more than one drink.

Strangely, after all these years of not being in his brother's presence, the first thing that struck Quentin was the humor of the situation. Here he was happy, sober, with the scent of Amelia still fresh in his mind, and his brother was striding forward angry, forlorn, looking as if he'd just climbed out of the gutter.

"So you think you can fool her? Do you think she doesn't know you're trash?" The words spilled from Damien's mouth, and Quentin hurried toward him.

"You don't need to do this here. We can take it outside."

"Good idea." Damien stood up straighter, and Quentin saw then it wasn't alcohol that caused him to slur his words, but jealousy. Damien's eyes were red, maybe from tears. He turned and stalked up the stairway to the deck.

When they got outside, the cold air took Quentin's breath away. It seemed strange to him that after five years, after losing his father's riches and after hiding from his brother's perusal, that the thing Damien was most concerned about—had finally approached him about—was a woman.

"Do you think she really cares about you?" Damien picked up where he'd left off. "She's a kind soul who likes offering a helping hand. If she really understood, knew who you are and all you've done, then she wouldn't treat you so kindly."

"You're wrong."

"Am I? Why don't you test it and see? Let her know what your life has been like for the last five years—really know—and see where that gets you."

"I did that."

"You told her everything?" Damien pointed a finger hard into his brother's chest. "How many months have you been living on the streets?"

"More that I want to count."

"And how many women have you slept with?" Damien huffed. "Yes, I bet the same answer."

Quentin lowered his head.

"Tell her that. Tell her the truth, and we'll see how far that gets you." With that, Damien turned and began to stalk away.

"Are you trying to ruin everything?" Quentin called after him. "Are you trying to strip away my last glimmer of hope?"

Damien paused at those words. He turned to face his brother. "Me strip it away? Did you just say that?"

His brows furrowed and his face reddened. He rushed up to Quentin, fists balled and hands raised up in front of his chin like a prize fighter. Damien repeated. "You took Mother away! And half of father's fortune. And now, when I find the one woman I have feelings for—"

Quentin didn't expect the punch. It hit his jaw like an anvil. His head reeled back. His neck snapped. His body propelled backward, and his feet scrambled to keep up, but it was no use. He slammed against the deck. His back hit first then his head. Pain coursed through his skull. His eyes blurred.

Without a moment's hesitation, he scrambled to his feet and rushed his brother. If Quentin had learned one thing on the street, it was how to fight. He lowered his shoulder and connected it with his brother's chest. Damien's breath released in a moan. Amazingly, Damien maintained his balance. Instead of tumbling, his knee rose up, catching Quentin under the chin.

Again Quentin felt himself reeling backward. He landed on his rear, hard. Obviously his brother had learned a thing or two during their time apart also.

Damien leaned forward, hands on knees, waiting for his brother's next move. Quentin rose to one knee, and just as he was about to lunge again, he heard a man's cry.

"Someone get an officer! Hurry! Fight!"

Quentin shuffled to his feet and moved to the doorway.

A sharp laugh erupted from Damien's lips. "That's right, Brother, run. It's what you do so well. And when you get yet another thing stripped away, don't blame that on me!" Damien shouted. "You've done it all to yourself. The only person you can blame for ruining your life is the one you see when you look into the mirror!"

Chapter 18

Sunday
April 14, 1912

Amelia awoke early, if that's what one called it. It was hard to use the term *awoke* when one had had so little sleep. She dressed quietly and made her way to the closest deck, noticing the sun rising behind them, spreading light to a bank of clouds. Bright red and pink, the clouds were a beautiful sight. Her eyes moved from the enchanted light to the swell of sea that extended outward from the ship. It continued on as if it touched the skyline. Did those who'd crossed the ocean a hundred times appreciate the beauty as she did? Or did they get used to it, just as she had gotten used to the sights and scents of Southampton?

Footsteps sounded from behind her and she turned. She wasn't surprised to see Quentin standing there.

"Amelia. I have to talk to you … before we go on. Before our hearts grow any closer."

Amelia nodded, and she approached him. She stared into his dark brown eyes. They appeared more troubled than before. She motioned to a small outside café table and they sat.

"You say you want to know everything, Amelia, but you have no idea. The depths of where I fell. The pain I've caused."

"I know things must have been hard…. I can't imagine what it was like. You've been through so much." She rested her forearms on the table, and her fingers inched toward his hands. He pulled his hands back.

She could tell he wanted to talk, but she also saw fear. A deep fear. Looking into his gaze was like looking into the face of a pained child.

"I told you that you don't want to get involved with me, Amelia."

"Why don't you let me decide that for myself?" she urged. She balled her fists and considered pounding them on the table. When would she get through to him? All night she'd worried about how things would work out if she gave him her heart, but at this moment a new worry struck—that he'd never give her the chance.

Dear Lord, help me. Show me a way to get through.

"I shouldn't do this." He leaned back in his chair, sitting straighter. He ran his hands through his hair. "Maybe later. I need more time to think."

He scooted his chair back as if preparing to stand. Instead of pleading with him, urging him, she looked into his face.

It was then she felt an answer stirring in her mind, a gentle peace. It was what Quentin needed, too—not her constant confrontation. He needed her gentleness and God's whispers of care.

She released her fists and opened her palms to him.

"You are still running, Quentin." Her voice was a soft breath of air. "And I have bad news for you."

He paused, surprised. Then he leaned forward to hear her words. "What's that?"

"We're on a ship, Quentin. You can't keep running forever. There's nowhere to go but into that water."

It was her whispered words that caught his attention. Many had tried to urge him, had argued with him, but she simply waited.

He studied her, studied the way the wind blew strands of blond hair across her face. He wanted to tell her she was beautiful. It would be easy to do. He'd learned how to woo a woman, but he couldn't do that. He couldn't sway her emotions to meet his desires. In just the few short days that he'd known her, he'd come to care more about her than he'd cared for any other woman in his past. At first those women had come to him because they'd wanted to be linked to his money, his fame. He'd allowed that in order to get what he wanted. The romances lasted weeks, some months, but they always ended badly. Just remembering those times brought him shame. It was as if Amelia's purity shined like the sun, casting penetrating rays into all the dark places of his heart.

He stared at her hands opened on the small table.

"What are you looking at?" she asked.

He glanced up guiltily. "My mother had soft, delicate hands like that. They're beautiful." He didn't believe he'd said that.

He leaned forward and kissed the back of her hand. Then he stopped himself. He knew what he had to do. He had to tell her what he'd been dreading.

"Amelia." He cleared his throat, determined to get this done with. Willing to share everything. "I've been with many women. I've hurt many people. I've stolen. I've lied…." Quentin felt a tear run down his cheek. "For so many years I made wrong choices—"

"I know." Her simple statement interrupted him.

"For so long I took what my flesh desired—"

"Quentin," her voice was gentle. "I said I know, and I have to say something."

She focused on him until his mind had settled. Until it was clear he was ready to listen.

"You have done many wrong things. All of us have. You have done worse than some...but when it comes to how God sees sin, no one's sin is greater than another."

He swallowed hard.

"That's why Jesus died for us, Quentin. He didn't sacrifice His life for those who've lived perfectly or those who've tried to. He died for all of us, and if you ask Jesus, He will forgive you now. At this moment."

Quentin lowered his head, a battle waging in him. When he was small, his mother had read him stories from the Bible and had often sung her favorite hymns. As he got older, it had been his father who'd told him about God. But Quentin hadn't listened. He hadn't wanted to think about God or imagine what God thought about what he'd done.

"Is it that easy?" he finally asked.

"Yes." Emotion poured out with the single word.

"And all I have to do is pray?" He glanced up at her, taking in the beauty of her face. The joy he saw there. "I'll do it."

Quentin lowered his head, and for the first time he could remember, he surrendered. He asked God to forgive him for the foolish mistake he'd made as a boy and all the millions of mistakes he'd made since then.

And as he prayed, something changed inside. It was as if his heart had been cracked open and the pain finally had a place to drain out—into the hands of Jesus.

When he finished and lifted his head, he looked to Amelia through his tears.

"Thank you, Amelia. Thank you."

Amelia's heart hammered in her chest. As she'd lain in her bunk last night, praying for Quentin, God had spoken to her spirit. As hard as it would be, Amelia knew God had another gift for Quentin that He wanted her to deliver.

Dear Lord, I can't do this, her heart prayed. *Give me the words to say. Help me to guide Quentin to healing for his pain.*

As her words echoed through her spirit, a new strength seemed to gird up her limbs. She rose and walked around her chair, placing her hands on its back.

"Quentin, I want you to imagine your mother sitting here." A bolt of lightning shot into her heart as she said those words. Quentin flinched. Gazing at him, she noticed that the cut he'd gotten on his cheek the day of the *Titanic's,* launch was mostly healed, but her words touched a sore spot in his heart that had festered far too long.

"Do you remember how much she loved you?" she continued, feeling God's strength as she did.

He nodded.

"What do you think she would say to you if she were here? Mostly, what do you think she would say about her death?"

He lowered his face into his hands. She could tell he didn't want to think about that. He didn't want to surrender that far. He glanced at her in desperation, as if saying, *Wasn't the prayer I just prayed enough?*

"I—I can't do this, Amelia."

"Do you know what I think she would say about her death?" Amelia stepped forward, and then she kneeled before him, placing her cheek on his knee. "She would say it was worth it."

"No!" Pushing her away, he scooted his chair back and stood. "No. You can't say that. Maybe if I'd led a good life. Maybe if I'd done things differently."

She remained where she was, on her knees. She didn't flinch, didn't budge at his rage.

"Even if she saw who you let yourself become and what you've done, she would still think it was worth it," Amelia continued in a soft voice. "Because ... because the truth is your life isn't over yet. From this day—today—you can live the type of life she'd be proud of."

A low cry escaped Quentin's throat, and a couple strolling by stopped and paused. Amelia ignored them. She wasn't there to impress anyone, and she didn't need to feel ashamed because of Quentin's tears. Because of her tears. She brushed her tears away.

Quentin's shoulders shook, and he looked to the sea. If only he could cast his pain and worries into the depths. If only she could help him.

Then he turned and walked back to her, standing before the vacant chair. He opened his mouth wide as if to say something.

Amelia rose and stood behind him. She lifted her hand, wanting to touch the sleeve of his shirt, but held it in midair instead.

Quentin drew a deep breath. He looked to the chair's seat, to the floor, and back to the chair again.

"You are right...." He turned to her. "My mother was a good woman. A kind woman. It would break her heart if she knew I'd run from my father's love."

Amelia didn't ask him what his next steps were. She didn't press for what she wanted him to do. She'd let God deal with Quentin's heart. She'd done what God had asked. Now she'd wait and pray.

Pray and wait.

Chapter 19

After breakfast Amelia strolled the deck, but the bitter wind hit her face. She remembered a similar wind when they approached Queenstown. She knew it was caused by the ship's movement, because in Queenstown it had died away as soon as they stopped, and it had picked up again when they got back into open water.

It also reminded her of God, and of what had happened to Quentin that morning. Sometimes God's Spirit hit like a bitter wind, but movement meant progress. It meant God was at work.

She studied a woman reading the French fashion newspaper *La Mode Illustree,* wondering what it would be like to think only of one's dress, one's social calendar. She was eager to see what America held for her—what God had in store once she got off this ship. In her opinion, one could only dress up so often. There was a time to enjoy a fine meal and a time to offer a meal to another.

Amelia wondered how Quentin was doing. After their time on the deck that morning, he'd gone back to his room to think, to pray. Amelia had told him she'd be meeting her aunt at the Sunday morning worship service in the first-class reception room. He'd mention he might meet her afterward. He said he had a lot to think about, but she could see the truth in his eyes. He worried his brother would be there, his father, too.

Outside, brilliant sunlight streamed across a clear sky, but her eyes were drawn to the covered corridor that was being used as the children's playground. Two small boys with curly hair played with their father. He chased them and they ran with squeals, staying just one step away from his tickles. A sad smile rose when she imagined C.J. like that with his boys.

Lord, restore what was lost. Heal what's been broken .... Whatever it takes.

She moved from the deck to the library and scanned to see the *Titanic's* position on the chart posted there. They neared America faster than she thought, and, in a way, faster than she wanted. From the moment she received word from Mr. Chapman and money for the passage, she'd been excited—about a new place, a new life, and hopefully love. And now? If she had her choice, they would stop the ship right here and allow her to pull her thoughts together. What awaited in America had not changed. What had changed was her heart and the person she'd chosen to love.

How can I trade my affections from a man of simple means, of character, of noble pursuits, to one who has spent the last two years stealing and hiding and running? Am I making a big mistake?

Even now she didn't know if she could completely give Quentin her heart. But could she walk away?

Two Catholic priests sat in the middle of the room. One chattered in German to a finely dressed couple. His Bible was open on his lap. She assumed he was sharing a scripture truth with them. The couple's eyes were focused on the man, and they nodded often. If Amelia spoke German well, maybe the priest could give her advice.

Passengers packed the library. They, too, seemed to be waiting until it was time for the Sunday service. She took in every detail of the room, the armchairs and small tables scattered about, all in mahogany. Some used the tables to write notes. Others played cards. Glass-cased shelves flanked one side.

She leaned against a white fluted wooden column and waited to head to the first-class reception room. All classes were invited to the church service, which was noble. The only thing was, like Quentin, she, too, worried about seeing Damien and C.J. there. She looked to the clock on the wall once again. She still had another fifteen minutes.

She approached the library steward. He was a thin man with a long, sad face. "I would like a book about New York City."

"Can you wait a bit, ma'am?" He held up a stack of papers in his hand. "I must serve these baggage declaration forms for passengers to fill out."

"Yes, of course." She held out her hand. "The nonresident form, please."

"It's hard to believe we will be in New York in two days, with calm weather the whole trip," someone behind her said.

Amelia turned to the female voice. It was the woman she'd been introduced to the night she'd had supper with Damien. What was her name? Then Amelia remembered—Dorothea.

"Yes, it has been a wonderful trip, hasn't it?" Amelia studied the woman's face, searching for any sign of the anger she had seen there the first night. There was none. Amelia guessed it was most likely because she no longer posed a threat to Damien's heart.

"The trip is better now." The woman grinned, showing off perfectly white teeth. She was dressed in a long red dress, and the stole around her shoulders appeared to be fur. "I was worried for a time. I thought Damien's affections were being drawn away." Dorothea placed an open hand on her chest. "Dear man, he was just getting cold feet. He assured me last night that I was the woman for him."

Amelia smiled, and she tucked a strand of hair behind her ear. "How lovely for you." Amelia nodded. "The two of you are perfect for each other." Then she glanced at the clock again and took a deep breath. "Would you excuse me? The church service is about to start, and I need to feel a special connection with God this morning. In fact, I have a feeling we all do."

Chapter 20

April 14. It was a day that was never far from Clarence's thoughts. It had been twenty-one years since he'd lost Jillian. What he hadn't realized then was he'd lost Quentin that day, too. It had been a slow loss. Quentin still breathed, but even as a boy his eyes carried a burden that weighed on his every action.

He hadn't been surprised when Quentin left home instead of going to college, determined to make his own way in the world. He hadn't been surprised when his son had demanded his inheritance with hopes of building an empire of his own.

It had all started when Quentin had seen his mother's body lying on the grass. Quentin had run and hid. It had taken Clarence three hours to find the boy hiding in a maid's closet. Since then Quentin had never stopped running, hiding. He ran not only from his father's love but God's love, too.

"Give your sons to me," a voice inside Clarence said, and he again prayed a prayer of surrender.

"Do you know what today is?" Clarence Walpole turned to his son. Damien's face was pale. Did that have anything to do with that woman, Amelia? Ever since she'd shown up at the library and had called Damien by Quentin's name, things had been different. Had Damien grown to care for the young woman? He wasn't sure. Did Damien battle with worry and concern for his brother as their liner steamed away from England? Clarence guessed this was the case.

"Of course I know what this day is," Damien stated flatly. "You ask the same question every year, Father. How could I forget? It's not every day you see your mother dead by your brother's hand."

The hairs on Clarence's neck rose, and he looked at him with shock. "Don't blame Quentin!"

Damien slid his arms into his jacket, preparing for the Sunday service they were going to attend.

"And who am I supposed to blame?" Damien's words shot from his mouth. "I've been angry for over twenty years...and you're just figuring this out? And he's not the only one I'm angry with. I don't understand, Father, why you'd asked *me* to be the one to stay with Mother's body until the undertaker arrived. Stay with her while you went looking for Quentin. It's a memory that haunts me to this day."

"I'm sorry. I didn't think of that. I needed you to guard her body. I didn't worry how it would affect you—though I should have. My thoughts were on your mother. She had dressed so carefully, done her hair just so. One of my last memories was of her applying the slightest amount of rouge to her cheeks and smiling at her reflection, pleased. It always satisfied me to see her content, and as she strode into the party that night, she had such confidence, as if she were the queen of England herself."

"What does that have to do with afterward—after the accident?"

"Don't you understand? I didn't want anyone else to see her that way—lying there with her dress and hair such a mess. It was as your mother would have wished. She would have been horrified to think of her guests' last memory of her being laid out like that. Instead they remember her walking down the stairs like a princess on her wedding day."

"I wish I had that memory, too, Father."

Clarence could hear the tremble in his son's voice.

"After all, I was only a ten-year-old boy."

Amelia entered the large first-class reception room, and her heart warmed to see passengers from all classes seated around the room.

Scanning the crowd, she found Aunt Neda seated in the middle of the room. Her aunt had saved Amelia a seat, and she waved her direction.

After weaving her way through the crowd of people speaking in low tones, Amelia sat. Those who weren't from first class marveled at the luxurious room. Amelia noticed a brightness in her aunt's eyes, but she soon discovered it wasn't because of the lush carpet and finely styled chairs.

"After you left the dining room, I met the most pleasant lady," Aunt Neda said. "Nellie invited me to join her family at their table. She's been living in India with her husband and three children—can you imagine that? Her baby is sick, and she is returning to America. Her husband is on the mission field still. What a brave lady for traveling with children alone, but, Amelia, I have to admit it does not seem right that a man should send away his family in order to stay and tell strangers about the Bible."

"It's a sacrifice," Amelia whispered, but her thoughts weren't on the family her aunt spoke of. Instead she considered what sacrifice God was asking of her. Was God asking her to walk away from the stability that Mr. Chapman offered? Or was he asking her to leave behind her mounting emotions for Quentin? If only she could be sure.

Quentin smoothed his suit pants and paused near the group of people filtering into the first-class reception room. His heart pounded and his mind told him to turn, to run. Instead he fixed his feet on the spot and focused ahead. If he could just make it through that doorway.

Ahead of him two women chatted. They wore fine clothes, and he guessed they were from first class.

"So did you get a chance to meet Mr. Walpole?" one woman asked the other.

Quentin's ears perked to their conversation.

"Mr. Walpole, yes, I met him last night. He's traveling with his son. I have never seen a more handsome fellow. Damien is his name. He has money as well. Tonight I might have to make an introduction." The woman fanned a gloved hand in front of her face as if just talking about Damien excited her.

"Doesn't Mr. Walpole have two sons?"

The second woman shrugged. "I thought so, but I heard a rumor that one died. Tragedy falls on the rich as well as on the poor, I suppose."

The crowd moved forward, and Quentin followed. His hand tightened around the doorjamb. In a way, the woman's words were right. He was dead. Dead to his family. Dead to ever being a son.

He knew from the moment he walked out on his family that would be the case. For a time, his father had tried to keep in touch, but the more he walked into dark places, the more he wanted to hide. What son would take an inheritance while his father still lived? He was worse than the drainage of waste on the city streets in the slums of London. So he'd told himself it was better not to allow himself to recall his father's love than to long for it. He had no right to yearn for what he'd thrown away.

He considered pausing, turning, but as his eyes scanned the room, he saw something—someone—he no longer wanted to run from.

His father was turned to the side, talking to the young man next to him, but as if an invisible hand tapped him on his shoulder, he paused and turned, as if he sensed Quentin's presence there.

Then, as if he moved in slow motion, he rose and his mouth whispered Quentin's name. His face brightened as he stood. His arms flung open. "Son, son!"

Quentin's feet felt planted to the ground, and he watched as his father staggered forward with shaky steps.

Intense elation started as a buzzing in Quentin's chest. He took a hesitant step. His knees softened. His father continued forward, his face beaming. Then, as if strength had been poured into his legs, Clarence Walpole set forth in a run.

They hurried toward each other, and tears filled Quentin's eyes. His father had aged—the gray hair and wrinkled face evidence of all the years lost. The crowd parted, letting them through, and before he could catch his breath, his father's arms were around him. Holding him. His father lifted slightly, as if Quentin were a young boy and he wished to sweep him into his arms.

His father's arms. Warm, strong. Quentin's throat thickened. Words refused to release.

His father pushed back slightly to look into his face. He held Quentin's cheeks, as if making sure he was real. And as Quentin looked into his father's gaze, he didn't see anger. He didn't see questions. He saw only an acceptance he didn't expect or deserve. He saw home. He saw love. He realized yet again what it meant to be a son.

Chapter 21

The room had just quieted, as if the Sunday service was about to start, when Amelia caught sight of a man entering the room. It was Quentin. He looked reluctant, and then his eyes widened.

"Son, son!" she heard Clarence Walpole call. The room stilled, and everyone watched as the older man rose and stumbled forward.

Amelia's breath caught in her throat as she noticed Quentin's eyes widen. Then as a tear broke through and trickled down his face, he stepped forward into his father's embrace.

C.J. wrapped his arms around his son, and he lifted slightly, as if Quentin were ten again and he prepared to scoop him up. The tears came. Amelia didn't know who was crying more, the two men or herself.

"Son," C.J. repeated. Even from where she was seated near the front, Amelia could hear their words.

Her hand covered her mouth. She'd hoped for this, but she'd never expected it.

C.J. touched his son's face, and he looked deeply at him as if trying to assure himself he was really there. All eyes in the room watched them, but they only had eyes for each other. Quentin's lips lifted in a smile, and Amelia wondered what brought the most joy... seeing his father again or feeling his acceptance. If

Quentin had doubted how much the older man cared before, there was no reason to doubt now.

C.J. moved his hands from his son's face to his shoulders. He opened his mouth as if to speak, but Quentin raised a hand to halt his words.

Quentin stepped back slightly. "Father, I have sinned against heaven and in your sight, and am no more worthy to be called your son"

C.J. turned to a man who had followed him. Amelia assumed it was C.J.'s butler. "And ask the steward for the best room still available in first class. I wish for my son to sleep as close to me as possible tonight. And if he needs clothes, we'll find some."

Happiness sluiced through Amelia, making her feel weak in the knees.

"That's Quentin, isn't it?" Aunt Neda tried to make sense of what was happening. "So he's also the brother of…"

"Damien Walpole." Amelia nodded.

"Oh dear." Aunt Neda lifted a hand and placed it on her cheek. "It seems the men trying to win your heart are brothers."

Amelia wasn't concerned about that now. All she cared about was the joy in C.J.'s face that brought a smile to Quentin. C.J. lifted a hand and squeezed his son's shoulder as if still trying to believe he stood there.

Amelia scanned the salon. Every person in the room was watching them. Some leaned awkwardly to get a better view. Some stood on tiptoes, trying to discover what the commotion was about.

"My son!" C.J. turned and raised Quentin's arm high. "My son whom I haven't seen in five years… He's here, on this very ship. Praise be to our Lord."

"His son? The one who left, robbed his very father?" one of the first-class men said, leaning heavily on his cane.

"His mother drowned, too. She died saving him. What a shame."

A murmur of disapproval carried through the first-class passengers. It was only then that Amelia understood what Quentin had risked coming up here. Amelia looked to C.J.'s face, and there was not one hint of hesitation.

As he returned to his seat, his arm wrapped around Quentin's shoulders, C.J. didn't notice the raised eyebrows and furrowed brows of his colleagues and friends, but Amelia could tell from Quentin's downcast eyes he'd heard. Every gesture, every word had been noted.

Tears filled her eyes, and she understood. She doubted a day passed during his growing-up years when he wasn't reminded of the accident. Many of these same people had been there when his mother had drowned. They knew that she gave her life for his, and if their gazes back then were anything close to what they were today, they didn't think it was a worthy trade.

"Tomorrow night, on the last day of the voyage, we will have a party on this ship like no one has ever seen!" C.J. called to the crowd. "There will be food and music ... a full banquet in the A La Carte Restaurant. Everyone here is invited. Bring your family, your friends! First class, second class, third—it does not matter. All must come to take part in the most joyous occasion!"

Cheers rose from around the room, mostly from the third-class passengers. It was one thing that they were allowed into the grand reception room to worship together. What would it be like to attend a party put on by one of the wealthiest men on the ship?

Seeing their joy displaced some of Amelia's anger from a moment before, and she decided that no matter what life held for her, she never wanted to be so wealthy that she forgot about the true treasures she had in family, friends, and the healing hand of God that restored what had been hurt and broken for so long.

The service started then, but Amelia's heart was already full. As they began singing their first hymn, she couldn't keep her eyes off of Quentin. The words echoed through her heart:

> *O God our help in ages past,*
> *Our hope for years to come,*
> *Our shelter from the stormy blast*
> *And our eternal home.*

It was the cheers in the room that caught his attention first. Damien had expected a solemn and traditional church service, but the noise from the room sounded more like a rugby game.

He entered the reception room, surprised to see most of the churchgoers on their feet. They were looking at something, cheering about something. He followed their gaze and a gasp escaped his lips. There, in the front of the room, was his father with his arm around Quentin.

Anger mixed with surprise pulsated through Damien. Surely many people in this room knew of his brother's deeds. He was shocked his brother had the nerve to show his face here of all places.

Quentin had lost and wasted what had taken their father years to earn. Losing the money was one thing, but the harm to his father's reputation was another. Yes, Clarence Walpole had a mind for business, but the man couldn't control his own son.

And now?

Damien balled his fists, wishing he could pound them into his brother's chest. If his brother were going to be the fool, why couldn't he have chosen another time, another place? Word of this *reunion* was sure to hit New York by wireless before they even reached the shore. More than one reporter had tried to get his father to talk about Quentin asking for his inheritance. Damien cursed under his breath, hating knowing what this would look like in print.

Over the years the society pages had produced photos of Quentin throwing lavish parties, and later lying drunk in the gutter. There were news stories of him entertaining a new woman every night. His father hadn't turned the reporters away, but each time they'd approached, he'd only offered one comment. "While my son makes choices that hurt my heart, he will forever be the son I love, and until he returns home again, I will display his photo upon my mantel."

As the church service ended, Damien ran a finger under his starched collar and attempted to control his emotions as he strode to his father's side.

"Father?" he said sweetly. His eyes scanned the crowd, noticing all eyes on him.

Clarence turned to Damien. "Damien. Your brother—look, he's here. He's been on the liner this whole time."

Then Clarence's smile faded just slightly. "Son, Damien, why don't you look surprised?

Amelia returned to her room, dropping her handbag onto the sitting bench. She pulled off her white lace gloves one finger at a time then plopped down on the bench herself. She noticed Aunt Neda hadn't tightened the faucet all the way closed, and the water dripped a drop every few seconds.

She replayed the disapproving comments of the first-class passengers. Each drip of water spurred her anger. She wanted to give them a piece of her mind for their harsh judgmental attitudes. They'd been at a church service, after all. She set her lips in a grim line and told herself this wasn't her battle to fight—as much as she would enjoy taking up arms. It was the life Quentin would have to face, whether he liked it or not.

Damien sat on the deck chair, staring into the inky black sky.

He heard footsteps approach, and he knew it was Arnold, his father's butler.

"Sir, your father has set up your brother in a fine room. He wishes for you to come see him."

"Arnold, I have no desire to see my brother."

"Sir?"

"You can tell my father that."

"Yes, sir."

Not five minutes later, he· heard another set of footsteps approaching. He could tell by the slow pace and the soft steps that it was his father.

"Son, do you not wish to come see your brother? We are making plans for the party tomorrow night. I could use your help with the menu."

"Use my help? Father, all you've taken from me in the last ten—twenty years—was my help. All these years I've been by your side. I have done all you asked. I've worked far more hours than I've rested to ensure that your business prospers. I've agreed with all your decisions. Not once have you thrown a party for me, and you never even suggested I have a luncheon for my friends. Now this..." Damien spit out the words. "Now this *son* of yours shows up. Did you forget he's the one who lost half of your holdings? You heard the rumors. Wild living, prostitutes, drunkenness. You're throwing a party that will be attended by some of the most influential men in this world...for him? For that?"

Only then did Damien dare to look into his father's face.

"Son, you are right when you say you've been by my side, and deep down you know that everything I have is yours. But this celebration—I have no choice but to be glad. This brother of yours was dead and is alive again. He was lost and now is found."

Chapter 22

The Sunday sun was not as bright as the previous days', and nippy air blasted Amelia's cheeks as she stepped onto the decks. The cold outside only served to make the cabins seem warmer, the salons more luxurious.

She had met Quentin's eyes from across the reception room during the Sunday service, but after that he'd been ushered away by C.J. She told herself he wouldn't forget her. She told herself Quentin was just caught up in the excitement of his father's acceptance, but she had to admit that after spending so much time with Quentin not having him by her side left her feeling terribly alone.

On the deck, a group of men gathered around the starboard side. They stared down to the ocean below, studying the water being churned up by the blades of the propellers. The watery foam spread like a thousand diamonds bubbling up. Amelia bundled a scarf tighter around her neck as she watched the diamond bubbles spread.

"Why is it doing that?" she dared to ask.

"We're closer to the ice fields," a steward explained.

Amelia glanced out over the waters, as if expecting to see chunks of ice floating there, but she only saw a dark haze rippling out in every direction.

"If ice is near, does it mean the ship will slow?" she asked.

"If the captain hears that ice is near, he will make sure we heed the warnings, but it's my guess it's far enough away that it won't affect us. Not that any ol' ice could hinder the *Titanic* anyway." The steward smirked.

The steward hurried off, and she listened to the sloshing of water against the sides of the liner as she replayed her last conversation with Quentin. They'd been so focused on his spiritual healing they hadn't taken time to discuss their feelings for each other. He hadn't asked if she felt differently about *them* now. He hadn't asked if she had more hope in their future together.

And she did have hope for a future with him.

Amelia had cared for many people during her years. She'd fed and clothed orphans. She'd stopped to talk to the beggars under the bridge. She'd visited new mothers and took them soup, but never in all her years had she witnessed someone who not only accepted her help but also heeded her advice. Her suggestion that Quentin put down his pride and reunite with his father had been hard for him to hear. Even harder to do. Yet he'd done it. He'd valued her words enough to put his own honor to the side. In return, she felt utterly cherished.

More than that, she hadn't seen the power of prayer at work in such an amazing way. She'd prayed for Quentin to do the right thing, and it was clear God had stirred his heart. And the more she prayed for him, the more she understood for herself that prayer made a difference. When she left this liner, she'd start praying more.

As a woman who loved God, Amelia knew she *should* pray. She did so at church and after her morning Bible reading, but she never really talked to God throughout the day, and for the first time she wondered why. Why had she thought she must store up all her concerns and take them before God in the morn or at night? Wasn't God attuned to her words and watching over her all day long every day?

"Lord, if I am to allow these seeds of love for Quentin to take root in the garden of my heart, won't You make that clear?" She whispered the prayer and felt it lift, carried away by the spray of the ocean. "Also, forgive me for not coming to You more often. Not only for this, but for all things."

Amelia finished her prayer and hurried back inside the liner to warm up. As she walked, she noticed that that sun setting on the watery foam glowed red, as did the *Titanic's* side. A strange sensation came over her, and she had a feeling God was not finished working yet. She didn't know what the days and weeks ahead held, but as the warm air enveloped her inside the doorway, Amelia had a feeling she would have to trust God more than she ever had before.

A steward had been waiting by her stateroom door when she returned. In his hand was a note from Quentin.

Amelia, darling, can you meet me at the first-class promenade deck? I'm overwhelmed by my father's love, but I'm missing you most. With care, Quentin

She entered her stateroom and saw that her aunt Neda wasn't there. Her aunt, it seemed, was yet again busy with newfound friends. Amelia checked her hair, put on her warm coat, and then hurried to find her way to Quentin.

He, too, wore a coat as he stood on the promenade deck. He must have heard her footsteps, for just as she approached, he turned and smiled.

"Have you been waiting long?" she asked.

"No, not very." He blew out a breath. "Besides, it was good to have some quiet. My father's been making quite a fuss."

As they looked out on the water, cold air carried his breaths up in vapor clouds. Her own breathing was quickened. She placed a hand over her heart, hoping to still it. The sea was calm, perfectly serene for miles. The ship cut through the dark glass. Only the broken surface lapped against the ship's side.

Amelia placed her gloved hand into the crook of Quentin's arm. As they stared out onto the waters, a solemn hush brooded over the sea. Her lips curled in a smile. It was good just to be together again—to know they could be comfortable like this without words.

Only the *whoosh* of the waters as they protested being pushed aside by the speedy vessel and the beating of her heart broke the silence. At least Quentin couldn't hear the beating of her heart.

She'd never thought love could happen so fast. Especially love for a person who lacked what she'd thought she wanted most. Yet in their four days together, he had become a different person. On the docks she'd found someone who'd run away from love. The man who stood alongside her now dared to hope love could be possible—she had seen it in his eyes as soon as she had walked out the door.

"Amelia, I have to ask you." His voice broke the silence. "Once off this ship, if you did not have to worry about means for supporting yourself, what would you do?"

She laughed. "Of all the people who should ask such a question!" Then, as she studied his face, she realized he was serious.

"Well, all right. I will entertain your question. When I was in London, I volunteered at a home for orphaned children. There were many there who needed food and clothes—that was actually the easiest part to remedy. As they grew, though, I saw many older children sent out on the streets ill-prepared. It seemed a shame to me that one would feed a child but not educate him. It seemed a shame to teach a young girl proper manners without giving her a way to support herself once she left the shelter of the children's home."

Quentin nodded.

"Why do you ask?"

He looked to her and shrugged. "I was just wondering. I'd just like to know your dreams."

"Is that the only reason why?"

He shook his head. "Not really. My father's been asking me the same type of questions. He tells me my experiences will not go to waste. He said that God can take all those broken parts of me and turn them into a beautiful mosaic. I'd never thought of things that way before—to think something good could come out of all my failings."

"It makes sense; your father is wise. Maybe that's why I dream of helping children. Because I was in their situation before, I understand what they're going through." She placed her hand over his and squeezed. "Thank you."

"For what?"

"For sharing your father's words. For helping me understand that my past shouldn't be forgotten .... Instead I need to offer it to God to be transformed."

His eyes scanned the horizon, but she could tell from his gaze that his thoughts were not on the sea.

"What are *you* thinking about?" she dared to ask.

He blew out a sigh. "I have seen children on the streets. I've also seen those kicked out of the orphanages when they came of age. You have a worthy mission."

"Is that all you'll tell me?"

He nodded. "Yes, lest I break your heart."

They stood for a while, smelling the cold ocean air that stung her nose, feeling the slight vibration of the ship. Finally, Quentin cleared his throat. "Amelia, I have never cared so much for a woman. I have wanted to tell you that all day. But telling you such is a problem."

"Why does it have to be a problem?"

"I sit here in borrowed clothes. I have nothing to offer."

"You have yourself. You have your heart."

"I am afraid neither is much. I've given my heart away to too many things, enjoyments, entertainers, people. The rest of my heart is small and as hard as a lump of coal."

"You say that, but I do not believe it. You have a kind heart. Every time we meet, I see more evidence of that."

He nodded, but Amelia could see he was distracted.

"There's something else, too," he confessed. "To provide for you—if that's where this leads—I will have to depend on my father's mercies. I've already taken—lost—my inheritance. I can't ask him for more."

"I don't think you should ask, but maybe there's a job for you. I imagine your father can find something." She cast him a soft smile. "Life when you exit this ship will be different than you thought, and that's okay. You've already accepted God's grace, Quentin. The hardest part for you will be accepting your father's favor, too. But that's what grace is—accepting what we don't deserve.

A shiver of cold had driven the other passengers below, and Quentin lowered his head and closed his eyes, still overwhelmed with the day's events. When he'd first climbed aboard the ship, he'd planned on hiding among the baggage and sleeping to the noise of the engines thundering with the might of a hundred thousand horses. *And now?*

His chin quivered. His knees softened, and he grabbed the cold rail, leaning on it for support. He'd felt his father's embrace; he'd been welcomed back into the family. He'd regained what he'd foolishly wasted. And if that wasn't enough, the God of mercy and grace brought Amelia into his life. She'd sought him on the docks and offered him an unexpected gift. Her heart was an offering he had no right to receive.

Quentin still hadn't made amends with Damien, but he hoped that would change. He'd seen his brother briefly after his reunion with his father. Only one emotion lurked in his brother's eyes—disgust. Would his brother ever forgive him? Would he ever earn Damien's trust?

The cold air blasted them again, rattling the glass enclosure. Quentin thought of the men in the crow's nest, wondering how they handled the cold. He scanned the waters and saw nothing... and told himself not to worry. Capable men manned the ship. His worrying wouldn't propel the liner to move any faster. He didn't need to fret about the weather. He didn't have to be concerned about his brother yet either. He only had to focus on the matter at hand—the beautiful woman who stood at his side.

He and Amelia stood only a foot apart, and his heart pounded like hammer blows. He studied her eyes and noted anticipation there. Pink tinged her cheeks, and her simple innocence nearly took him to his knees. She'd never been attracted to anyone as she was to him at that moment—he could read it all right there in her gaze.

His head dipped, and her face slightly lifted. But something inside caused him to pull back. Though the man he'd been before he'd boarded this liner would have taken her kiss and much more, the man he'd become once he fell into his father's embrace paused. She offered him a gift. By taking her kiss, he would also be taking a piece of her heart.

He pulled back even farther and stroked her cheek with his finger. Her eyes fluttered down, as if embarrassed by her desire for a kiss, but when she looked back into his face, he saw something there that he hadn't seen in years. A decade even. Respect. His chest swelled with emotion, and his chin quivered slightly. His eyes grew moist.

Embarrassed, he looked away.

He turned to the glass window, unsure of what to do or say. This woman treated him like a human. She not only looked past his flaws, but she seemed to look deeper, at the potential he hadn't realized he possessed.

"Amelia, I have to ask you something, and I'm just going to say it before I change my mind."

"Yes, I'm listening."

"What do you see when you look at me? I want you to be honest."

"Quentin, of course I will be honest." She took a deep breath and focused her eyes on his hands. Finally, she looked up into his face. "When I first saw you, I felt a bit of worry. You were so disheveled, untamed. But you didn't fight as they dragged you off board. It was as if you'd already accepted your fate. Then when you glanced up and looked at me ... Well, your look passed through me more than *at* me. I've seen that look before in the faces of children I work with. I saw someone who felt very scared and alone."

Her words ground in his heart, like salt in an open wound, causing it to sting.

His stomach clenched, and he didn't like that feeling. Standing before this woman was like being stripped down. Baring his soul. He wore a fine suit—his father saw to that—but as he listened to her, he again felt as if he were in rags.

"I see you're struggling with what I just said," she continued. "I don't want to make you feel uncomfortable. I also want you to know that I'm not finished. I still see some of those same things in your gaze, but I also see more. I see a man who faces his mistakes, who turns and walks away from a past that held him in chains. I know it was hard to accept your father's embrace today, but you did it. And in the coming weeks, I hope you grow closer to your father ... and God, too. And maybe someone else you've gotten to know on this journey."

She flashed him a brief, nervous smile. Then she shyly looked away and wrapped a curl from the base of her neck around her finger.

Hearing her heart, he finally felt brave enough to ask the question he'd been wanting to ask all day. "Amelia, do you think there can be anything more between us? I know you feel it. Feel the attraction. Could this be the start of something... of a new beginning for both of us, together?"

She bit her lip, and he could see sadness in her gaze. "I would be lying if I claimed I did not look forward to each moment that I spend with you, but I need to trust God with what is next. We both need to trust God. He will show us. As we both grow closer to Him, He'll make a way."

Quentin nodded, and he waited for Amelia to continue, but there was only silence. She didn't say more. She didn't point a finger and tell him that though he'd cleaned up on the outside he had a long way to go within. She didn't need to. A woman like Amelia deserved a man who had much to offer—someone who could guide and lead with confidence. And that was why he hadn't kissed her, because deep down he'd known.

And just when Quentin thought he should suggest they go inside, she glanced up at him with a grin.

"I have made some decisions I think you should know about. I've already written a letter to Mr. Chapman and told him I can't see him and me as anything more than friends. You see, Quentin, the man who paid my passage follows every criteria on my list for what I wanted in a husband. So what I don't understand is why another man has captured my heart."

"Me?"

She blew out a breath and offered an innocent smile. "I'm afraid to say, but if it's not you... well, then I'd be a fool to be talking so freely to another."

She lifted her head, and their eyes met. Hers were hopeful—hopeful that he'd become all she needed.

As he studied her, a smile tugged at one corner of her mouth, a smile as sweet as her heart.

Inside, relief built and rose from his stomach to his chest. She didn't expect him to transform overnight. He liked that, and he would do all he could not to disappoint her. Besides, he was tired of running and hiding. Even though opening himself up came with pain, Quentin was ready to once again be known.

Chapter 23

Soft cadences from the ship's orchestra drifted up to where they stood, reminding Amelia that they weren't the only two people on this ship, no matter what her heart told her. She felt as if the journey she and Quentin had been on the last few days had taken them even farther than the voyage of this liner, and suddenly a weariness overwhelmed her.

"Would you like to go to a party?" Quentin asked. "I could lie and tell you that I'm in the mood for dancing, but the truth is, what I'd enjoy the most is holding you in my arms again."

"Who says we need to be on the dance floor to do that?" Amelia took a step toward him, and Quentin placed a soft hand on her shoulder, then on her back, pulling her close.

Heat rushed through Amelia's lungs, and she paid no mind to the cold wind brushing against her. Her heartbeat quickened, and she placed her chest against his chest. She found peace there and excitement, too. The two emotions were twisted around each other, and she didn't know where one ended and the other began.

Stars and planets twinkled above them, and beneath their feet the mighty engines pulsed and throbbed. Propellers churned up a fast and thick wake.

"I heard some officers talking today. They said we were going to break the record for being the fastest ship to cross the Atlantic," Amelia said, leaning her cheek against his chest.

"I know. Passengers were talking about that, too."

While most people wanted to be part of breaking the record on this maiden voyage, she'd be perfectly content to remain on board for months, years. To arrive in New York would mean telling her cousin Elizabeth that she'd worked so hard to find Amelia a suitable mate for nothing. It also meant having to look into the face of dear Mr. Chapman and thank him for the passage, but also declare that their romance would not be progressing, that she'd already given her heart to another.

"As much as I'd like to spend the night dancing in your arms, I'd better get below." She yawned. "It's getting late."

"Tomorrow then?" he asked.

"Of course. You're not going to get rid of me now." She playfully punched his arm. "I've looked for someone like you for so long. My aunt would always remind me, 'The future is unrolled in God's good time.' I just never believed it until now."

Amelia took a step back and hunched her shoulders against the cold. "But it is late, and I should say good night."

"G'night." He smiled.

She waited for him to escort her inside, but his feet remained fixed. Then, as if finally accepting their time together must come to a close for the evening, he placed a gloved hand on her elbow, and a thousand goose bumps rose on her skin. Quentin led her inside to the warmth of the reception area, and she'd never been so thankful for the warmth.

Amelia turned to give Quentin a brief glance, but then a hard rocking under her feet jarred her. "Did you feel that? What do you think it was? Maybe one of the engines went out?"

Shouts sounded from the outside—on the decks below. Surprise mixed with excitement.

"I'll check it out." Quentin stepped away from her.

"I want to go with you."

"You've just got in from the cold."

"I think I'll survive." She wrinkled her nose. "And maybe it's just another excuse to spend more time with you."

"Is it?"

She lowered her head and looked up at him from under her lashes.

"Okay..."

They rushed back outside. Stepping out into the cold after feeling the warmth was like walking inside an icebox and holding her hands over blocks of ice. As they rushed to the deck, Amelia noticed a large, white shape glide by. The sight of it caused Amelia to jump back. Her heart pounded, and goose bumps rose. It hovered over them like a ghost. She turned away.

"It's an iceberg," Quentin declared.

"It's so close!" Fear gripped her heart.

They wandered down to the boat deck, and soon it filled with people in various stages of dress. "They must have felt that jarring, too. Do you think we hit it?"

"If we did, it was just a glancing blow," Quentin's words sounded more convincing than his gaze.

Amelia looked around. The perfectly calm sea and brilliant starry night reassured her. All seemed to be well. She blew out the breath she'd been holding.

Then, as they watched the iceberg slip into the distance, the engines slowed and then stopped. The dancing vibration that she'd known for the last four days was gone. She felt as if she were walking on air, floating almost. As if her legs were no longer connected to the floor.

Quentin hurried back inside, and Amelia followed. They approached the steward who stood by the staircase. The man was most likely waiting for the few passengers still lingering, listening to music, to head to their staterooms so he could turn out the lights and go to bed.

"Did you feel that?" Quentin asked the man.

"Feel what?"

"That jolt."

He shook his head.

"The engines aren't running. Do you know why we stopped?"

The steward shrugged. "I don't know, sir."

They walked through the vestibule to the deck and again stared down at the sea. Black, still.

Just when Amelia was sure it was a false alarm, Quentin turned and grabbed her shoulders. "Amelia, listen to me. Go to your room and wake your aunt."

"Do you think there's been damage? You said it was just a glancing blow. And they say the *Titanic* is unsinkable."

His startled eyes met hers, and he grabbed both of her elbows. "I can't be sure if this ship is indeed unsinkable, but I've learned on the streets to expect the worst. Just have her get dressed, and we'll wait for news. She might be upset for being awakened, but that iceberg was large." He leaned down and kissed her forehead. "You trust me, don't you?"

"Yes, of course."

"Good. Just do what I say, and I'll meet you back here."

She hurried down the steps, but something felt different. With each step she felt off balance as if the ship was tilting slightly to one side.

As Amelia looked closer, she could not see any visible tilt to the stairway, and she was sure it was all in her mind. Maybe it was simply the rising fear that caused her heart to pound in her ears and caused her feet to stumble.

When she reached the second-class hallways, she noticed they were mostly deserted. A few stewards on night watch stood at their stations, still not acting as if they'd felt anything, heard anything. As she hurried on, heads started appearing as passengers peeked out, asking questions from half-closed doors. With a trembling hand, she pulled the key from her pocket and knocked as she put it in the door.

"Aunt. You must get up and get dressed. There has been an accident."

She opened the door and hurried into the room, flipping on the light.

"Aunt Neda, you have to wake up. Something has happened. The liner has stopped, and I'm pretty sure we hit an iceberg."

Her aunt sat up and rubbed sleepy eyes. She cocked her head as if listening and then snuggled back under her blankets.

"You won't catch me leaving my bed on a cold night. Tell me what happened in the morning."

"Aunt, listen to me. Quentin told me to come for you. I think we should dress warmly and head up to the deck to see if there is any announcement."

Amelia's teeth chattered, and her fingers fumbled as she removed her coat and layered another simple dress over the one she was wearing. It was cold outside, and if she was going to wait there, she'd do what she could to stay warm.

"Honestly, Amelia, I'm not sure about all the fuss. Even if we did hit an iceberg, I'm sure the ship has barely a scratch."

Quentin waited until he saw the door to Amelia's stateroom close, and then he quickly moved to his second-class stateroom and entered. Even though his father had provided a room above and filled it with fine things, he kept the things that mattered most here.

His eyes immediately moved to the top drawer of the bureau, and he hurried to it, pulling it open. Inside there were only two items, his mother's pearl necklace and a letter he'd started writing to Amelia. He'd planned on giving both to Amelia tomorrow night, after the party his father was giving to him. Amelia had given him the greatest treasure he could imagine—hope for a reconciliation with God and with his father. Both had been gifts to him. His chest felt light and full at the same time.

He slid both into his coat pocket and then patted it.

He did love her. He'd been afraid to admit it before. But now...

Could his confession wait until tomorrow?

He worried that it couldn't.

Quentin moved back into the hall and heard Amelia talking as she helped her aunt dress. He thought about knocking at the door, but his mind carried him another direction, to third class. Was anyone down there rousing them? Helping them? Telling them they needed to head up to the boat decks? Even if there was nothing seriously wrong with the ship, it was better to be safe.

He turned and jogged down the hall, thinking through the best maze of passageways that would take him to third class. He couldn't help everybody, but he had to do his part. God had done so much for him... it was the least he could do.

Chapter 24

From the first-class decks, Damien looked down onto the forward well. Dorothea's kisses were still warm on his lips, but his mind was on another. He didn't want to think about where Amelia was now—who she was with. It was bad enough to hear his father talk about Quentin without stopping. It pained him to hear his father's prayers of thankfulness. How could he be thankful to be reunited with someone who'd caused so much pain?

His eyes widened as he spotted chunks of ice scattered across the deck, ankle deep. Laughter filled the air and, below, a group of boys spilled out of the third-class doorway, throwing the ice at each other. Within seconds their throwing turned to kicks, and they started up a game of American soccer. At least they knew how to have fun—how to liven things up.

He strode to the smoking room and saw three gentleman playing cards. "If you're wanting to know what we hit, it was an iceberg. Seems to have passed now."

One of the men glanced up. "Maybe that's why they've slowed the engines—because more are ahead."

A man from outside rushed into the room. "It was an iceberg, all right. Saw it with my own eyes."

One of the other card players shrugged and then fixed his eyes back on his game.

"How big?" Damien asked.

"Sixty feet, maybe more."

Damien nodded, glancing down at his suit and wondering if he should go for his coat. He might want to venture out later, and a coat would help against the cold. "My guess is that we swiped an iceberg with a glancing blow and they stopped to examine her," he said, even though no one seemed to pay him any mind.

One of the card players laughed. "Poor vessel. Such a pretty thing, and now some of her paint has been scratched off her side."

"Well, look at it this way," the final card player piped up. "It appears we have more ice for our drinks, gentlemen. Now back to our brandy."

As the men continued their game, Damien returned to the deck, walking vigorously to keep warm. He glanced over the rail a few more times, as if the answer to why they stopped could be found in the waves.

Minutes passed, and the ship began to move again, slowly, creeping through the water. Just then he spotted something out of the corner of his eye. An officer climbed up on a lifeboat and began to throw off its cover.

Damien crossed his arms over his chest, considering if he should warn anyone. The first person who crossed his mind was Amelia. He shook his head and sighed. Quentin would take care of her, he supposed. His lips lifted in a sarcastic smile, again unsure of what someone like her saw in someone like his brother.

Pushing her from his thoughts, Damien approached one of the officers who was milling around.

"We struck an iceberg, but there is no need to worry," the officer explained even before he asked.

Damien knew the best thing to do would be to return and reassure his father. There was no need for the old man to get up and dressed for no reason. Still, he hurried to their stateroom, and a foreboding came over him. What would happen to his father if he wasn't around? His father had embraced Quentin, that was to be sure. But where was his younger brother when Father needed help?

He moved through their shared sitting area and knocked on his father's door. The light flipped on, and his father opened it. Just as Damien was about to tell him of the iceberg, a loud pounding sounded from outside.

"It's ordered that everyone must put on their life belts!" a voice called. "Then head up to the decks as you are able!"

His father looked to him, concern filling his gaze. "What's happening?" "We hit an iceberg, Father, but I'm sure all will soon be well. You know how important safety is to our captain. I imagine once everything is checked out, they'll be sending us back to bed."

His father's butler entered the room and pulled out clothes.

Damien dressed, putting on an extra layer of clothes over the ones he was wearing. Then, with quickened movements, he gathered up their watches, wallets, and trinkets that they'd picked up in London—putting them in their trunk and locking it tight, lest anyone try to sneak in and rob them of their things during the confusion.

"Are you ready, Father?"

"I am, but what about your brother?" Panic seized the old man's face.

"I'll check his room again, but I've been watching, and he hasn't returned. I believe he's with Amelia." "Yes, please check, and then search the decks, will you, Damien? Now that I know your brother's on this liner, my heart's not going to settle until I know he's safe—until I know we're all safe together."

A man's voice echoed through the halls. "All passengers on deck with life belts on!"

Amelia put her lifebelt on over her coat, tying it firmly. A shiver ran up her arms, and she turned to her aunt, helping to tie her life belt, too. Then they left their room as quickly as they could.

Other passengers filled the halls and passageways now, yet none of them seemed alarmed. All spoke in low tones as they filed up to the deck, wondering what this could mean.

Amelia took her aunt's hand, and they walked side by side. Before and behind them, fellow passengers chatted as they walked. No one seemed in a hurry. Some joked of their midnight drill. Amelia's stomach knotted, and she thought she would be ill. Only the officers' anxious faces looked alarmed.

She led her aunt to the place where Quentin had told her to meet him, but he was nowhere in sight. Around them, the shouts of officers and sailors filled the air as they hurriedly prepared the lifeboats.

"Amelia, this deck is cold." Her aunt's chin quivered. "Maybe we should go in there." Aunt Neda turned and pointed to the reception room. Following her gaze, Amelia saw that indeed most of the passengers were inside, enjoying music, drinking. Fur coats draped over their life belts, and men and women huddled in small groups, laughing and talking.

Amelia lowered her head and said a quick prayer for wisdom. If only Quentin were here. Where had he gone?

"All right, Aunt." Amelia blew out a sigh, and her breath hung in the air. "We can go in for a little while. No use standing in the cold."

They hurried inside and huddled with the others near the grand stairway, listening to the musicians play. Amelia crossed her arms over her chest, anger mixing with her worry. Where had Quentin gone?

As the minutes ticked by, Amelia thought about returning to the deck to look for him. Just then she felt a hand on her arm.

She turned and immediately recognized the red-headed steward, one of those she'd chatted with on the journey.

"Don't you realize this ship is going down, ma'am? We've struck an iceberg. They've already launched some lifeboats. You must get in the first one you can."

She opened her mouth to reply, but what could one say to that? With urgency in his gaze, he hurried off without mentioning the lifeboats to any others.

"Aunt, can you wait here one moment? Mr. Walpole's stateroom isn't far. I just want to go take a look."

"Yes, dear." She nodded. "But hurry. You heard what that young man said."

Amelia quickly strode up the stairway and then found herself jogging down the hall where the first-class staterooms were. As she continued on, an eeriness passed through her. The rooms were lit so brilliantly, their doors were opened, their contents scattered.

Down the hall she heard a woman calling to a steward, frantic that she could not find her life belt. The steward removed his own life belt and hurriedly rushed toward her.

Arriving at the Walpole staterooms, Amelia let out a cry. They were empty. Rushing back to her aunt, she grabbed her arm and guided her outside.

"Did you find Quentin?" Aunt Neda asked.

"No." Her voice quavered. "There was no one there."

"Maybe they put the first class into lifeboats first. Maybe he's already left."

Amelia shook her head. "No, he wouldn't do that. He wouldn't leave me."

Aunt Neda looked into Amelia's face. "Of course not, dear. Of course not."

Chapter 25

On the top deck, many passengers had assembled. Women in coats and wraps. Others with blankets wrapped around their shoulders, shivering. Thankfully, with the ship's engines stopped, the breeze caused by its movement had died down, too. Amelia peered at the ocean below. It seemed so vast and dark. The air was frigid, and she guessed the water was colder still. The *Titanic* seemed large and steady. She questioned if the steward had known what he was talking about. The ship under her feet seemed far safer than the small lifeboats setting off.

The men and women around her stood quietly on the deck, watching the crew as they prepared the lifeboats. They arranged the oars and coiled ropes on decks. One man adjusted the ropes that ran the pulleys, preparing to lower a boat to the sea. No one questioned what was happening. No one offered to help.

The atmosphere was quiet, and stars filled the sky. She glanced around and noticed that there was no moon. So she hummed her favorite song to calm her nerves. More people poured from the stairs and filled the deck.

By the light of the silvery moon . . .

"Lifeboats? Why are they lowering the lifeboats?" A woman's voice called out. "This ship could smash a hundred icebergs and not feel it!"

I want to spoon, To my honey I'll croon love's tune . . .

As if responding to the woman, an officer cried out, "Get on your life belts, there's trouble ahead!"

Honey moon, keep a-shinin' in June. Your silv'ry beams will bring love's dreams, We'll be cuddling' soon, by the silvery moon...

Just then Amelia turned and saw Quentin approaching. He led a woman with three young daughters. Quentin fastened the life belt on a girl who appeared to be around ten years old as they approached. "Here, see how that fits. It's the latest fashion. Everyone will be wearing them soon."

The girl approached Amelia, tugging on her arm. "Do you think they'll have a life preserver for my doggie? He's in a crate down below." Amelia turned to the girl's mother. Tears filled the woman's eyes. Then she turned back to the young girl.

"I'm not sure they have one his size, dearie. But look at those people getting on the lifeboat. Would you like to join them?"

The mother crossed her arms and pulled them tight to her chest. "No, we're waiting here for my husband. He's coming up just now with our son. Should be here any moment."

Amelia turned to Quentin, her eyes pleading for him to help.

He stepped forward. "Ma'am, if I were your husband, I would feel better knowing you were on a lifeboat. If you go ahead, I'll make sure he knows you're safe."

The woman looked around as if hoping her husband would suddenly appear. "Are you sure?"

Quentin nodded. "Yes, ma'am, go ahead and get in the boat."

Relief filled the woman's face, and she hurried to the nearest boat. Within a minute's time, they were safely aboard.

"Did they come from third class?" Amelia asked Quentin.

He nodded. "Yes, that's where I came from. I did what I could to lead some people up to the decks, but there was too much confusion. Many didn't want to leave their things, their large trunks. It's all that they own."

Beside them, a young man led his wife to the awaiting officer who manned the next lifeboat. "You go, and I'll stay awhile," the young husband said. He stroked her long hair.

"You'll get in another boat, won't you?" Her words released as sobs.

"Of course." He nodded. "When they let me, I'll be the first to board."

Next to the young woman an older woman stretched her hands out to her husband. "Please, won't you get in with me?"

He sadly shook his head. "Darling, what type of man would I be if I allowed women to wait while I found my way to safety?" He shooed her with his hand. "Don't worry. We'll meet up soon enough."

Seeing that the woman wasn't leaving her husband's side, Quentin took her hand and led her to the next lifeboat. As soon as he helped her aboard, he stayed there, assisting the frightened women as they stepped from the firm foundation of the *Titanic*'s decks to the lifeboat that swung by ropes hooked to rigging.

Amelia stood with her aunt, wondering if they should board a boat, too. She glanced around and noticed a steward standing among the passengers. A cigarette dangled from his lips, and it seemed he, too, was waiting his turn to board the life vessel. Surely if someone who spent his life on the seas believed it was best to get into the boat, she should trust that. Amelia closed her eyes and imagined what her mother would do. Would she hang back, feeling security in the ship?

Get on the boat, she felt something in her say. *Trust... trust you will be carried to safety.*

A woman with dark hair falling from its bun approached the steward, grasping his arm.

"Sir, my mother is elderly. She's still sleeping below. Do you think I should wake her?"

With slow movements, he pulled the cigarette from his lips, flicking ashes onto the deck. "Listen ma'am. I know it doesn't seem like an emergency, but I've worked on liners long enough to know that they don't launch lifeboats unless they believe this ship is going down."

The woman gasped. "That's impossible. It's an unsinkable ship."

The steward shrugged, and it was clear he wasn't going to argue. Reluctantly, the woman entered through the doors and moved down the hall.

Amelia peered into the icy ocean. The woman had a point. What about the watertight compartments? Had they been compromised? She rubbed her hands together, trying to warm them. Weren't the many safety precautions supposed to keep the ship afloat?

As they waited patiently, the line lengthened, and both Amelia and her aunt took a step back. It seemed wrong to push their way to the front. She was sure they'd all get their turn.

As they stood, a white-haired stewardess approached, and through the fog of her thoughts, Amelia realized it was Geraldine.

Geraldine's face was pale, and she grasped Amelia's arm in a vicelike grip. "I heard Mr. Andrews—the designer—talking to Captain Smith. The ship will sink, Emma. You must get on a lifeboat as soon as possible."

"Geraldine, I am Amelia, Emma's daughter," she tried to explain.

The older woman nodded. "Yes, Emma, of course." Then she hurried down the deck, approaching another passenger with the same news.

Just then, a roar blasted through the funnels, sounding like a line of train engines roaring down a tunnel. Amelia jumped and tried to control her emotions that carried her away like wild horses. Fear gripped her heart. Her stomach ached, and she was sure she'd lose her dinner.

Just when Amelia felt her legs would no longer be able to hold her up, Quentin approached with a blanket, wrapping it around her.

"Amelia, I need to leave. I must go find my father. My brother. But I can't leave the deck until I know you're safe. It is time. I want you and your aunt to get on the next boat."

She looked into his eyes, seeing love there. "Yes." She nodded, not wanting to be like these other women. She wanted Quentin to know that she trusted him. She was determined not to argue.

"I want you to know something." He stroked her cheek. "Never regret giving me that ticket, do you understand? Even if I don't make it—"

Her hand reached for his. "Don't say that."

"Listen." He placed a finger to her lips. "Even if I do not make it, I will always be thankful for meeting you. For having the chance to love you." His eyes glistened with unshed tears.

"All women and children head down to the deck below. We'll board there. Men stand back," a voice called, interrupting.

"But more than that." He swallowed hard, his Adam's apple bobbing. "If I hadn't been on this ship, I never would have found my way into my father's arms. If I'd never made it to the ship, I never would have discovered that God still loved me, that I could be forgiven. God used you, Amelia."

He smiled at her. It was a sad smile. "Now, do what the man says and head to the deck below."

She nodded, but she didn't move.

"Amelia, you must go." He placed a kiss atop her head, hugged her tightly—adjusting her coat to make sure she was snug—and then gently pushed her back.

TRICIA GOYER

With a tear-filled gaze into his eyes, Amelia took her aunt's arm, and they followed the others. Near the bottom of the stairwell, a woman next to them clung to her husband, refusing to leave. Another young woman pleaded for her father to join her.

"He must wait," the officer said simply. "Once the decks are cleared of women and children, he will be put in a lifeboat, too."

Amelia's knees quivered at the scenes around her—fathers parting from their children, giving them an encouraging pat on the shoulders. Men kissing wives.

"I'll be with you shortly," one man whispered as he helped his pregnant wife into the boat. His wife nodded, but Amelia could tell she didn't believe him.

Another woman cried as she hung on to the lapel of her husband's jacket.

"Darling, it's just a precaution. There is no danger," he stated simply. "Don't you remember? This is the finest ship ever built. With the water-tight compartments, we won't sink."

"Then let me stay with you," she cried.

"Darling, please. Just do as the good officer says."

The husband waited as she climbed in and then tucked the blankets carefully around her as if she were preparing for a motorcar ride.

Just then a loud roar sounded and a hiss filled the air. Amelia clung to her aunt and looked around. "It's one of boilers, I suppose."

A child's cry split the air, and the women around her spoke in hushed tones.

Amelia looked back to the deck where they'd just come from, and she noticed Quentin was gone. Maybe it was better that way. She hoped he'd find his father. And after that she guessed he'd help more people—it was what he would do.

Another deafening boom sounded, and Amelia jumped. The strains of the band's song gently reached her ears, and she saw they'd moved onto the deck. Did they hope to cheer up the passengers by playing outside? She imagined that if this was a false alarm, they'd have a fine story to tell in the morning.

"Did you hear that?" someone called out. "Men are being loaded on the port side." With hasty steps, most of the men moved that direction. Only a few others remained.

"Amelia!" A woman's voice filled the air.

Amelia turned to see Ethel Beane moving toward her. Her husband, Edward, was one step behind.

"Ethel, it is you." Amelia grasped the hands of her friend. Had it been only four days ago they'd pranced around the first-class deck together, taking in its opulence?

"Amelia, do you think the ship will go down?"

"Maybe not. Maybe it will only sink so far. They say it's unsinkable after all. Still, I promised a friend I'd get in a lifeboat just the same." Amelia thought about mentioning Quentin's name but realized Ethel wouldn't know whom she spoke of.

Ethel looked to Edward and then back to Amelia. "I left my jewels on the nightstand and my beautiful linens and embroideries in my bride's trousseau."

"Ethel, that's not what's important. You must go with Amelia and get in the lifeboat," Edward urged.

"Are you sure?" she looked to her husband.

Edward smiled. "It's good-bye for a little while."

Noticing the next lifeboat was filling, Amelia led her aunt to its side.

Looking back, she noticed the deck was nearly empty. Many of the women had stayed on the deck above, she guessed.

An officer approached. "It is your turn now, miss." Amelia stepped in, helped by the man's guiding hand. Her feet caught on the tackle and oars, but she righted herself. The lifeboat swayed. Aunt Neda gasped and clung to Amelia. They hurried to their seats, and she gripped the wooden bench with her hands.

TRICIA GOYER

She sat in the boat, shivering, her aunt near her. Ethel was in the seat in front of her.

"Any more ladies?" one of the officers called out.

As Amelia looked around, she saw that they were among the crew, some stokers, and a few men passengers. Her heart pounded. Maybe Quentin would have been able to get on board if he were near. She scanned the decks but didn't see him—hardly saw anyone.

The call for ladies followed again. One sailor looked up and pointed. Amelia looked up and noticed C.J. Walpole looking down from the deck above.

"Any ladies on your deck?" the sailor called up to him.

C.J. looked around "No. None."

"Come now, you sir. We still have room."

C.J. hesitated. "But my son. He told me to go to the first-class promenade, but I'm afraid I got lost. He's going to be looking for me. Both my sons will be looking for me."

Amelia stood, placing a hand on her aunt's shoulder to balance herself. "Please, Mr. Walpole, I am here. We'll find your son—your sons—together later, but for now please come on our boat, there is room."

He paused for only a brief second and then hurried down the stairs and climbed into the lifeboat. Behind him a young couple with a baby climbed in, too.

"Did you see Quentin?" Amelia asked.

C.J. lowered his head. "No, I was with Damien. I told him to find his brother. He told me to go to the promenade. What if he goes there and doesn't find me?"

"He'll know. He'll know you are safe. Perhaps they even got in boats, too. I heard they were loading men on the other side."

Even as Amelia said those words, she knew it wasn't the truth. She could tell by the look in C.J.'s eyes he knew, too, but neither said a word.

"Edward, you should join us!" Ethel called.

"I'll wait for the next one, darling. I want to help these others first."

An officer in a long coat strode by. "Lower away. Once afloat, row around to the gangway. Wait there, and you'll receive orders."

"Aye, aye, sir!" a sailor's voice called. Then with soft swinging, they began their descent.

"I love you, Edward!" Ethel called up to her husband, waving. He smiled, but he didn't wave back. Amelia could tell he was trying to stand strong. Trying to hold in his emotion.

Her eyes moved to the old man as they lowered. She didn't know who was supporting whom with their gaze, but it helped to know there was another person whose heart ached for the same people she ached for.

The boat continued down in jerks. The ropes squeaked under the strain of the boat laden with people. One side started to lower faster than the other. Amelia gripped her seat, praying they wouldn't spill into the icy waters.

The crew in the boat called to the sailors above. "Lower aft! Lower stern!" The boat leveled out. "Lower together!"

They passed by brightly lit cabins, empty of their residents.

Light from the portholes brightened their faces for a moment until darkness enfolded them again. It was a slow journey through the levels, and Amelia thought her heart would pound out of her chest.

As they descended, a hissing roar sounded and a rocket sped into the sky. It burst in the air, filling the blackness with what looked like a thousand candles. A second rocket followed, and not much later a third. Amelia's stomach clenched as she watched.

"They're signaling for help," Aunt Neda whispered, only loud enough for Amelia to hear.

When they were near the water, someone pointed upward. They watched as a boat above them lowered in jerks. It continued downward until it was level with B deck. Women and children climbed over the rail, filling the boat quickly. Soon that boat began to be lowered, too.

Amelia looked to another woman who was sitting across from her, a stewardess with a black dress and a white apron and cap. Beside them, the ship groaned as waters engulfed the *Titanic.*

"Look how far down she's sunk," Amelia whispered to her aunt. Stretching out before and behind them more lit portholes glimmered ... from under the water. *Dear Lord, help us all.*

Finally, they reached the water and floated with the ropes still connected. The officers worked quickly to free them, slicing the ropes with their knives. The boat from above bore down. Finally, the knives sliced through, and they drifted into the dark waters.

"Amelia, do you think Edward will make it?" Ethel asked.

"Of course, Ethel, of course." But as a shiver moved up her spine, Amelia knew that if he did, it would be nothing short of a miracle.

Chapter 26

Quentin thought about finding his father and brother, but instead it was Damien who found him. A hiss and loud bang sounded as a rocket shot into the air. An explosion of white stars filled the sky. The sparkles of lights tumbled toward the ship as Damien approached.

Damien looked to his brother. "You know what that means, don't you?"

Quentin sighed. "Where's Father?"

Damien shrugged. "You care?"

"Of course I care."

"After all these years?" Damien asked.

Quentin studied his brother's eyes. Damien hated him, but even he knew Quentin wouldn't leave their father helpless. He guessed their father was on one of the lifeboats. There was no other reason for his brother to be so calm. Knowing that caused Quentin to release a breath.

"Tell me, Quentin." Damien held his arms behind his back as he strode closer. "Tell me, what did Father say to you today?"

"When?"

"When he settled you into your new stateroom. Did he promise you half of his kingdom once again? The half of the half that remained?"

Quentin thought back to the day—had 'it only been just this morning? His father had promised many things, but he had focused not on what he could get. He only wanted to think about them being together.

"I told him I didn't want anything. I asked for a job at one of the shipping depots."

"Of course you did." And with that Damien lunged forward.

A flash of silver caught Quentin's eye. A knife! A second later it plunged into his leg.

Pain shot through him. More pain shot through his heart. His brother...how could his brother do this? Wasn't it bad enough they were going down on the ship? A small cry escaped his lips.

"Why?" A moan escaped his lips.

"Why? You weren't the one who had to look into our father's eyes every day and see emptiness there. To know that what I offered wasn't enough. To know *I* wasn't enough."

"This has nothing to do with you!" Quentin gripped his leg, and blood flowed over his fingers. My leaving had nothing to do with you. So don't do this. Don't make this about you!" He hobbled backward, attempting to put space between himself and his brother. He felt light-headed, and the deck around him seemed to sway. *Amelia.* At least she was safe. He could die tonight knowing he'd done at least one good thing.

"It's not about me, Brother. If it was, I wouldn't do this," Damien hissed. Then he bent over, lowered his shoulder, and rushed forward. Quentin gasped and tried to turn, to run, bracing for the blow, but it was no use. The wind escaped his lungs, and he felt himself falling, just as he'd fallen into the pond so long ago.

With all the strength in him, Damien lowered his shoulder and rushed his brother. He connected with Quentin's sternum. Quentin's breath escaped in a low grunt.

Around him voices stilled as passengers and crew all turned. Gasps filled the air.

Damien stepped back, meeting Quentin's eyes with his. He expected to see anger there but instead noted defeat.

"You think you deserve this, don't you?" The words seethed through clenched teeth. "I'll show you what you deserve."

He pulled back a hand again, balling his fist. He ignored the blood already seeping through Quentin's pants. Then, just as his fist was to connect with Quentin's jaw, his younger brother jerked his head. Damien's hand smashed the metal wall of the salon.

"Listen. Do you really want it to end like this? We're both going to die tonight as it is." The words shot from Quentin's mouth.

"Not if I can help it!" Grabbing his brother around the waist, Damien spun Quentin around, plowing him toward the rail of the A deck. A woman's scream split the air, but Damien wasn't sure if it was from the scuffle or from the tilt of the ship as it plunged deeper into the water.

Releasing slightly, Damien felt Quentin stagger back. He attempted to put weight on his injured leg, but it crumpled.

Struggling for breath, Quentin leaned forward, pressing his hands on his knees. "Damien, please! I ask your forgiveness again."

"I forgive you, Quentin." With those words came tears. "Now I just pray you can forgive me."

Then, with all the strength in him, Damien rushed forward. Arms opened, he wrapped them around Quentin's legs and lifted. Damien jerked upward, lifting, pressing, pushing.

A cry escaped Quin's lips as his calves caught on the rail, but there was nothing to keep him from falling.

Damien released. Shock registered on Quin's face. His arms flailed as if he swam through the air. The crowd called out protests. Quentin's body hit the deck below with a thud.

Damien turned and rushed down the steps, taking them two at a time.

His brother still struggled for consciousness as he approached. "Why?" Quentin murmured.

Instead of answering, Damien turned the knife and struck the handle against the side of his brother's head. Quentin's head fell back onto the deck. His eyes closed and he let out a moan. He'd been waiting a long time to do that. A gasp escaped Damien's lips as he realized what he'd done. He pressed his lips together and pushed against his brother's shoulder, ensuring he was indeed unconscious.

Fellow passengers pointed, but Damien paid them no mind. From the moment he knew the ship was going to sink, he also knew what he had to do.

Hunching down, Damien mustered all his strength, and he picked up Quentin's limp form. His brother was lighter than he'd thought, and Damien realized how hard the last few years had been on him. With staggering steps, he carried his younger brother to the nearest lifeboat, which was only half full. The sailor lifted his hand. "Women and children only."

"I saw men being loaded on the other side. I'm not asking to get in. But my brother's been injured by another man. It'll be too hard for me to carry him all the way over there. Won't you just let me lay him in?"

"I'll care for him," a seated woman said.

The sailor appeared unsure, but Damien didn't hesitate. He rushed over and placed his brother into the floor of the boat, at the woman's feet. Then, not waiting for a response, he turned and jogged away as quickly as he could. With each step, he asked God to forgive him for his lie.

His brother had been found. His father couldn't lose him again. To do so would break his father's heart. For the last twenty-one years, he'd always been the one to care for his father's interest. There was no use stopping now.

Damien neared the promenade deck, looking for his father, but he didn't see him.

Maybe he'd made it into one of the boats. He hoped so. It was the only reason why his father wouldn't be here. Unless...Damien considered how easily his father got lost. Why hadn't he walked him to a boat himself? Why had he left to search for Quentin instead? *Did I make a mistake?*

Passengers filled the decks. People cried out in despair as they realized the decks were full and there were only a few more lifeboats.

A young man leaped into the next lifeboat, jumping ahead of the ladies in line. The sailor onboard leveled his pistol. "I'll give you just ten seconds to get back onto that ship before I blow your brains out!"

"Please, my father is waiting for me in New York. My mother just died. He needs me."

"For God's sake, be a man. We've got women and children to save."

With his head hung low, the young man climbed from his seat.

"Look, another one!" someone shouted, pointing. Another man was curled on the floor behind a seat, hiding. The sailor grabbed his arm and pulled him up, shoving him back onto the deck. Angry cries filled the air as men turned their fists on him. Wincing, Damien turned away.

Just then a steward approached. His eyes were wide, desperate.

He grabbed Damien's arm. "Can someone help me, please?"

"What's the problem?"

"There are women and children below! I need help bringing them up. I can't do it alone!"

Damien nodded. "I'll follow you and bring up a group."

He was thankful the lights were still on as he followed the man through a maze of tunnels. When they reached the third-class staterooms, the halls were filled with people. Water sloshed around their ankles.

"Why are they still here?" he asked the steward. The liner was listing to the side, and still they remained by their things. Maybe they believed some safety device would kick in and they'd all be saved.

Damien rushed toward an older man. "You have to leave your suitcase."

"I can't. It has everything. All I own. I'll wait." He lifted his chin in determination. "When I can bring my things, I'll come."

"You'll die if you don't come!" he said. But the man wouldn't relent.

He approached other people, urging them to follow, but they couldn't seem to understand English.

"I come with you, *ja!*" a man called out then spoke in German to those near him as he rushed forward with his family. Tears filled Damien's eyes as he glanced at the man's wife and their children. More passengers saw what was happening and joined them.

With Damien leading the way, they walked up the stairs to the third-class lounge. Next they passed the well deck, and soon the second-class library. Along a stretch of corridor they moved past the surgeon's office. Then he led them into the private dining salon and finally to the grand staircase. Mothers urged children to walk faster as they climbed to the top, but even then he knew it wasn't any use. What good had his help accomplished?

They would all still die in the icy waters. There would be no use in going back below to lead any more up. They all had to wait now. Wait until God's angels carried them to heaven.

When no boats remained, Damien knew his time on earth neared the end. Like a moth to the light, he moved toward the orchestra that still played on the deck. A hymn started that he recognized, and his voice lifted with the others standing there. As he sang, he looked around at the men who still stood on the ship. Major Butt, Colonel Astor, Mr. Case, Mr. Thayer, Mr. Moore, and Mr. Widener. All multimillionaires. Around them stood hundreds of other men. At that moment, money did not matter. Status did not matter. Rich or poor, they would die together.

He approached Colonel Astor. "Sir, have you seen my father?"

"Damien, yes. Yes, I believe I have. I saw him in one of the lifeboats as it was rowing away. There were no more women near, so they invited him in." Colonel Astor smiled bravely.

Why hadn't the colonel joined them?

"Thank you." The words escaped in a breath. His father was safe—or as safe as one could be on the waters. His brother, too, was in a boat. And Amelia? Quentin had seen to it she had made it. As much as his brother still angered Damien, Quentin had done the right thing. And maybe...maybe with Amelia by his side, he would continue to do so. Damien had hope in that. He would not be there to see it, but he prayed they would be there to care for the old man.

His lip curled up in a small smirk. It was the first time he'd allowed his father to travel without him. Maybe his father wasn't as delicate as he'd thought.

The ship creaked under his feet and sank lower. The deck tilted slightly, and the orchestra played another song. Damien lifted his voice with a few of the others. The rest stood around in stony silence, no doubt a thousand thoughts and worries filling their minds.

God of mercy and compassion!
Look with pity on my pain:
Hear a mournful, broken spirit
Prostrate at Thy feet complain;
Many are my foes, and mighty;
Strength to conquer I have none.
Nothing can uphold my goings
But Thy blessed Self alone.

Saviour, look on Thy beloved;
Triumph over all my foes;
Turn to heavenly joy my mourning;
Turn to gladness all my woes.
Live or die, or work or suffer,
Let my weary soul abide,
In all changes whatsoever
Sure and steadfast by Thy side.

When temptations fierce assault me,
When my enemies I find,
Sin and guilt, and death and Satan,
All against my soul combined,
Hold me up in mighty waters,
Keep my eyes on things above,
Righteousness, divine Atonement,
Peace, and everlasting Love.

"Sure and steadfast by Thy side," Damien whispered even after the last note was played. And then it happened—water rushed over the ship's side, running over his feet and ankles.

He looked around and noticed that no one panicked. No one cried. They all knew their fate. They stood as quietly as if they were in church, and the fact was they most likely would all soon meet their Maker.

Even though he knew most wouldn't last long in the water, something told him to try.

Walking toward the rail, Damien stumbled and fell in the icy water. It sloshed around his legs, stealing the breath from his lungs with its chill. His body numbed as the cold pierced his skin. He rose and staggered like a drunken man toward the rail. Questions plagued each step. Why hadn't he gotten into a boat when he had the chance? Maybe if he could swim to one they'd pull him in....

Panic set in as he looked to the dark ocean. Colonel Aster had told him his father had made it into the lifeboat. He'd believed him, but what if he was mistaken? What if his father was still somewhere on this ship? After all the years Damien cared for him, always staying by his side, he couldn't imagine his father dying alone. His stomach clenched and heaved, and he didn't know if it was from the cold or worry. Probably both.

He had to trust. He had to have faith that his father was indeed safe on a lifeboat. His mind couldn't think of anything but that. He crossed his arms over his chest, and his teeth chattered. Amelia had been right about many things. She'd been right about his desire for approval, but more real than that was his love for the man who had given him everything. And as he closed his eyes and considered jumping, Damien knew where his faith lay. Not on this ship—not any longer. The fact was, even if he never made it out of the icy waters, he'd find himself before the throne of his God. His father had given him many things over the years, but more than anything else, C.J. Walpole had passed down that belief in God to his son. No matter how Damien had stumbled, he still believed. That was his inheritance.

His eyes fluttered open, and the deck shifted even more under his feet. The boat creaked and groaned; the sound of metal crushing and wood splintering filled his ears. The cries—a hundred cries—pealed out where silence had been not long before. Damien turned to the rail and held on with all his might. Icy water splashed in his face, and he looked to a distant lifeboat.

This is it. I'm going in. It's my only chance.

He secured his life belt. He'd swim with all his might toward the boat. Maybe they'd let him aboard. He was sure if he stayed here any longer he'd be pulled down into the depths with the ship.

Then, taking a large breath, Damien stood on the rail and leaped. *Dear Lord, be with me now . . . .* Then with all his might, he jumped, thrusting himself as far from the ship as possible.

His body hit the water, and a thousand needles pierced his skin. The world around him was dark. He propelled forward, looking for air. Finally, he bobbed to the surface, and he sucked in a sharp breath.

The lifeboat. I have to make it to the lifeboat.

He moved his arms and legs, feeling as though he were swimming through wet concrete. The cold punctured him, and every inch of his body ached. His limbs were already succumbing to the cold, making it hard to feel, to move. His teeth were beyond the point of chattering. His ears felt oddly warm.

Others around him had jumped in also, splashing with all their might as they swam.

Have to get away from the ship. His mind grew numb. His body seized up.

Then, behind him he felt it—the ship taking a dive, reeling, plunging. Damien turned back to watch its descent into the depths. As he did, his eyes caught sight of the large funnel. It headed straight toward him. *No place to go. No life to fight for.*

Sure and steadfast by Thy side.

Chapter 27

As Amelia watched the *Titanic,* the lights flickered low and then brightened again. Its glow reflected off the liner in ripples, and if not for the horrific event taking place, Amelia would have considered it a beautiful sight.

She winced as bodies fell from the ship—jumping or tumbling—it was hard to tell which.

"Please. Someone help me, please!" Cries filled the air as water swallowed up the liner. Even from the distance, she could make out men struggling to cut the ropes of the last lifeboat. Others ran up the slanted decks, attempting to stay on the ship, and out of the water, for as long as possible.

Amelia turned to check on her aunt, and when she turned back she noticed the forward part of the ship was lower now—far lower than it had been just moments before. Her heart leaped, but she tried to remain calm.

They watched, stunned. A word or two was muttered in the lifeboat. There were scattered phrases, simple sentences that couldn't describe what their eyes were seeing. What they couldn't fathom as true.

Just then Amelia heard splashing in the water, not far away. A form neared.

"Edward!" Ethel called out. She rushed to the side and reached for him. Others helped to pull him in. A soaking, shivering mass crumpled into the floor of the boat.

"Saw boat leaving with room." His teeth chattered as he spoke. "Thought to swim for it..."

"Oh Edward, don't try to talk." Ethel kissed his face over and over again.

Amelia removed the blanket from her shoulders and handed it over. Ethel quickly wrapped it around her husband. Tears filled her eyes. At least Ethel's love story would come true.

Shivers overwhelmed her. She looked to the man who was rowing. Should she ask to take a turn—anything to warm her. But her efforts wouldn't be enough. It would be their strength that would take them away from the *Titanic,* lest they be sucked down with it when it finally went under.

The officers continue rowing them out. When one woman asked where they were rowing to, the officer gave a simple answer. "Away."

Amelia dared to look back at the *Titanic.* It stretched longer than it appeared at Southampton at the dock. The dark around it formed a black outline against the starry sky. Light blazed from every porthole and salon. Had it been just hours ago mothers had been tucking their children in for the night and whispering sweet prayers? And hours ago, too, when she'd relaxed into Quentin's embrace?

Quentin. She closed her eyes, not wanting to think about him now. Her heart ached from her loss, but she whispered a prayer, thanking God for the time they had. Thanking Him for the change in Quentin's heart, for He knew what mattered most now.

Amelia's heart clenched at the sight of the ship, just as it had when she first saw it. She tried to remember every detail, knowing it wouldn't last long. Even in its death, the *Titanic* was beautiful. The structure of her lines and the lights were set against the moonless night sky.

The water was now up to the highest row of portholes, and the bow tilted ominously downward.

They rowed in the quietness of the night, and Amelia prayed that when dawn stretched its rays over the horizon, the *Titanic* would still be floating there. She would rather feel a fool for not trusting those who engineered its design than see it go down. See so many lives lost. So many people who needed help, and her unable to do a thing.

"It's designed to stay afloat," a sailor assured them.

If you believed that, would you really be rowing away? Amelia wanted to ask, but the words stayed on her tongue.

"Look at that!" someone gasped.

Amelia watched the *Titanic* settle rapidly as if a large, invisible hand had pressed her down in the water.

"The bow and bridge are completely underwater," C.J. mumbled in shock. "My sons," he whispered.

A great floating palace, she'd heard a woman describe it before as they had strolled on the decks. The palace would soon be gone.

Music carried on the cold night air. "Nearer, My God, to Thee" the orchestra played. Did God's angels surround the ship? Maybe to hold it up? Or to take God's children home?

One of the stokers turned to the oarsman. "It's time to row harder. We need to get as far away as we can."

Amelia imagined again what could happen if the large ship sank. It would surely cause a great wave to flood their boat. Or the suction from its sinking could pull them down with it. Or, if there was an explosion, debris could shoot up into the air—much like the flairs that had been shot up earlier.

As Amelia watched, it was clear their oarsman was unskilled, because their journey was erratic. At times she, too, wanted to tell him to row faster. Other times she wished to whisper, "Go back. Go back."

The stern tilted more, nearly upright, looming black against the sky. People slid off the deck into the water. One of the smokestacks crashed.

Blackness engulfed them, and Amelia sucked in a breath. Then, as a miracle, the lights flashed once—just long enough for their hope to peak and then plummet as it went out again. The ship cracked and groaned before splitting in two.

A mighty rumble filled the air. The sound of machinery and furniture roaring and rattling down. The ship groaned as if crying for her life, and Amelia watched in horror as the bow sank. Cries and groans echoed through the darkness.

Then the stern settled, flattening again, and only then did Amelia release her breath. Maybe it was designed to stay afloat. But soon it, too, began to go under.

Then suddenly, like a pebble dropped in a pond, the huge liner disappeared into the black darkness. The blue ensign on the flagpole of the *Titanic's* stern slipped under the water with barely a ripple.

With a quiet sinking, the water swallowed her up. All those in Amelia's lifeboat waited, tense, but the only evidence of the great ship's sinking was the ripple of the sea, gently heaving around them.

A thousand cries filled the air. Thrashing bodies struggling in the cold. Sobs shuddered within Amelia. A light gray vapor rose into the air like the ship's ghost. Across the surface of the water was wreckage, or so she thought. But as Amelia looked closer, she noticed it wasn't pieces of the ship that floated in the water but bodies.

"We have to go back! We have to help them," she called out.

"We are too far. We'll never get back in time. It is no use." One of the officers shook his head.

Moan upon moan filled the air.

"We can't just sit here. We have to do something," she pleaded with the women around her. "What about your husband? Your son?"

"If we go back, they will swamp us," one young woman said. "They'll cling to the sides and pull us in, too."

Aunt Neda lowered her head in agreement. "We cannot save them. By the time we get there, it'll be too late. Too late."

Somewhere in the night, a sailor's song filled the air, as if he was trying to distract them, but the cries were heard over his voice.

The cries lessened, and the sounds of gasps rose. They were the sounds of men and women struggling for their last breaths.

"My God. My God."

"Help! Help!"

"Boat ahoy!

Amelia pressed her hands to her ears. The moans quieted, one by one.

Tears streamed down her cheeks, and she thought of those she'd come to know and love. She thought of Quentin and Damien, of the men and women who'd strolled the decks, their faces full of smiles, laughter on their lips. She thought of the children playing. She considered the brave stewards, and—did Geraldine make it into a lifeboat?

Why this? Why? Why? In all her years, Amelia had never questioned God. Her aunt had always taught her that He was there—only a whispered prayer away. She had talked about God as if He was a part of her life. Amelia had always assumed that, too. She'd told Quentin that very thing.

But if there really was a God—if He was there and He cared—why would He allow this to happen? How could a liner like the *Titanic* sink?

"Where is God?" she whispered into the night. "God, where are you?"

The heartrending cries floated over the surface of the waters. The voices grew quieter, the pleas weaker and weaker until they died out.

The silence cut deeper than any cry for help.

God was there but maybe in a different way than she had thought. Maybe it was His whisper that hovered over the waters, calling His children home. Calling Damien home. Quentin home. She covered her face with her hands, wishing she could have had five more minutes with Quentin. Time to remind him of her love. Of God's love.

Minutes passed. She didn't know how many, but silent sobs shook her shoulders. C.J. leaned forward and grasped her hands, holding them tight within his. He was brave, even though they both were aware that his sons were gone.

There was no more sound, only silence. Amelia ached from the cold. She ached from the realization of what had just happened.

"Look over there!" Ethel pointed. "I see a steamer. They are coming. We will be rescued!"

One of the stokers shook his head. "No, it's just a low star."

"I need to find my husband," one woman gasped as if finally just stirring to life. She held a small boy on her lap. The boy was bundled in a blanket, and thankfully he slept. "If you don't go back, I'll jump in and go back myself."

The officer's voice was stern. "Maybe your husband has already been picked up. Then what good will your death be? Please, ma'am, consider your child."

Amelia stared up at the quiet sky filled with brilliant stars. Not a cloud could be seen.

Cold wrapped around them, icy fingers shot needles of pain through her limbs. Only the red-faced sailor who rowed seemed anywhere close to warm.

They sat in a somber silence. The boat trembled as everyone shivered from the cold.

The child woke up and started to cry. With numb, cold fingers, Amelia removed her coat and handed it to the mother. "You can have this for your son."

The woman nodded and bundled her child. As minutes passed, the child's cries ceased.

They rowed for what seemed hours, and then they drifted in suspense. Women wept for everything lost. Her tears joined theirs.

Through the night, as the boat drifted, she tried not to think of what they'd left but what waited if they were ever rescued. A new life in America. She tried to forget the tenderness in Quentin's eyes, but it was no use. She saw his face even when she closed her eyes.

With the promise of dawn came a realization of where they were and what had happened. With dawn came a resurrection of their pain.

Women around her sobbed. Their cries ripped at her heart.

"My husband."

"My son."

The sailor with them cried, though he tried to wipe away the tears as fast as they came. "The great ship," he muttered now and again. Their pride swallowed up in the depths of the water.

An older woman next to him trembled. The sailor wrapped an arm around her, and she closed her eyes, perhaps remembering a son's embrace.

Before and behind them a line of lifeboats stretched. As light dawned brighter, Amelia counted sixteen in all.

"I should have given my seat to another," C.J. mumbled.

Amelia patted his hand. "No one else was getting in. They didn't know there weren't enough lifeboats. No one knew."

The young mother with the boy sleeping on her lap jutted her chin into the air. "There were more boats on the other side. I'm sure of it." Her bloodshot eyes peered at the waters. "The men are in those boats. They've gone off another way."

The stewardess beside her nodded, but Amelia could see in her eyes that she had no hope of such a thing.

"We're lost. All's lost." A young woman looked around at the sea stretching in all directions and then buried her face in her hands.

Amelia took the woman's hands and squeezed tight. "A rescue ship is coming," she said offering hope, praying she was right.

She closed her eyes again and tried to remember each moment from the time she first saw Quentin being dragged off the ship. She would rather have had four days with Quentin than four years with a common man. There had been nothing common about him.

Tears filled her eyes and ran down her cheeks, but she was too numb, too weary, to wipe them away. Knowing this end, would he have boarded the ship? Would he have said death was worth reconciliation with his father and his God? Would he have said meeting her was worth it, too? Yes, he had told her all that. He had told her it was worth it.

Because of his willingness to set aside his pride and surrender everything, Quentin now stood in God's presence. She tried to picture that—picture Quentin strolling at the heavenly Father's side just as he'd strolled with her on the decks of the great ship just yesterday. Her shoulders shook more as she attempted to hold the emotion in. Death was never easy, but that image in her mind made it easier.

The wind rose, and Amelia wasn't sure if she could move. Her body felt numb, half dead. Her emotions, too. How could life change so dramatically?

She looked to the old man who sat by her side. A father of two sons—one just recently found. How did he have the energy to breathe in the cold, ocean air at this moment? Wouldn't it be easier to give up? To turn his soul over to God than to feel such pain?

Silence filled the space and seeped into her soul. She let her eyes flutter closed, wondering if this boat was where she'd breathe her last, too. It might be easier that way. Easier to die now than to live with the memories of what they'd just experienced.

They huddled together, and she could tell by C.J.'s face as he looked straight ahead that he thought of his sons. No father should outlive his wife and now two boys.

Amelia tried to tell herself that perhaps one or both had survived, but deep down she knew it wasn't the case. C.J. had raised men of honor. Men who would go down with the ship.

Someone passed around a bottle of water, and Amelia took a small sip.

As the sky lightened, it looked as if many ships had come for them all with their sails set.

"Look at all the help that has come for us!" one woman proclaimed.

But not five minutes later the pink dawn brightened the air. "Those are not the sails of a boat. They are icebergs." Amelia sucked in a breath as she took in the towering forms. She looked to the side of her, behind her. More icebergs rose up from the water as far as she could see. A shiver traveled through her. There had been no hope for the great ship. If they'd missed the first iceberg, they would have hit another.

She thought of the book of Job. Her aunt had been reading it just last week. "Who are we to ask?" she whispered, and Aunt

Neda turned to her, a sad, acknowledging smile lighting her face.

Aunt Neda nodded. "The Lord giveth, the Lord taketh away. Blessed be the name of the Lord."

Her stomach seized as her aunt said those words, and for the first time Amelia allowed herself to acknowledge what she had lost—love.

As clear as the rays of dawn stretching over the water, she knew that in the span of a few short days she'd met the man God had planned for her. She also knew that as kind as Mr. Chapman was, she wouldn't give him her heart. She'd worry about the excuses and about what she and her aunt would do in a new country, but she couldn't imagine considering a new relationship now. How could she when the man who took her heart carried it into the sea with him?

"Maybe he lives," her aunt spoke aloud, understanding what Amelia had been thinking about. A dozen eyes turned. Though she wanted to offer hope, it wasn't something the women could grasp. They'd left their men on the boat. They'd seen it go down. They'd heard the cries in the water. What use was hoping now? She closed her eyes, the pain of what they'd experienced settling deeper in her aching heart.

Gasps from others in the boat caught her attention. She opened her eyes and noticed the glow of rockets.

"Do you have any paper? Any handkerchiefs?" a woman next to her asked. "We can light them on fire so whatever ship is looking for us will find us."

In the distance the form of a ship neared. They didn't need to light anything, as the sailors from the large vessel waved their direction. They were seen!

Tears filled Amelia's eyes. They'd be safe soon. They would make it. A song of joy broke out of one stoker's lips, but few joined. Amelia was silent as she listened to those who attempted to sing with quavering voices. Her jaw and teeth chattered too heavily to allow her to sing any words.

The ship appeared sooner than she expected. With its cabins alight, they could see it was a large steamer. Soon it stopped, sitting motionless on the water.

"We have to row to her. She cannot get to us because of the ice!" one man called out.

Dawn broke completely and tinged the thin clouds with pink. In the distance, the crescent of a new moon touched the horizon. Where had that moon been all night?

An image came over her as she sat there. Quentin's smile had been broad when she'd sung along to her favorite song, "By the Light of the Silvery Moon." Pain pressed against her chest. Why had she opened her heart so quickly, only to have it crushed?

Their steersman laughed as they rowed closer. "Never again can any of us say that thirteen is an unlucky number." Amelia was confused until she remembered they were in lifeboat number thirteen. "Why, it's the best friend we've ever had."

As their boat rowed alongside the *Carpathia,* Amelia attempted to shift, but her frozen body felt stiff. She turned to her aunt, and she too looked chilled. Her face was pale. Her hair plastered to her forehead. She looked like a statue of the lively woman she used to be, and when Aunt Neda turned and looked into Amelia's eyes, she saw a reflection of all the heartache she felt deep inside.

But it was Clarence Walpole's face that surprised her. His cheeks were flushed.

She reached over and took his hand. "Are you all right?" It was a foolish question to ask a man who'd just lost two sons.

He nodded and squeezed her hand. "Days ago Quentin was dead to me. Knowing that he found true life at the end—that he allowed himself to be embraced and to fall in love—that brings me joy mixed with pain. Both of my sons loved God. Both of them … may they rest in God's arms for eternity."

Hearing his words plowed an iceberg into her heart. God had placed her within the arms of the first man she wanted to spend her whole life with—could imagine spending her whole life with—only to have him stripped away.

Tears came, springing up in her eyes. A soft moan released from her lips, even though she had tried to keep it at bay. Other whimpers joined hers, and she understood. They were going to be rescued. Knowing that made them consider those who never would. Consider those who lay in the icy water as floating forms devoid of life.

As they reached the side of the ship, Amelia saw ladders and ropes. The ache in her chest now seemed to cover every inch of her. Did she have the strength to carry herself up? She needn't worry. As their lifeboat approached, a sling was lowered. They each waited patiently for their turn. Clarence helped her place Aunt Neda in the sling, and then he helped her next. He was silent, holding her hand until the last moment.

When she reached the top, Amelia was ushered to the crowd in the forward deck where she joined her aunt and the others. As she watched, their now-empty lifeboat was hoisted up and stored on the deck. Discarded life belts tumbled back into the water below.

One by one more lifeboats approached, and Amelia watched as the survivors were carried aboard. Amelia recognized some of the faces. The couple whom she and her aunt had dinner with. The two boys who had been playing on the promenade deck. Stewardesses carried them, but their father was nowhere in sight. The red-haired stewardess that Geraldine had introduced her to—the woman's eyes met Amelia's as she boarded.

"Geraldine?" Amelia mouthed.

The woman dabbed her eyes and slowly shook her head.

After they were empty of passengers, some lifeboats were left adrift. They looked so small as they floated away, yet the cargo they'd carried had been so great.

One lifeboat was full of first-class passengers. Margaret Brown, whom Damien had introduced Amelia to, manned one of the oars as it approached. Dorothea sat beside her, trembling in her red coat and life belt. Behind their lifeboat others waited, but she needn't wait around to watch the passengers disembark to know that neither Quentin nor Damien were with them.

She turned to go find warmth in an interior salon when the mother and boy who'd ridden in her lifeboat approached.

"Ma'am." The woman handed her the coat. "Thank you for letting me use your coat. I'm not sure my son would have survived without it."

Amelia took the coat from the woman's hands and then watched as she hugged her boy to her chest. "Yes, of course. You're welcome."

At 9:00 a.m. an Episcopal priest conducted a service in *Carpathia*'s first-class salon, in memory of the dead and in thanks for the living. Someone said that seven hundred survivors had been rescued, but looking around, Amelia saw that few registered what was happening, so great was their shock. Following the service, and throughout the morning, officers walked around, taking down the names of the survivors.

Amelia was on her own mission, too. She moved around the decks, searching the faces and listening to survivors' stories. Almost anyone whom she paused to talk with was willing to tell their experiences. Many miracles had taken place. Her survival was a miracle. If it hadn't been for Quentin's quick thinking, she and Aunt Neda would have gone down with the ship. He'd insisted they get in the boat just in time.

After she'd searched every face, she approached one of the stewards who guarded the captain's area.

"Sir, is there anyone in the doctor's cabin?" She held her breath as she asked.

"Only Mr. Ismay. I hear they've given him a sedative."

"Thank you." Amelia's heart sank in her chest, and she hurried away toward the spot where Aunt Neda rested.

"Ma'am?" A man approached as she entered the reception room. A woman stood next to him, and Amelia could tell from the look in their eyes they weren't survivors. *They must be from the* Carpathia. Those who had been on the *Titanic* had a different look about them, as if part of their souls had died within those waters, too.

"My name is Mr. Hurd, and this is my wife Katherine. If you have time, I would love to hear your story."

Her gaze met his. "Are you a reporter?"

He briefly lowered his eyes, and then lifted them again. "Yes, ma'am. My wife and I have been vacationing aboard the *Carpathia*."

"I do have a story." She placed trembling hands to her lips. "I haven't heard from my mother for many years, you see. Yet I met a woman—a stewardess on the *Titanic*—who knew her. Don't you think that's a miracle, sir, to meet someone who knew my mother?"

His eyes stayed on hers, and she could tell he was disappointed, but as Amelia took in a deep breath, she knew that was the only story she could tell. Sure, he'd be thrilled to hear of the romance between her and C.J. Walpole's long lost son, but she wouldn't give him the satisfaction. The memories were too precious to her. Their time together too precious.

"Do you wish to tell more? Of the voyage or...the sinking?"

She folded her arms before her and pulled them tight to her chest. How could she tell him? Where could she start?

"Many are finding some relief in the telling," he urged.

Heartache filled Amelia's chest, and she thought she'd faint from the pressure. "Maybe later, sir. Right now I must go find my aunt. She's my mother's sister-in-law." Amelia offered him a smile. She couldn't even tell of their survival without mentioning Quentin's name.

Later, as they waited in the warmth of the reception room, Aunt Neda's face was pale, and worry rose in Amelia's gut.

"We've lost everything," Aunt Neda said. "And those poor, poor people. I don't think I can close my eyes without seeing them, those shapes thrashing in the water. Their cries! I can still hear them." She turned wide eyes to Amelia. "I think I envy them in a way. I'm not sure how I can ever live with these memories."

Amelia pulled a blanket back around her aunt's shoulders, tucking it under her chin. "There's a reason we're here," she whispered to her aunt. "Look around."

Aunt Neda allowed her gaze to scan the room. Men and women sat, some in the fine clothes they'd been wearing the night before. Others in nightclothes. They spoke in low voices. They huddled in groups.

Amelia leaned her head on her aunt's shoulder. "Some are laughing. Some are crying... but even their tears prove they are alive." She let out a low sigh. And I believe the fact that they're alive is proof God still has plans for their future."

Aunt Neda offered the slightest nod.

"Aunt, we cannot let this experience take our lives—rob our hearts. The icy waters have claimed enough lives today, don't you think? You have to hold on. You have to fight."

Her aunt nodded again, and Amelia was sure she saw a tint of light in her eyes. Then, as if coming to life, Aunt Neda grasped her hands.

"Amelia, did you look around at everyone from the other lifeboats? Quentin wasn't among them, was he?"

Amelia let out a low sigh. "I'm afraid I did not see him. Damien, either. Nor did I see them on the decks—with the rest of the survivors. I'm afraid they've both been lost." Her words quivered, as did her chin, as she spoke.

How is C.J. handling his loss? she wondered.

Damien had been such a good companion to his father all those years. He'd given up his own pursuit of love and a family to make sure his father was not alone. And Quentin—he'd just recently been found.

Amelia covered her face with her hands. "Do you remember the last time we saw him on the deck? He made sure we were in the right line for the lifeboat, Aunt, as if he was just parting for the evening. I didn't see him after that, nor did I see him today." Her throat grew thick, and she tried to swallow down her sobs. Those around her had just settled down on their make-shift beds. A few had already fallen asleep, and she did not want to wake them.

"You loved him—you have to remember that, Amelia." Her aunt took her hand and pulled it to her cheek. "Years from now you are going to look upon that time, and you are going to wonder. You are going to think that the story of how you saved him at the docks and how you fell in love with him walking the decks was just a fairy tale, just something you made up. But even if you marry and love again, a love like that deserves to be remembered."

"But don't you understand? I can't…I can't think of him ever again, because if I do, I'll realize it's all my fault." She lowered her head and looked into her hands. "No matter what Quentin said, it is."

"What's your fault?" Aunt Neda seemed confused.

"It's my fault he is dead. I'm the one who gave him Henry's ticket. If I hadn't, he'd be—"

"On the streets? Sleeping under a bridge? I'm sure if he could, he would say that God had planned it. You need not carry any blame upon yourself. He got to see his father one last time. He got to be reunited. God planned that. If ever a story of joy found in the midst of pain could be written, it would be this one."

Amelia nodded, and she tried to tell herself her aunt's words were true. Then, closing her eyes, she rested her head on a borrowed pillow.

"Ma'am, I have some clothes for you." A woman approached with some clean clothes folded in her hands. Amelia had heard that the passengers of the *Carpathia* had been gathering them up for the survivors.

Amelia looked down at her dress and coat.

"These are fine." She looked to her aunt, hoping the older woman would understand. These were the last clothes she'd worn—the last Quentin had seen her in.

"Amelia, honey, a bath would be in order." Aunt Neda cocked an eyebrow, and her gaze seemed to say, *Remember what you just told me.*

Amelia nodded. She took the clothes and hurried to the bathing room. It was only as she slipped off her dress, preparing to take a bath, that she noticed a piece of paper inside her coat's pocket. "What is this?"

With trembling fingers, she lifted it out. Opening the paper she saw that it was signed by Quentin and it bore Saturday's date. Had he tucked it in there last night when he'd been straightening her coat?

Saturday, April 13, 1912

Dear Amelia,

This day spent with you I can honestly say is one of the best days of my life. Amelia, darling, you have captured my heart. More than anything I wish to ask that when we disembark off this ship you will kindly but firmly tell Mr. Chapman that your heart has turned to another. When I look into your eyes, I believe it has. Tonight with you, I believed you care for me, but then when I returned to my room and lay in the quiet of the night, I convinced myself I was just seeing things. I convinced myself it was only wishful thinking. After all, how could one such as you be in love with one such as me? Impossible. You saw me for what I am . . . what I am without these borrowed clothes and room. You saw me at my worst, and you looked upon me with compassion.

And yet . . . still my love for you cannot be bottled in. I am sure that if I were to tie my love to an anchor and drop it to the bottom of the ocean, it would somehow find its way back to my heart.

I have nothing to offer yet everything to gain.

I have nothing to provide, but your smile has provided peace that I haven't known.

I believed that by walking away from my father that I'd ruined all chance of reconciliation, yet because of your words, your encouragement, I would like to go to him. To seek his mercy.

Tomorrow, if I am brave enough, I will approach him. Not as a son, but as a man in search of a decent job. I'd be happy to work in one of his rail yards. I'd shovel coal if that was the only job available. I will approach him, first because I must ask his forgiveness for what I've done. I'm tired of carrying the burden. Seeing your lightness in life has encouraged me to let it go.

I will also approach him because, more than anything, I wish to provide enough of an income to provide a small home for our future. Oh . . . a future I'd like to think we could have someday.

The letter ended there, and a gasp escaped Amelia's lips. She bathed quickly, dressed in borrowed clothes, and then hurried to her bed.

She curled against the pillow and pulled the blanket under her chin. It was then she heard Aunt Neda's whispered words. Her aunt was praying—for Amelia—for the other survivors. Finally, after a night of heartache, Amelia found herself falling asleep. If she could dream of Quentin alive—that would be enough for tonight.

Chapter 28

April 18, 1912
New York City

Amelia stood at the deck. Even though she entered New York in a manner she hadn't expected, she yearned to see the city lights. The land. As the lights of the city filled the horizon, she had a strange longing for Southampton. Would she ever enter its harbor again?

A flotilla of small craft circled the larger ship, and Amelia placed a hand over her mouth, worried the small boats would be run over by the *Carpathia*. Men in suits and hats—whom she assumed were reporters—shouted questions. The intensity in their gazes and the gloom of the evening light caused a shiver to move from her neck to the base of her spine. Magnesium flares and flashes from photographers' bulbs brought back memories of the emergency flares from *Titanic,* and in an instant, scenes from that dreadful night played through her mind once again.

Amelia watched in horror as a pilot ship neared and more reporters attempted to climb *Carpathian*'s side, but *Carpathia* didn't slow. C.J. stood at the deck rails, also looking at the lights of the city. He glanced at her and then glanced away. She could tell from his eyes he didn't want to engage her with words. His eyes said he wanted space to mourn. She didn't blame him. She imagined that seeing her brought him too many memories.

The wind picked up, and rain started to fall. Thunder rolled through the sky, and Amelia moved back inside to where Aunt Neda waited. C.J. remained outside, the rain washing away his tears.

They continued on through the bay, and with each minute that passed, weariness overtook her. The loss she carried was great. The worry of what waited pressed. The memories. Oh, the memories.

The cries and tears of fellow passengers over the ocean miles had sapped her energy and tired her soul. She wanted to be alone—to have a quiet place to think and pray, but if the reporters in the boats were any indication of what was to come, that wouldn't be the case.

As the ship continued on, they outdistanced the newspaper boats till only open harbor stretched ahead.

Aunt Neda pointed. "Look."

Amelia watched a flash of lightning illuminate the Statue of Liberty. Soon the statue, too, was behind them, and they parked at the White Star Line pier. She watched as the lifeboats from the *Titanic* were lowered into the water to be towed away by another ship. She thought she and the other passengers would disembark there, but instead they continued on farther. It was then Amelia noticed the crowds.

A mass of men and women stood behind portable wood fences as misty rain fell on their heads. All those people had come for them. Was Mr. Chapman among them? Did he know she was alive? He would be relieved to know she was, but what filled her wasn't relief.

Suddenly the idea of trying to make conversation with a stranger seemed overwhelming. Surely he'd understand that it would take time before she would be ready to open up. Tears filled her eyes. What she couldn't tell him, what she was sure she'd never tell anyone, was how quickly she'd fallen in love with another. And no matter what she did, she could not change things. That love would be forever lost.

Finally, the gangway was lowered, and Aunt Neda took her hand. Without a word, they descended, Amelia wearing the thin dress she'd been given by a kind passenger with her coat over the top. Quentin's letter was in her pocket. Her aunt wore the same dress and coat she'd been wearing since she'd climbed into the lifeboat. Tears flowed from the faces of those who waited.

Cries of joy gave evidence of many happy reunions. Amelia was pulled into numerous hugs as strangers welcomed her, welcomed them.

Amelia searched the faces, looking for Elizabeth. She had yet to see a photograph of Mr. Chapman, but still she searched men's faces for any sign of recognition. At the street, a line of cars waited.

As they reached the pier's front entrance, spotlights lit their walk down the gangway, and the clamor of dozens of reporters filled the air. Explosions of photographers' magnesium flares caused her to wince, and Amelia continued to search the crowds for a familiar face.

As they waited, Bruce Ismay parted through the crowd and climbed into a waiting automobile. Mrs. John Jacob Astor crumpled into the arms of a young man who led her to another waiting automobile.

"Her husband went down with the ship. He helped women and children into the lifeboats," she heard one passenger telling the press. "John Jacob Astor is a hero."

She smiled slightly, remembering the man's conversation with C.J. Walpole.

"Today is a new day, a day to make a difference, to do what's right," Mr. Walpole had told him. Perhaps that declaration had been on John Jacob's mind as he chose not to save his own life, but to put others first. No one would ever know for sure, but at least in the man's death he'd have more honor than when he still lived.

Other families were reunited, and most of the reunions were met with tears as mothers climbed into waiting cars with their children, their fathers nowhere in sight.

When Amelia scanned the line of cars again, a door opened and a tall, thin woman jumped out.

"Mother! Amelia!" Elizabeth approached with hurried steps. She pushed past the wooden fencing and pulled them both into a tight hug.

"Is Len here?" Aunt Neda peered over Elizabeth's shoulders.

"There wasn't room in the auto, so Len is waiting at the hotel. Mr. Chapman's cook, Betsie, is waiting there, too. And, Amelia..." Elizabeth offered a soft smile, "Mr. Chapman is here. It was his auto we drove up from New Haven."

Elizabeth ushered them toward the car. A man stepped out of the vehicle. His face was a mix of sadness and excitement. He was a giant of a man with broad shoulders and thick blond hair with hints of gray at the temples. His Adam's apple bobbed once, but he said nothing. He didn't need to. His gaze was filled with compassion, and she noted tears in the corners of his eyes.

Her tongue felt thick and her throat tight. She assumed on any other occasion she would appreciate meeting Mr. Chapman, but at this moment, she wanted nothing more than to turn and hurry back to the waters of the bay. To look into the darkness that lapped against the dock and peer into the depths. She wanted to speak into the water and remind Quentin of her love, but it was too late. It would forever be too late.

"Amelia?" Mr. Chapman said, a hint of German accent highlighting her name.

"Yes." She extended her hand. "I am Amelia."

He smiled. "And I am Earl. Earl Chapman."

Behind Earl's shoulder an ambulance pulled up and two men in uniforms hurried out of it. The medical bag that one of the men carried read, St. Vincent's Hospital.

She moved toward the open door of the car, and just then, out of the corner of her eye, she saw two stewards from *Carpathia* carrying a man on a stretcher into the ambulance. His face was turned away from her, but his dark, rumpled hair, his ear, and even his neck looked familiar. Her heart pounded, and she took a step in that direction.

She felt a hand on her shoulder, and Amelia turned to face her aunt.

"Sweet Amelia," Aunt Neda's words came out heavy with emotion. "It's not him, my dear, although we both wish it was so."

She turned back to Earl and took in his thick eyebrows and the way his light hair curled at the base of his neck. Tiny beads of perspiration formed on his brow, and he studied her, a pleasant smile touching his lips. "We should get you back to the hotel. You need rest. It's—" He paused. "It's been a hard journey."

She looked back to the ambulance once more, just in time to see them closing the back doors with their patient tucked inside. Her aunt was right. She had searched the decks and studied each face. It wasn't Quentin. Her heart ached at the realization of that.

Amelia turned back, nodded, and climbed into the car. She touched her hair. She hadn't done much to care for it in the last few days. Now, that no longer seemed to matter. She thought about the dresses her aunt had sewn for her dates with Mr. Chapman. They were lost, too. Nothing could be done about that. They rested somewhere at the bottom of the ocean. Maybe it was even better that way. Mr. Chapman knew her to be a simple woman born from questionable means. It seemed right in a way that there would be no layers to peel back to reveal her true self. All he saw was all she had to offer—a broken woman with a pained heart.

"We bought you some things—clothes, shoes, toiletries— Mr. Chapman was so kind to make sure all your needs would be cared for," Elizabeth said. "Full suitcases are waiting back at the hotel."

"I—I wrote you a letter on the ship." Amelia managed to say to Earl. She'd actually written two, but the second one was the one she spoke of. It was one that told him they could be no more than friends. That she had grown to care for another.

April 19, 1912
New York
Amelia wore all black as she stood outside the doors of a tall church, waiting for Earl Chapman to park the car on the streets of New York.

Len and Elizabeth, her aunt, and Betsie stood next to her. Her eyes scanned the crowds of people who'd come to the memorial service to remember the victims of the *Titanic.* Amelia noticed a hand in the crowd waving. A face brightening. It was the mother she knew from the lifeboat with her son.

"Amelia!" The woman hurried up to her. The young boy walked beside her with quickened steps. "I am so glad I found you. I was worried I wouldn't. I have something...something that belongs to you!"

The woman reached into her purse and pulled out a pearl necklace, pressing it into Amelia's hands.

"I am so sorry. When I was washing my son's pants, I found this in his pocket. He told me he got it out of your coat pocket when he was on the lifeboat. Please forgive him. Roger is only five, and with everything that happened..." Tears filled the woman's eyes, and her voice trailed off.

Amelia looked down at the string of pearls, and her brow furrowed.

"I'm sorry, but..." She shook her head, preparing to give them back when a memory flashed in her mind. It was Quentin with tears trickling down his cheeks, telling her about his mother saving his life. Telling her about her string of pearls that he'd found in his hand as he raced up to his house to find her father.

Had he slipped them into her pocket with the letter? She remembered his last smile. His last look of love. Suddenly she realized he had.

Amelia sunk to her knees on the ground as silent tears shook her. "Thank you. Thank you."

"Dear child. Are you all right? I don't understand." Aunt Neda grabbed her arm. And then Len's strong arms helped her to her feet. "Thank you," she said to the mother and son again, and they hurried inside the church. She didn't follow them. Something inside told her she had another destination to go to instead.

When Amelia saw Mr. Chapman exiting the vehicle, she rushed up to him. "Sir, I need to—want to—go someplace else. Do you happen to know how far St. Vincent's Hospital is?"

"Are you ill, Amelia?" Earl looked from her, to Betsie, back to her again. Amelia nodded and forced a smile. Betsie was a lovely young woman, and the more Amelia had been around her, the more Earl Chapman's affection for the cook was clear. Because of that, Amelia was going to tell him about Quentin— about her own change of heart—but first she needed to get to the hospital. Something inside told her she could not leave the city without checking.

Elizabeth approached with eyes full of questions. "Aren't you going to the memorial service, Amelia? All the survivors are expected to be there."

Amelia shook her head. "Elizabeth, I have to go to St. Vincent's. I know survivors were taken there. I have to go…. I have to check."

"I'll take you." Earl stepped forward.

"Really?" Amelia reached her hand toward his and squeezed it tight. "Thank you."

When she got to the hospital, guards were stationed by every hall. She guessed that reporters were still trying to get in—to get a unique scoop on the tragedy that had captured the world's attention.

Amelia approached the nurse's desk with Earl by her side. "Excuse me. I am looking for someone."

"I'm sorry, miss, but you'll have to go to the White Star Line and talk to a clerk in their office."

"You don't understand. I have to know. I was on the *Titanic*. Lifeboat 13. I'm a survivor, and I thought I saw them bring someone in—my cousin." Amelia knew what the chart was going to say—that there was no survivor named Henry Gladstone—but she thought this would at least stall the nurse until she could think of another way to get inside.

"I'm sorry, ma'am, I did not know. What is your name?"

"Amelia Gladstone."

"And your cousin?" The woman lifted a list of names.

"Henry Gladstone." She watched the woman's eyes scan the page.

"Amelia," Earl leaned close, whispering in her ear. "Your cousin did not make it onto the ship. Don't you remember?" A worried expression crossed his face.

Amelia ignored him.

The nurse stuck out her bottom lip and shook her head. "I'm sorry. There is no one by that name."

A man rose from one of the chairs in the waiting room and strode toward her. She guessed from his hat, suit coat, and the intense look in his eye that he was a reporter.

"Wait, Nurse, can you check on one more name?" The words spilled out before she was interrupted again. "Quentin Walpole. Can you look one more time, please, and tell me if his name is on the list?"

Out of the corner of her eye, she saw Earl stiffen beside her. He cleared his throat, and she wished she could explain. But there was no time.

Instead of answering, the nurse turned to the approaching man. Amelia turned to him, too, and noticed a small smile.

"Ma'am, may I talk to you for a moment? I work for Mr. Walpole's estate."

She nodded to him, but as she turned to follow him back to the waiting room, she noticed another man—an older man—walking out of a patient's room just down the hall. She immediately recognized his white hair and his mustache. Her heart leaped.

Mr. Walpole wore a fine suit, but the thing she noticed most was his smile.

"C.J." She rushed past the surprised guard. Mr. Walpole's arms opened to her. As she reached him, she fell into his embrace.

"When we disembarked, I tried to look for you. I couldn't see you anywhere," she said. "Where did you go?"

"Just as I have been looking for you over the last day. New York is a big city. And to answer your question, I didn't disembark right way from the *Carpathia*. I was down in the infirmary. He was conscious by then, you see. He was able to tell the doctor who he was. When he saw me, he asked about you. That was the first thing out of his lips, your name."

"He?"

With her question, Mr. Walpole stepped aside. Amelia dared to look into the room.

He appeared so thin and frail in the bed. His feet stretched to the end, and when she gazed into his face, she noticed his eyes were open, fixed on her.

"Amelia." He lifted a hand to her, and she saw that it took most of his strength to do so.

"Quentin! Quentin!" She hurried toward him, wanting to wrap her arms around his neck—to hold on—but she told herself to be gentle. Instead she pulled up a chair and sat by his side. With joy coursing through her, she took his hand between hers and pressed it to her lips.

"You're really here," she whispered.

"I was just going to say the same thing. My father told me you were alive. He told me you were the one who urged him to get on the lifeboat. Thank you. He hired a dozen men to find you. I was hoping...." Quentin let his voice trail off. "I had faith that they would." He smiled.

She looked down and noticed one of his legs lying on top of the blankets. It was wrapped in a wide bandage.

"Did you get hurt? How did you survive? I didn't see you on the *Carpathia*."

He smiled.

"I'm sorry. Those are more questions than you can answer at once."

"My brother..."

"I know. He didn't make it."

"I was going to say, my brother did this to me." He motioned to his leg. "He knew I'd never get on a lifeboat on my own. I'd never take the place of a woman or child. The last thing I remember was him lunging at me with a knife. Then I woke up in the infirmary."

"He injured you—"

"So he could save me."

Quentin's eyes blinked slowly, and she was sure he was blinking back tears.

"You're alive. You're really alive!" Unable to contain herself anymore, she leaned forward and gave him a kiss on his cheek.

He took her right hand and pressed it hard against his chest. Quentin didn't speak, but the message was clear in his gaze. He never wanted to let her go. His heart beat wildly beneath her palm. And she imagined wrapping up in his arms, laying her cheek on that very spot, and soaking in the realization that he was alive.

Quentin is alive.

His gaze moved from her eyes to the pearl necklace she wore around her neck. With her free hand, she touched it, running her fingers over the pearls.

"So you found it?"

"The letter and the necklace ... yes. You should be applauded for your sleight of hand. I didn't know I had anything in my pocket until I was on the rescue ship. I'm honored, and I wanted you to know something." Her face grew serious. "I just want you to know, Quentin, that I love you, too."

She would never question her feelings for Quentin again. It didn't matter if they had to wander this earth to find a place where they could lay their heads. At least they'd be together.

A man cleared his throat from behind her, and it was only then that Amelia remembered Earl. He'd brought her here. He'd done so much.

She turned around and saw him there, mouth open. His eyes were wide, filled with questions.

A deep sadness came over her then, because she understood. He was seeing her love for Quentin firsthand without any sort of preparation, any word of warning. It was like a slap to his face.

Quentin released her hand, and she rose and moved to the door, approaching Mr. Chapman.

"Quentin and I, we met that first day on the *Titanic.* We became friends and ... I thought he was lost to the ocean depths, but he's here. He's alive." It was all she could manage to say.

Earl removed his hat and turned it over in his fingers. "I can see that."

"I am so sorry. When I left Southampton I had every intention ..." She let her words trail off. "I can work to pay you back for the fare."

He shrugged. "There is no need. Actually you've given me hope."

"How's that?" she asked.

"If you can find someone you care that much about on such a short voyage, then maybe I can dare to ask the woman I've come to care for about certain matters of the heart."

She closed her eyes and swallowed. She wished she had more to say. Opening them, she looked into his face. He was a kind man, handsome even. She grabbed his hand. "Betsie does care .... I saw it in her eyes."

Mr. Chapman's jaw dropped in shock. "How did you know?"

She smiled. "I could read it in your letters. It was very clear you were becoming friendly with your cook. She seems to be a wonderful woman."

He nodded and took a step back. "Your aunt, she's with Elizabeth. I can help you both until you're on your feet."

"There's no need." C.J. Walpole stepped closer. "I appreciate your kindness, sir, but you can be sure this young woman and her aunt will be well cared for. She—" His voice caught in his throat. "Because of her care, I was given a great gift—the return of my son."

Earl nodded, and a smile lit his face. "I'll go to the memorial and find your aunt. Then I'll return."

"Thank you."

He nodded and strode away with shoulders squared. She wanted to tell him more. She wanted to tell him that it was because of his kindness that she was here at all.

"To think it was only nine days ago when we were in Southampton at the docks." Quentin's voice spoke to her from behind. "I didn't know you existed. I just wanted some bread and maybe a free passage. Now you're ... you ..." He sighed happily. "I can't imagine life without you. I can't imagine not knowing I have my father's love, and my brother"—he shook his head—"he cared enough to save me when he was certain I'd be lost."

She returned to the chair and sat again. "I can't believe it." She placed her fingers over trembling lips.

"You saved me, too, you know," he said. "You opened my eyes and made me look back on what I'd been running from."

"No more running now. You promise? Because if you do ..."

He put a hand on her jaw, silencing her words with the softest touch of his thumb.

"No more running. I promise," Quentin whispered. "And what about you? Are you willing to risk your heart with a man who doesn't even own the clothes on his back?"

She looked over her shoulder and noticed C.J.'s smile. She had a feeling that with him around they'd never want. Then again, even if he never offered a penny, God would be with them, watching them. If God could save them, He could guide them, too.

"It's not what I put my faith in, it's *who* I put my faith in," she said.

Tenderly, Quentin looked into her eyes. "'Sure and steadfast by Thy side.' That's from a hymn my mother often sang. It was her favorite line." He smiled tenderly. "It was my brother's favorite line, too...." Quentin's voice choked up. "I'd like to think he's singing that now with the angels as we speak."

"I have a feeling he is." Amelia offered a sad smile. "I have a feeling he is."

Tears filled her eyes as she thought of Damien. He'd been so stubborn...so, so stubborn. He'd worked so hard to do everything right...and in the end he'd done exactly that.

The End

By the Light of the Silvery Moon

The original lyrics of the song "By the Light of the Silvery Moon" are now in the public domain due to expired copyright. They were first published in 1909, and the lyrics are as follows:

Verse 1

Place: Park
Scene: Dark
Silv'ry Moon is shining through the trees,
Cast: Two,
Me, you,
Sound of kisses floating on the breeze;
Act one: begun,
Dialogue "Where would ya like to spoon?"
My cue: with you,
Underneath the silv'ry moon.
Chorus

By the light, of the silvery moon,
I want to spoon,

To my honey I'll croon love's tune.
Honey moon, keep a-shinin' in June.
Your silv'ry beams will bring love's dreams,
We'll be cuddlin' soon,
By the silvery moon.

Verse 2

Act two.
Scene: new.
Roses blooming all around the place.
Cast: three
You, me,
Preacher with a solemn looking face.
Choir sings, bell rings,
Preacher: "You are wed forever more"
Act two, all through.
Ev'ry night the same encore.
(Repeat chorus)

$\mathcal{T}$ricia Goyer has published numerous articles, novels, and nonfiction titles. A former teen mom, Tricia founded Hope Pregnancy Center in Kalispell, Montana. She now lives in Little Rock, Arkansas, with her husband and four children, including a newly adopted daughter.

Printed in Great Britain
by Amazon

71732384R00185